Sunrise Sunset

Christina L. Barr

Become a fan on Facebook

www.facebook.com/sunrisesunsetthebook

For my number one fan,

Tina

Table of Contents

Chapter One

Every morning started the same. I had absolutely no recollection of what transpired the night before. I only had the gut-wrenching feeling that I hurt someone I loved, with words that came out my own mouth, from a person who wasn't quite me. My body was still numb from sleeping uncomfortably on a cold, concrete floor. I could see a small bit of light pouring in from the window in the corner, but it was still so dark and cold. I was damp from sweat and from other things I'm too embarrassed to talk about. I'm grateful that my parents caged a monster, but it upset me that it cost my dignity to do it.

I began to get up slowly, and the chains tugged on my wrists and ankles. It wasn't a lot of space to move. It's a wonder how She ever managed to fall asleep. I hissed at the pain I felt. It must have been a rough night for Her. If not for the enchantments on my chains, She might have very well escaped.

"Roxy?" I heard the door open, and my mother began to walk down the stairs. Each step had its own distinctive creak, like the screams my mother was actually too afraid to let out. I didn't say anything until I could see her foot stepping down slowly from the last step. She should have known it was safe, but I couldn't really blame her for being terrified.

"It's me, Mom."

She breathed a sigh of relief and came into my full vision from behind the wall. "Of course it's you!" Mom said with a shaky voice. "It's like clockwork."

"Sunrise," I smiled. "It's the best time of the day." I reached out my arms as much as I could manage, so she could free me.

"Give me one second." Mom rushed over to the hook on the wall to the side of me where she kept the keys. It was in sight but too far out of my reach. It was one of the cruelest things they could do to Her, though I'm certain it wasn't wise.

"I set out some clothes for you. Your backpack is packed and at the door." Mom's voice was still jittery. She told me once that she could always tell the difference when she looked into my eyes, but I noticed she was often too afraid to look into them.

"Where's Dad?" He usually unchained me in the morning. He wasn't afraid of Her like Mom was.

Her fingers were shaking as she put the key in the hole. "He needed some space."

As soon as my hands were free, I rubbed on my wrists. They were bruised and cut. She usually wasn't that difficult. "Do you want to talk about it?"

"No. Everything is alright." Mom never liked to lie to me. It was an effect that I had on people. She was instantly wracked with guilt, but I knew she was still suffering from the effects that She had.

"You can talk to me, Mom."

She hid her glistening eyes from me as she unlocked the chains from around my feet. I feared what might have happened, but I was strong enough to handle it. I knew I could make them feel better. That's what I was made for.

"Mom?"

"Breakfast is in fifteen." She rushed away quickly, but she underestimated how strong my ears were. I could hear her starting to sob when she reached the top step.

I didn't understand. I woke up chained like I was supposed to. Mom didn't have a scratch on her. I told Mom and Dad never to engage in a conversation with Her. She was a liar, and She knew exactly what words to say to make them sound like truth.

It wasn't easy getting up every morning knowing that someone had stolen my face and tried to ruin my life, but I did it with a smile. Everyone has burdens to bear. Mine was particularly heavy, but there was no point in going through life with a frown. There was too much in life I cared about to let someone so vile drag me down.

I hurried up the basement stairs and up another flight to my bathroom. Mom had a towel and a fresh pair of clothes set out on the hamper for me. That was enough to be grateful for. I had a shower and cute, clean clothes waiting for me.

I threw off my clothes and considered trashing them. They were only a black pair of sweats and a grey T-shirt. It wasn't something I would miss. I didn't let Her wear my nice things just so She could ruin them. If She could ruin my wrists and ankles so carelessly, there was no telling what else She would destroy if anyone gave Her the opportunity.

She was so devious! I wouldn't be surprised if She plotted leaving me scarred, so I could go to school looking like an abused child. Eventually, child services would come to our house and see Her strung up like the innocent victim. Luckily for me, God gifted me with a handy capability to defeat that plan before it could ever see fruition.

I looked down at my wrists and realized that the abrasions were gone like magic. Sometimes healing required a bit of concentration and sometimes it happened effortlessly. It didn't matter how many times She tried to hurt me. I could always recover from it.

When I was clean and dressed, I looked myself over in the mirror. My hair was naturally curly, and it was a bright and vibrant blonde. My eyes were so blue that they practically popped out the sockets. I had been told there was something inviting about them, and I've heard that my smile was charming. I hope I don't sound like I'm vain, but I thought I was pretty. I knew I didn't look that intimidating either. I bet if anyone ever ran into Her, they'd be pretty knocked off their feet. I'd like to think I was born to be good. She's just an infection meant to slander my kindness.

"Roxy?" Dad called my name from beyond my door. "Your food is gonna get cold."

I smiled and ran out of the bathroom into his arms. "Good morning!"

"Hi." He slowly wrapped his arms around me and kissed my forehead. "It's nice having you back." Dad was such a cheery person. I assumed he was where I got it from. I don't mean to say anything bad about Mom. There was just a difference between the two of them.

"I don't plan on ever going anywhere," I sighed, "besides between sunset and sunrise."

"I know, Roxy. We just miss you when She comes around." Usually he appeared unscathed in the morning time. I wondered what was so different about the night before. "Hopefully, everything will change."

"Is that possible?" I squealed from the thought of it!

He smiled, and it wasn't a smile to make me happy by covering up any sadness. It was a genuine smile that meant all of my suffering wasn't in vain or permanent. "We have to talk about some things after you get home from school today."

"Is it bad?"

"No, I just think it's time for you to find out why you're the way you are."

I had only been asking Mom and Dad about that ever since I could remember! "I'll be looking forward to that conversation."

We walked downstairs for breakfast together. It wasn't anything too fancy, just bacon and eggs. Mom really didn't have a lot of time to

8

make breakfast, but she took the time out so we could have a little bit more time together at the kitchen table.

I had to sit next to Mom. I knew it made her uncomfortable that I had the same face as the person who made her so miserable, but I couldn't let that be what she thought of me. She didn't say much. Dad and I had casual conversation, but I noticed she was slowly beginning to smile a little bit more.

My cell phone began vibrating in my pocket, and Mom and Dad both gave me friendly glares. There were no cell phones allowed at the table, but I didn't have any intention on answering it.

"You better get that," Dad said. "We should get going anyway."

I looked at my phone and immediately started to smile. I hoped I wasn't being rude answering it at the table. I didn't mind if my parents heard my conversation. "Hi, Adam."

"Hi, Roxy." I could hear the smile in his voice when he said my name. "Tell your mom and dad good morning for me."

I pressed the phone down to my chest to block the sound. "Adam wishes you both a good morning."

"It's scary how well he knows you," Mom said.

I had to do my best to hide my giggles when I spoke into the phone again. "What's up?"

"I thought I'd give your dad the day off and take you to school."

I looked over at Dad. I would have tremendously enjoyed riding in Adam's car, but I didn't want my dad to feel uncomfortable. "That's incredibly sweet of you, but you don't have to do that. I'm about to head out soon, and you live closer to the school than I do. I'd hate for you to go out of the way."

"I know, but I've already thought about those facts. I knew you'd be your sweet and darling self, so I thought I would con you a little bit and drive to your house and hold off on asking until I arrived at your front door."

My heart skipped a beat. "You're at my front door right now?"

"Absolutely right now."

I started blushing incredibly hard. I knew Mom and Dad didn't want me to get too attached to Adam—considering my condition—but it was hard not to want someone that spectacular. "Excuse me," I told them.

I knew I was totally giving myself away, but I ran out of the kitchen and slid across the hardwood floor at the risk of busting my head wide open just to see him. Even if I would have fallen, it would have been worth it once that door flung open. "Adam!"

He was still holding onto his phone, smiling adorably. "May I escort you, Ms. Harris?"

I giggled into my phone. There was just something dazzling about him. There was goodness within Adam that resonated all throughout me. "I don't know. If you conned me, how can I ever truly trust you again?"

"I suppose you'll have to let me earn that trust back."

"Do you deserve that chance?"

"I believe I do." He smirked, and I almost melted into a puddle on the floor.

"I would love for you to escort me."

He hung up his phone, and I did the same. We were not capable of hiding our true feelings, and it was most inconvenient when I heard my parents coming up from behind.

"What's going on?" Dad asked.

I turned around and clasped my hands together. "Is it alright if Adam takes me to school? He's already here. Nothing bad will happen, I promise!"

Dad kept looking at me and then Adam, back and forth as he tried to figure everything out. "I know I can trust you, Roxy."

"Thank you, Daddy!" I ran up to him and Mom and kissed them both before trying to bolt out the door.

"Wait!" Dad yelled before I could close the front door behind me.

"Yes Sir?"

"Our morning joke! You can't leave before the morning joke."

"Honey, please…" Mom begged.

I stood there with a little smile, preparing for one of his horrible jokes. "I'm ready."

"Where do cows go on the weekend?"

I smiled, already guessing the terrible answer. "Where, Dad?"

"To the moo-vies!"

I genuinely laughed. It was awful, but it cracked me up how excited he was. Mom rolled her eyes, but she at least chuckled. Adam smiled to be polite. "I'll see you later, Daddy."

"Be careful," Mom warned.

Adam laughed as soon as the door was closed. Then we were on our way to his chariot. "Your parents are quite the characters."

"My dad is cheesy, but I like it. At least I know that they love me."

Adam frowned just enough for me to catch how he felt when I said that. "That's worthy of envy."

"No need for envy." I grabbed his hand and held it tight. "There are enough people that care about you."

"'People', meaning *you*?" He stepped behind me, and before I knew it, my back was pinned against the door of his remodeled beauty. Everything about him was right. It was one of those moments in one of those movies I refused to watch because I found most film too immoral. If I remembered correctly, that was the part where he was supposed to kiss me and make me fall into happily ever after.

I couldn't lie about how I felt. "Of course I care about you."

11

He smirked and his gorgeously blue eyes flashed brilliantly. "How much?"

I could see my parents peeking out of the window and I knew I couldn't let him lean into my lips like he was totally doing! "A considerably generous amount." I played it sly, and I sank into the car coolly. Dad was still probably having a heart attack, but I was going to remain the wholesome girl.

My heart sure was pounding from my first almost kiss. I figured I probably would have liked it. He seemed like he would be a good kisser. I wasn't sure if he had any experience. I had never seen him kiss another girl. The girls at school certainly were interested in him though. He was smart, funny, and he smelled good every day. That's all most teenage girls cared about. It helped that he was on the honor roll, and he was impressive at track and basketball. He was a great catch, and with all the nets laid out across the ocean, he wandered into mine.

He wasn't always perfect. When I first met him in middle school, he was a little dreadful. He didn't say much to me for a while. I just knew that the teachers would always hold him after school for pranks or back talking or something dumb like that. When I finally got to know him, he turned into an entirely different person. I wasn't that acquainted with his dark side, and I hoped he never got to meet mine.

"Have you thought anymore about the dance tomorrow?" We were silent for the first couple of minutes until he had to ask that.

"I've thought a lot about it and I've spent a lot of time reconsidering my decision, but I'm afraid it's still the same."

"Why exactly?" Adam didn't get upset with me too often, but the prom was a bit of a touchy subject for us.

"I told you. I can't stay out late."

"You're nearly eighteen. You can't stay until eleven or ten?"

"No."

12

"Nine?"

"No."

"Your parents honestly don't seem that uptight. Protective? Yes, but I don't think they chain you to the house like you pretend."

If he only knew! I couldn't tell him the truth about what I was and the reason why I didn't know what the world was like when it was blanketed by darkness. I had never even seen a constellation in the sky with my own eyes. I wanted to be with him, but there was no way he could have known the repercussions of the darkness. "Can we please not talk about the dance?"

He tensed up his mouth, stopping himself from saying something he probably didn't want to. I knew I kept him happy, but there were some emotions I couldn't make go away, especially when I had the same ones.

"If you wanna go out, maybe we can do it on Saturday morning. It could be like an early birthday celebration."

"I have to take care of my grannie on Saturday."

I felt the weight that was on him. "Is she doing any better?"

"No."

Just as he had weight, I had some also. Within my hands, I had the power to alleviate that terrible burden he felt. Just like I healed my own wrists and ankles, I could heal his grannie from the cancer eating her away. I wanted to help Adam. I truly did, but my parents warned me a million times what could happen if I revealed my powers to anyone.

I might not have been able to save her, but I was optimistic. I had to believe that something good would happen to Adam. "Have a little faith."

"My faith is us has proven ineffective. I'm not sure I can muster up anymore."

I kept my mouth shut after that. There wasn't anything I could say to make him feel better, and that included the truth. I probably would have been sent away to a looney bin if anyone ever met Her—not that they could hold Her.

For what school was, I enjoyed it. I didn't know how much of what I learned could be applied in my everyday life. There was no algebraic equation that could help me solve my problem with Her. If there were a physics explanation, I was certain I wasn't smart enough to figure it out. My parents said I could be homeschooled if I actually wanted to, but I wanted to go so I could learn about people. I had faith that I would one day be free from my bonds—literally and figuratively. I wanted to be a normal human being and some social skills were required.

Most everyone liked me. The teachers gravitated toward me, and I was a little old to be referred to as a teacher's pet by my peers. There were some that didn't like me and couldn't put their fingers on it. I had classmates that held onto their negative emotions and fed off of them like a drug, while other problem cases like Adam got better around me. If I allowed myself to be more social, there was no telling how much of a difference I could have made.

I just couldn't. She would ruin it all. She would ruin them.

I had a bit of an off day though. I couldn't get Adam out of my head, and he was in a few of my classes. We were somewhat avoiding each other. We sat right across from each other during lunch, but we barely looked at each other. I didn't want us to be that way, so I did the only thing I thought I could help. "You can take someone else."

"I can what?" Adam asked distracted while playing with his mashed potatoes.

"You can ask another girl to prom." He and the kids who sat around us all began to stare at me. It might have seemed weird, but I thought I was doing the right thing. "I'm sure there are lots of girls who want to go with you. We're not even boyfriend and girlfriend."

14

There was a friend at our table who had just suffered a breakup. It would have been nice for him to go with her. I thought it was brilliant, yet Adam looked at me as if I were an idiot. "I don't want to go with anyone else."

I didn't want him to go with anyone else either, but I knew he really wanted to go. He thought I was going to break. If it wasn't for Her, I would have broken already. "You don't want to waste the ticket."

"I care about you, not the money." He reached across the table and grabbed my hand. "I want to be together, but you keep pulling us apart."

Everyone was still looking at us. He was usually such a private person. I was flabbergasted that he was too upset to care. "I don't mean to. My life is just complicated."

"It can't be any more complicated than mine!" He got up and walked around the table just to be close to me. I couldn't believe that he was being so open and persistent about his feelings in the middle of the cafeteria, but everyone else never crossed his mind. When I looked into his eyes, I could only see me. "You simplify things for me, Roxanne. You complete me."

I heard a few swoons. One of them might have been me. It broke my heart that I meant so much to him, yet I knew that we could never be together. "I can't go." I could barely speak it, but I had to deny him again for the hundredth time.

There were gawkers and gaspers that were beginning to make me feel awkward. They didn't get to Adam, but the rejection certainly did. He left me after that and disappeared for the rest of the school day. He even missed our English class during fifth period.

When it was over, I had to rush to my locker and get my stuff before the bus pulled away. I got teased for being the only senior who rode the bus, but I didn't want to bother Dad in the afternoon. She was so difficult that I didn't want to make him rush home after work. It was bad

15

enough that he had to adjust his work schedule during the year when sunrise got later and later. I wanted to simplify people's lives.

Complete them…

I honestly did feel terrible.

"Roxy!" Adam called my name from down the hall. I didn't want him to be angry and start yelling at me. He had never done that before, and I didn't know if my heart could take it.

"Adam—"

Then it happened. As soon as I turned around, his lips made a crash course collision with my face. It wasn't more than two lips touching, but it was much more than I had ever encountered. I was stunned, and I wasn't sure what was next after he pulled away.

"Now you listen to me!" Adam said.

I braced myself. I couldn't yell back at Adam. I liked him too much.

He furrowed his brows and pointed his finger right in my face. "I am in love with you!"

"You're in love with me?" I thought I had misheard. He was yelling after all.

"Yes. I am madly in love with you and I will only be in love with you. Ever. There is no one else." He started to lower his voice, but the passion still remained the same. He grabbed my hands again and looked into my eyes. "I don't want to sound like I'm a teenage boy with a school crush, but there is no one else in this world like you, Roxy. You are good and pure, and you make me feel like a better person—a decent person. Let me help you with whatever problems you think you have."

I was starting to cry just thinking about it. "I think you'd be a little out of your depth." I wasn't trying to be cruel. We were too impossible.

16

"I've known you for six glorious years of my life. The life I have now, I would have never thought it was possible. It's not perfect, but that's only because I can't be with you every second of the day."

It was so hard going through life every day not telling my best friend the reasons why I had to decline just about every invitation that he ever extended toward me. He didn't owe me his love. "We've never even been on a real date!"

"You're my best friend, but I'd be lying to you if I didn't come out and admit how I really feel about you." He spoke with such an assurance that I believed him, and no force on earth could have ever convinced me different. "I am in love with you."

Then Adam—the boy who always liked to hang out alone with me because he didn't want anyone to see him express any true feelings— announced to the entire hallway filled with our peers: "I am in love with Roxanne Harris and I don't care who knows it!"

I laughed and I cried too. He had changed so much over the years, and he claimed it was all for me. "I love you too."

He bent down to kiss me again. It was another peck on the lips. The kiss left me wondering what a true kiss was like, but it was sweet and satisfying enough for the time being. "Then will you go to the prom with me?" Adam asked.

All of that beautiful affection and I couldn't do a thing about it. "I literally can't."

All of his hopes and dreams instantly began to fall off his face.

"But I still love you!" I held him and hoped that was enough to make him feel better. I knew I made him happy. It was an effect that I had. He had that effect on me too.

"May I take you home?" Adam managed a smile through his disappointment.

17

I was giddy again. "Yes, you may." I reached out my hand for him. I knew he was a little upset, but the two of us could work it out. I was going to make it up to him somehow.

We made quite the spectacle, but we escaped high school hand-in-hand and made it to his car. I wasn't sure what my mother was going to do when she saw us pull up together, but I had no intention of hiding anything from her or my dad. I believed in love no matter how complicated it might have been. They would find a way to accept the both of us.

Adam could barely keep his eyes on the road. He kept looking at me, and he couldn't wipe the smile off of his face. "I'm gonna marry you one day."

I was nervous, but I felt incredibly amazing when he said that to me. "That's quite the proclamation."

"I know, but it is true." He pulled up to the front of the house and parked. He looked at me for a while. Perhaps he wanted me to change my mind about the dance, but I couldn't do it. "No matter what you're hiding from me, I can take it."

"I'm not sure that you could. I'm not sure if anyone could." I mumbled, "I barely can."

"That's actually the reason why you need me," he said. "In life, when you have a partner—someone you can rely on and trust with everything that you are—there isn't anything you can't accomplish. I will always be there for you, if you let me."

I wanted to believe him so badly. "No matter what?"

"No matter what."

He couldn't possibly understand what that meant, and it wasn't fair to lead him on with no intention of coming clean. I'd have to tell him everything eventually. "No matter what I am?"

Adam laughed despite being confused. "What are you exactly?"

18

It was a terrible conversation. I didn't know how to start explaining, and I didn't have the time either. "Someone who has to get inside before Mom goes ballistic." Mom was standing in the doorway, and I knew how much she hated for flies to come into the house. "I'll see you tomorrow."

I reluctantly got out of the car, and he kept stepping on the gas pedal just to make an impression. The sound of the engine made me jump, but we laughed. I liked how confident he was and his cute smirk. He was playful and probably the sweetest boy I would ever meet.

"I'm guessing you had a nice day," Mom said sarcastically.

I caught a glimpse of Adam's smile before closing the door behind me. "It was lovely and frustrating. Thank you for asking."

"Lock the door," Mom spoke annoyed. She had to remind me just about every day.

"Sorry." I guess I didn't have a real sense of danger because our house was about a mile away from anyone else, and we lived in such a small and friendly community. Maybe I was being naive, so I locked it.

Mom wasn't only upset about the door thing. Mom and Dad weren't used to me taking any interest in boys. Adam had been around for years, but it was still probably a shock for her.

I was going to avoid the confrontation about him. "If it's alright with you, I'm gonna do some homework before Dad gets home and commences the biggest conversation of my life."

As I began heading toward the stairs, Mom said, "We'll discuss it another day."

I twirled around on my tiptoes until I was facing her head on again. "Why?"

She sighed. "We're afraid that you might be in danger."

"In danger of what?" I didn't get the sense that she was concerned, but rather disappointed in me.

"Of changing!" I don't think I had ever seen Mom that upset before. "You cannot be with a boy. You are to remain chaste and pure!"

"Just because I fall in love with someone doesn't mean I'm not a virgin anymore!" I would never dream of doing something rash with Adam and with all the time I had known him, he never hinted once that he would pressure me either. I knew how important purity was for my self-preservation and for stopping impending world destruction. The fact that I had to remain a virgin was the only thing Mom and Dad was honest about. "Adam and I will take this slow."

"He can't know about Her, Roxy! He wouldn't understand." Of course that was a concern for her. It was a concern for me as well, but she didn't know Adam as well as I did.

"Maybe he would." Perhaps it was my naivety working against me again, but Adam was remarkably understanding and forgiving. He had to be in order to love me after I made so many excuses why we couldn't be together. "He's different. I think he could love me in spite of Her."

Then Mom shook her head as if she knew something that I didn't. I think she pitied me. "I'm also afraid of what might happen if he were to meet Her. You don't know how She is. She could seduce him into her way of thinking. Don't ever think that you can have some sort of normal life as long as She's with you."

I was finally beginning to understand their burdens. Mom and Dad were the ones who chained me up and had to deal with Her. I couldn't experience the effect that She had on people, but if it were anything like the one I had, I could only imagine the worst.

But I had my own life, and I couldn't let Her ruin it. "I'm not afraid of Her."

"Sweetheart," she laughed, "you're too afraid to speak Her name."

Mom was terrified and some of it began to rub off on me. I felt that darkness and it made my voice quiver as I silently spoke. "Lyla." I composed myself before saying another word. "I'm not afraid of Lyla."

Then I saw the fear in my own mother's eyes as they glistened. "You should be." But even worse, I saw that she was still afraid of me. "We all should be."

She walked away. I had noticed a little bit every day that Lyla had been destroying a piece of my mother's happiness. I tried to restore it, but it was becoming more difficult. Even with knowing that fact, I still didn't want to believe that the same thing could happen to Adam. But for the meantime, he was going to stay far away from Lyla.

My day was wasted with much homework. I had to work on it as soon as I came home, or else I would fail school. Lyla couldn't remember anything that I experienced or learned, so I imagined her to be a loveless and illiterate beast. She couldn't finish my homework for me. She'd probably write down the wrong answers on purpose if she did somehow understand.

There were times when I felt sorry for her, but other times I was a little more self-righteous than what I perhaps should have been and thought that she got exactly what she deserved. Mom said Lyla wasn't suicidal, but I would sometimes wake up with cuts and bruises. She wanted to hurt herself just to hurt me. I guess she failed to realize that I could heal myself.

I finished with just enough time to go outside and swing on an old tire tied up to a large oak tree in the backyard. I liked to sit there and look out at the lake. Mom and Dad would take the rowboat and watch the fireworks during the fourth of July. I, unfortunately, couldn't join them. Even if Lyla would act decently enough for the occasion, I wouldn't remember what she saw. I liked to imagine all of those colors bursting in the air as the sound exploded in my chest.

21

I did love those long summer days, but I did wish that I got to see at least one nighttime before I died. Just one would be enough.

"You should come eat," Dad said from the back porch.

I was a little disappointed with Dad, and I turned around so I could let him see that on my face. "I'm not very hungry."

He began walking toward me. "Well, you know we can't feed Her."

I shrugged my shoulders and turned away to face the lake once more. "Lyla will live."

Dad stood close enough to be in my peripheral vision. He looked a little surprised. Was it really that shocking that someone dared to speak her name? "It's you too," he said.

They couldn't let her eat, they couldn't let her use the bathroom, shower, or sleep anywhere except where her chains were. No wonder why she was an animal. "I'd rather be alone for a little while longer."

Mom and Dad couldn't trust her, so I had to suffer because of it. "I'll never know what it's like to have a full day to myself, so I might as well enjoy what I can."

Dad furrowed his eyebrows and pouted his lip, something he often did before he tried to lecture and apologize at the same time. "Roxy, I do like Adam. It's just that—"

"You're afraid I'll have sex?"

"No!" Dad said offended. "I trust you."

That made me smile and feel a whole lot better.

"I'm afraid that Lyla will get in the way, and you'll get hurt." Dad didn't like to show fear, but it was obvious. "She's powerful, Roxy. She's more powerful than you can imagine."

"Well, good trumps evil!" I smiled and swung the tire swing just enough to bump Dad in the hip.

He smiled at first, but my charm wasn't as effective as usual. "Only in the fairytales."

Dad was thinking about telling me the truth about my origin and Lyla seemed to be getting more desperate. Something was happening. I could feel it.

"I'll be in soon for prison duty."

Dad kissed me on the forehead before heading back inside the house. I knew he and Mom liked to eat as many meals as humanly possible with me, but I couldn't go inside yet. I loved how the warm sun felt on my skin as it was bathing me with life. I loved how the wind whipped my hair back and forth as I bravely soared higher and higher on that rickety, old swing. I loved how each blade of grass tickled my feet as the dirt squished between my toes. But one of the greatest things that I loved about the day was watching the sun fall below the horizon. The sky was filled with so many beautifully rich colors. The orange speckled through the clouds as the rest of the sky was covered in blues, pinks, and purples. I was always curious to see what would happen next, but it would forever remain a mystery to me.

"Roxy!" Dad came running toward me, screaming my name. I hadn't noticed until he grabbed me and shook me. "Roxy!"

I snapped out of my trance and wrapped my arms around him as he carried me off to the shelter of our home. "I'm sorry."

It was hard to explain what happened in the twilight. Sometimes I would feel myself go, and other times, I just went. I could feel my mind going and the darkness consuming me. "I've never felt like this before."

"Hold on!" Dad yelled.

He rushed me down into the basement. Mom was there, practically shaking. She helped me with my clothes. As I took off one thing, she was there to help me put on another. As soon as I got both of my arms into my shirt sleeves, a shackle was there. I knew it was for the best, but I never could get rid of the gut-wrenching feeling that they were chaining me up because I was a monster.

It didn't hurt. It never hurt when She came. I know that I claimed not to be afraid of Her, but it did frighten me how easy it was to let go and for Her to take me over completely.

Every night began the same. Mommy and Daddy cowered away in fear of their beloved daughter, and I reviled in the thought of their sorrows soon to come by my own hands.

"Lyla," Daddy said with such disdain. It tasted so yummy!

"Have you missed me?"

Chapter Two

"I can't say that I have, Lyla." Daddy was an entirely different person at night, one who that silly twit would never be able to comprehend. He hated me, and that's what I loved the most about him.

"I've missed you." I smirked and set my sights on Mommy. "I've missed her too."

"Good evening, Lyla." Mommy was terrified, which was hysterical to me. It was wise of her, but I was locked up in those cursed chains. I very well couldn't do anything as long as the engraved enchantments kept my powers dormant.

"You should relax," I chuckled. "Go have another drink."

Daddy became enraged and got close to my face, practically nose to nose. "Don't you dare talk to your mother like that!" His nostrils were flaring and everything.

It was quite insulting to me. "Just because someone is a whore doesn't give them the right to be a mother!"

I looked over at Mommy again. The poor dear was shaking, and tears were beginning to well in her eyes. It amused me that she held her head up high, trying to appear strong. "You've got some twisted concept of what a whore is, but that doesn't surprise me. What would someone like you know what it means to be pure?"

"Well, if you remember correctly, I'm the only virgin in the room. Unfortunately..." They went through a lot of trouble to make sure their darling poodle didn't give away her special treat to any of the many dogs that came barking. "But don't try to convince me that you two junkies are any kind of righteous."

"How did you know that?" Their faces were so funny—the horror, the shock!

It would have taken so much of me not to laugh, so I didn't bother and I laughed at all of their displeasure. "I've got a talent, but I'm sure you know that." I finished my laughing fit with a smirk. "I know about all of that wine Mommy likes to take to relax herself and I know it doesn't quite hit the spot."

"That's our past," Mommy lied. "We're not those people anymore."

I rolled my eyes, purposely over dramatic. "Just because a couple of priests offer a chance at redemption doesn't mean that you get to change. After all, you two idiots are raising a great evil along with the good." I offered them my thumbs up approval. "Fantastic job there!"

"You will behave yourself!" I think Daddy had an ulcer. He was dreadfully angry about the stupidest things. I was only pointing out the obvious. They were screw ups eventually about to destroy the world.

"Or what?" I asked.

He smiled, as if he were actually capable of coming up with some kind of decent idea. "Or I don't give you your bucket back."

It's pretty humiliating when an all-powerful being is forced to piss in a bucket in the first place. Then he decided to take it away after too many honest conversations. Whoever knew men were such babies! I knew all the right buttons to press when it came to Daddy. If I wanted, he could have thrown himself off a cliff right after bleeding Mommy Dearest dry. I would never be weak enough to be controlled. "You've chained me up to a wall every night since I was a kid and you're trying to control me by offering me some small piece of dignity by giving me a bucket to piss in? Real smooth," I said sarcastically. "I think I'd rather have Mommy scrubbing the floors every day."

Mommy's nostrils flared up. I knew she hated it a little more than I did. That was a much better consolation.

"Let's go upstairs." Daddy made sure to jingle the keys in front of my face. If I were quick enough, I could have reached out and caught it with my teeth. I wasn't going to try and give him the satisfaction of feeling victorious in case I failed. I didn't even flinch or look at him as he placed the keys back where they belonged on that idiotic hook. Sooner or later, making me a mockery would be their undoing.

"You know I'm going to kill you both, right?" I watched for Mommy's reaction. She was so terrified, and she shook and had to hold back tears. She begged me with her eyes to take it back or to be joking, but I wouldn't kid about something like that. "No one gets to treat me this way and live."

"Come on!" Daddy ran to take Mommy's hand, but she pulled it away.

"Take that back, Lyla!"

I wished I had a mirror present to watch my own twisted smile, but the sheer horror on their face reflected my malevolence perfectly. "I'm going to slit both of your necks and watch your blood stain that clean carpet that Mommy loves so much."

"We won't let that happen!" Daddy was such an esteemed liar. He pretended to be the valiant hero so much that he was beginning to convince himself that he was. Deep down, we both knew he didn't possess the stones required for victory.

"Then kill me," I challenged. "You both know it's the only way."

The sad part about it was that I knew them well enough to know that they were not only considering it, but they certainly had already. They were simply too riddled with guilt to go through with it.

"Oh." I pretended to be confused. "Is that pesky emotion for that fairy princess getting in the way? What is it called?" I laughed. "Oh yeah! *Love*." They claimed they loved their precious, little Roxy. Why couldn't they be like normal people and love a dog or something? I know that they shed, they make a lot of noise, and they piss everywhere when they're not trained, but it would be less of a hassle than a teenage girl. "Would you honestly forsake this entire world for the life of your daughter? You know the one you two prefer?"

"You don't know anything about Roxy," Daddy proclaimed so dignified! "She is strong enough to defeat you."

Mommy was just a foot behind Daddy, cowering behind him. "Mommy doesn't think so."

He looked behind him to see her. Daddy felt so betrayed, so she put on a brave front and tried to be the hero. "Your end is coming soon, Lyla."

"If that's true, you two won't live to see it."

Perhaps some part of them thought I was only making idle threats. I had been for a very long time. However, I believed what I was saying was actually a prophecy about to come to pass. If only they knew what was soon to come! I was going to sow so much destruction into the world. Too bad Mommy and Daddy weren't gonna live to see the benefits.

I began to sing a little song for them. "I'm gonna slit your throats, slit your throats, slit your throats. I'm gonna slit your throats and watch you bleed dry." I had a very lovely singing voice. I was a little hurt that they both looked so mortified, and they began walking slowly until they got to the stairs and left me all alone in the basement. Oh well. I had my little song to keep me company for the next twenty minutes.

The worst part about being chained up every night was the fact that I got bored. I could only imagine how I was going to skin my parents alive so many times. I had been plotting their deaths since I was six. I needed a new hobby or a new victim of interest.

It was fun breaking down Mommy. I heard her arguing with Daddy about what they should do with me. She believed all of my threats. She wasn't sure whether or not she should kill me or beg for their miserable lives. I was pretty sure I was going to kill her regardless of whatever deal she tried to make with me, but she didn't need to know that until it was far too late.

Miss Princess thought her life was so hard. Ha! I was chained to a freaking basement every night. The chains were barely long enough for me to lay on the ground and place my arms in a comfortable position to sleep. Of course I hated that she got to live her life while she expected me to rejuvenate her by sleeping. In some ways, she rejuvenated me as well. My wrists didn't hurt anymore. The twit actually thought I couldn't catch onto that nifty healing power of hers. My ability was a lot more useful, but it was out of commission as long as those stupid chains were there.

The twit and my parents also believed that I couldn't remember anything that happened during the day. I was only about ninety-nine percent positive of the reason why she couldn't remember me, but I remembered every nauseating detail about her mundane life. I especially wanted to kill Daddy for those blasted morning jokes. Mommy had to die for her runny eggs.

One bright spot about her day was that gorgeous, light skinned, dark brunette. Adam and Roxy probably thought they would run away and start their own adorable country music band. He also had quite the lovely singing voice whenever Roxy could weasel him into singing a few notes. I had other plans though. I wasn't sure if I was going to gag, maim, or take off that pretty honey skin of his one inch at a time.

29

There was also the other option. I could have spelt with him and defeated Roxy by sabotage. I was not above it. He could be easily corrupted. I rather enjoyed the thought of it.

I desperately wanted to mention Adam aloud to Mommy and Daddy so word could get back to Roxy. She would go mad from worry, completely push him away, and make both of their lives miserable until I murdered him anyway, but I thought it was better that Team Good thought I was totally ignorant of what my annoying half did.

Hours passed by very slowly. Roxy was depending on me passing out, but I wasn't going to do that. If she was going to be a terrible inconvenience and pop up every dawn, then I was going to stay up all night and watch that moron bumble through her pointless high school about to pass out from lack of sleep. I didn't always have to kill to be satisfied. Sometimes, the simplest annoyances were all the evil that I really needed. If everyone knew that, we wouldn't have wars.

Seriously! The problem that I had observed about human beings was that they felt certain negative emotions, and they continuously held them in until they exploded all over someone else or hurt themselves. Mommy was a prime example. It wouldn't take too much longer for her to kill herself or let me go so I could do it for her. The only one keeping her tethered to her sanity was her dear husband.

Daddy eventually did visit me. I estimated that it was around midnight when he finally came down those creaky steps. He was holding that metal bucket in his hand as if it were the hope of all humanity. "Let's strike a deal, Lyla."

I eyed the bucket for a millisecond. I didn't want him to think he had some kind of advantage, but it would have been nice not to alleviate on myself. "Why? You weren't bothering me. I'm locked up so I can't bother you. Why flatter yourself with my presence once again?"

He smiled as he came closer, but it wasn't sweet or sincere. Daddy was so much crueler than what he led on. "I'm trying to show you some compassion."

"You're trying to get me to earn your compassion, which makes it void of compassion. Therefore, you can shove your compassion right up your—"

"Am I to understand that I'm getting on your nerves?" He smirked, much too overconfident for my taste.

"Of course you are. You, your wife, and your heaven spawn all make me extremely sick." I smiled blissfully while thinking about the day when they'd be choking on their own blood. "But I'll be rid of all of you soon, so what's it really matter?"

Daddy chuckled. "You're in no position to give threats." That old snake even pulled on my chains to make a nice rattling sound. "You're trapped here."

"I've escaped your neglectful eyes before. Twice. Once when I was three and the other when I was six. You're not exactly Alcatraz. "

"So you're getting pretty rusty then, aren't you?"

"Or maybe I'm just biding my time." I smirked. "I can't perform the ritual until I turn eighteen, remember?"

Daddy's thin armor was finally pierced. "You know about that?" He honestly believed that he was above me, and it was just so precious!

"I had quite the adventure when I was six." Mommy had left a broom too close to me, and I managed to get the keys. They tried to stop me, but I sent Daddy flying through a wall easily enough. That put them out of commission long enough for me to find some idiot to manipulate long enough to make it into the next state. Roxy resurfaced, but she cried until the early sunset. Thank God it was the winter time. I was able to stay away from my parents long enough to find some of my adoring fans. "Some of my followers found me and told me everything."

31

I loved watching Daddy squirm. He thought he had everything properly situated simply because he considered himself to be good and had hope, and someone like me could never understand that. Little did he understand that evil loved hope. It made do-gooders extremely lazy while the bad guys swooped in and got what they needed done.

When he composed all of his rightfully placed fear, he smiled. "Roxy has people who want to protect her too."

"Too bad your wife isn't one of them." It was a sore subject for him, but it was something we both could agree on. Of course, he didn't want to admit that out loud to me, but he very well couldn't deny it! "She's tired. Why don't you relieve her of her burden and let me go?"

"You'd kill us both."

"Only a little," I giggled.

Daddy didn't think it was funny, yet he still knelt down in front of me and set the bucket down close enough for me to reach. I suppose he wanted to prove that he had compassion after all. "Have a nice night, Lyla."

As soon as he stood up straight, he kicked his bucket over, and it slid across the floor beyond my reach. I, unfortunately, let my anger show through a glare and a pout, which resulted and a very smug and satisfied smirk from him.

He started walking away with his righteous attitude, but I knew better than that. "You know, I didn't quite know what I was when you first started chaining me up like an animal."

He stopped right in front of the steps. I'm not sure why they always stopped to listen to what I had to say, but it was such a useful flaw on their part.

"The only thing I knew was that my Mommy and Daddy hated me. I thought you two were the monsters." They thought they were so holy! They were told one of us was evil and the other was good. Children don't know of such things. They're the ones who taught me how to hate. "But you know what, Daddy? I'm too big to be afraid of monsters anymore."

Instead of choking on his own blood, he began to choke on his tears. "Good trumps evil, Lyla."

I was satisfied enough for the time being. "You're just as dammed as I am."

That upset him enough to send him up the stairs again. Once again, the last laugh was mine. "Night, Daddy!"

I laughed and tried to relax myself enough without falling asleep. I was getting tired, but I was determined not to give Roxy the satisfaction. I didn't want to sleep through all of my existence, despite having nothing better to do. Resisting the urge to pee distracted me a little bit, but my body eventually forgot that I had to go. It would remind me later in a bladder crunching rush, but hopefully that wouldn't happen until dawn. Sweet Roxy had thankfully been easing off of so many liquids. I suppose she was about as humiliated as I was.

I was going to kill them very soon for all they had done to me.

I knew it wouldn't be much longer when Mommy came squeaking down the stairs so apprehensively. There was no reason for her to come see me so much. Roxy even told her not to, but Mommy couldn't help it. She was drawn to me.

"I won't bite you, Mommy."

The witch was already crying, and I hadn't even done much to her yet. "Hello, Lyla." The more I wore her down, the stronger I knew I could make her. It was Roxy and Daddy who forced Mommy to live like a coward.

"What brings you to me?"

She came out from behind the wall and revealed a plate of snacks. She hadn't done that since I was a very little girl. "Roxy didn't eat dinner, so I thought you might be hungry." She sat on the ground far away enough so I couldn't reach her. Then, she sat the plate on the ground and began scooting it closer to me so I could reach it.

My chains did grant me enough space to pick up the plate and feed myself, but I never made a move for it. "Feed me, Mommy."

The abundant fear rushed away and she immediately scooted close enough for me to touch her. "Alright." She smiled meekly and began to feed me the plate of cheeses, fruit, and lunch meats. I could have easily bitten her fingers off, but it had become so easy to manipulate her that there was truly no need.

"Thank you." I was starving. Roxy could really be an inconsiderate whore when she wanted to be.

Mommy began to smile and stroke my soft cheek as she would do to Roxy when she used to wake her up in the morning when we were small enough to sleep in a bed. "My little girl…"

I did love her fear, but I did prefer her adoration just a little bit more. Perhaps it was the bond that mothers have with their daughters. "I am yours, just as much as Roxy."

She smiled at me as she would at Roxy. "I know."

"And I love you." I reached out and wrapped my arms around her. My legs were chained so close to the wall that it was hard to move forward at all, but I had just enough room for a good squeeze.

"I love you too." Mommy wrapped her arms around me as tight as she could, as if she were making up for all of our lost time. I could have bitten her neck so hard that she bled to death. That's how much trust and affection she had for me. Deep down, she genuinely did want to help me. That's how I knew we would work out all of our problems. Daddy was in the way.

"That's why you should let me go."

"I should what?" Mom asked confused while pulling away from my grip.

She wasn't quite as ready as I thought. I tried to sound as adorable as possible. There was once a time when she was more afraid for me than of me. We needed to revisit that place again. "You should let me go."

I looked directly into her eyes, and I knew that I had her in my clutches once again. "What will happen?"

I had every intention of killing her, but I very well couldn't tell her that. She wasn't quite in that deep yet. "If you set me free, I will do the same for you."

"You'll set me free?" She was so hopeful! Mommy didn't even know what it meant, but she longed for it.

"Yes." I smiled, hopefully not too wickedly. "I'll set you free."

"You won't kill me? Mom asked surprised, yet still willing to follow through on whatever I asked.

"No."

"Or Rick?"

I pouted stubbornly. "He's not negotiable." I should have lied, but I hated Daddy far too much to even consider it.

"Please!" Mom begged.

I rolled my eyes and sighed. "Fine," I lied. "He can live, if he accepts me."

"I promise he will!"

That was debatable. Daddy loved Roxy and he accepted what she could do. He let go of his past sins and he liked living stuck-up. It was hard to work with someone like that, but it wasn't impossible.

I grabbed a hold of Mommy's face, and I made her stare into my eyes as I poured my desire into her soul. It was so easy to do. She didn't believe that Daddy was the greatest man in the world. She didn't like how he treated me, and she was forced to betray me for his unjust verdict. All I had to do was find that resentment in her heart and carefully cut the strings that bound it in her subconscious. "But he'll have to die if he tries to kill me. You'll have to kill him. Do you promise me?"

"I promise you."

I held up my right pinky. "Pinky swear?" I reminded her of a time when I was so tiny, my hands would barely fit in any chains. Daddy hated me. I frightened him, but Mommy loved me. She would hug me and kiss me while we sat in my bed, and I asked her to promise me that she wouldn't let Daddy hurt me. She pinky swore that she wouldn't let anything bad happen.

"Pinky swear." She smiled, and her pinky made a firm agreement with my own. Her promises didn't mean much to me anymore, but I wouldn't need her to follow through. If she didn't have the stones, I would kill him along with her. After all, what was a mother worth if she couldn't keep her children safe?

"Now get the keys and set me free."

Our pinkies unclasped and she did just as I commanded. She stood on her feet and began walking slowly over to the keys.

The house began shaking from the quick stomps of Daddy running as fast as he could to try and stop me.

"Hurry up!"

Mommy did as she was told and grabbed the keys just as I heard the basement door open. There was no squeak from the steps—only the thud from Daddy heroically jumping down and diving into Mommy just as the tip of the keys grazed my shackles.

"No!" Mommy screamed as she tried to fight him off. "We have to be free!" I could only use a bit of my power in my current position, and it was more than enough to make Mommy go downright insane.

"Get a hold of yourself!" He shook her violently until she began to snap out of it. "She's controlling you!"

She stopped struggling as the realization washed over her face. She couldn't breathe at first, but then she breathed as if she were exasperated. Then Mommy began to cry, and she dared to look at me as if I had betrayed her. "You…"

"You pinky promised that you would kill Daddy."

I watched both of their priceless expressions. Daddy didn't quite know what to do. It was unfortunate enough he had a daughter living in the basement who wanted to string him up by his intestines, but it was even worse that he couldn't trust the woman who slept next to him.

Mommy had another reaction entirely. She became enraged like an animal and broke free from Daddy long enough to slash me savagely in the face from the top of my cheek to my lips. "You stupid, evil, whore!"

Daddy grabbed her again before she could inflict anymore damage on me, but I knew he wanted to let her go and turn her loose on me.

My face stung. She cut far enough to make me bleed, but I laughed. "I was only going to kill the both of you, but I think I'll settle when everyone you ever loved is dead." I tasted the blood dripping on the side of my mouth and smiled as malevolently as my face could manage.

"You're not going to win," Daddy seethed.

I ignored him altogether. "That was your last chance, Mommy."

I imagined their terrified face and closed my eyes as I once again began to sing my song. "I'm gonna slit your throats, slit your throats, slit your throats. I'm gonna slit your throats and watch you bleed out dry."

Mommy burst into a fit of tears, so Daddy had to help the raving lunatic upstairs to her room.

I sat there squirming a little bit from my body remembering that I had to pee again, but that wasn't the only reason. I enjoyed their strife so much. I thrived within it. I also knew that very soon I would be free, and they would be dead.

Then I would move onto my next exciting project.

Chapter Three

Holy cow! "Dad!" I squeezed my legs as tight as I could. It felt like my bladder was going to explode! "It's sunrise!" That wasn't all. My face hurt too, and my eyes were really heavy. If I didn't have to pee so badly, I would have probably collapsed. What had Lyla done to me? "Dad!" I screamed.

He came running down the stairs. "Sorry."

As soon as he unlocked me, I blotted up the stairs and to the downstairs bathroom. Thank goodness Mom wasn't occupying it, because I don't think I could have made it in time on my own. I could not live like that. Dad was going to have to give Lyla the stupid bucket back!

But after having that sense of relief, my whole body felt exhausted. She must have literally stayed up all night. Thank God it was prom night. All the teachers felt they had a moral obligation to let us off the hook with no tests.

I got a good look in the mirror and that sort of startled me into being awake enough to function. Mom told me once that Lyla was a pretty vain person, so I found it hard to believe that she could tear up her…Or rather *our* face like that. How could she even manage it? I always chewed off my nails. It was a lousy habit of mine that I'm sure she must have disliked. She must have really dug at me.

"Wow." It wasn't that big of a deal. I just thought it away and as easy as it came, it went. It was a good thing I had the ability to heal or else I'd have to start holding a grudge against her.

I did not like waking up like that. I had to make some kind of arrangement with Lyla somehow if that's the way she was gonna treat me.

I walked out of my bathroom, and I heard my phone ringing from my bedroom. I usually didn't get a lot of callers, especially that early. I figured that it could only be one person. As soon as I opened my bedroom door, I jumped flat on my stomach on top of my bed so I could be close enough to reach out to grab my phone sitting on my night stand. "Hello?"

"Roxy?"

"Adam!" My morning was already a hundred times better. "You're quite the wonderful wake up call."

"I'm sorry if I woke you."

"I was awake already. You just made my morning better." He certainly did. I was so giddy talking to him.

"I'm sorry to bug you so early." Something was wrong. I could tell by his voice. "The doctors are saying that my grandmother will be gone in a few hours and..." Adam became silent for a couple of seconds, but it felt like forever. "I really need you right now, Roxy."

"Sure." I didn't even really think about Dad or asking for permission. I just needed to be there for him. "I'll get dressed, and I'll be ready by the time you get here."

"Thank you, Roxy."

"You're welcome." When I hung up the phone, an incredible load of problems fell on my shoulders. I couldn't let him lose his grandma when I could heal her. She was a very personable woman and honestly, she was all that he had. If she died, he would have to spend the rest of the night alone. I couldn't even be there to comfort him. I just couldn't let that happen!

Mom didn't sit my clothes out like usual and I didn't smell breakfast or hear her in the kitchen. I decided to creep across the hallway to see if she was in her bedroom. The closer I got, the more I wished I hadn't started trying to sneak my way in. Just as I could hear her sobbing behind her bedroom door, I could feel the darkness around her like a ghost haunting us. I had felt it sometimes, but never as strong. I almost felt as if it were ready to reach out and choke me.

"Mom?" I knocked gently and maybe a little hesitant. I didn't want to see my mom in any sort of distress, so I had to help her. "Mom?"

I pushed the door open. My parents had two giant windows in their bedroom, but the curtains were covering them both. There was only a sliver of light peeking through the window and hitting Mom lying on the bed. She was tossing and turning as if something had a hold of her. I slowly walked to her bedside until I was close enough to see the tears stained on her face. "Mommy?"

She stopped struggling and looked dead at me, terribly afraid. "Lyla?" She gasped as she spoke her name and not mine. How could she look into my eyes and not know?

"No, Mom." I reached out and grabbed her hands. They were still shaking. "It's past sunrise. It's me, Roxy."

She looked at me for a while, but I don't think she understood. I could see her eyes, but they looked glazed. The lights were on, but nobody was home—at least anybody that I knew.

"Roxy," Dad called from the doorway, "come on."

Mom sank back into her bed and began whimpering once again. I couldn't just leave her alone like that. "But she needs me!" I squeezed onto her hand tighter and began to wish her well. Everything that I had, I tried to give her. Any other day it worked just as well as my healing abilities. I just thought about it, and it happened. I didn't understand why she wasn't getting better.

Dad came into the room and placed his hand on my shoulder gently. "She needs to be alone for a little while."

Why weren't my powers working? I couldn't even feel it starting to work within her. That haunting aura continued in the room, strangling my mother and making her suffer.

"What did Lyla do to her?" If Lyla was standing in front of me, I would have slapped her good! She would have deserved it too.

Dad shut the door behind us and began nudging me away. He didn't want me anywhere near her. "From what I know, they only talked, but Lyla has a way with words."

I understood that Lyla was dangerous. Mom warned me about her, and they obviously had to lock her down for some reason, but I refused to believe that her powers were stronger than mine. "I have to help her, Dad."

"I don't think you can." He furrowed his brows and sighed again, and I almost broke into a fit of tears before he even spoke another word. "When she sees you, she only thinks of Lyla."

Mom told me that she knew the difference. She could look into our eyes, and it was like clockwork. It didn't make any sense why she couldn't just snap out of it!

"It's better that I get you to school," he said. "I'll stay home and take care of your mother."

It was better that he didn't leave her alone at all. "I hope it's alright with you, but I'm going to the hospital with Adam. His grandmother is going to pass soon, and he needs someone to be there for him."

Dad was probably going to lecture me in seven different languages until I got him with the sympathy bit. Still, he gave me that stern look that I didn't get that often, but all kids knew what it meant. "Roxy, you cannot heal his grandmother."

41

I opened my mouth to try to come up with some kind of excuse, but it only became a gasp instead of a full word. I just didn't have it in me to lie. "She's all that he has!"

"I'm serious, Roxy. If you do this, you will cause so many repercussions." He grabbed my shoulders and looked me straight in the eye. "You have to trust me."

I understood that I had the power to help people, but he didn't want me to. I trusted that Dad would always keep me safe, but I didn't always believe that he was doing the right thing. "If I don't do all that I can for good, how am I any different than Lyla?"

"I think Lyla would be insulted if she could hear what you just said. Lyla is pure evil, Roxy. You're the only one who can stop her, so let me keep you safe until the proper time arises."

I frowned. "I trust you, Dad." But I wasn't sure what I was going to do yet.

I got dressed and grabbed a bagel and a cup of coffee before I left the house. Before I could run off to Adam's car, Dad stopped me at the door. "Morning joke."

I looked behind me and saw Adam waiting. He literally had someone dying waiting for him to show up and I was holding him up. "I'm running out of time."

"You'll miss these jokes one day, Roxy!" Dad looked sad and sounded miserable like he was about to lose me.

I wasn't in the mood, but he had a more terrible morning than me. Far be it from me to make it worse by not taking two seconds to listen to one of his silly jokes. "Go ahead."

"Why do obese people suck in their stomachs when they get on a scale?"

I took a guess. "Because they mistakenly believe it will alter their weight?"

42

"No." He smiled. "It's so they can see the numbers."

It took a second, but I laughed. "That was actually pretty good." I noticed that he didn't enjoy his tradition as much as he usually did. He must have been real upset about Mom. "I'll never have to miss your jokes because even when I get married, I'll call you every day so you can tell them to me."

He pulled me in for a nice bear hug after that. "I'm counting that as a promise."

"Well, you know I'm not the type to lie." I got a bad feeling. I usually didn't have bad feelings. It was odd, and I truly didn't like it.

Dad loosened his bear grip, but he wouldn't let me go. He grabbed my arms and kept looking at me sympathetically. "I think you should know that you're going to save the world." After all the times I wanted to know, he just spat it out.

"Oh." That was so not the way he was supposed to tell me that. "No pressure. Right?"

"I'm not joking, Roxy." I knew he wasn't. Dad couldn't fake out anybody. He always smiled too much. "When you're eighteen, some people who are on your side will come and take you to where you need to be. There's some sort of ritual you have to perform."

Then he shook me while his fingers desperately clasped onto me a little bit tighter. "You have to succeed so Lyla doesn't."

It was a little hard to believe. "Because, she'd destroy the world?"

He nodded.

It was too much. "Wow." It was easier to blame her for all of my problems if she was that bad, but I didn't want to believe that I actually had a pure evil being inside of me. "Really? Wow!"

"We'll talk after you get home from school today, but I think it's important for you to know that you might have to leave everyone you know behind." He finally let go of me and I felt alone and cold. "Your life

43

is so much bigger than that boy and your friends at school, Roxy. It's time that we prepare you for what you were meant to do."

I always wanted to know what I was born for and why Lyla was the way that she was. It was gratifying finally knowing my purpose, but I wasn't ready to accept it if I had to leave Adam behind. I had to hold back my tears. "Thanks for being honest with me."

I began backing away slowly from my dad. I didn't want to leave him. I didn't want to leave Mom. It was as if I was tugging at a loose thread of my life, and it was becoming undone with each step that I took. When I came back home, was I not supposed to be with Adam anymore? I didn't know. The only thing I knew for sure was that I couldn't let Lyla hurt him like she hurt my mom, so I had to hurt him first.

I wished he was having a better day. All of the butterflies I had were gone. The only thing I had inside of my stomach was guilt about his grandmother and rejection about the prom.

"Morning, Roxy."

"Morning." It was a totally different dynamic. The previous day, Adam was dressed in a light-blue, button-down dress shirt with a pair of khakis. We rode to school with the top down and professed our love to one another. That day, he was dressed in a pair of jeans and a T-shirt and his neat wavy hair was a little curly and messy. He was tired.

Adam's mom had died when he was just a kid and his dad wasn't in the picture. No one from his dad's side wanted to take him in. I guess they were an unruly bunch. He didn't have any aunts or uncles. He only had his grandmother. It wasn't like she had lived a long time and she was ready to go. She was only fifty-two. I guess she had sowed some wild oats in the past, but she had done more than make up for it after being so generous to Adam.

"You look really upset," Adam said.

That made me quite nervous. I couldn't lie to Adam! "Aren't we on the way to the hospital to visit your dying grandmother?"

"Yeah, but you look particularly upset and now you're nervous." Darn him! He knew me too well. "What's the matter?"

"I wish there was something I could do." I couldn't even manage to speak out that one sentence before my eyes welled up with tears.

"These things just happen, Roxy. You live and you die..." He didn't want to accept that. He was stubbornly trying to hold in his tears. He didn't have to try so hard around me. I fully understood.

"My family is having some problems. Most of the time I can solve them, but things were real miserable this morning when I woke up." All it took to make my mom better was being in my presence, and somehow, Lyla made it so that my own mother couldn't look at me without freaking out. "Today was the first time in a long time that I felt completely powerless."

"I know what you mean. Grannie has done so much for me that I feel terrible that I'll never be able to return the favor." Every time he mentioned her, it felt as if he were twisting a knife in my heart. If I didn't do something, I wasn't going to be able to forgive myself. I didn't know how I was going to last going inside of the hospital and looking at her.

"I must say, I'm a little disappointed. I thought everything with your parents was perfect."

"Really?" I was a little surprised. I thought everybody thought I was a freak who lived in a cage because of psycho parents. No one says that stuff to your face, but I wasn't that naive. I still went to high school.

"I think they're a little uptight most of the time, but I thought you guys had the perfect home."

A charming, cheery, cheesy dad and a mom who made me breakfast, lunch, and dinner might have seemed like a dream come true for someone like Adam. Too bad there was so much more to us than that. "It's more dysfunctional than you can imagine."

I reached out and grabbed Adam's free hand. "I don't wanna talk about my family though. I wanna be here for you."

He smiled, which was enough to put all of my negative feelings on hold until we got to the hospital.

The way I felt walking into mom's room was the similar sense I got when we walked inside. There was heaviness and a hopelessness dwelling in that place. It was expected with so many people dying there. I never had to go to a hospital. I never got sick, and Mom and Dad didn't get sick often, certainly not sick enough to go to the hospital. I always wanted to walk up and down the halls relieving all of the patients and families of their troubles, but Dad forbade it. He said it was too dangerous for me.

When we hit the fourth floor where his grandmother was, that's when it all hit me like a punch in the face. There was so much suffering, and I was doing nothing. I walked by rooms of old men struggling to catch any breath and a room where one woman just screamed until a handful of nurses got off their coffee breaks and rushed inside to help the poor woman. I should have been one of the people running inside, but my father's warning continuously kept buzzing in my ear, and I deemed myself too much of a coward.

"She's in here." Adam grabbed my hand and tugged my arm along until we were inside of his grandmother's room. It was a two person room, but the first bed was empty. She had so many different tubes sticking out from different places that it was hard for me not to look away. I felt extremely nauseous and since I couldn't get sick, I knew it was because I was being a baby.

Adam was a pro. "Hi, Grannie." He smiled and came to her bedside as if he were seeing her for the first time in years at a family picnic instead of at her death bed.

She slowly opened her eyes. "Adam?" Even her voice was weak. "Shouldn't you be going to school?"

"I thought I'd stay with you."

"It's that bad, huh?"

"You're gonna be just fine."

I didn't know how to act in that situation. Ms. Owens was so important to Adam, and it was difficult to see her with that bald cap on her head. I wasn't strong enough to walk closer for her to see me. I was ashamed of what I could do for her, because I couldn't do it.

"Enough with the bravery act," she told Adam. "I've still got good ears. I hear the nurses' whispers, and my doctor doesn't have very good bedside manner. I know I'll be dead in a few hours."

Adam clasped her hand tightly. "Don't say that—"

"Now listen. I don't have any life insurance policies. I took my life savings, and I've already had it put in your bank account. There should be enough to cover my funeral. I don't need anything fancy. Just bury me in the cemetery and be done with it."

"You deserve more than that!"

"If only I did..." She chuckled, but it quickly turned into a harsh cough. Adam's brave composure was lost, and he was a helpless child as he watched the person he cherished most in the world begin to die.

"Grannie!" He grabbed a tissue and covered her mouth as she coughed into it. I could see the blood beginning to soak through it even from where I stood. All I had to do was touch her and will her sickness away. It wouldn't hurt me. It wouldn't drain me. It was effortless, and that's what made it the worst.

47

I couldn't hold back my tears when Adam's shaking hands started wiping away her blood with another tissue. I'm not sure how he managed to keep himself from collapsing on top of her in a hysterical cry. I knew I would if my parents died.

"Use the rest of the money and live your life," she begged. "Make something of yourself, Adam. I always had faith in you."

His face was red, but he held himself together with a smile. "Thank you for taking care of me, Grannie."

I was struggling to hold in all of my emotions, but I couldn't breathe. When I did manage, it was a big gasp. That was when they remembered I was in the room. "Is this her?" Ms. Owens asked.

"Uh oh," I said as playfully as my tears would allow. "I'm being referred to as a pronoun, and everybody still knows who I am."

"Adam won't stop talking about you!"

"Don't embarrass me, Grannie," Adam begged.

I smiled and took the seat next to Adam. "I'm sure she can't do any worse than what you already do on your own." I admired him a lot. I didn't think I had it in me to be as strong as he was. He deserved to be rewarded for his strength. If I loved him, I should have been the one to help him.

That was when I made up my mind. "Do you think you could get me a coffee?" I asked him. "I didn't get any sleep last night and—"

"Sure." He leaned over and pecked me on the lips. I wasn't expecting it, but it was marvelous. It birthed instant smiles. "I'll be right back."

Ms. Owens observed Adam as he got up and walked out of the room to get me a coffee, and I could see that she was impressed and a little surprised. I didn't think he was whipped or anything. He was just a polite, sweet man. "You know," she said, "when you've got a man who completely adores you so much to the point where he would leap off the highest mountain and swim through shark infested waters just to meet your desires, you've got something worth holding onto."

"I know." I felt like a little girl trapped inside a fairytale.

"I tried to tell my daughter that, but she never listened." There was a hint of bitterness in her voice. I bet she had a lot of stories that I couldn't even begin to imagine. "Of course if she had, I would have never gotten my Adam."

"What is his father like?"

Her eyebrows rose. "You've never asked Adam?"

"I've always been a little afraid of the answer." I didn't like sad stories, and I knew his dad was a touchy subject. I didn't want to bug Adam about it if it would upset him. Maybe that was wrong of me considering how long we had known each other, but I guess I figured he would tell me when he was ready.

"I'm surprised he hasn't told you, but it's not my place to say."

I didn't know where the closest place to get coffee was, but I was beginning to get nervous about when was the proper time to heal Ms. Owens. I definitely didn't want Adam to be in the room, but I didn't want Ms. Owens to notice that it was me either.

Then as if on cue, Ms. Owens began yawning and breathing heavier and deeply. "I'm sorry. I've been so tired lately."

I shrugged. "It's early." I reached out my hand and placed it on top of hers. "Why don't you go back to sleep? Adam and I will be here until you wake up."

"Thank you." She smiled, which took about all of the strength she had left. "I can see why he's so in love with you." If I had any doubts before, she certainly erased them all. I waited a couple of more seconds until she drifted off to sleep.

I concentrated and imagined her getting better. I had never healed anyone before. I healed a bird that had crashed into a window when I was around seven, and Dad was even mad about that. Who was the bird gonna tell? If it weren't for that bird, I wouldn't have been positive that my abilities could work for anyone other than myself. I could feel my power going inside of Ms. Owens like warmth resting on both of our chests. Then when I felt what I had for Ms. Owens completely pass over, I left her and started rushing out of the hospital room before Adam caught me.

I didn't know where else to go, so I stood outside of the door in the hallway. I didn't know if I had made a mistake, but I couldn't just let her die! I couldn't do that to Adam. Whatever the consequences were, I just had to deal with them.

Adam came from around the corner with two coffees in his hand. "Why are you out here?"

I almost spilled all of my secrets from my mouth, but I scolded myself since Dad wasn't there. "I needed to leave the hospital room." That was the truth. I did need to leave the room.

Adam joined me and pressed his back against the wall next to me. "It's a little too much, huh?"

"I'm sorry." I took my coffee and just stared at it. I didn't know how to act casual. I had been keeping my abilities a secret from Adam, but it never felt like I was lying before. I was totally deceiving him!

"No. I understand." He leaned over and pecked me on the cheek. I started blushing, but I kept looking at my coffee cup instead of facing him like an adult. "Thank you for at least being here for me." He wouldn't be thanking me if he knew how long I let him suffer unnecessarily. I really didn't deserve him.

"Adam!" Ms. Owens yelled.

His eyes bucked and he zipped right to her beside, clutching onto her hands as tightly as he could. "What's the matter?"

I walked in slowly. I didn't want her to know it was me who healed her, but she was undoubtedly better. Before, her skin was so pale that it almost had a grey tint to it. It had returned to its beautiful mocha color and her voice was crystal clear. She could barely raise her arms or keep her eyes opened, but she had enough strength to pull at her IVs and fight Adam as he tried to stop her. "I feel fine!"

"What?"

"I'm fine. I feel fine!" She laughed, and her eyes shimmered. "I swear I feel fine!" It was difficult to hide the truth when I saw her finally well again. It was too soon for Adam to believe, but the pure joy on her face was enough to break my smile from its dinky prison.

"Just lie down, Grannie!" Adam had to push on her shoulders to force her to rest on her back. "I don't want you to strain yourself."

"I've been dying for the past three years of my life! I know what it means to be finally well again."

Adam was still finding it hard to believe, but there was a small part of his brain beginning to open up to the idea that miracles were actually possible, and he was one of the few that got to stare it right in the face. "Let me get the doctor for you."

She grabbed onto his arm quick and tight, something she could have never done before. "You should go to school."

"No!"

Ms. Owens sat up in her bed and pointed at him in guardian mode. "You've already missed too much this year, and finals are coming soon!"

"I can't leave you here alone, Grannie! They said you were going to die."

"And I'm telling you that I'm going to live!" She grabbed his face and kissed him on the cheek, incredibly cheery. "I feel better than I've felt in a very long time."

Then it happened. "I don't know if God finally answered prayer…" She looked dead at me. "…Or if Roxanne is truly an angel sent from heaven."

51

I was already smiling. I think she was only suggesting that because she liked me and she wanted me to marry her grandson, but Adam zoomed in on me too. There was no way he could have known that I was able to do it, but for some reason, he became more open to the idea of miracles once it was a possibility that I could be used to create them.

"I am fine. I promise!" She patted Adam and shooed him away. "I promise you."

He looked at me again, somewhat suspicious. I didn't think he figured it out, but I wasn't going to be able to hide it for long. "I guess we'll go after I talk to the doctor." He kissed his Grannie on the forehead, and he took my hand and led me out. I waved a few fingers at Ms. Owens as a goodbye, since the rest of them were clasped onto the coffee that I didn't want to drink.

Adam found her doctor and talked to him for a couple of minutes. I watched from far off. I couldn't hear them, but it looked like they had a minor argument. Then the doctor walked into Ms. Owens's room and Adam started pacing back and forth. It was evident how desperately he wanted his grandmother's healing to be true. I wondered what it would be like to just outright tell him. Maybe he wouldn't have been mad at me. Maybe he would have been grateful. I didn't do it for any praise or anything, but it was already amazing being held so highly in his eyes. If he knew what I was truly capable of, then maybe it would have been enough of a balance for him not to bail on me when Lyla surfaced.

The doctor came out of the room and began talking with Adam again. The news must have been fantastic, because Adam hugged the doctor. His bedside manner must have been exceptionally awful, because he barely knew how to hug the boy back. Adam ran back inside the room, and I heard laughter and yelling. The other patients probably didn't appreciate it, but it was music to my ears.

I didn't want to intrude on their moment, so I walked back down the hall and stood by the elevators for a while. With that mess taken care of, I had another monstrous situation to conquer. I didn't know how I was going to break up with the perfect boy. I loved him a lot, and he said that he would never be with another person. It wasn't right to take such a giant leap backwards after finally getting over a six year hurdle. I didn't know what I was gonna do.

"Roxy!" I raised my head and spotted him running toward me. "It's a miracle!" He lifted me up into his arms without any reservations and spun me around. "She's okay!"

I smiled. "That's good."

I'm not sure why that busted his bubble, but it did and he set me down. "I mean the doctors have to run some tests, but from an immediate observation, she's okay."

"That's really great."

He was reading right through me somehow. The elevator door opened up, and I shuffled inside and tried to hide behind a big man, but there was just enough space between him and the wall for Adam to glare even more suspiciously. I knew that was my fault because I wasn't being cool and collected, but it was hard.

The burly guy didn't ride with us all the way down and he got off on the second floor, leaving me trapped inside with Adam and our awkward silence that he just had to break. "You don't seem too surprised about my grandma."

"It's amazing!" I smiled as wide as I could and lifted my hands up in the fake celebration. "I told you to have some faith."

As soon as the elevator opened, I hurried out of there while trying not to be too fishy, but I was nervous and he wasn't even running after me. He was calmly walking behind me through the hospital and outside to the parking lot and that actually made everything worse! Then when I got to the car, I didn't have anywhere I could actually run to. I had nothing to do but bounce around all fidgety until he slowly cornered me. "Roxy—"

"What?" I screamed on an accident.

"Did you somehow..." He got this super cute detective look in his eye as he walked over to my side of the car. "...Did you heal her?"

I laughed hysterically and way too nervous to pull it off. "How would I do that?"

He smiled like he knew and I seriously needed him not to know! "I can't explain what it is about you, but at the risk of sounding cheesy, you make me feel better inside." He threw up his hands like it was crazy, but he actually believed it. "Maybe you made her better inside literally."

I was stuck on the whole "feel better" thing. He looked up to me, yet I felt like I let him down for hesitating for so long. "If I could do that, do you think I'd be selfish enough to let you and her suffer for the past three years?"

"Why are you deflecting instead of giving me a straight answer?"

I started stuttering. I didn't know how to lie. It was something utterly beyond my capabilities, especially when it came to him. "Will you please take me to school now?"

Adam didn't want to back down. He was stubborn that way, but I guess he didn't need to bug me. "Sure." My inability to tell a white lie probably said the truth better than my actual words ever could anyway.

I don't know why, but he let it go after that. He didn't say anything during world history or physics. He kind of ignored me with words but told everything with his eyes. When he was talking with other people, he was actually looking at me with a cute curve in his mouth that made his eyes smile too. There was a vibrant joy overflowing from within him, and I got the feeling that he knew that it was partially due to me.

I was jumpy and paranoid the whole day, and instead of sitting across from me during lunch, he sat right next to me. He was flirting a lot

54

without actually flirting. He kept bumping into me playfully and making suggestive movements with his eyebrows. The way he was acting, it was like the two of us were about to run off and get married.

That would have been nice. I could make him a hot meal every day and have it ready for him after coming home from a hard day of work. He could tell me about his day and say that it all went fine, but he really couldn't wait to get home to see me. I'd giggle and then we'd…Well…We'd make love.

"Am I ruining a moment?" asked Nancy. She was an underclassman friend of mine.

"No!" I said embarrassed. I couldn't blush harder than I already was. "Nothing is going on."

"Good." She scooted in between the two of us and Adam made room for her, which was weird. He'd usually be a little upset about something like that, but I guess he was just in an extra happy mood.

"Hi, Roxy. You're looking lovely today!" Nancy was not a generally cheery person, and she could manipulate people on occasion and often used them. She wasn't a bad person, and she didn't mean to be selfish. She was just a tad inconsiderate sometimes.

"Nancy, is there something that you want?"

"We sort of need more bodies to help with prom decorations."

"The junior class is supposed to take care of all of that," Adam whined.

"Yeah, and we suck. I know that." She grabbed my arms and shook me. "It's your prom! Besides, you're not going."

"Why would you say that?" I might have changed my mind!

She rolled her eyes. "You actually came to school today!"

There was a scarcity in the amount of seniors that showed up. Physics was pretty much a desert. "Sure. I'll help."

Adam leaned forward enough so that I could see his cocked eyebrow. "You can help with prom decorations but you can't go to the actual dance?"

"Can we not have this conversation again?" I did the baby face pout. It was another notable power that I wielded quite effectively.

"No need." He smiled and turned to Nancy. "I will stay and help as well."

"Thank you!" Nancy got real excited and hugged and kissed Adam on the cheek. He smiled, but why wouldn't he? Then he saw me looking at her hug him, and he almost started to laugh. "I won't forget this!" Then Nancy ran off after she had what she wanted.

I didn't know what Adam was up to, but I could see that it was no good. "I find it hard to believe that a man who practically built his car from the ground up wants to blow up balloons and hang streamers."

"I find it hard to believe that a girl is willing to decorate the gym for prom, but isn't willing to actually enjoy it."

"What can I say? I'm very mysterious."

He scooted closer and leaned lazily in front of me with a big grin, waiting for me to say something. "Did I make you a little jealous right now?" He was pretty cocky, and he liked to show that on occasion.

I shrugged. "I don't know." I wanted to deny it, but I didn't feel like that would be one hundred percent honest. "Maybe you shouldn't bring another date to prom, if you don't mind."

"The thought literally never crossed my mind. I'll probably go back to the hospital after I take you home."

I moaned. "You really want to decorate the gym?" I did technically agree to help Nancy, but I shouldn't have spent any unnecessary extra time with Adam.

"No, but I'd like to spend some time with you." Darn him. I couldn't resist his charming smiles. It was like he had his own super powers.

I mostly agreed to help Nancy out because I did want to show my school spirit somehow before I left high school. I got to go to a couple of tennis matches and track meets and the pep rallies that were during school, but I never got to go to any of Adam's basketball games or school dances. I probably could have had a little bit more of a social life if my parents weren't deathly afraid of me getting too attached to anyone.

I did want to go to prom. I mean, what kind of girl didn't want to get dressed in a pretty dress and get their hair and makeup done for that special guy who would pick her up in a limousine with a corsage in his hand? It was romantic if not downright magical. It was a girl's right, and I was going to miss it due to Lyla party crashing. If I couldn't be at the prom, I could at least make sure it was the greatest night ever for those who could experience it.

The gym sort of looked like a party store threw up on it when I walked in after school. There was stuff everywhere, but it didn't look like anything, and the juniors were running around like chickens with their heads cut off.

As soon as Nancy spotted me, she ran toward me with a paper in her hands. "It's not supposed to look like this mess! It's supposed to look like this." She unfolded her paper and revealed a beautifully colored sketch of the gym transformed into a starry night sky. I was able to understand why there were so many lights piled up and tangled everywhere. The bleachers were stacked up against the wall and covered by the biggest black drapery ever, a couple of banners were hanging, balloons were being blown up, and a stage was built and set up with all the instruments, but there was still tons to do.

"This is a lot of work." I didn't mean to be a downer, but I was trying to be honest. "I don't know how we could ever manage to get this done. It would take a miracle."

"Well, Adam told me that you were a miracle worker." She hit me in the arm before running off to greet Adam as he came through the door.

I stood there shocked and by myself for a little while. Just because he told Nancy that I was "a miracle worker" didn't mean that he gave anyone any specifics. If he did, then I should have heard something else from someone. Adam was probably just trying to be cute and mess with me a little bit. Even when I watched him talk to Nancy, he was overlooking her shoulder and smirking at me.

I decided to dismiss it. I wasn't going to overanalyze what was probably our last day together. I got to work right away on untangling the lights. They were pretty much glorified Christmas lights, but it was going to look spectacular when everything was hanging on the ceiling. The entire gym was going to be encompassed in black drapery so we didn't have to see the ugly roof of the gym. It was literally going to look like a night sky, probably the closest I'd ever get to seeing one.

With all the heavy lifting Adam could have done, he came right next to me and started working on a pile of lights. The silent smiling was a little unnerving, and I couldn't even last more than one minute before asking, "Why did you tell Nancy that I was a miracle worker?"

He chuckled. "You're quite obsessive."

"Something we have in common, I guess."

He shrugged his shoulders a little bit, but kept his eyes on his insanely terrible knot. "You do work miracles. Look at the job you did on me. I was a delinquent with a future in prison. If it weren't for you, I'd probably be on the run, being tried as an adult, or dead."

"That's not true!" He was handsome, intelligent, and charming. He could become the president if he wanted to one day, or at least a very popular senator.

"It is." He had a breakthrough on his knot, and his string of lights began to straighten out. "I haven't quite told you everything about my past."

I had a little bit more trouble with my pile, even though mine was a little less complicated. "I'm listening."

"Maybe somewhere private. Maybe tomorrow in the morning?"

"I thought you had to take care of your grandmother."

"Well, I got a call from the doctor, and there's no trace of cancer." He smirked and our eyes met. "How do you think something like that happened?"

My heart blasted through my chest so hard and fast that it could have been down in Mexico by the time I managed a cheesy wink and a smile to cover it up. "I guess somebody up there likes ya."

I'm glad he liked me. My classmates said I was charming, but I knew that some people found me to be annoying. I knew Dad was cheesy, but I was no better than him sometimes. If Adam was as bad as he claimed, it seemed a little weird that he'd like me. Maybe it was only because of my powers. Maybe he had such a bad life outside of my aura that he just didn't know any better. He thought I was the only way he could be happy. If I were just a normal girl with the same personality, would he even be into me?

"Let me see that." He took the lights out of my hand and saw another way to untangle the knot, and it came loose easily. He smiled at my astonished expression before moving back to his own. "What would you do without me, Roxy?"

I wasn't sure, but it was only right that I gave him the opportunity to figure out what life could be without me. I was unintentionally impacting his every decision. He didn't know how to be his own man. I was the angel on his shoulder constantly nagging him on what was right without ever saying a word. Maybe that was good, but was it fair? Did he even truly love me? "There's something I have to tell you once we leave here."

He smiled and nodded. "Good." No doubt that he thought I was going to reveal my secret powers. He was going to be devastated once I broke up with him.

We got done with the lights and started to hang them. Adam was quick, strong, and fearless. He didn't mind standing up on those high ladders to hang stuff. I was a little bit more of a chicken and stayed on the ground arranging tables and chairs. We were lucky that our graduating class was so small that we could have prom in the gym. Some of the kids were bummed we weren't having it in a fancy place, but a majority of them were glad that the tickets were only going to be twenty-five dollars.

I kept checking the clock on my phone so I wouldn't be trapped at the school too late. I wouldn't want Lyla tearing the dance floor apart and ruining the black, white, and silver decorations with blood splattered everywhere. It would ruin the classy *Night under the Stars* theme. We were working pretty fast, so it was about six when we were putting the finishing touches on everything.

"We're ready for the test!" Nancy yelled.

Adam climbed down the ladder and ran by my side. He obviously had a mischievous smile on his face. "Let's see what we're missing."

The lights flicked off and everything went pitch black. I clasped onto Adam in a terribly embarrassing kind of way. I was a tiny bit afraid of the dark, and it happened all of a sudden. He took full advantage of my fear and wrapped his arms around me. I wasn't going to complain while I was still frightened. He had big, strong arms. I felt safe with him.

Then, the lights came on and my breath was taken away instantly. The lights draped across the black cloth roof were phenomenal and in the center of the room, there was a star shaped light display that flooded the floor with star spotlights. It was more gorgeous than what I imagined a night sky to be like. "This place looks pretty fantastic."

Adam hugged me tighter into his chest and kissed my forehead. "We make a good team."

"Yeah, we do." I did have some doubts about us, but I couldn't say that it felt wrong. It actually seemed pretty perfect.

Nancy was clapping and jumping up and down. The other juniors were too pooped to show much excitement, but everyone was pretty happy with the room. My fellow seniors were going to flip when they came to the dance! "Why don't you test the dance floor?" Nancy asked us.

I had never seriously danced before with a boy other than my dad. That was pretty depressing, wasn't it? "Did you set me up?" I asked Adam. That devilish smile made all the sense in the world.

"Once a conman, always a conman."

I wasn't upset. I wanted to go to the prom and dance with him. I just couldn't. "Thank you." I rested my arms and head on his chest. I wasn't sure what the appropriate form was, but I was comfortable and the moment was sweet.

Nancy ran to the stage and began tinkering with the equipment until music began to blast out of the speakers. She started skipping through a couple of pop songs until she found a lovely, slow song to dance to. It must have all been Adam's idea, but she was a sweetheart to go along with it.

"Since Grannie is okay, I can focus my attention on other things."

I was trapped inside of a dream. "Like?"

"Starting my life with you."

I lifted myself from off of his chest. It was a beautiful statement that made my heart flutter, but it was a childish thing to say. "You're not suggesting we get married, are you?"

"No, but you don't tell a girl that you love her and that there's no one else if you've never thought about it." He looked a little sad. "You haven't?"

Of course I had imagined a perfect life with Adam at least a thousand times, but with every dream of us, there was also a nightmare of Lyla. "I can't." We could have the perfect morning and then in the twilight, I would be scared to death that I would lose him and wake up at dawn finding him dead. Lyla didn't know how to be happy. She despised the idea of it. She couldn't let someone as wonderful as Adam live. It would mean the end of her. "There's too much I have to work out."

"Like?" Adam was too cocky not to meet the challenge head on.

There was no point in prolonging it anymore. "I'm supposed to break up with you."

His eyes widened in a quick moment of shock, but he hid it well and laughed it off. "It's a good thing we're not boyfriend and girlfriend then, huh?" He waited for me to say that I was joking or toying with his emotions, but all he got from me was awkward and guilty silence. "Why?"

I couldn't even look at him. "My dad thinks it's for the best."

He was offended. "And what do you think?"

I couldn't lie to him. "I think you're for the best." I leaned back into his chest, closed my eyes, and tried to pretend like everything was going to be alright. The more I tried, the more upset I got until I finally started to cry. "No. I'm being selfish!" I couldn't even lie to myself.

I backed away from him, and Adam was so heartbroken. That made me cry harder. "I need to go home."

He was literally perfect, and I was going to let him go. "Okay."

The juniors were extremely nosey, so I rushed out quickly and waited for Adam at his car. I looked at my cell phone. I had several missed calls from Dad. I was a little surprised that he didn't run off to find me. I guess Mom was in seriously poor shape. I still had some time to get home. It was about a twenty minute drive to my house, but I'd get there with still another hour until sunset.

We had another silent ride for the majority of the time. I didn't want Adam to feel bad about losing me. I wasn't the greatest catch in the world. I was perfectly proportionate, but maybe he wanted someone a little taller or someone with a crooked smile. I was only an average student as far as grades. He could find another girl smarter than me or prettier than me. "I can't have sex."

He did a double take. I did announce it out of nowhere. "Ever?"

"I don't know." Mom and Dad didn't tell me that part. I didn't want to be a nun, but I could take an oath of chastity forever if I needed to. It wasn't fair to ask Adam to take it with me. "Definitely not soon."

"Okay."

"Okay?" I was confused and surprised. That was supposed to be our deal breaker! "What kind of boy are you?"

"I'm one who's *in love* with a girl. I'm not *in lust* with you."

I was amazed. I heard girls talk about boys. Sex seemed like the way of the world. "And it's never crossed your mind?"

"I'm a boy!" He laughed. "It's crossed my mind, but that's not what we're about. Don't try to cheapen what I feel for you." He understood me, but I think I insulted him. He was already frustrated about the breakup. I didn't mean to pour salt in his wounds.

"I'm not trying to do that. I'm just telling you that it's tremendously crucial that I'm a virgin."

"Fine. You'll be the next one in this relationship to even bring up sex."

63

It couldn't have been that simple! That was supposed to send him packing. How was I supposed to break up with him if he was really as spectacular as I suspected? "Even if I wore a belly shirt and booty shorts over your house?"

That made him laugh for some reason. "You would never wear that, but sure."

I didn't get it. If Adam was that marvelous, the universe shouldn't have made me leave him. "I need you to stop being so perfect when I'm trying to break up with you."

He smirked. "I'll try." He was so cocky! He thought he had fixed everything, but I was still going to break up with him as soon as he parked that car.

Then the moment came. We pulled up at my house. We were done. Over. There would be no more rides, no more dances, and no more kisses! "Okay." I got out of the car and slammed the door. "This is it." I leaned down and spoke to him through the rolled down window. "We're over."

"Okay," he said casually.

"Okay?" That was disappointing. I was expecting a bit more of a fight.

"Okay." It was like he was waiting for me to leave, like I had been bothering him the whole time.

"Okay." I started walking away with my head hanging low. I knew it had to be done, but I didn't expect him to give up that easily.

Then I heard his door slam shut. "Wait!" Adam began running toward me. "You left something in the car."

That was weird. I had my backpack and my purse. I didn't remember carrying anything else unless my phone or something fell out. "What did I leave—"

As soon as I turned around, his lips were there to meet my own, but it was more than the lips. Oh boy, it was more! I don't know if I was ready for it. My eyes bucked at first, but I kind of relaxed and let it happen after that. It was a good first kiss—a *real* first kiss.

His lips parted from mine and everything on my body was still tingling—my tongue, my lips, my skin…Everything! My mind was warped in the craziest kind of way and part of me wanted to do it all over again, and then there was still a part of me that wondered what I had left behind.

"Me," he said.

"Oh." I blushed and giggled. I hardly felt like a woman, but whatever I felt like was in a really happy place. "You really have to stop that or I might not be able to break up with you."

He cupped my face with his hands gently and pecked me on the lips. "I'll be here to pick you up tomorrow at noon."

Then I became mush! "Okay."

"Okay." Adam walked away with his head held high and a little swagger in his steps. I guess he wasn't upset about prom anymore. That was much better than a silly dance anyway.

I would have stood on my porch dazed all night if my dad wouldn't have opened the door and pulled me inside. "I thought I told you to call it off with him!"

I closed the door so Adam couldn't hear my dad yelling. "I tried, but I couldn't." I didn't like to be yelled at. I didn't need that for someone to get their point across. I knew I didn't do what he told me to, but I wasn't going to march outside and break up with Adam just because he yelled it in a command. "I'm in love with him."

"You can't afford to let Lyla find out about him!" Dad was such a kind and compassionate person. Sometimes I forgot he had anger in him. "Your mother hasn't gotten any better."

I felt bad again for not being able to help her, but I probably could have done it if Dad would had given me more time. "Can I see her?"

"You can't use that much of your power. It's too dangerous." He was so sure of it, but I didn't get it.

"It doesn't hurt me. I got rid of Adam's grandma's cancer without breaking a sweat!"

Dad's eyes bucked. "You healed his grandmother?" Dad yelled. Again!

"I had to." I felt trapped against that door while he screamed, hovering over me like some kind of monster.

"You didn't have to!"

"What's the big deal?"

He grunted to himself while he tried to calm down, but all he did was lower his voice. He was still just as mad. "Just as Lyla leaves an impression when she uses her abilities, you do also. It's possible that those who know about you and Lyla can track you."

How was I supposed to know that if they never told me? "No one has found me yet."

"You seeping out your joy or whatever it is that you give to people don't make as big an impression as when you force it on people or when you heal."

No wonder why he was so angry about that bird. We had to pack up everything and leave after that. "Is that why you didn't want me to fix Mom?"

He didn't even look guilty about it! "Even if you could save her, the energy that you would have to put out—"

"Would be worth it!" I was a little disgusted with him. I had never felt that way about him before, but it wasn't right to let her suffer. "If Lyla put out that much energy, then we're in danger anyway!"

"No. Just as Lyla's chains suppress her full powers, I have similar markings on this house. It will keep the outside world from tracking her here. I couldn't do the same for your powers or it would have disrupted Lyla's cloak."

Lyla could do what she wanted, but we were in danger if I fought back? It wasn't fair! "So what now?"

"Do they know it was you?"

I mumbled. "Adam is suspicious." I wasn't sure what Dad would do to him, and that scared me a little bit.

Dad took a couple of steps away from me and moaned to himself. I guess I really messed things up. When he got himself together, he took a deep breath and faced me again. "I have to find a way to mask your energy and I have to do it now. I have to chain you up before I leave."

He knew how much I hated that! "Can't Mom do it?"

"Absolutely under no circumstances is your mother ever to speak or see Lyla again. She can't handle it anymore." He blamed me. I don't think he ever had before, but it was getting harder for him to separate the two of us. "Please go change."

It hurt me like he had just taken the rustiest knife he could find and plunged it into my back. I didn't create that situation. I was born with Lyla. I wasn't crazy. She infected my life, and they chose how to deal with everything. They chose to keep me ignorant. "You know, I wouldn't have made such a mistake if you had been honest with me about everything!"

"Yes, you would have." Dad was sure of it. "I should have kept you from this boy."

"And lock me up like you do to Lyla?" Adam was one of the best parts of my life. Without people like him, was it worth it to save the world? For him to suggest that all those memories weren't worth it…

I had begun to cry. Usually Dad would hold me in his arms and kiss me on the forehead, but he didn't do anything besides walk away from me.

I followed him into the basement and changed into an old, gray dress. It was big, ugly, and depressing. It was basically a more comfortable burlap sack. Dad got the bucket and sat it down in Lyla's spot, except it was for me. I hated being chained up early, so we didn't do it. I never had to wait more than ten minutes for Lyla to take over. When they shackled me, I didn't feel like myself. It reminded me that I was two people, yet we were one in the same. The chains were cold, and they were tight. I would have caught up on my sleep if I wasn't too uncomfortable. I didn't want to be trapped there for an hour like an animal. "I'm sure everything will be okay," I told Dad. "Please don't leave me like this."

He was a little sympathetic, but he was mostly duty bound. "I'm sorry, Sweetheart." The only compassion he offered was a kiss on the forehead. "I'll see you at dawn." I watched him set the keys on the hook, and I wished they could have flown over to me so I could set myself free. It must have been even worse for Lyla, who was truly capable of such a feat if it weren't for her chains.

Dad walked up the creaky steps, and I counted them until he had reached the top step and closed the door behind him. From then on, I began to cry. It's not like I wanted to. I was tired. I might have been the one to walk around in the day and have a life, but just because I wasn't trapped to a wall didn't mean I didn't have chains. As long as Lyla was a part of me, I would never be free. That's all I truly wanted. I wanted to be free.

Chapter Four

I laughed. The twit finally understood what I had to go through for an hour, and she had a mental breakdown. Good. The more the selfish brat broke down, the more powerful I would become.

I licked my lips. Roxy had a fabulous day with her little boyfriend. I finally got to kiss a freaking boy, and it went considerably well. When I finally got to meet Adam, I'd have to keep him alive for at least a little while. If Roxy found it hard to believe that he was willing to be patient about sex, far be it from me to doubt her.

I was a little disappointed that she hadn't fallen asleep. She pumped herself full of coffee and energy drinks to stay awake through that pointless establishment for higher education. Oh, please! The most fascinating things she could learn, she covered her ears and yelled, "La! La! La! I'm a virgin," to block it out.

I was determined to remain the insomniac. Roxy couldn't keep her do-gooder tendencies to herself and she healed Adam's grannie, meaning that one of my followers would soon be able to track it. Daddy didn't know how to defuse her energy. He was a chicken with his head cut off in the matter.

It wasn't long before I heard something. My ears worked better than most people, but I couldn't quite make it out. I assumed it was Daddy coming back from his futile journey, but it was much purer than that. I could almost taste his optimism and kindness like a kiss on my lips.

"Help!" I screamed. "Help! Please!" I screamed and rattled my chains until I started bruising my wrists and made my throat go raw. I conjured up tears as well until they streamed down my face and down my neck. It was my best chance of freedom, and I wasn't going to let him walk away.

"Hello?" I faintly heard his voice and the door flew open. "Is someone down here?"

"Adam!"

He marched down the steps, and the look on his face was simply priceless. It was unquestionably terrible what Mommy and Daddy did to me every night, and it was finally liberating to meet someone else who believed that. "Roxy!"

"Please help me!"

"Hold on!" He was so heroic. He didn't even stop to wonder why I was chained up to a wall. I mean even if I had confessed my love to someone, if I found them chained up to a wall, I'd have to ask myself why. It had to be for some kind of good reason. I was in a basement, not a bedroom. Still, my hero ran to me without the slightest bit of suspicion. His only concern was to set me free.

"How did this happen?" He tugged at my chains and held my face. Oh, he cared for Roxy so much. I could see it in his blue eyes. It was cute. He was cute…Incredibly sexy even! Roxy didn't know how to see what was right in front of her for the past six years. What a moron!

"My dad doesn't want me with you. He doesn't want me with anybody…" I was blubbering with snot and all. "He's in love with me. That's why I couldn't go to the dance. That's why I had to break up with you." I should have gotten an award.

70

Adam certainly bought it. He was shocked, disgusted, but the moment I lived for was when he indulged me with his hatred. One little lie and he was ready to rip my Daddy's throat out. "He'll pay for this!" It was pretty hot.

"The key to the chains are on that hook over there!" I motioned my eyes toward the prize and he followed. I smirked while his back was turned. I just couldn't help it. "Hurry!"

Adam grabbed those keys and plugged them right into the keyhole of the bonds on my right wrist. I watched as the shackle became free and I felt so much lighter. It was like taking off an uncomfortable and heavy jacket. For so long, I hadn't been able to use my abilities. I could already feel my true strength coming back to me. "He could be back at any time, Adam."

"Where is he?" He loosened the next shackle and my hands were set free.

It was so hard not to smirk! "He's looking for you."

"Then he'll find me!"

The shackle on my left foot came off, and I felt something sensational resonate all throughout me. Roxy was nothing compared to me. Even with my shackles, I could still use some of my power on Mommy over time. Adam would be child's play. "I don't want him to hurt you, Adam!"

"I'm not afraid of him, and I won't let him hurt you again." There was a rage inside of Adam that Roxy wasn't able to notice. Whether I was myself or her, he'd still be bloodthirsty after such wickedness entered his ears. If he wanted his chance to kill Daddy, I wanted to be kind enough to arrange it.

My last shackle fell, and I was reborn. My skin was tingling. I was itching to do something spectacular, but I wasn't quite ready to blow my cover with my dear Adam. I had extensive plans for him.

71

I rubbed my wrists. They were red and about to turn a nice shade of blue, but Roxy would take care of that in the morning. The most important thing was that I was finally free. "Thank you."

Adam wrapped me in his arms. "I'm so sorry this happened to you." Oh I had never hugged a man like that before. He had a strong, firm chest and his arms were ripped. Those sports teams treated him exceptionally well. "I'll protect you."

I smirked. I didn't exactly need a big, strong man to protect me, but it was going to be nice. "I was afraid to tell you."

"We'll go to the police. He'll get what he deserves, and you'll be free."

"I'm already free, and it's all because of you."

He took my hands and helped me on my feet. He was quite the gentleman. I liked being adored and treated with respect. Adam held my hand tight and walked in front of me prepared to fight if he needed to. My precious knight was going to play right into my hands. I could easily use his adoration for Roxy against him.

Daddy wasn't home yet, but I could sense him drawing near. He was going to be inside in a few minutes. I needed to stall Adam until he arrived.

"Where's your mother?" he asked.

She was still nestled safely in her room while she mumbled and cried to herself like a lunatic. She was no threat to me, but she was too much fun not to kill. "She didn't like what Daddy did to me." I hid my face in my palms while I pretended to cry. I even shook my shoulders for that extra something special while I conjured up the water works. It wasn't exactly easy crying over that traitor. I needed a couple of seconds before I had produced enough tears to show him my face. "She finally tried to protect me, and he killed her."

I noticed something intriguing about the expression on Adam's face. "That's terrible…" Rage? I understood that. Shock? Oh, most definitely. But that's not what it was. I was looking into the eyes of an understanding man, like he could relate to my pain. He was becoming much too amusing to kill! Roxy never had the stomach to ask Adam about his mom and dad, but I was going to when the time was right and when opening the wound would fester it.

Adam was thrown off the mission. I swear he had an interesting flashback that I deserved to know about.

Daddy had his own private den, and where it seemed he had put in a liquor cabinet, there was actually a variety of weapons locked up tight. Adam breathed out heavily and frustrated once he saw the lock. He grabbed it, and I predicted he was about to yell out all of his anger. That was the perfect time to demonstrate what I could do without him growing suspicious. As soon as his fingers collided with the lock, it opened up in his hand.

"Daddy didn't lock the cabinet?" I asked while faking to be surprised.

"Good for us, huh?" Adam opened the doors, and he was a bit speechless at the amount of guns Daddy had stored away for a rainy day. Most of them were assortments of hand guns and ammunition. Adam picked one up and began to load it with such speed that I questioned if he had any military training. "Do you know how to use one of these?"

I had actually never fired a gun, but it wasn't rocket science. That wouldn't have been a good impression of Roxy though. "I don't know if we should. Someone could get hurt."

"I'm trying to protect you, Roxy." He grabbed a gorgeous, radiant butterfly knife and placed it in the palm of my hand. "I won't apologize for that."

He was getting hotter by the second. It looked like I was going to be able to keep my promise to Mommy and slit her throat after all. "I'll do my best."

I heard the garage open and in order to keep my excitement bottled up, I pretended to be afraid. I clutched onto Adam's back, and his spine straightened up a little bit. The more you make a man feel like a hero, the more he'll begin to think it's actually true. "He's going to lock me back up."

"No, he won't." He took the safety off the gun and began to walk slowly out of the den. We could hear Daddy's keys jingling as he set them down on the kitchen counter, as he did every time he came home. Adam was extremely careful with each step he took, not giving away our position. He actually knew what he was doing. He knew that gun better than he did a woman, and he was quite the crafty spy. He didn't make a sound.

We eased out of the den and treaded through the hall, making our way toward the kitchen. Then I heard the unmistakable sound of those creaky basement stairs. Daddy was about to find out soon enough, so I nudged Adam in his back, and we rushed for the basement door. By the time we got there, Daddy was pounding into those steps as he ran back up them. He was so surprised when he came to save the world and was instead met with a gun pointed at his chest.

"Just let me go, please!" How could anyone not believe me? I was so proficient at playing the victim. I partly was. The only thing I genuinely pretended was being afraid. "I swear we won't tell anybody! Just let me go!"

Daddy was angry at me. I was hoping he would lunge and try to wrangle my neck, but I'm certain he must have run through that scenario before. He barely looked at me for two seconds before pleading with the boy. "You have to listen to me—"

74

"Shut up!" Luckily my dear boy wasn't hearing any of it. "You don't deserve to live!"

"Whatever she told you was a lie." Daddy was surprisingly calmer than what I would have expected. He was nonthreatening as he slowly stepped forward to us and we took a step back. He possessed a finesse that was similar to an animal tamer. "I'm not the enemy, Adam. She's manipulating you."

"Were those chains a lie?" I had to keep myself from laughing after Adam blurted out the obvious. There kind of wasn't a decent way back from that.

"That's for everyone's protection, Adam. She's a monster, and she'll destroy this world if you let her go." That was even funnier. Daddy sounded like a complete lunatic! Adam had spent six years falling for Roxy because she was pure and innocent. He'd never believe anything different until I chose to reveal it.

Adam was shaking, filled with fury and disgust. It was clear to him who the villain of the story was, and it didn't all have to do with finding me strung up in the basement. "And what was the reason for killing your wife?" Adam yelled in a soul wrenching scream.

There was silence. Daddy wasn't mad anymore. He was awfully confused. "My wife?" When he left the house, his wife was alive, helpless, and resting in her bed. She was still exactly where he had left her, but he didn't know that. He couldn't.

"You…" Daddy's eyes began to glisten when he set his eyes on me. He had been through hell and back with that woman. I might have played a massive part in dwindling her sanity and deteriorating their happy marriage, but it was always very evident to me that he loved her.

That's why I couldn't hide my smirk from Daddy.

"You!" He snapped. The fool lunged forward with his arms extended and fingers prepped to choke my neck until I was dead.

I had taken note of Adam's composure. He was steady with that gun at first, but he had become terribly upset. His hands were shaky, but I didn't know if his trigger finger was quite happy enough. Maybe he needed a little push.

Bang. Bang. Bang.

Daddy didn't even have time for one good squeeze. Through the smoke of the nozzle, I watched my daddy stumble backwards, and he fell down the stairs with three bullet holes where his questionable heart was supposed to be.

I wanted to dance or at least stand over his body and gloat, but no! I was still pretending to be that twit, and I couldn't do any celebrating while my boyfriend slowly began to suffer from a mental breakdown.

"I…" He dropped the gun and fell to his knees. The big baby had tears in his eyes and everything. I thought he might have been a killer. It was a bit disappointing. "I didn't mean to…"

I began to scream and forced out as many tears as I could manage for Daddy. It wasn't a lot, but I was hoping I would get points for the screaming. Mass hysteria was better than tears anyway. I thought Adam would totally buy it. "You killed my daddy…"

"He was gonna…" Adam pounded his fist into the floor, cracking his knuckles and beating them bloody. He was taking the whole murder thing pretty hard. I was going to get offended.

"He was gonna kill me." I fell to the ground. "Or worse…" It's not like any court wouldn't have let him get away with it. Three bullets might have been a little much, but who didn't like drama? "You did what you had to do, Adam."

"I didn't think I was gonna pull the trigger. I wasn't sure, and then I didn't mean to do it so many times and…" He really wasn't a killer…Not yet.

"We should call the police."

He reached his hand out and grabbed my arm. "No!" Adam was afraid. Of course he was startled that he just killed a man who had to tell horrible jokes just so he could see his family smile every day, after believing a fabrication that the man was going to molest his daughter. That would freak anybody out, but it was more than that. "They'll never believe me…"

"I can confirm it." Things were moving in my favor remarkably quickly, but I had to milk it a little further. "You'll be okay, Adam."

"No, I won't be." The poor thing was so distressed! He was rocking back and forth as he breathed heavily into his clasped hands with bucked eyes. He must have had a deliciously detrimental secret on his hands. "I have to leave. I have to run away." He looked so pathetic that it was actually kind of adorable.

I needed to help my dear boy. "I'll come with you."

He shook his head and spoke through his tearful voice. "I can't ask you to do that, Roxy."

I held his face and made him look into my eyes because I sincerely meant what I was about to say. "I just lost both of my parents all because I love you. I can't lose you now!"

I wasn't sure if Adam was eventually going to commit suicide after what I had said, but it was enough guilt to push him out of the realm of reason and into the arms of my insanity. "Leave your cellphone behind. We can't use credit cards. Is there any cash we can take?"

"Maybe a couple hundred upstairs, but Daddy kept everything in the bank." There was no need to worry. I remembered that Fate was on our side. "Can't we stop by the bank and get your money out?"

"My Grannie's money?" He really felt like a tool for even considering it. "I guess we'll have to." It's not like she didn't owe me anyway. If it weren't for Roxy, the old bat would be dead.

"Let me change and grab the money. I only need five minutes!"

"Please hurry." Adam was so distraught; he probably would have done just about anything I said. Who needs to be evil when good is such a baby?

I hurried upstairs. Daddy kept some money hidden in a safe in the closet, so I figured it was time to finally off Mommy. I mean I was going in there anyway. I might as well.

Eventually the police would show up, if only for a missing person's case regarding Adam after his grannie started getting worried. They'd find the bodies and the theory would be a lover's quarrel thing. We ran away to be together. I didn't know how they would work in the basement chains.

I wouldn't touch the doorknob with my hands. With the slightest bit of my imagination, the knob turned by my will. It made for a bunch of neat pranks when I was little, but my powers had grown far beyond merely opening a door.

"Lyla..." Mommy was still mumbling my name. It felt so dark inside. My own presence was there to greet me when I walked in, and I felt quite welcome.

"Hi, Mommy," I whispered.

She was only mumbling my name because she had cracked. Her truest, most predominant emotion was fear; she didn't have the will to overcome it. When I actually responded, she awoke and rose up frightened and preparing to scream. "Ly—"

Her right hand slapped her mouth tightly. She screamed as loud as she could and her tears rolled onto her hands, but she was nothing more than a muffled sound. Mommy tried to pull her right hand down with her left, but I kept it firmly pressed against her face. Any harder and I would have broken her fingers off or destroyed her jaw.

"Remember when I used to play with my dolls, Mommy?"

She couldn't answer.

"Of course you do." I slammed her body back down into her bed. She tried kicking her feet into the mattress to make all sorts of noise, so I had to restrain her legs. "You thought it was fascinating how I could make my dollies do what I wanted them to do."

She was so horrified that it began to make me giddy. I loved her fear. It was like a yummy dessert satisfying my soul with its sweetness, yet it gave me a craving for more. I wanted to hurt her more. I needed to terrify her to make up for that night when she let Daddy drag me down into the basement for the first time. It was only a cage back then, but it still felt like I couldn't breathe. She needed to know what it felt like.

"The terrible thing about my dollies though, was that no matter how I made them move, they were still dead." I climbed into her bed and stood on my knees, one on each side of her waist. I revealed the knife from behind my back, and I got that flicker—that sparkle of fear. It was astonishing. I wished I could have put it in a jar and saved it for a rainy day.

"My dollies didn't have souls. They couldn't speak to me. They couldn't love me." I traced the tip of the knife against her chest—not hard enough to pierce her skin. I only wanted to freak her out and watch her struggle to beg some more. "I couldn't look into their eyes and see anything, like I see in your eyes right now."

I enjoyed watching her so much that I considered keeping her alive so I could do it all over again. "But do you know what I did like about my dollies?"

She ceased the struggle and decided to play along, shaking her horror stricken face from left to right.

"My dollies were mine. They would never betray me. They would never think I was some kind of freak, like my mommy." I lifted the knife, prepping to stab her to death, and then she closed her eyes. It was no fun if she closed her eyes!

79

"Does Mommy actually think that her dear Lyla would kill her after she protected her for all those years?" Of course I was only joking. I didn't need to convince Mommy that she had failed me. It was evident.

Mommy opened her eyes again. They were positively radiant!

"I told Adam that Daddy killed you. Do you think Daddy would kill you where he screws you?" I wanted her genuine opinion.

She couldn't form any real words, but I think I was able to make out a satisfactory answer through her mumbled screams.

"You're right. He's not that poetic." I jumped off of her bed and headed for the bathroom. "Follow me then."

Mommy's body flung from off the bed and hit the floor rather hard. I should have been more careful or else I'd alert Adam, but I was finding it difficult to show restraint. Out of everyone, she deserved to pay the most. I dragged her body along while she kicked and tried to drag on the carpet, but my mental powers were far too strong for her to stop me.

The bathroom was freezing; the tiled floor was nice and cold. She was only in a short nightgown. Her bare legs were suffering from carpet burn and the cold. It was brilliant!

Then it was time for our final moments. "I think he'd kill you in the bathtub."

With my will alone, I raised her from off the floor and flung her into the tiled wall. The clacking of the busted tile was loud, but I didn't really care anymore. It was fun watching her bounce from the wall and in the tub like a pinball. She landed on the side of the tub on her left rib cage. If I wasn't forcing her to hold onto her mouth so tight, she would have spit out a ton of blood. Even a little bit managed to seep through the cracks between her fingers.

"I guess playtime is over, Mommy. You're not recovering from that—not without Roxy—but that's not the way you're supposed to die." I bent down so I could get a close look at her. She surprisingly looked like what I would have looked like if life wasn't kind, and it was about twenty years later. That's another thing that really bugged me about her. We weren't actually that different, yet she couldn't see anything other than a monster. At least Roxy got to know what that felt like before I put Mommy out of her misery.

I smiled. I might have been a lot of things, but I could keep my word when it was important. "I'm gonna slit your throat, slit your throat, slit your throat." I took my knife and pierced her neck flesh with the tip of the blade. I watched for Mommy's eyes, but by then she just wanted me to get it over with. I wasn't as cruel as some people thought I was, so I obliged her request. "I'm gonna slit your throat and watch you bleed out dry."

I swept my blade across her throat, and blood began to spill all over the floor. I took a step back, not wanting to get any on me. I didn't have time for a shower. I didn't honestly have time to watch her bleed, but I promised Mommy that I would.

I decided to take a minute and made my knife squeaky clean. I wanted to keep it with me as a memento, and I very well couldn't have Adam questioning whose blood was on it. Talk about awkward!

It was off to the safe next. Mommy told Roxy the code once, but it was much more fun to pull the door open. There was a bunch of different papers inside, so I pulled everything out until a black pouch slid out with it all. I unzipped the pouch and floated a couple hundred dollar bills up to my hands. After not being able to use my powers, I was quite impressed with how much control I had. It was as easy as imagining the world in the way that I wanted it, and then I could make whatever I wanted happen. It was all simple telekinesis.

Something else caught my eye. There was a white photo album that Roxy hadn't looked at in a long time. I lifted the book with my mind and placed it in my hands. It was Mommy's and Daddy's photo album of their wedding. That would come in handy.

I did start to hurry after that. I didn't want Adam to follow me upstairs and our agreed upon time had already gone. I knew what was in Roxy's closet so it shouldn't have taken long, but I hated her clothes. They were just as bright and cheery as she was. Everything was preppy and playful. She had so many baby doll dresses and light colored shirts with adorable characters on it. Her room was also filled with stuffed animals. They were ridiculously cute in a terrible kind of way. I had to change into something. I found the only black shirt she owned, and it still had a penguin on it. That and a pair of jeans was just gonna have to do. I got a duffle bag out of the closet and stuffed it with a couple of different things.

Before I left out of the room, I looked at it. I never got to spend any time in there, and she didn't either. That's why I didn't get all the teddy bears, monkeys, penguins, unicorns, and heart shaped pillows. Roxy was way too much of a sissy to be attached to me. She was in for quite the rude awakening at dawn. Even though she wouldn't see what I had done, I decided to let out some of my built up frustration for Roxy and in one thought, all of her stuffed animals exploded. Cotton, beads, and beans flew all across the room and I smiled. I'd have to leave Roxy a note or something. She'd get quite mad about it.

"Roxy!"

"I'm coming, Adam." There was nothing left for me in that house. In time when people learned about what happened in that house, they would probably say it was haunted because of the misdeeds I had done, but it was already cursed before. They had no right to treat me that way.

Adam was waiting at the bottom of the steps, still pacing back and forth with the gun in his shaking hand. The poor dear needed to be saved. I wouldn't even need to do much, just a few suggestions here and there. I wouldn't even need to use my powers of persuasion to make him unconditionally mine.

"Are you having regrets?" I asked because it seemed like a very "Roxy" thing to do.

"I didn't mean to…" Adam was trying to compose himself. He was a strong man, not willing to waste any more time on angst while there was a task at hand. I liked that. "I can't stay here, Roxy. There are things you don't know about me."

I hugged him tight so I could smile behind his back. "We'll be okay. I know we will."

Oddly enough, I think he smiled. "You're always so optimistic."

"The universe has done so many terrible things to me that I figure it owes me a couple of favors." I let go of him and tried to imitate Roxy as much as possible. "We're all each other have now. That's why I know it's gonna work out."

I'm not sure what was wrong with what I said, but Adam seemed a little uncomfortable, or maybe it could have been the weight of everything. "Let's go."

And it was that easy. After nearly eighteen years of captivity, my parents were finally dead because Roxy forgot to lock the door…Again!

I was curious as to why Adam came to the house. He knew Roxy wasn't supposed to have late night visitors. It was bugging me, but I waited until we had already started driving. "Why did you even come back to my house?"

"I wanted to know the truth about you." I sensed a hint of anger and frustration from him. "I was sick of the lies." Since he was the one who just killed my daddy, I thought it was a wee bit unwarranted.

"I never lied to you."

"But you weren't honest!" Typical. After his shock, he had to blame his troubles on me. "Look at your life, Roxy. Think of what just happened. We could have prevented it. I should have."

"It's too late for regrets. We have to just go on, Adam."

I did something wrong, because he kept looking at me like he couldn't believe me. "You seem a little calmer than what you should be."

Oh yeah. I suppose it would have been better if I kept up a little bit of remorse or something. "I'm still in shock!" I didn't mean to fall out of character. It was just hard being sad for Daddy. "Can we not talk for a while? I can explain everything, I promise I can. I'm just a little overwhelmed right now."

"I understand." Adam began to hold off some tears. His lip even quivered a little bit. "I'm really sorry about your parents."

They had it coming. "Mom's in a better place." Out of my hair. "I wanna make sure you're safe now."

He nodded and kept his eyes on the road. I couldn't wait to break him. I was pretty sure that I wasn't going to kill him. Roxy wouldn't last on her own. Besides, I was dead tired. I hadn't slept in over twenty-four hours, and I needed to rest if I was going to have enough focus on my mission.

Soon, everyone would be free.

Chapter Five

We drove all night. We only stopped when we needed gas or when Adam needed an energy drink to keep going while I slept a majority of the time. He stopped at an ATM before we left the state border and drew out a couple thousand dollars. The poor dear was so upset about taking his Grannie's money, but he did it anyway.

I wasn't quite sure where Adam was going, but it was probably toward a place he thought he could be safe. I wasn't going to question him or make him go where I wanted until after I returned. The sun was going to rise soon, and I didn't know how Adam would react to finding out that he hadn't been with Roxy the whole time. She was confident that he would love and stand by her regardless, but it was going to be annoying having two people plot behind my back right in front of my face.

"I need you to pull over."

"Why?" Adam was afraid to go just a little bit over the speed limit in fear of cops pulling him over and linking him to a murder case that couldn't possibly be under investigation yet. If he didn't have to worry about that, I'm sure he would have been flying down the highway without stopping at all.

"Please," I asked sweet and calm. "I need you to trust me and pull over."

He grunted, but he did it anyway. "Fine." We were kind of in the middle of nowhere, which was excellent. I predicted that Roxy was going to have a monumental freak out. It was most appropriate that Adam pulled up to an empty dirt lot. "Now what?"

"I've been hiding things from you, Adam." I wondered how it was possible that he had so much trust for Roxy after he knew she had kept secrets from him. She betrayed him daily, yet he stood by her side constantly. "It's more than what my father did to me and my mother letting him. You never asked *why*." That was perhaps the most puzzling thing about him.

Even with my baiting, he didn't change his opinion of Roxy. He was curious, but he hadn't even begun to worry about the obvious problems. He merely asked, "Why?"

I looked off into the distance to peer into the rising sun. Roxy didn't really feel much when I came. It was such a simple change that it scared her. It made her feel like she wasn't in control and then she'd lose herself completely to me. Well, I was a different story. I could always feel her coming as I was being shoved into a dark abyss. It was like my mind couldn't breathe anymore. One day I would be rid of her, but she was my burden to bear for the meantime. "I don't really have time to answer that question accurately. You're gonna have to ask her."

"Who?" Adam asked confused.

I made sure to turn to face him and smile as creepily as I could manage. "Roxy."

I wish I had a camera for his face. "What do you mean?"

I didn't have time to answer him. I opened the car door and stood up to face the dawn. No, I wouldn't be able to speak or react in any sort of way that would be a representation of how I felt, but I would be able to see precious little Roxy collapse as she realized her entire world was stripped away from her. That was worth the momentary hell I felt in my head as I slipped away into the abyss and stood trapped behind a glass wall.

Everything was different. Nothing was like how it should have been in the morning. I couldn't feel the chains around my wrists and ankles. I only felt the pain from them like a shadow of a tall tree stretching across the ground. The bruises faded away, just like the assurance I had of waking up to a wonderful world. The smell of the basement dust wasn't tingling my nostrils. The basement wasn't dark with the tiniest sliver of light peering through a small window. Worst of all, Mom and Dad weren't there to greet me with their relieved faces. "Where am I?"

There was nothing but flat land going on for miles and miles. I lived in a little town, but there was forest all around. Nothing was remotely familiar. There was no way I could have been there. No one could have moved me unless they knocked out Lyla and that was highly unlikely.

I didn't feel like I was dreaming. I hoped I was dreaming, but my panic felt too real. I had terrible dreams before, but my heart had never pounded so fiercely. It couldn't have been a dream, but I couldn't accept that Lyla had escaped. There were too many consequences that I could never face.

I stepped backyards and ran into something big and hard. I looked at it an immediately recognized the remodeled red and black stripped Dodge Charger. "Adam?"

I turned around and I saw him standing by his door with a very baffled look on his face. "What's going on?"

I had to be careful about what I was about to say, but I just couldn't think straight. There were too many terrible possibilities rushing into my brain. "What are we doing here together?"

Adam looked at me like he didn't know what was going on. Things weren't weird between us until I just made it weird. How was it possible that he could be with Lyla for so long and not notice the

87

difference between the two of us? Why would she even keep him alive? Why would she not even corrupt him? I couldn't feel her presence choking out the goodness within him as she had been doing to my mother. I didn't understand how Adam could be just as he always had been.

"I think this has been too hard on you."

"What's been too hard?" I asked.

"You mean you don't honestly remember?" Adam slowly came from around his car to approach me with his arms outstretched as if he were about to chain me up and throw me in some kind of mental institution.

I stepped away slowly. "Remember what?"

I could tell from Adam's eyes that his heart was breaking from what he was about to tell me. "I found you locked up in the basement, so I helped you escape."

"No..." I didn't want to hear anymore. I was too afraid. Lyla free was the greatest fear I ever had. I didn't know how to fight her. Mom and Dad talked about how powerful she was. They said she was an abomination that I couldn't reason with.

"Your dad tried to stop us and..." He was doing his best not to relive his words, but it was too painful. I had seen him close to crying when he was with his grandmother, but this was different. It wasn't grief overwhelming his beautiful soul. It was pure guilt. "I killed him."

I couldn't breathe. I literally couldn't and at the time, I couldn't even think to do it, and I couldn't remember that I needed to. My chest ached so much that I clenched onto it and fell to my knees. How could the man that I love kill my father? He knew my father. He should have known that he wouldn't hurt anyone, especially me. I didn't know how to look at Adam knowing what he had done. "What about my mom?"

"He killed her before I got there."

"No!" That didn't make any sense. "He wouldn't have done that." I didn't know Lyla, but I knew she was evil and a manipulator. "She must have killed her."

"Who?"

"Lyla." It wasn't that farfetched that she killed my dad. Adam would have never hurt my dad. She must have tricked him and made him do it. Adam didn't have it in him to kill anybody.

"This is getting too crazy!" Adam yelled. "Tell me the truth, Roxy. All of it."

I foolishly led myself to believe that I could one day be with Adam peacefully and that I could tell him my secret, but how could I have ever believed such a thing? How could he ever accept me after Lyla forced him to kill my father?

He still deserved to know the truth. With Lyla free, we were both her prisoners. I needed him if I was going to defeat her. "I'm not the only person living in this body."

He laughed at first. I don't know why. I would joke with him, but never in a way that would make me tell a lie. I guess it was too crazy to believe. "Are you saying you have a split personality?"

"I'm not crazy!" I yelled as I got back on my feet. I couldn't even let him think it! "It's not a personality disorder. I literally have two different people—like two different souls inside of me."

I was desperate for him to believe me, but I think that just made things worse. He didn't think I was joking, but I honestly think he thought I was crazy. "I can't believe this."

"I'm not crazy, Adam!" I was more desperate with tears still streaming down my face. Just because I sounded sincere and serious, didn't mean that what I was saying wasn't insane. It was! "Every sunrise, I gain control. When the sun falls, Lyla comes back."

He didn't believe me, and I didn't know how to explain it any better. How could Lyla have pretended to be me so well if she didn't know anything about my life? Adam didn't suspect a different person at all. "She's devious and wretched, and she's trying to destroy the world!"

I think he regretted being with me. Two minutes ago, he blamed everything wrong in our lives on himself and I opened my mouth for a few sentences, and he regretted knowing me. "You believe me, don't you?"

He exploded. "This is too much!" He threw his hands up in the air and stepped away from me on the verge of tears. He needed to know that it wasn't his fault that my dad was dead.

"I can prove it!" I looked around for anything sharp, but I didn't see anything except a jagged rock on the ground. I hated pain. I was sort of a baby about it, (even though I could be healed) but I sucked it up and dug the sharpest rock I could find into my hand.

"Are you crazy?" Adam snatched the rock out of my hand and threw it as far away as possible. "Have you completely lost your mind?"

"Look!" I held my bloodied hand up toward his face. He was repulsed and tried to look away, but I waved my hand in his face until he stayed still long enough to watch the cut begin to close. The pain didn't last long, but the blood still remained all over my hand and dripped down my arm. He could still tell that the cut was gone though, and he slowly and gently grabbed my hand to stare into something that had already disappeared.

There was still a lot to explain, but he calmed down a lot. I guess he understood that I was special and not extremely insane. "So, you did heal Grannie?" Adam looked at me with such gratitude that I didn't deserve. I let her suffer for so long, and there was no telling how bad Lyla had just screwed up his life. He didn't need to stare at me as if I were as glorious as the sun.

"Yeah. I did." I could barely look at him. I didn't want to see Adam admiring me. I wasn't a god or an angel. I was just a girl with a terrible demon attached to my soul.

"Then I owe you so much." He was trying real hard to make a moment when we didn't have any time. I didn't even know where I was.

"Apparently I owe you a future, since Lyla took it away." I had to maneuver my way past him to grab a couple of napkins out of the glove compartment and wipe away the blood. I hated that it didn't just go away. The sight of blood made my stomach do flips. I was not cut out to be a warrior. I didn't know how I was going to make it without Mom and Dad guiding me.

"You gave me a future in the first place, Roxy." Adam grabbed me by my arms until I had to look at him. It didn't matter if I was bloody or that I very well might have been bonkers. He still thought I was his muse. "Do you have an ability…To make things better?"

I was afraid he might have thought I manipulated him. I only ever wanted to help when I could. "I do."

He smiled. "Then you made me a better person, Roxy. I'm the man I am because of you." The whole world was crumbling around us, yet I somehow managed to completely retain his affection and admiration. Adam began to lean into me for a kiss, but I couldn't. I turned my head before he could ever touch my lips.

"Lyla lives to make people miserable. She enjoys it like a drug." It was dangerous for Adam to be around me and for him to have so much love for me. Lyla would kill him if she ever found out how truly magnificent he was. "You couldn't tell the difference between the two of us at all?"

He jerked his head back, a little surprised. I guess he didn't think I'd be offended. I didn't mean to be, but how could I not be a little bit? "I

91

thought something was weird with you, but I was too upset about what happened to your parents."

Then I realized how silly I was being. It was true that I was going through a lot, but he was too. "You didn't kill my dad, Adam. Lyla somehow did it."

His eyes widened. I'm not sure if he believed it, but there was a speck of hope in his eyes that was powerful enough to cut right through me. "Are you sure?"

"I'm positive!" Why would he even think he was capable of such a thing? "She's got special powers too, more impressive than mine."

"Then I didn't kill your dad?" He was tearing up again, but I knew he wasn't going to cry. He wouldn't want to show me that, but I knew how afraid he was of himself and the possibility that he had done the unthinkable.

"No." I gently wrapped my arms around him and held his face as he looked into my sincere eyes. I was tearing up, thinking about how my parents were gone, but I couldn't hate him for it. I knew within my heart that it wasn't his fault. "You could never hurt anyone, Adam. I know you."

I'm not sure if he believed me though. I think he wanted to, but he didn't even know that Lyla was real yet and he surely didn't know how evil she could be. "We can't go back home, Roxy. If what you say about having another person inside you is true, then you'd be taken to jail—at least for questioning—and Lyla would jeopardize your freedom." He took my hands and placed them at my sides, making my stomach fully sink into my knees. "Besides, they wouldn't believe that she made me do it, and even if they did, they wouldn't make you innocent."

I did want to go home and sleep in my own bed, but I never got to do that anyway. When I was little, Dad would unshackle me at dawn and carry me to my bed—so I could wake up feeling safe and comfortable—

but he hadn't done that in a long time. The only thing that made my home happy was my parents, and their bodies were lying dead on the floors. "There's nothing back home for me anyway."

I did my best to hold in my tears. I truly did, but when I tried to hold them in again, I exploded with so much emotion onto Adam's chest. I moaned, and my shoulders shook, and I could barely breathe again. I could never hear one of Dad's terrible jokes. I could never have any of Mom's home cooked meals again, despite it not always being the best in the world. They had their flaws, but I was the most trouble anyone could ever have, yet they loved and protected me still. I would take them at their worst, just to be with them one last time.

"Roxy…" Adam wrapped his arms around me, and I was grateful. It was the only safe place left in the world. "We have to keep moving," he told me.

I had to be a big girl. Even though I wanted to curl up into a little ball and cry my eyes out until everything made itself better, I knew I didn't have that luxury. Lyla wouldn't waste her free time. I couldn't either.

We both got inside the car and he started driving off again. I kept biting my nails and shaking my leg. I was just so jumpy; I couldn't stay trapped in that car. It felt like I couldn't breathe and every light I saw behind us on the freeway, I thought belonged to a cop. Every time I saw a police car parked on the side of the road or driving by, my heart started pounding. I didn't know how I was going to make it living on the run.

After a while, I had to ask, "Where are we going?"

"My dad's."

I was surprised. I always had the assumption that his father didn't care about him or was an immoral person, not the sort of man you would go to in a time of crisis. "Where is he?"

"I think he's in Kansas."

"You think?"

"I'm not sure. I got a postcard once and…" He hit the steering wheel, and I jumped. "It's all I know to do, Roxy!" I didn't mean to make him so frustrated. I guess it was better to keep my mouth shut. I didn't have any better ideas.

"You've got to tell me some more, Roxy, especially about Lyla."

"She's powerful and manipulative, but she's ignorant. Mom and Dad don't educate her, and we can't remember what the other one does. She's nothing but a beast!" I couldn't stand the thought that she was a part of me.

Adam looked confused and then he shook his head slowly. "I hate to break it to you, but if she's smart enough to manipulate me into killing your dad while murdering your mother and making me escape with her, I think she knows more than what you think."

"What do you mean?"

Adam was trying to dance around what he had to say. Even when he eventually spoke, it was a dragged out thought. "I couldn't honestly tell the difference between the two of you, Roxy. She knows you enough to pretend to be you. Plus, she knew stuff that only you would know. She's much smarter than what you think."

That was impossible! "But my parents told me that she doesn't have memories of the day. I don't have any memories of the night."

"Someone as smart as Lyla probably thought it was an advantage not to let on to how powerful and clever she truly is."

"So she knows me?" Every single thing I did, she saw. Every rotten thing I ever said about her, she heard. Every plot against her, she knew about. Every time I held hands or kissed Adam, she felt it. "If she knows me, she knows you."

I remembered what she did to Mom. She had lost her mind and Dad didn't even want me to see her again. Dad wasn't even quite himself.

I couldn't let her ruin my sweet Adam. "She's going to hurt you. You have to get away from me!"

"She won't hurt me," he said casually. "She must need me for something."

"Like what?"

"You still can't drive, remember? Maybe she needs a driver." He smiled. I think he was joking.

"Or maybe she wants to corrupt you before she kills you!"

"I can handle her."

"You didn't see what she did to Mom!" I didn't even want to think about it. Mom must have been so afraid when Lyla came into her room and killed her. I should have been able to stop Lyla somehow. It wasn't fair!

"I'll be fine, Roxy." I'm not sure how Adam was so confident or calm. Nothing was natural about what I had shared with him. It was almost like he wasn't human. "Now tell me more."

I shrugged my shoulders at first. "I'm supposed to save the world. Lyla wants to destroy it."

He cocked his eyebrow, looking a little worried. "How?"

"I don't know," I said embarrassed. It was too bad I couldn't restore Adam's faith in my capabilities of saving the world. "Dad was supposed to tell me, but he never got the chance."

He frowned and shook his head. "You're seventeen! Why wouldn't they tell you all of this sooner?"

"Maybe they were afraid of accidentally letting Lyla know."

"That was real stupid of them."

I had to wipe a tear from my eye. "Please don't talk about my recently deceased parents that way." I knew that they were wrong about keeping me in the dark for so long, but there must have been a legitimate reason!

"I'm sorry." Adam didn't really sound like he was apologizing. "They just left you blind."

That was fair. Maybe they should have opened up before, but they were going to. If I hadn't been hanging out with Adam, Dad might have come clean about everything.

"What can Lyla do?"

They did let me know about that piece of information. They had to justify chaining her up every night. "She can make things happen just by thinking it, and it's really creepy."

Then Adam was seriously worried. "Are we talking 'turn you into a jack-in-the-box' creepy or 'spill over a glass of water when she's mad' creepy?"

"She can move things. She really hasn't had the opportunity to use her powers since we were six. I don't know if that makes her more powerful or less." It's not like I had ever seen her use her powers before. "I'm sorry, Adam. I don't know her. I've never met her."

"Is there anything else you can think of that I should know?"

There wasn't a lot that I knew, but there was something else important that he needed to know. "She has followers that can track her every time she or I use our powers."

"So that's why you don't go up and down the hospital, huh?" I knew he had wondered about it! How could he not?

"It still seems pretty selfish," I said quietly.

"Not if you're gonna save the world." He sighed. "You risked a lot for me and I let your greatest enemy free."

I guess he thought we were pretty even as far as guilt, but it wasn't fair for me to think that way. "Well, I'm sorry that Lyla has become both of our burdens." As long as Lyla was a part of me, I'd always be the bigger problem.

"Why didn't you tell me all this before?" I knew he felt a little betrayed. He must have had an idea and understood why I kept something so crazy a secret. I was surprised he believed it so easily. It was simply too much to expect anyone to take.

"I was afraid you wouldn't love me if you knew the truth." I could barely make it through my confession without choking up. I didn't know how he still felt about me. Just because he was stuck, didn't mean that he loved me.

Adam looked so terrible, like he was riddled with guilt. I expected that he was going to take his confession back. "I know I ruined whatever you considered a life and I know I don't deserve for you to even look at me." His eyes welled up with tears, and his voice began to break up. "I am so sorry about your dad."

I had to turn my head from him. I couldn't look at him while he was so emotional. I had never seen him cry with real tears rolling down his cheeks. It wasn't even his fault. Lyla did it. I don't know why he couldn't accept that!

"I'm so sorry, but you never have to worry about me loving you, Roxy."

I blinked hard and let my tears flow down my cheeks before turning around to face him again. He was broken up about the role he had played in Lyla's escape. He was being strong because he had to be, but it still ripped something up on his insides. He was hurting, but he was sincere when he looked into my eyes, and he told me, "I will always love you."

In the midst of that terrible morning in that godforsaken world, I smiled. No matter what was going to happen, I knew the two of us could get through it. Our love was stronger than Lyla's hate. "So what do we do now?"

Adam cleared his throat and wiped his eyes, trying to appear invulnerable again. "We have to lay low."

About an hour later, we stopped at a large department store. I pushed the basket while we went up and down the aisle. He got a couple of toiletries for us like toothpaste and deodorant. He asked what kind of soaps I used and made sure not to get them, and he picked up some different body sprays. "Why are you getting the opposite of what I tell you?"

"Because you have to be totally different from what you were. You can't look like how you used to, smell like how you used to—"

"Act like how I used to?"

"No. You can still be yourself. I need you to be."

I almost started blushing. At least he was still sweet to me. I guess he had to be in order to make up for what was coming next. He also got a couple of T-shirts, hoodies, jeans, caps, and beanies. He usually dressed so clean-cut and preppy, but he was going for more of a skater boy wardrobe. I understood where he was going with everything until we got to the hair products. He got some scissors and a razor.

"You're cutting your hair?" I asked horrified.

"I have to." He seemed unusually detached from it all, even when he started going through the hair dye. "What do you think about being a redhead?"

"I absolutely think you shouldn't be one!" He would look ridiculous!

He laughed. "I was actually talking about for you."

"Me?" I grabbed my hair like I was protecting it for dear life! I loved my curly, blonde locks. I didn't want him to mutilate it. "I can't."

"You have to." He held up a box of black coloring as well and shook them both in front of my face. I didn't want to be that dark, but I certainly didn't want to be red! "You have to choose," he said annoyed.

"Fine!" I took the red box and threw it down into the basket. I couldn't believe I was soon to be a deep, ruby redhead! That's not all he got though. He picked up a flatiron and some dark makeup that I usually wouldn't wear. "You wanna change me completely?"

"It's the only way." He found a bunch of other stuff too, like fake piercings for your mouth, nose, and eyes, fake leather bracelets with metal studs on them, and clunky jewelry that I would look ghastly in.

Then there was one other thing he needed for himself. There were some colored contacts that would turn his beautiful blue eyes into brown. "Not your eyes!" I begged. "Please!"

"A brother with blue eyes it too memorable. It's got to be done."

There wasn't anything I could say. I could have cried, kicked, or screamed, but I didn't know what I was doing and I needed to listen to someone who actually knew what to do. "How do you know so much about being on the run?"

He shrugged his shoulders. "I guess I watch a lot of TV."

I guess he might have had a point. I didn't watch any TV, so I didn't know anything that came on it. It was weird to me that they would teach that sort of thing. "Let's hope that Lyla is as cooperative as I am."

"Let's not leave it up to fate." We walked together over to the pharmacy section, and he started pacing up and down the aisles until he found a bunch of different brands of sleep medicine. He started looking through them, reading the back of the boxes, and trying to find the ones with the biggest dosages in them. "Do you think this will work?"

"How will you get Lyla to take it, especially if you think she can hear us right now?"

"I was thinking you could get drugged up before sunset."

I didn't like that suggestion. I hated to be reminded that we were one in the same. "It won't work. Nothing really affects me."

"We have to try." He put a few boxes in the cart, and we were done with the shopping. For the most part, we did the self-scan so the employees wouldn't get suspicious about what we were buying, but they did ask to see his I.D. when we got to the medicine.

"Sure thing." He started searching for his I.D. like he knew where it was, but then it wasn't in his wallet. "I'm sure it was here!" He started patting down all of his pockets and searched everywhere on him. "I know it's somewhere!"

When he started to unbuckle the belt on his pants, the poor cashier raised his hands up to stop him. "That's okay! I believe you!"

Adam continued on with his buckle. "I don't wanna get you in trouble!"

"You're fine!" He yelled. "I promise."

Adam and I both struggled not to smile until we left the store. That was pretty brilliant of him. "So what now?" I asked.

"We try to become these new characters."

Of course we couldn't do that somewhere nice though! We went to a crummy motel right off the freeway, to a place where they wouldn't be suspicious when he used all cash to pay for our room, which was only about forty-nine bucks. I was a little afraid to sit down or bring any bags in that we had to take out due to stowaways, but Adam commanded that we took everything out of the car. "I'm gonna dye your hair first, and then there's something I've got to take care of."

"Like what?"

"I'd rather not say." Whatever it was, he was obviously upset about it.

I decided to leave it at that. "Okay."

It was weird having my hair dyed. The product was cold and slimy, and it was strange watching Adam work on my hair in latex gloves. I would have never imagined that he knew how to do such things. The only thing I knew he loved to work on was his beautiful car. He even dyed my eyebrows. "Where'd you learn this?"

"My mom." It was a short answer, spoke shortly.

I didn't know a lot about her. I was surprised he acknowledged her at all. "You don't talk about her much."

"There's not much to say. She's dead." He was frightfully cold. I knew she had been dead for a long time, but I didn't understand how he could be so detached from her memory.

"What about your dad?"

"What about him?" He didn't raise his voice, but it felt like he snapped at me.

I had never actually asked about his dad, not persistently. I was always afraid to pester him about it, because I didn't want to offend Adam and risk losing him over someone who wasn't even in his life. I figured that his dad hurt him real bad, and it wasn't worth bringing up those old scars. But if we were on our way to see him, it was necessary to know what kind of mess I was getting in. "I guess I always assumed he wasn't a good guy. That was the impression your grannie gave me."

"He is," he said casually.

My eyes bucked. "Then why are we looking for him?"

"Because I don't know where else to go and what else to do." Adam lashing out at me and getting irritated was precisely the reason why I didn't want to bug him about it. "I'm not saying he would let us crash with him or that it would be a good idea, but he could probably get us some fake identification that would pass for real."

"Is he a criminal...Like a professional one?"

"I'd rather not talk about my parents."

I kept my mouth shut. I didn't know where else we could go. I only knew that it would be awful if his dad were a terrible guy and he got around Lyla. She could make anybody worse than what they were. We honestly didn't have any other options though.

We rinsed my hair out and blow-dried it, and it was indeed a dark, ruby red. I frowned once I saw myself in the mirror, but Adam was smiling. "I kind of like it."

"It's not me." My hair was pretty poofy. I didn't know where I got my voluminous hair from. My parents' were pretty flat. I guess it didn't matter anymore since I would have to flatten it for the rest of my life.

Adam hugged me from behind and kissed me on the cheek. "You're still adorable."

I hugged his arms and smiled. He always knew the right things to say. "I guess I'll start straightening my hair and complete the transformation."

"And after that, start trying to take the pills."

"It's still a couple of hours until sunset."

"I know, but just try it. Take about eight of them every hour."

"Eight?" I didn't know if I could swallow one!

"And if you're not asleep by the time I get back, you'll have to shove a handful in your mouth before sunset. If she's as bad as you say—"

"She is!" I didn't want Adam making the mistake of thinking he could somehow tame her. "I don't want you around her."

"Then this is what we have to do." He kissed me on my cheek again before leaving the bathroom and heading for the door.

"Don't be gone too long!"

"I'll try." He grabbed the only key to the room that we had. "Don't leave and don't answer this door for anybody!"

"I won't!"

And then, I was alone. I was finally alone, and then it dawned on me how much I had completely lost. I had shed tears for Mom and Dad before, but they weren't the only people I had lost. I could never see my classmates again. I could never be in my house. Adam might have been a sweetheart, but how could he not somehow resent me for separating him from his grannie? I couldn't even look like myself if I hoped to survive. Lyla had taken just about everything from me, and if I wasn't careful, she would take Adam too.

I broke down in a rickety chair while I straightened my hair and tried to douse myself with sleeping pills that I knew wouldn't work. I wished that it would, so I wouldn't have to deal with my nerves. Every noise I heard, I thought it was someone coming to the door. We were in a rougher part of town, so I heard a couple of sirens and I always got so scared that it was someone coming for me.

I had to shake off my feelings and hope for the best. If Lyla was knocked out, then I would need to change for the both of us. I started going through the bag of clothes Lyla had packed. The first thing I found was a folded up note and a knife that I knew belonged in Dad's weapon cabinet. I was apprehensive about touching it. I could feel a trace of her on it. It wasn't strong enough to draw any attention toward us from outside forces, but it was distinct enough for me to sense that she had done a great evil with it. I couldn't even touch it!

I was curious about the note though. She had never left me a note before. "Dear Roxy, I just thought you should know that I killed all of your stuffed animals…" Even though I knew I could never see them again anyway, the fact that she did it upset me. I crumpled up the note and threw it across the room. "What is wrong with you?" I screamed. I dumped the bag on the bed and started sifting through for anything to wear.

While I was frantically lifting up a long tank top, I found Mom and Dad's wedding photo album. "Why would you pack this?" I sat it to the side until I finished changing. I put on the long tank top and a pair of black

103

leggings. I wouldn't normally wear something so scandalous, but I wasn't trying to be myself.

Then I took some more sleeping pills and sat in the bed with the photo album. Mom and Dad were so young in the pictures. They didn't have any wrinkles or worries. They looked in love with one another. They had more family than I realized. I didn't get to see them. They didn't think it was a good idea for me to be attached to my family. It was too dangerous, and they might not have understood how to take care of Lyla. I never even got to meet my grandparents. Mom had bridesmaids that looked like her. They must have been sisters. I didn't know that. They left them all behind for me. They couldn't have predicted that taking care of me would be so hard or that it would cost them their lives so early on.

I couldn't look at the album anymore. I decided to lie down and close my eyes. Just because the pills wouldn't work didn't mean that I couldn't go to sleep all on my own. Sleep was the only way I could see them again. I hoped I could dream of them and tell them how truly sorry I was for being such a burden.

Chapter Six

I opened my eyes slowly, being careful not to make even the slightest sound. I remembered what those two schemers were trying to do to me. I applauded Adam for trying, but Roxy should have known better. As long as we were one, we were invincible. I could protect myself, and her body would protect her for us.

Adam had returned and fallen asleep on the next bed. The poor dear hadn't gotten any sleep since we started our journey. He was probably exhausted. He wouldn't have to worry about getting a good night's sleep after I carved his heart out.

I didn't want to wake him, so I floated my body off of the bed until I hovered above him. I suppose I could have ripped his rib cage open and every layer of his insides until I pierced his skin so I could crush his heart with my bare hands, but there was no point in being that messy. I knew my knife was lying peacefully on the floor, and I made it fly right into my hand.

It was a shame Adam decided to plot against me. He was quite handsome, and he kept that idiot alive while I couldn't be the brains. She honestly did need him, but I didn't need the trouble. I raised my arm and prepared to strike him!

Then again…It would have been a shame to lose such a fine looking specimen. He kissed Roxy so well; it would be terrible if I never got to taste his succulent lips myself. He wouldn't need to die if I could train him right. All I had to do was show him who was truly in charge and that death awaited those who defied me.

I let him keep his life that one time. I then floated back to my bed, placed my knife back on the floor, and pretended to sleep. I would play along with his little scheme until the proper time.

In an hour, his alarm went off, and he woke up quickly so he wouldn't wake me. It was terribly sweet of him. I opened my eyes when I felt it was safe so I could observe him. He packed everything away and started moving everything to the car. He was still tired. He had to keep moving and chugged energy drinks just to stay awake. He must have wanted to get on the road while he thought I was passed out.

I was the last thing he bothered to pack into his car, except it wasn't his car. I didn't risk opening my eyes when we got outside, but it smelled like motor oil and the seats certainly weren't leather. It was around the same space. When the engine turned on, I knew it wasn't as good a car as his former masterpiece. He probably felt he had to get rid of it. Too many people would be able to identify a car as wonderful as his.

Poor Adam. The prince fell for the princess and wanted to live happily ever after, and he ended up with the witch instead. I could feel his mind swirling with worries. I could practically taste his conflicts. He didn't want to leave Roxy, but it must have certainly crossed his mind. Then there were all of his family problems that he wouldn't tell Roxy about. He would tell me. We were sure to bond.

"I'm bored now."

"Ah!" Adam freaked out and turned the wheel, swerving into another lane and then back into our original. "You're awake?"

"Yep! Roxy tried to tell you that it wouldn't work, but nice try though." I felt a bit chipper. How could seeing that horrifying expression

106

on Adam's face not make me happy? He looked like he was going to have a heart attack.

He was such a cool, tough guy. He calmed down pretty quick. "You're Lyla, I presume."

"You presume correctly." I looked around at his new car. I felt sorry for him. It was an old, four seat car with only two doors and not a lot of space in the back. "You traded your baby for this?"

"I didn't have much of a choice. I needed no paperwork and no questions."

"Is that why you didn't want to wait for the sunrise? You wanted to distance yourself from your beauty before the police could find you from it?"

"I guess you're clever." He smiled. Adam wanted to be as friendly as possible with me, even somewhat flirtatious. How delicious of him!

"Much more than you can imagine." I smiled and leaned back into my seat quite comfortably. He was already making me have so much fun. "From now on, you do what I command."

He laughed. "Oh really?" I was there. Roxy told him what I could do. He had no reason to take my threats so lightly. He must have been a real fool or just that manly. It was quite sexy.

"Really." I wondered how attracted he'd be after I made him piss his pants. "I'm sure it'll be satisfying resolving your daddy issues, but I'm afraid we're gonna abort that mission. Unlike Roxy, I actually know a thing or two about myself, and I do know people that will actually help us."

"Help you? No, thank you!"

I glared at him, but it wasn't quite threatening enough. I couldn't wipe the smile off my face. "You will not defy me."

He leaned his head over so sexily and smirked. "Watch me."

107

Adam didn't deserve another warning. His foot collided with the gas pedal, and the car jerked forward into a nice zoom. "What are you doing?" Adam yelled.

I laughed. His face was so hysterical! My big, strong man was instantly terrified. "I'm showing you who's in charge and who wears the panties in this relationship."

He didn't like that at all! He struggled to reach out to grab me, but I forced his hands to the steering wheel and made him grip it tight. "Stop this!"

"Were you trying to hit me?" I was a little shocked. I thought he was a little bit more civilized than that. "Why don't you keep your eyes on the road?"

He was about to hit a car. He gasped as soon as he noticed, so I had to take matters into my own hands, and I turned the wheel and swerved us out of the way in time. "You have to stop this!"

"Oh hush! I'm only playing a game." It was a dangerous game, but not as dastardly as it could have been. It was two in the morning. There weren't many cars on the road, and if there were, they were trucks. They were hard to get around, but it's not like they would zoom right into us.

"Let me go, Lyla!"

"You know, some people don't respond well to yelling." I forced his foot to push even harder on the gas, and the speedometer rose from ninety to one hundred twenty. I released his hands from my will, only because he needed to be fast enough to dodge all of the traffic down the freeway.

"You have to stop, or we're gonna die!" He used his left foot to hit the break and we started skidding along the highway. He was losing control, and we were going to crash into a semi right in front of us if I didn't do something drastic. "Lyla!"

I took control again, and I forced Adam to turn the wheel until we were off the road and drove between the break in the dividers. We were bouncing up and down from going off the road to the little dip in the grassy hill, but that was nothing compared to the rush of when we crossed to the other side of the highway, driving the opposite direction of the traffic flow.

"Stop this!" I couldn't blame him for being terrified. He didn't know how powerful I was yet, and he certainly didn't know that it was more dangerous to deny me of my fun than to let it see fruition. "Now!"

"No."

The cars coming at us did the best they could to dodge us. When they got too close, I helped them along. Some were swerving off of the road and crashing into dividers or other cars. I didn't bother looking back to see all of the people getting hurt by my madness, but I did enjoy the terror in Adam's eyes when I saw that he glanced into the rearview mirror. I imagined it should have been a mess. It sounded terrible. There were tires screeching, metal crashing, and screams. I think I smelt the burnt rubber.

"Stop this now!" Adam yelled right in my face. He made my ears ache a little, and I certainly didn't appreciate the spit, or the fact that he thought he could tell me what to do.

I heard the horns from two trucks in front of us. One of them was a semi, and the other was an oil tank. I was hoping Adam would give a good scream, but he tensed up even tighter and just froze. The lights were so bright, he probably thought he was seeing that final flash before he journeyed into the afterlife, but I wasn't about to let him off that easily.

I concentrated. I hadn't attempted moving something that large before, but it was always fun to experiment. As I begun the attempt, I tensed up and dug my fingers into my chair. It did feel like a weight on my mind—like an instant migraine—but it did what I wanted, and the oil tanker lifted right above us.

I heard Adam finally gasp, somewhat relieved. It was more work than I thought, and I didn't have the energy or frankly enough motivation for a soft landing and I sort of tossed it front first into the road. As soon as the tank hit the ground, a fire exploded from behind us. I was being reckless. Perhaps I should have tried the semi instead. The flames were coming fast, and it was such a powerful force. It was like the fury of hell was at our heels. I dug into the chair and gritted my teeth. I imagined a wall between us. When the explosion hit that wall, my head ached as I could feel my mind closing in on me. I didn't want Adam to see me struggling, and luckily he was too distracted by his own fear to pay any mind to me. I closed my eyes and dug deeper, pushing us forward and away until we were at a safe enough distance.

I had to let go of Adam, and he drove across the freeway safely to the other side. I was able to recover myself and appear unaffected, but my head was pounding and I was tired. Those regeneration powers were wasted on Roxy. I needed them for times when I wore myself out. However, it could have been due to not being able to use my powers for such a long time. Not even I was aware of my true depths.

Adam was silent. I could still tell that he was afraid since both hands were still tightly on the wheels. He drove a little while longer, not even acknowledging my presence until a few exits down where he got off at an empty rest stop. He parked the car and began breathing deeply into his hands before turning it off and getting out.

I smirked. My head was throbbing, but it was well worth his mental breakdown. "Adam!" I got out of the car and joined him on the driver's side so I could properly watch him snap. "Is something wrong?"

He was pacing back and forth and the fear had washed out his pretty yellow glow, and he had become pale. "You killed all those people..."

"What?" I was expecting him to sing anthems of my magnificent power and beg for my forgiveness and mercy.

"All of those people on the freeway who crashed or got caught up in that explosion!"

"Oh…" I hadn't thought about it like that. "Collateral damage."

Then something snapped inside of Adam. His eyes narrowed in on me, and he had a very feral look about him. It was kind of hot. "How could you do that?" He grabbed me and pinned me to the car. He was really angry! It was even worse when I started laughing. "How can this mean nothing to you?"

He was beginning to squeeze a little too tight. I had no other option but to use my powers again and force him off of me and to the ground. It did put pressure on my mind again, but I had to be superior to him. "Because, they're ants."

"They're people!" Adam yelled. He was terribly distraught about it. I didn't think Adam would be that much of a humanitarian.

"And an ant is like a person to another ant, yet you would squash one just the same." I bent down beside him. I knew he wasn't going to reach out to hurt me—not yet. "You fail to see that I'm not one of you. I'm so much better."

"You're nothing but a murderer," he seethed.

I smirked as malevolently as I could. "It takes one to know one."

I upset my dear Adam with that one. After Roxy did all of that convincing to make him believe I was behind her father's death, he certainly didn't want anyone else bringing up the possibility that she was wrong. "I know about your powers. You made me kill your father!"

I chuckled to myself. His desperation was so adorable! "Do you really believe that?"

"Then deny it!"

"Why? Do you think lying is too beneath me?" I began to stroke his cheek as delicately as I could. He was such a magnificent creature. He was so full of fear and hope while externally masculine and sexy. He was a masterpiece. "I could tell you that I forced you to point the gun and pull the trigger three times, but it could very well be a lie. It doesn't matter what I tell you. It matters what you know."

I think he knew the truth. He was shaking from it. "I'm not a murderer." He spoke determined, but barely loud enough to hear above all the sirens from the ambulances, fire trucks, and police cars driving by.

"Then I suppose you have your answer." He was one of the few human beings that were capable of making me smile. I looked forward to making him bend to my will. I wouldn't even need to use my other powers on Adam to get him to lighten up. The two of us had more in common than he and Roxy ever could.

I stood back up and struck a flirtatious pose for him with my hands on my hips, and my chest leaned forward toward him. "Now I don't know how to drive, so I'd very much appreciate it if you drove me to Florida."

It was obvious that he wanted to deny me, but he was afraid of the consequences. He covered it well. "I saw what you did. You could just fly the both of us if you wanted to."

I couldn't let him know that I had limits or that I was in pain already from my exploits and probably would be until Roxy had healed us. "It's not about the destination. It's the journey that matters." I lifted Adam off of the ground and helped him onto his feet. He wanted to panic, but he didn't speak a word and he caught his face. He was an obedient boy. "I want you to be there by my side."

"Why not just make me agree?"

"Like Roxy makes you like her?" He looked a little surprised. Had it never truly crossed his mind? "I'm not that cruel…At least not when I don't need to be." I wrapped my arms around my scrumptious man. Everything about him was perfect, even his shoulders. I even liked his newly shaved head. His buzz made him look so much harder. "You and I can be good friends all on our own."

Adam wouldn't play along though. I knew good and well that he desired Roxy, and that meant he also desired me. That's the only reason why I didn't force him to wrap his arms around me. It would all happen in time. "And if I refuse?"

I was impressed. He wasn't just a terrified mouse. He was more like a lion, but it made no difference as long as he was still terrified. I looked around me for some incentive and found a small pebble lying on the parking lot next to my foot. I lifted it up to Adam's eye level so he could get a close look at it. "Then I'll shoot this little rock straight through your skull. Is that understood?"

Adam took a tremendous swallow of his pride and forced it back down. "Crystal."

I let go of him and clapped. "Goodie!" We were going to have so much fun together that I had to start spinning all the way back to my side of the car! I was already beginning to feel better from my feat of strength. I felt like I could do anything.

Adam wasn't as excited as I was. He slammed his car door when he got inside. It almost hurt my feelings. "Florida..."

"Yeppers." But I was still physically tired. "I'm hungry. When was the last time you ate anything?"

He moaned. "I don't know!" No wonder why he wasn't excited about hitting the road with me and being my servant.

"Find us someplace we can eat."

"This late?"

"Yes. I'm hungry." Besides the platter of cheese and crackers that Mommy gave to me, I hadn't personally tasted anything since I was a child. "You know Mommy and Daddy never fed me. Isn't that terrible?"

"Criminal." It was terribly sarcastic, but a decent start.

He had to do some searching, but we did find a place about twenty miles away. It was a diner that wasn't too far away from a truck stop. There was actually quite a bit of traffic inside. I hadn't been around that many people in a while. It was odd. I could feel them all constrained like fizz trapped inside a pop bottle. They were full of fear, pride, sorrow, joy, and lust. There were so many telling lies with their smiles and laughter when all they wanted to do was scream and run blindly into the night. They were all so restricted, as I used to be.

"Adam," I grabbed his arm to get his attention, "what do you see?"

He looked around quickly. "I see people trying to enjoy their meals, not expecting to be killed by you any time soon."

"Is that all you see?" I asked amazed. No one could see the world as I could, not even Roxy.

"Please, don't hurt anybody," he begged quietly. "I just want to eat and go."

"Well if I killed anyone, I'd never get my food at a decent time!" I truly did want to eat first. Everything else could wait. I watched the waitresses and waiters as they brought out trays of so many delicious smelling fatty foods and I wanted to go berserk. "I think I want it all, Adam!"

"Oh joy…"

I grabbed a hold of his arm when the server led us to our seat. He didn't need to be so upset. I was doing him a favor by giving him a break. "You're only grumpy because you haven't eaten and you've barely gotten any sleep."

"Really? Is that why?" He didn't need to be so sarcastic!

"Now I know this isn't an easy adjustment, but if you can get used to Roxy, I'm certain you can get used to me." I was the sexy, powerful one. Roxy was so sweet that she could make your teeth fall out, and she wasn't even graceful or poise. I was the perfect woman. She was nothing but a little girl. "You'll learn to like me better."

"Roxy is the sweetest, most kind person I've ever known!" I couldn't tell if he was trying to compliment her or insult me.

"Yuck!" And to think he actually liked her idiocy! "Do you really love her?"

"And what would you know of love?" Adam asked, sticking his nose up at me.

"Oh, I know of lots of things, Adam." I reached out for his face, and he knew better than to draw away from me. I kept my eyes focused on those pretty lips of his. "Roxy's first kiss was my first kiss, and it was with you."

My eyes quickly left his lips and focused on his beautiful eyes. He hadn't put his contacts in yet to cover them up, and they certainly were gorgeous. It was also easier to see him for who he was when I looked into them purely. It was like his soul was a map book. It was quite beautiful.

In the midst of my admiration, Adam mistook my gestures of interest and attraction for something more, and he cocked his eyebrow at me confused. "Are you saying you have feelings for me?"

"Sure," I said simply. "Is pity considered a feeling?"

"I can't believe this..." He mumbled while turning his head away. He was extremely frustrated for some reason!

"You'll feel better once you eat." I tugged on his arm when the hostess signaled us to follow her to a booth in the corner of the restaurant. I pushed him down naturally, and he rolled his eyes. I ignored him because I was a good person. I tried sitting next to him, but he was on the edge and he wouldn't budge. It was a round booth, and I certainly wasn't about to get in on the other side and scoot all the way around. I didn't have a choice. I forced him to move over with my mind. He was caught off guard, and he gritted his teeth and dragged his feet on the carpet as he tried to stop it, but he couldn't stop me from sliding him down and plopping right next to him with a gigantic smile plastered on my face.

Our dear waitress must have seen the altercation. She was quite confused. "Can I get you something?"

"Sure!" I snatched the menus out of her hand before she could drop them on the table. I wasn't going to read through it. I glanced at a couple of pictures. "Give us pancakes, bacon, a cheeseburger with everything on it, French fries, onion rings, chocolate milkshakes, Buffalo wings, your best slice of pie—"

"And that'll be all for now." Adam snatched the menu out of my hand and handed both of them back to the waitress. "Thank you."

She smiled as politely as she could before rushing away.

I pouted. "Maybe I'll want some more."

"You're not even gonna eat all that! I've seen Roxy eat. She's a featherweight. You'll pick at everything and be done."

That might have been true, but I didn't appreciate his tone. "What's your problem with me?"

"Besides the obvious?"

"Yes. Besides." It was odd how he got in my face and dared to argue with me after I destroyed so many lives with a thought right in front of his eyes. I was capable of things that he dared not to even dream about, yet he challenged me. I didn't understand it. I found him too intriguing to rip his throat out.

"Roxy is supposed to save the world, and you want to destroy it!" He kept his voice down, yet he found a way to yell at me quietly. "I feel a bit like I'm turning my back on humanity right now, so excuse me if I'm not having the best time of my life!"

I laughed. I didn't mean to laugh as loud as I did, but human beings were just so hysterical! I mean, I busted a gut. Adam might have been a little embarrassed that I was drawing so much attention to us. He might have also been worried that I snapped and was going to slaughter the entire restaurant at any second, but I could do that sane. He didn't need to worry about that. "Save the world, destroy the world…Do you even know what that means?"

He blinked a few times. "It's pretty self-explanatory."

"Really? It sounds quite vague to me." He made his own assumptions about me based off of a girl who admittedly knew nothing. "Why would I want to literally destroy the world? I live on the same planet you do, breathe the same air."

I watched the epiphany on Adam's face. It was a little bit like cracking the perfect egg carefully and watching the yoke spill over into the frying pan. "Then what are you specifically planning on doing?"

I smiled. "I'm going to free humanity."

Adam didn't believe me, but he was certainly curious enough. He was going to speak, but our waitress came with our drinks and set them down. She said some meaningless drivel that I didn't listen to about our food being up soon. I blocked it out and watched Adam stew in his curiosity until the old bat walked away far enough for us to be alone. "Free us from what?"

"Lying to yourselves daily." I smiled and stirred my drink with my straw. He would never believe my sincerity. "I'm going to make them incapable of lying to one another by making them not care about the repercussions of the truth. It'll be complete justice, all the time."

I had offended him. "And who gives justice to you for what you deserve?"

"Humans cannot judge what they cannot understand."

"And you're putting yourself above humanity?" He chuckled to himself. "You may be powerful, but you're still human. You still have weaknesses."

There was no need to remind me. I understood them better than he did, but I also knew the facts. "You're too weak to kill me and Roxy can't be killed. Even if you were somehow able, you wouldn't be able to go through with it." If he thought destroying me would save the world, all he had to do was strike me down while I slept or found a way to poison me while I ate. Cutting off Roxy's head might have worked, but he could not live in a world without Roxy. He was afraid to face himself without her. "I understand much about the concept of love, and the thing I understand most is how it hinders."

Oh I knew my dear Adam all too well. He didn't enjoy it. I was certain he detested me, which was fine. It was almost as tasty as that sweet lemonade tingling my tongue while the sourness pinched my cheeks. He hated me, but not even he realized that he was clinging onto me. "But I do know how much you crave freedom."

"Freedom?" He knew not what he had spoken, yet it resounded all throughout him. There was no thought behind it, yet his soul was captivated with the possibilities of what it could mean.

"You want to be with Roxy, but you're afraid to be honest with her. You're afraid the truth would push her away." It was silly considering all she had hidden and the dreadful repercussions of it. It only proved how worthless his faith in her was. His faith would be much better suited in me. "And you're afraid because I know you better than she ever could. I can see right through your bull, and I think you're beautiful."

Adam slowly began to look sick. "You don't really have feelings for me, do you?" Adam whined.

I smiled. "I like that you're a smart aleck and that you're choosing not to cower in front of my mighty and spectacular presence. I just want you to remember what I can do and that if I feel like it, I'll kill you."

"I can't possibly forget what I just saw you do." And yet Adam kept his composure so nicely. He was going to come in handy once I converted him willingly to follow my commandments.

"Goodie!" I clapped my hands together once I spotted our waitress coming out of the kitchen with some helpers. "The food is done."

It was so scrupulous! I decided to be courteous and share with Adam, even though he was being coy. The cheese on my burger was so gooey, the bun was lightly toasted and buttered, and the meat was perfectly seasoned. It melted in my mouth and sat my senses on fire. I had never eaten anything like that before. Mommy couldn't cook like that and Roxy didn't usually order unhealthy things. Daddy wanted her to take care of her body, even though her body took care of itself. It was stupid. I was glad they were dead. I ate, and I ate everything that I possibly could and then it looked like I barely put a dent in any of it. The only thing I ate all of was the cherry pie.

"I told you," Adam said smugly. "Roxy picks. You pick."

I wanted to finish the plates, but I just didn't have enough room in my tiny stomach for it. "You've barely eaten anything."

"Would you share a plate with the devil?"

"I'm sure he doesn't have cooties." I laughed, but Adam would do nothing but glare at me. "I don't have cooties either, Adam. Eat. I know you're hungry."

He didn't want to. I suppose I understood his hesitation, but I knew he was starving! I had heard his stomach rumble a few times. He hadn't forgotten that he was hungry. Adam picked up a fry and started to dip it in a little cup of ketchup and ate it cautiously, as if I had found time to speed away in the blink of an eye to poison it in the kitchen and come back to the seat without being noticed. He chewed slowly as if he were waiting for a heart attack at any moment. Then he gulped it down in a hard swallow with a frown like it was the most disgusting thing in the world.

"It's not so bad!"

"I think I'd rather dine with the devil."

"Oh, please! I want you to stop fooling around and eat. We've got plenty here, and you know that we've got a long journey. Besides, wouldn't you rather stuff yourself now so you don't have to do it later? That way, you can spend more car time with Roxy."

That was all I needed to say. He barely had time to finish swallowing one thing before he put another in his mouth. Adam shouldn't have been so selfish. I already knew he was starving. He was only hurting himself. He ended up eating everything I had left on the table, including five refills. It was impressive.

"Next time, just do what I tell you."

"I could say the same thing about you."

I glared at him playfully. We were going to have loads of fun. "I'm glad Roxy never listened to Daddy and decided to get attached to you. Now, I've got a very good pet." I scooted closer until I could lean on his shoulder. He moaned loudly and rolled his eyes, but he was only playing hard to get. "Soon, I'll teach you how to play fetch, lie on your back, and wag that sexy tail of yours. Hopefully we'll never get to play dead."

"Why are we even bothering with this?" He sounded like a whiny, little boy who was upset that he had to stay after school and clean off the chalkboard while all his friends were roaming about playing, but I knew good and well he had nothing better to do. Nothing else could have been as interesting as me. "You don't even need me."

"But Roxy does, and whether you realize it or not, you need the both of us." He grumbled or something like it. I'm not sure. I just knew he didn't believe me. "I'll have to wean you off of her, of course. You don't wanna be alone in this big, scary world, and we both know that if your dad cared about you, he would have been there for you."

120

"It's not exactly like he can be." It was quite yummy that he responded. I didn't expect him to.

"Let me guess." I tapped my finger on my chin, just to play along. "He's a criminal and the cops are after him."

"It's a little bit more complicated than that." Grumpy, grumpy, grumpy!

"No. It's not. If he cared about you, then he would have made an honest living for himself so he could have given you a safe and stable home. Instead, he screwed you over. Your grannie said that your mom was an ingrate who wouldn't listen to common sense about men, so your whole conception was screwy. Did your mom ever remarry?"

"Shut up," he seethed.

I giggled. If I weren't capable of ripping his brain through his skull, he probably would have been strangling me. "How can you marry Roxy and not be totally honest with her?" It blew my mind how he could want to kill me so badly, even though part of him must have known that I made perfect sense. "You wanted to run away, because you had dirty little secrets—not because I suggested it. So what is it about you that's so awful?"

Then Adam started acting like a little psychopath and started shrugging and shaking his shoulders until it was too uncomfortable to lean on him, forcing me to get up. "I'm not opening up to you. You're not my girlfriend. You're not the woman I love. I don't have to tell you anything!"

I shook my head at him in disbelief. "Poor Adam." He was so angry that it was just downright funny. "You think so little of me when all I want to do is help."

He grumbled, crossed his arms, and leaned back into his seat. I was the ball and chain wrapped tightly around his ankle. I can't say I wanted to be. I knew better than anyone what it was like being trapped

121

with no way out. I had to show him the depths of my greatness and let him decide.

I spotted two couples in the restaurant sitting a couple of tables away from us. They were all middle aged. The two men sat next to their spouses. They had been in the restaurant for a while, yet I did not see much of a spark from those they sat next to. I could mostly tell from their wedding bands that they were married. "Look over there!" I pointed to them so he would see exactly who I meant.

"What about them?"

"They're on a double-date. They're probably traveling across the country together. They must be extremely close friends to do that."

"So what?"

One of the women got up to go to the bathroom, while one of the men left to go outside to their car to get something. A man was left sitting across from a woman; neither of them married to the other. Their body chemistry instantly changed. It was so much stiffer before. They were obviously attracted to one another. I could sense it. Why wouldn't they be? They were more physically fit than their spouses. They looked a little better. The man said something that made her laugh louder than what her husband was capable of doing. They were only torturing themselves. "They want to have an affair."

"Why would you say that?"

"Because, they're too afraid to speak it themselves." They only needed a little push. I could sense their desire for one another like a tiny bubble living inside of them. There were so many walls built up to stop them from acting out on their true desires. I could crumble them one at a time and make them topple on one another like dominos. I didn't know if they were compatible or whether or not they had children. It was likely, but I didn't care about something like that. What was the point of living if you couldn't live in the moment and give into what you truly wanted?

Their walls collapsed, and one more look of desire and admiration was all it took before they reached across the table and started shoving their tongues down each other's throats.

Adam's eyes bucked and his mouth dropped. "Are you doing this?"

"No. They are. I only helped them accept it." I smiled at my handy work. They looked happy. That was all that mattered.

"Stop it!" Adam's hand grabbed onto my shoulder, and he began to squeeze it. "You're going to ruin their marriages!"

I was not immune to pain, and it was unexpected. I hissed before forcibly removing his hand and placing his own chokehold around his own neck. "What's that even mean anymore?"

He looked rather silly choking himself. His eyes looked like they were gonna pop out of his head. It was kind of funny. With all of his might, he managed a command for me. "Stop it!" He should have asked me nicely, but I assumed he wasn't thinking rationally while he lost all of that oxygen for his brain.

I let him go and he collapsed on the table gasping for air. I bet he never thought he'd almost choke himself to death! That's one reason why he should have appreciated me. He could experience something new every day.

The new couple had grabbed the attention from everyone in the restaurant. There were only a few children, but their eyes were beginning to be shielded. They were becoming wildly inappropriate for a restaurant setting. They were beginning to take their jackets off, content with having sex in front of all of us. "I can't stop them," I told Adam. "They're already free."

I was waiting to see what would happen between their true spouses. I was hoping the absent wife would be first and would begin to cry, but it was the absent husband who came back in the restaurant and howled with a fury that was intended for bloodshed. And just as I freed the friends of their inhibitions, the jealous husband shredded his walls like pieces of paper and lunged over his table to tackle his once beloved friend.

"Lyla!" I felt Adam's desperation. He wanted to strangle me until I made everything as it once was.

"Is this not what he deserves?" Two friends gave into their dark desires and betrayed their loves. Was the husband not honor bound to fight for his woman? "Were you not speaking minutes ago about justice?"

"You provoked this!"

I rolled my eyes. "I don't bring anything to the surface that's not already beneath."

It was a violent fight, but the man betrayer didn't stay down forever and was able to flip the righteous man over into another table. Their rage transferred quickly into the table of bikers who were enjoying their early breakfast. They had no reservations and quickly joined the fight, not caring about who was justified. They only wanted to hurt someone for interrupting their peaceful meal. The other wife came back from the bathroom, and the two wives joined in on the fight. The one involved in the affair cared too strongly for the men to stand idly by just because she was a woman and the one who was betrayed was not yet aware of the betrayal. A fight of eight couldn't last in one spot in a crowded diner. It all began to spread. Everyone who was touched or deeply entranced by their actions was all prey to my powers. They all fell in a chain reaction, and they began to fight and cry, love and scream—all because they felt it.

Adam was not touched by the madness. He somehow avoided it and watched it all with horror. "We need to leave!" He pushed me until I had let him out of the booth and then he grabbed my arm and began pulling me to the door.

"Hey!" The hostess tried to block the exit. "You can't just leave without paying!"

"Do you honestly care about this job?" I asked her.

She looked confused at first, but then wildly indignant. "No. I hate this job!" She threw her apron on the ground. "I quit!"

I laughed at my glorious deeds. Could Adam truly not see that I had done that girl a favor? Did he have to pull on my arm so tightly? "These people would thank me if they knew what I was doing for them."

"You're creating hell on earth!"

We had made it safely to our car by the time glass began to shatter from chairs flying through the windows and people started escaping by them when the front door wasn't working fast enough. I could feel someone's fascination with fire when I entered into the building. Most people were captivated by it, and many people had random thoughts of setting things on fire. Perhaps people like that shouldn't have worked in kitchens.

Adam watched as the restaurant began to be engulfed in flames. The number of people running out was not equal to the number of people once inside. Most notably, the wedded couples were nowhere to be found, nor the bikers. Through the broken windows, I could still see them fighting bitterly to the death to defend something that didn't matter and to fight for nothing at all.

"This is what you want to do to the world?" he asked.

"Isn't it wonderful?" I outstretched my hands and begun to dance and spin around. It was lovely to me. The people trapped inside weren't even afraid anymore. They were incapable of feeling it. How much freer could you get than being without the fear of death?

He pointed to the building, channeling all of his rage into his finger. "This is insane!"

I stopped dancing. I didn't feel like celebrating if he was going to ruin it! "If you don't like what I do, you can leave."

"Oh, I can leave?" Adam yelled sarcastically. "Just like that, I can go?"

"Yes. You are free to leave." I meant it. I didn't want him around if he was going to try to ruin my fun all the time. Besides, I didn't want any prisoners. I either had servants or trophies, but no slaves.

Adam wanted to go. I knew he did, but there was a burden of obligation on his shoulders weighing him down. I was curious as to what would happen if I set him free. He probably wouldn't even care about all of the mischievous things that I did, which meant he could stay with me and be happy, because I would be willing to please him physically. I could sense his lust for Roxy. If he weren't so angry at me most of the time, he'd be even more attracted to me.

Oh well. I wasn't going to free him yet. I wanted his restricted mind to make the most momentous decision of his life.

"I..." He took in a deep breath and exhaled slowly and jagged. His eyes were glistening as well. "I can't let you roam around free, and I can't let you drag Roxy around to only God knows where."

I smiled, but I wanted to be clear. "So, your choice is to stay with me?"

He looked back at the burning building. I knew the possibilities frightened him, but he wouldn't need to be afraid for much longer. "Yes."

"Yay!" I clapped and jumped up and down. I was so glad! I had a willing servant and not a slave! It was so vital to get those chains off of him. Sure I could sense that he would resent Roxy for it, but he was coming out of love and loyalty.

That's how I knew he'd never kill me. "On to Florida!"

Chapter Seven

I opened my eyes and sensed that it was a little past the dawn. If something bad had happened, I assumed that I would have been awakened at dawn. I sighed with relief. It must have worked. Adam must have had a safe day without Lyla bothering him at all.

I sat up and realized that everything was once again different. I didn't have quite as much space, and I wasn't as comfortable in that small car. The dashboard, the seats, the windows…Everything was different.

I turned my head and Adam was gone. Before I panicked and began screaming for his name, I took a deep breath and looked around. There were other cars and gas pumps around, and I was parked at one.

I also had a massive headache. "Ow!" I held my head and it faded away quickly. I was beginning to worry about the success of the plan. I knew I fell asleep, but I didn't feel like it was an induced drowsiness. Then I didn't think a headache was a side effect when I read the box of medicine. If it wasn't from something I did, then Lyla must have been the reason why I had a headache. But if Lyla was in charge, how could Adam be alive?

I saw him walking from out of the gas station and rushing over to the pump. He had bags under his eyes. He might have needed me to help him, so I got out of the car. "Adam?"

He turned around quickly, almost like he was about to jump. Nothing usually scared Adam, but he was frightened and prepped to punch me if necessary. "Roxy?"

"Of course, it's past dawn. Who else would it be?"

He met me halfway and embraced me at the back bumper of the unfamiliar and sort of sad looking car. "I'm so glad to see you again!"

"What happened to your car?"

"I had to get rid of it."

My mouth dropped. "Adam! You love that car!" I couldn't believe he was being so nonchalant about it. He slaved over it for hours for years making it absolutely perfect. It was the longest committed relationship he had ever been in!

"That's not important! What's important is that you're here." I was glad he was happy to see me, but he was sort of creeping me out. He looked like a mess. His hair was gone, his eyes were bloodshot, and he smelled like coffee and smoke. He obviously needed a long shower and a nap.

"Did our plan work?"

Then Adam's eyes got real big, but they seemed pretty empty. "No." He held onto my arms, almost hurting me. "Lyla was totally unaffected. She made me drive in oncoming traffic and basically killed the entire freeway. Then I saw what she does!" I was almost afraid to hear anymore. I had never seen Adam so out of control. "She takes away inhibitions until we all act like wild animals, giving into our instincts. There's no judgment or restraint. Even wild animals have some kind of order to them. This...This could end our world!"

Adam was talking so fast and crazy that it was hard to process it all. Mom and Dad never told me that Lyla could strip inhibitions away. I thought she just made people evil and tormented them. But whatever it was that she did, I couldn't let it continue. "We have to stop her."

128

"We?" I had never seen Adam nervous before. It sort of made me scared too. "I don't know what I'm supposed to do, Roxy. This is so much harder than I ever thought it would be. I don't know how to stop her. I don't know if you can stop her—"

"Hush." I placed my finger on his lips to make him stop. I couldn't listen to him bring the both of us down. If he was failing in being the strong one, I was going to pick up the slack. I was not going to lose to Lyla, and I refused to let her destroy Adam! "I'm gonna make you feel better."

Adam stepped away from me! "You're gonna force your powers and me again?"

"Did she tell you that?" Of course she would tell him that. It was worse that he seemed to believe it. "I have never misused my powers when it came to you. I promise."

Adam was shaking. I didn't understand how Lyla could make him so afraid and miserable. Most of all, I didn't understand how she could make him begin to doubt me. I could sense all of his frustration and traces of Lyla, but she didn't force her powers on him. She was weakening him the old fashioned way. "I don't know what I'm supposed to do, Roxy."

"I know." I grabbed his face and pulled him to me until our foreheads touched. "Just clear your mind."

I could sense that he didn't know what I was talking about. His mind was whirling around with too many unpleasant memories. I couldn't see them; I only felt his pain and torment. He was so frightened while trying to be so strong. He fought her, because he was too good to let her win. Even if he couldn't do much to stand against her, I sensed that goodness in him and I focused on it. It felt like a warm light covered in darkness until I made it grow bigger into an overpowering force.

Adam smiled and began to laugh uncontrollably. He had such a beautiful smile and his joy reflected on my face. "I feel really good!"

"I'm glad." I didn't know if it was safe to use my powers, but I couldn't refuse Adam after I put him through so much with Lyla.

"I even feel a little better." His eyes were so much brighter and the bags under his eyes were gone. He had a spring in his step, having energy he didn't have before. "I've got a little bit more strength!"

I took his hands before he started doing cartwheels or something. "Yeah, but you should get some real sleep! Maybe we should check in another motel."

Adam sighed heavily and his shoulders dropped. "Lyla wants me to drive her to Florida."

"Florida?" I didn't remember it extremely well. I only have half a memory for each day anyway, but it was such a traumatic time. "She has followers there."

"How do you know?"

"When we were six, she ran away." I kept waking up in different places across the country with men I didn't recognize. They took care of me, but they would barely say a word or stay around me. I stayed the longest time in a house built like a fortress in Florida. I remembered I never left a specific room with red walls and white curtains. I wanted to, but I couldn't. I spent most of my time napping or watching from the window as The Master of the House played with his children. He seemed so kind from afar, but he never spoke one word to me. I remembered his odd blue eyes. They almost looked silver.

I stayed in that room for nearly a month. Each morning, I had another doll lying next to me. I didn't like to play with them because I knew they were Lyla's. She started placing them on shelves too high for me to reach, so they would always stare at me with their dead eyes while I wished for a single soul to stay with me. I hated dolls ever since. Maybe that's why I started collecting stuffed animals instead.

130

Even though the odds were stacked against me, and my mother and father were nowhere to be found, I didn't lose faith in them. I knew that they loved me, and unless they were dead, they wouldn't stop until I was safe in their arms again. Then one morning, I woke up on an airplane next to them smiling at me. "I was lucky my parents found us and took us home."

"Are you saying we shouldn't go?" He almost acted like he wanted to go!

"You sound like there's no choice."

He threw his hands up in the air, exasperated. "I don't know if there is one!"

I crossed my arms and pouted. It was a childish habit, and I didn't wear that stubborn face often, but I always meant it when I used it. "I can beat her."

"You're not even around to fight her when she's here. You lose by default!" I realized then how much Adam was involved in the fight, and honestly, he was the only one fighting. I was his damsel in distress, and I hated it. It was neat to read about those girls, but I never wanted to be one of them.

Something needed to change. "Whatever it is that she's supposed to do, I'm not gonna let her do it. I'll find a way to save this world from her!" I had no information, no way to meet her face to face, and no way to fight against her even if I did. I didn't care. I was not afraid of Lyla!

I was terribly disappointed that Adam was. "I'm at a disadvantage, Roxy. I wanna be here to protect you. I need to stay alive, but some of the things that she does…" He wasn't only afraid. He was appalled with whatever she had done to him. "I don't know how much I can take before I lose it."

"I don't expect you to stand for her injustice." Maybe I was being unfair with him. I didn't know what I would do without him, and Lyla was going to kill him as soon as he outlived her amusement of him. It was more than a difficult decision. It was impossible! "I know that we can find a way to stop her together."

Adam was doing his best not to look terrified, but I could sense the fear starting to come back. "I'm afraid that she'll use her powers on me. I don't wanna turn into the person I think I am."

"Then remember the person I know you are." I leaned into him, and it was the first time that I ever tried to initiate one of our kisses, but he looked uncomfortable and took a step back from me.

"I think I do need some rest."

I shrugged my shoulders. "You're the driver." I was trying to ignore the fact that he wouldn't kiss me back, but it only got me thinking that there was something seriously wrong that he didn't want to talk about.

He found a brilliant way to ignore the topic; he had me play co-pilot! Not only did I not ever go anywhere, but people usually printed up directions or had a GPS. Who knew how to work a map book anymore? I was too busy struggling with directions to figure out a way to pry the dark secrets from his mind.

I did notice that we were still heading toward Florida. I think the map plot was only to distract me, and Adam really knew where we were going anyway. He didn't know any side streets, but the freeway wasn't hard for him to figure out.

When it was noon, we stopped at a motel somewhere in Alabama for check-in. We were so close to where Lyla wanted us to go that my stomach was all in knots. Whatever she was planning, it couldn't be good. I had to think of a way to convince Adam not to go through with Lyla's commands. There had to be a better option. I wasn't going to try and convince him otherwise until he had gotten some rest. I didn't want to upset him and risk keeping him up when he needed a nap.

It was odd sharing a motel room with Adam again, especially in such a rundown place. I guess I hadn't thought a lot about it, but it would have been nice if our first time sharing a room was when I was lucky enough to marry him. My life wasn't turning out at all as I expected, even though I didn't have much hope to work with Lyla attached to me. My white picket fence life with Adam was nothing but a pipe dream. He might have said that he would always love me, but it was selfish of me to accept any sort of proposal from him. He was probably by my side because there was nowhere else to go. He was doing his best to survive.

Adam didn't seem to care about how the room was and how dirty it might have been. He collapsed right on his bed and started resting his eyes without even taking off his shoes. He had been working harder than me or Lyla, and he couldn't rely on any special abilities.

I could sense some negativity inside of him. I might have made him feel better earlier, but I couldn't keep his true feelings covered forever. I didn't have the right to. "Adam?"

He kept his eyes closed, still trying to fall asleep. "Yeah?"

I was shaking just thinking about all of the pain I had caused him. "I'm really sorry about everything."

He opened his eyes and slowly began to sit up. I didn't know what he was gonna say. He didn't seem angry, but he was certainly upset. I could feel that, and he had a furrowed brow. "Stop apologizing. It's not your fault."

"But it is my fault!" I didn't mean to play the martyr, but there was no point in being naive about it. I was partially responsible for Lyla and I led Adam onto my secret by not being careful enough, so he came back to my house. I probably even left the front door unlocked! Maybe Lyla was always destined to get free eventually, but it was my fault that Adam was involved. "My parents warned me about forming bonds with people, but I couldn't help myself when it came you."

133

I started blubbering. "I fell in love with you and it has cost you everything! You don't even have your car, and you probably can't ever see your grannie again."

"But you lost your parents," he spoke quietly. "It's not like I'm the only one who's suffered."

"But that's Lyla's fault! She even tried to drag you into her lies, and you believed it for a short while." I took a deep breath. I was so upset that it was becoming difficult to think and to speak, especially with Adam's negative emotions continuously building. I couldn't even figure it out. He didn't sound like he resented me and I didn't quite feel that, but I couldn't pinpoint the emotion either. I always had trouble figuring out negative emotions.

"We can't go to Florida, because we'll be doing exactly what she wants us to do." All of our troubles were because of Lyla! I was gonna find a way to make her sorry for what she did to Mom and Dad. "We can't ever do what she wants!"

Adam's emotions continued to strengthen, and he turned away from me. "I'm not in a position where I can disobey her, Roxy."

I was shocked. I understood that Lyla was dangerous, but I did not believe she could control Adam! "I don't think she'll hurt you."

"She'll do something much worse!" He snapped all of a sudden. It made me gasp even. He calmed down after he startled me, but his negativity was coming to a climax. "I've seen what she can do. I can't let her use her powers on me."

I was bewildered. I took a seat next to him on his bed and grabbed his hand. I prepared myself to use my powers if I needed to, but I was confident that we could talk about our problems. "What are you afraid of?" I smiled and even laughed a little. There was no reason for him to be afraid of himself. "I know your nature, Adam. You're one of the best men I've ever met."

134

Usually, that was all that it took for me to lift his spirits, but the feeling inside him only became stronger as he shied his eyes away from me in…Shame? "There are things about me that you don't know, things that you could never forgive."

After all I had put him through? It wasn't possible. "What do you mean?"

I didn't think there was anything Adam could say to make me ever hate him. I doubted that he had it in him to ever truly hurt me. I liked to count my blessings in a world where they were so few, and he was one of mine. I didn't believe there was anything he could ever do to make me feel differently, but he did, and it was eating him up inside. He was shaking!

"Adam?" I believed he was only exaggerating, but I couldn't help the little bit of fear and anxiousness that came over me. "Please tell me!" I didn't care what it was. It couldn't be as bad as what he was trying to make me think.

Adam's eyes were glistening, and it wouldn't be long before tears began to fall from his beautiful eyes. "Your dad…" He got choked up, and I held my breath from the absence of thought from the thing I dared not to think while my heart ached and felt the truth I wasn't brave enough to face. "Lyla didn't kill him," he said. "I did."

He certainly thought he did. He looked pitiful, wanting to ask me for forgiveness while believing that he had no right to ask at all. He didn't need to feel that way. There was no way he could have killed my dad, so I wasn't upset. I knew he was innocent! "That's not true. She—"

"You keep defending me, but you don't even know any of the details! I pulled the gun out on him."

"And she made you pull the trigger!" He was starting to get on my nerves. I knew it was hard to accept the fact that Lyla could manipulate people so easily, but at least it wasn't his fault! He'd just have to accept that.

"No!" He squeezed on my hand and looked me in the eye—with all of the seriousness and truth he could gather up—while he was completely breaking down. "She might have tried, but she was a little too slow. I know for sure that the first shot was my own, maybe even the second one. I was surprised about the third shot, but all it took was the first one in his chest. It was me, Roxy. I killed your father."

How? Maybe he believed that Lyla made him do it after I brought up that it was a possibility, but he must have figured it out eventually. How could he have kept something like that from me?

I finally figured out why he felt so negative and it began to feel too overwhelming for me. If Adam spoke another word to me, I would have lost it. I would have started screaming at him at the top of my lungs, even though I didn't have the words to express what I felt. I was so angry and disappointed.

I had never felt that way in my life. I felt cold inside, but my face was so hot. I released his hand and rose off the bed. I couldn't even bear to touch him! I didn't want to see him or smell him or even think about him! "I have to be alone for a while."

"Roxy!" Adam reached out to grab my arm, but I pulled it away as soon as I felt him reach for me and bolted out of the door.

I didn't know where I was running to. There was nowhere for me to go, and it wasn't fair to abandon him. I didn't know how I'd manage without Adam anyway. I couldn't drive. I didn't have much money on me. I wouldn't know what I would do if the police questioned me! But I couldn't think about all that. I just needed to get away and clear my thoughts.

Once again, we were staying somewhere right off the freeway out in the middle of nowhere. I guess there was a less likely chance we'd get spotted by someone, but it didn't leave me with much to do. The only places around were these two gas stations and one of them had a diner attached to it. It was as good a place as any to sit by myself. I wiped my face as much as I could before going inside.

There weren't many people in there. There were probably two people in the kitchen, one waitress, and a burly man enjoying a hardy plate of pancakes with a little girl. The place looked a little scary, especially with all of the animal heads plastered on the walls. I didn't see why a deer head needed to be displayed on the wall so it could stare into my soul as soon as I took a step inside the building. It was creeping me out, but I couldn't take my eyes off of it.

The waitress saw me staring up at the deer, and she slowly stood next to me without me even really noticing, and we both stared at the dead creature together, only she admired the handy work while its very existence boggled my mind. Finally, she smiled and asked, "You're not from around here, are you?"

"Is anybody?"

"We get a lot of strangers pass'n through, especially truckers. The locals don't usually come 'til night. There's no work in town, so they're gone dur'n the day." She was certainly getting a kick out of seeing me so uncomfortable by the deer head. "We make great burgers!"

I wasn't much of a meat eater, and I didn't think I could stomach a cheeseburger while an animal was continuously giving me guilt about it with its black, soulless eyes. "I am hungry, and the pancakes do look delicious, but I don't have any money on me."

The man sitting with his daughter raised his hand up quickly and with barely any effort or energy. "I'll cover it," he said.

I smiled and ran over to the man's face to properly thank him. From a first glance, I wouldn't have thought he had much money to spare. "Thank you, Sir."

He smiled at me, but he was really too engrossed in his meal to mean anything more than a kind gesture. His daughter was also too busy

137

making a mess with her syrup to notice I was there. It was all over her face and hands. My dad would never let me eat pancakes out in public for that reason.

Dad...

"What can I get you?"

I wiped my eyes before I started crying again and drew even more attention to myself. "I'll have a stack of pancakes and an orange juice, if you don't mind."

"Sure thing." She touched my shoulder gently and smiled. "I'll even throw in a side of bacon on me. Okay?"

I nodded and kept my face as hidden as much possible. If I would have spoken or smiled back, I would have burst into a fit of tears and I was so sick of crying! If I didn't somehow gain control, there was no way I was going to defeat Lyla.

I took a seat in one of the few corner booths, and she brought my juice out to me quickly. "Thank you." I knew I was hungry and thirsty, but my sadness was masking it. I kept looking at the glass knowing that I should take a sip and then another one would follow until it was gone. It was a very simple process and yet I didn't have the will to do it.

"You okay?" The waitress asked.

I hadn't noticed that tears had rolled down my face until she asked about it. There was no sense in lying. Besides, I just didn't have it in me. "No."

"What's the matter?"

I certainly couldn't tell her that my soon to emerge evil self manipulated my boyfriend into murdering my dad, and now I was on the run because of it. I didn't know what to make up, so I remained quiet.

"It's men troubles, ain't it?"

I raised my head up at her surprised. It was more complicated than that, but Adam certainly was the reason why I ran away in such a fuss. "Yeah."

She sighed heavily and rolled her eyes before sliding into the booth across from me. "Of course it's a man. It's always a man! So what's the problem?"

"He did something unforgivable!" I caught myself. After all of my promises, I didn't mean to say that. It was even worse that I meant it. "I want to forgive him, but it's so hard with how I feel right now, especially when he was dishonest about it."

"He cheated?"

"No! He'd never!" It was odd that I was so offended with that suggestion considering that he had killed my dad. I didn't want to think about being around him, but I couldn't imagine him with anyone else. "But I am afraid that if I leave him, he'll leave me for this disgusting woman whose been eying him from day one!" Adam was already in a state of weakness. If I didn't work things out with him, I was confident that Lyla would use it to her advantage.

The waitress was glaring and pursing her lips as she thought about my problem. "Honey, I don't need no more details to solve your problem. All you gotta do is ask yourself one single question." She held her index finger up, and I nearly gulped as I looked at it. I was waiting anxiously for her to continue, because she was so confident in the setup of her speech and something about her southern accent made her seem so much more determined to get it through my skull. "If you dumped him for what he did to you, and five years go by and he's walking down the street with that little hussy, would you be happy for him or would you be a bitter hag?"

I yelled out my answer without considering it for one second. "I certainly don't want her to have him!"

139

She pursed her lips into a smile and nodded her head before speaking so nonchalantly to me. "Then forgive him and take him back. Obviously, you're not ready to lose him. If he's trash, let the garbage collector dispose of him."

What she said made sense to me, but it wasn't all that simple. He betrayed me. It was hard to come back from that, especially with something so serious. Adam had killed a man, a man who happened to be my dad. Maybe having Lyla inside of me was worse than anything he could ever do, but that didn't excuse what he had done. If anything, Lyla was more reason to stay away from Adam.

But Lyla would never leave Adam be. She was going to use him until there was nothing left but scraps for me to remember how he used to be before she tainted his world. My best option was to stay with Adam so he wouldn't willingly fall into her arms.

Then it occurred to me how much I still cared for him, regardless of what he had done to me. If I loved him, it was best to stay by his side and protect him from Lyla and himself. I had no choice but to forgive him. It was the only way to keep him safe.

"Is he a good guy?"

"He's a great one." Although I knew it, my words didn't feel like they were real. I suddenly couldn't stop thinking about my dad and the last moment I saw him. He was heartbroken after having to watch me cry after he locked me up in my chains too early, because he had to clean up my mess. My dad had to die because he loved me.

"Good guys are hard to find." She pointed over toward the man dining with the young girl. "The man who offered to pay for your meal— Frank—might not look like much, but he quit his job for one with less pay so he could take care of his daughter."

No, he didn't look like much. He was an obese man, real scrappy looking. His clothes were wrinkled, and it was only an orange tank top and a pair of blue jeans that were a little too snug. He needed to shave his beard or at least cut it neatly instead of being a bushy mess. He had more hair on his face than he had on his head. I don't want to sound rude, but he was a physically sloppy guy, yet I couldn't really notice that until the waitress had pointed out his appearance. The overwhelming affection he felt for his daughter masked his flaws, because love was the only true beauty in the world anyway.

I could tell the girl was his daughter. They did look alike, except she was adorable in her own way. She had chubby cheeks and the greenest eyes. Her hair was thick and light brown and forced into a puffy ponytail that lacked a woman's finesse. "Where's her mother?"

The waitress made sure to speak quietly enough for only me to hear. "He doesn't know."

That explained something else that I felt from the man. There was a heavy load on his shoulders, and it was more than the burden of taking care of his daughter. There was something really pressing on him—a worry that was immediate that he couldn't shake. "Is there anything…" I didn't know how to properly pry the information, but I felt like I needed to help him. "Is there anything wrong with him?"

She sat up straight, quick, and double blinked as if she were offended for the man. "What do you mean?"

"I don't mean to offend! Something just feels…" I looked at the man again and noticed him grab onto his chest and rubbing it. His daughter was too young to notice the expression of pain on his face that he tried to hide, but I caught it. "He's sick."

"How would you…?" She didn't need to say another word. The floor and our table shook from the large thud of him falling onto the ground.

"Daddy!" His daughter immediately began to cry, and she rushed out of her seat to look at him passed out on the floor. She was so bound in fear that she couldn't do anything but stand over him. The poor thing didn't even know to ask for help.

"Somebody call nine-one-one!" The waitress ran over to Frank's side and put her ear to his chest to search for his heartbeat. The people in the kitchen also ran from their stations to watch in a panic as Frank struggled for his life.

I sat in my booth for a couple of seconds, but they felt like hours. Each one that passed by was another I failed Frank. He offered me kindness, and I let my parents' cautious fear that was rooted into my existence hinder me from making the right choice. It shouldn't have mattered if I could have been caught by trackers. I couldn't let a kind man die, and I most certainly couldn't leave his daughter fatherless.

Someone in the kitchen had called for help and another one came out to grab the little girl and pulled her in a safer room, but she became responsive and began kicking and screaming all of the way outside. "Daddy!"

If I could bring my dad back, I would. I wouldn't let her experience the emotional scars of losing a father, especially since he was so kind to me.

I slid out of my booth and walked over to Frank. "Let me help." They were all involved in their panicked bustling. I had to bend down to his side and get in their way before they would acknowledge my offer.

"You can't possibly be a doctor!" The cook said, covered in grease stains and sweat.

They had no reason to believe me, but they had no reason to refuse me either. "I know what to do." No one got out of my way or gave me any breathing room. Even though they were shocked and didn't know what to think, I could feel them doubting me. It wasn't really nerve wrecking, but it was disappointing. Instead of a bit of hope, they gave into all their fear.

My powers didn't depend on them. Most of the time, I healed myself without any thought at all. With others, it only required a bit of concentration. I placed my hands on his chest and closed my eyes. I felt him fading away into cold darkness. There was only a speck of light that I could feel that was hiding inside of his regret. He loved someone so much—probably his daughter. I held onto the light as tight as I could until it consumed his entire body.

He opened his eyes and looked right at me. Frank was practically back from the dead, yet there was calmness on him. I knew he was better on the inside. He might have still been a big man, but he was still healthy. But it was more than just his body. He was different. I had made him different. "Thank you."

The restaurant workers all stared at me. I never had admirers before—not normal ones that I knew about. There was only Adam, but he grew to love me. I had never felt that instant *aw* before, and it was highly enlightening.

"That was amazing!" My waitress yelled. "How did you do that?"

I giggled like a child. I was filled with such inexplicable joy. I knew deep down that I was at risk for using my powers, but I couldn't get over the feeling that was covering the room. There was gratitude, love, and such hope. To wash away doubt and fear was a powerful gift indeed. If only I could make everyone feel the way we all felt in that room!

"Daddy!" The little girl ran back into her father's arms, and he held her tight into his chest. "Are you okay?"

"I'm fine, Sammie." He hugged her, but he was still looking at me with that cheerful smile. None of them had reactions I had imagined. I thought people might think I was weird, or they would kidnap me and put me in a lab somewhere. I suppose they didn't have the authority to do something like that, but they could have started throwing out dozens of names of people I needed to help. I didn't mind doing it, but I couldn't.

"If you don't mind," I got up as slowly and started heading for the door, "I'll be going now." I felt their eyes still on me, and their joy was like a power trying to burst out from within my stomach. It was so powerful!

I took off running back to the motel with a huge smile on my face. I had to hide myself before everyone started chasing me or wanted to ask me a bunch of questions I couldn't literally answer.

I hadn't forgotten that Adam had murdered my dad, but I couldn't let the feeling pierce my heart. Whatever I had done to heal that man of his damaged heart, I somehow healed mine. I knew I could forgive Adam, because I didn't want to die with regrets when I could live with his love.

I banged on the door, and he speedily opened it up. "You're back."

I immediately started to blush. "And you're not dressed."

I had never seen Adam with his shirt off. I was very, very prude. When I was in middle school, I asked the basketball coach to tell his boys to put their shirts back on because it was indecent. I didn't really see guys with their shirts off and seeing Adam there with his muscles rippling and his body glistening was…Very awkward.

"I finished a shower not too long ago." He noticed how flustered I was and even though he was still in a down mood, he struggled not to laugh at me. "I'll put on a shirt."

He moved out of the way to let me inside, and I made sure to slide in as close to the wall as possible, so I wouldn't run into his perfect body. I don't think I had ever seen a six-pack of abs before. I wasn't sure if I should cover my eyes or leave the room or what.

After healing that man in the restaurant and seeing everyone filled with such joy and how it empowered me, I figured out something valuable that I needed to tell Adam. So what if Lyla could bring out the worst in people? I could make them happy. Wherever she spread her poison, I could fight back. It wasn't a war we would lose. As long as the sun would rise, I would fight.

"I didn't mean to run off," I said. "I was just scared and—"

"Angry?"

I wasn't terribly angry anymore, but the reminder of it started to kill the immensity of my positivity. I didn't want to seem like a monster and tell him that I was over my father's death. That just wouldn't be true anyway. It was only buried in a shallow grave.

"I know you don't wanna hear this, but I figure I should explain."

I honestly didn't want to hear it. I didn't him need to. "Please don't—"

"I found you chained up in the basement, and you were so scared. I believed your dad was hurting you, and Lyla created a story about him being obsessed, and it made sense why you couldn't go to the prom or why he wanted you to break up with me. When he showed up, I thought he was gonna fight me to keep you. I thought I was protecting you."

Adam's eyes were welling up with tears, and my pain was resurrected. I couldn't hold my tears in and they fell from my eyes. I tried to be stubborn and fight them off like he always did. I didn't wail or whine, but tears were still shed nonetheless.

Then he said something that I couldn't understand. "I'm sorry that I was wrong, but I can't apologize for trying to save you." I could never understand taking another human being's life, even if it was for me, yet he spoke with such passion and with such conviction. "I'd kill any man to save your life, and if I failed you, I'd fight through the depths of hell until you were in my arms again."

I guess I should have thought he was romantic. It was. His dedication toward me left me breathless, but I was scared. Lyla heard every word he said to me, and she'd use his love for me to her advantage, the same way she tricked him to kill my father.

"Maybe you don't understand, and I know you can never forgive me—"

"I forgive you." I had to say it quickly. I wouldn't dare take it back after giving it to him.

"You do?" His eyes lit up, and he began to smile. The way he looked at me…The way he needed me to take him back or his life would be rendered meaningless…What woman wouldn't want a man like that— whether he was flawed or the truest perfection?

It reminded me how much I wanted him. "How could I not?" Adam could barely look me in the eye, but I held his face and made him look into my eyes steadily. "I won't pretend like this isn't the most painful thing that's ever happened to me, but I do know that you're a good person, and you acted on your best judgment at the moment."

I smiled. "But for an even easier explanation, I'm not ready to lose you." I didn't wait for him to analyze what I had said or for my brain to stop me from giving us what we both needed. I leaned into him and kissed the man that I loved. I promised myself that no matter what happened, I would love him fearlessly and unwavering. If I had no loyalty in love, then there was no truth in my life and no reason for my breath. Because I truly had someone who desired nothing but my perfect happiness, I could be brave enough to storm the gates of any hell in his heart to save him from himself.

We held each other, and my head rested upon his chest. I listened to his heartbeat and felt his emotions. I had pleased him, but there was a piece of grief that he was holding onto. I wondered if I should take it from him. Perhaps I didn't have the right to take it. Perhaps our suffering is part of our humanity. It was sad to think about, but if we completely let go of every consequence that ever made us care, we'd be exactly who Lyla wanted us to be.

"There's more to tell you—"

I placed my finger on his lips before he would speak another word. "And I believe that I'm strong enough to handle it, but not today."

Adam looked relieved. "Okay."

"And no more kissing with your shirt off. I have to be chaste and innocent to complete the ritual. I do know that much."

He sighed and started to laugh. "Of course," he said sarcastically. "What exactly is this ritual?"

"I don't know, but it's whatever I have to do in order to save the world. Oh, and I have to be eighteen to do it."

"That's uncomfortably soon."

As he turned around to walk to his bed to pick up his shirt, I noticed something I had never seen before. On his back, he had a scar about eight inches away from the bottom of his neck. It was a circle with an odd circular shape inside. It was meant to be a specific design, but nothing I could recognize. From how it healed, I could tell that it had happened years ago. The scar was lighter than the rest of his body, but the edges were brown, and the texture was different too. "How did you get that nasty scar?"

Adam grabbed his shirt and quickly put it on. I could sense a great deal of shame suddenly. "My stepfather decided to be creative with one of my punishments."

It was way beyond my comprehension! "What did you do to deserve this?"

"I learned that cigarettes were bad for you and I tried to save him by tossing his out in the garbage." He chuckled, but it was bitter. "I guess he still had one on him."

"I didn't know that you ever had a stepfather." I was afraid to ask any more questions about it. I did tell him that I wanted to wait to talk about anything heavy, but I didn't want him to think I didn't care.

147

"Well, he and my mom died on my twelfth birthday, so it's kind of hard to talk about it."

It sounded like quite the terrible coincidence. "We should talk about it, but—"

"You should freshen up and rest and I should take a nap myself." Adam crossed his arms. He wasn't ready for that part of the story. I couldn't blame him, and I felt a little fortunate. I was such a chicken.

"Okay." I gathered some clothes out of my duffle bag and got into the shower. It was a little gross and yellow where it probably should have been white. I guess it was silly of me to be so scared of germs and bacteria when it could never affect me, but it still didn't stop me from being grossed out. Oh well. The jets were pretty powerful, and after the water began massaging my shoulders and neck, I got over it.

I felt like I was failing with my conclusion. I had decided that no matter what, I could fight off negativity. I had made up with Adam, but I was still afraid to confront certain issues. No matter how amazing I felt doing good for Frank, it all could come crashing back down if I let it. I couldn't wipe out Lyla in one swift blow. I'd have to keep fighting. I wasn't going to give up, but it would be quite the battle.

She must have known that though. Lyla must have been planning something big if she thought she could destroy the world or something like it. It couldn't just happen. She would need time unless she found a way to maximize her abilities and spread. If that was true, then I had a real serious problem…Unless I could do it first!

But that was a whole lot of speculation. However, it seemed like the only plausible option. If she couldn't do it in one swoop, the government would send the military and a bunch of different tanks and missiles after her. She was powerful, but she couldn't fight off an entire army, and if she could, surely she couldn't take the second wave. The only way the world could accept her was if they didn't know she existed.

I closed my eyes and relaxed. I sort of wished I could somehow peek into Lyla's mind. It was probably a less pleasant version of hell, but at least I would have figured out some information. She must have known something important. Something monumental was surely about to happen, and she must have known more about the ritual than I did.

"Roxy!" Adam started yelling and banging on the door.

"What?" I instinctively covered my breasts and my...Women's area. Even though he wasn't literary breaking the door down or trying to, I was already blushing.

"Get out here, now!" There was something definitely going on that made him very worried.

"What?" I still couldn't come out of the bathroom naked. No way!

"Now!"

I jumped out of the shower as fast as I could. I didn't even turn off the water, but I couldn't leave the room without some clothes. I at least put on my bra and panties. I was not running out totally naked!

"Roxy!"

"Hold on!" It was hard to get my clothes on when I was completely wet, but I didn't bother unlocking the door until I had my underwear on. I grabbed my shirt next, but the door flung open just as it was going over my head. "Adam!"

"Come on!" He grabbed my arm and started pulling on me. "We have to leave!"

I looked at my pants that I had accidently knocked on the tiled floor during my panic. I reached out for them, but I couldn't reach and he wouldn't let me. He wouldn't even stop for my duffle bag with all of our things inside. He wanted me to march outside with no pants. "What's going on?"

"Something is here!" He wouldn't stop running for the car, and he started trying to get the door open, patting down his pockets for the keys.

I looked around, but I didn't see anyone. The only thing suspicious I could see was a bread truck in the parking lot. No one else was outside. If I was in danger, I would have been able to sense some kind of emotions surrounding me. "We're safe, Adam."

"Get in the car, now!" He opened his door and unlocked my own. I knew there was no arguing with him, but I at least wished he would have let me put on a pair of shoes.

"Who do you think is here?"

"Don't patronize me, Roxy! I heard them."

"Heard who?"

Adam wouldn't stop. He pulled out of our parking space so fast, I gasped when I thought he was going to hit the car behind us. Luckily he didn't, but I knew to put on my seat belt as soon as he switched gears into drive. "I don't know. They just said they're coming for you."

"Who?"

The car shook, and the hood of the car was shoved down violently as something crashed into it and I screamed. It was a normal looking man dressed in khaki pants and a red buttoned-down shirt. When he smiled viciously at me, he didn't have fangs like a monster. He was even quite handsome, looking to be somewhere in his mid-twenties. His only abnormal feature was his silver eyes.

"Drive!"

Adam stepped on the gas pedal even harder, but the man did not budge or flinch. He smirked and sent a chilling all throughout my body before punching the windshield and forcing his hand right through the glass. The windshield was still intact, but his hand had clasped Adam's neck, and I was too stunned to react. Adam began hitting and pulling on the man's arm, but Adam couldn't do much while trying to navigate through a narrow parking lot.

The struggle only lasted a few seconds. Adam lost control and hit the grass and started heading for the road. Adam's face was beginning to turn red, and he was grunting from trying to breathe. The man's hand was so tense and firm; I knew his strength was more than Adam could ever hope to fight off.

Then, the car suddenly jerked from Adam pressing against the break as hard as he could. We skidded forward, and my seatbelt had to catch me, but the man had dug his feet into the hood of the car so much that he didn't budge. I gripped onto my seat and my handle as tight as I could on instinct from my fear. This man was invincible, and we were stopped in the wrong lane with a minivan fast approaching us.

The minivan blew their horn and the man looked behind him quickly and turned around with another evil smile. Then within a blink of my eye, Adam was pulled from his seat right through the glass. "Adam!"

I was frozen again in that moment with my heart beating so loudly that it was the only thing I could hear apart from Adam's screams like a muffled sound in the distance, as well as the honking horn of the van and it's screeching tires. If I was Lyla, I could have stopped him in midair while he was flipped upside down and frightened. Instead, I was glued to my seat and did nothing while his back made a collision with the van's windshield until he bounced right off and into the street.

"Adam!" I snapped back to reality and tried to leave the car before I had even unbuckled my seatbelt. I was so frazzled that I just couldn't concentrate. I had to focus and heal Adam before it was too late. As soon as the belt unfastened, the man grabbed my arm and pulled me up through the missing windshield. I screamed and tried to kick and pull myself free, but I couldn't stop him from pulling me against the shattered glass and cutting my bare legs. It hurt and I bled, but I healed instantly as soon as the man held me in his arms. Adam didn't have that luxury. "Let me go!"

"Roxanne Harris!" He said in my ear. His voice was too kind to be that cunning and cruel. Even the scent of him was pleasant, like the wind on a warm summer's day. "It's been a long time."

I fought harder. I couldn't let him take me back to that horrible place with all of Lyla's followers. They treated her like a princess, and I was the freak. I couldn't imagine what they would do to me now that they thought she was a god. "Let me go!"

He squeezed a little tighter and it became harder to breathe. "My father says it's okay to hurt you, Roxanne. No matter what I do to you, you'll always heal."

I didn't want to be tortured, but I would do anything just to save Adam's life. "Please let me heal him!"

Adam had lost consciousness. If he were still alive, he must have had a concussion. I wasn't sure. I had trouble sensing anything from him after he crashed into the van and sent the van crashing into a ditch off the road. There was a large gash on the side of Adam's head where he had hit the road, and his back must have been broken from how he had hit the frame of the car. From where I was, his left arm appeared to be broken too.

"The boy is of no concern."

I was being pulled away from Adam back toward the bread truck, and I wasn't strong enough to fight against my captor. I couldn't even sense a speck of goodness in his heart to convince him to let me go. There was nothing I could feel. Nothing!

I had to think of something in order to save Adam. I couldn't leave him in the street to die. "Lyla would want him alive!"

He stopped instantly. "And how would you know what Lyla would want?" He was insulted for her.

"Because she wants to turn him against me!"

That wasn't enough and he began walking again. I kept looking at Adam. It wasn't a busy road, but it wouldn't be long before someone might have run over him. Even if the person in the minivan was conscious and called a hospital, the police would take him in as soon as they discovered his identity. I couldn't abandon him!

"She'll kill you if you let him die!"

He stopped again. It was so nerve-wracking not being able to feel any emotion from him. I had never met another human being that I couldn't read, besides when I was a child and wasn't as powerful. He was something different entirely. "How did you know I was coming?"

"Adam knew."

"How?" He asked surprised, if not a little angry too.

"He said he heard you."

He let me go, but just as I began to run for Adam, he grabbed my wrist. "You don't get to heal him yet." He squeezed my hand once more to teach me a lesson until I hissed. When he released me, I saw his red and blue hand impression deep into my skin, but it faded away quickly like a breath on a glass.

He started walking toward Adam. I kept wondering if I should make a run for it and try to heal him as quickly as possible. The man was too fast, but I didn't know if I could afford to let Adam wait any longer or if he planned to let me heal him at all. I should have tried, but it just wasn't possible to do it before he stopped me.

He grabbed Adam and slung him over his shoulders like he was nothing. Adam was probably incredibly injured by that lack of compassion alone. I did finally noticed that he was breathing, and that gave me some small bit of gratitude.

I began reaching out for him the closer the man got, but he pushed my arms away as soon as I was close enough to touch Adam. "No." He continued walking past me, expecting me to follow.

I could see Adam's face. His whole entire right side was covered in blood from a gash. I couldn't bear to see him in such pain. "Please let me heal him!" I reached out to touch Adam's face, but the man turned around quickly and struck me until I had fallen off of my feet. My face was hot and stinging, and my mouth was filling with blood.

"You don't get to fix him until I say so." The man wouldn't look at me and wouldn't help me up. He continued heading for the truck, knowing that I would follow as long as Adam was in his custody.

I spat up the blood in my mouth onto the road. I had never been hit like that before. My jaw began to feel odd, and I swirled my tongue inside my mouth until I found a loose tooth. I spat that up as well and felt the pain in my gums as a new one instantly sprung up from nothing. It was extremely uncomfortable!

I looked back at the minivan still in the ditch. The driver must have been out cold. If I couldn't help Adam, I should have at least helped her. I got up and nearly lost my balance and fell down on the ground. I didn't know that I had sprained my ankle during my fall. I continued limping, ignoring the pain the best that I could until it faded into absolutely nothing.

"Get back here," he warned.

"I have to help her!"

I stopped in my tracks after a loud boom cracked my ears and echoed all around me. I was too frightened to turn around and see if he had shot Adam because of my disobedience. I turned around slowly. His gun was pointed up into the air and the nozzle was still smoking. Adam was no more harmed than before, but I could not take any more chances. "Move."

154

I took a deep breath and continued walking forward, trembling with each step. He turned around and motioned for me to hurry. I started running and got out of the road. I saw a car coming from far off, and our car was still in the middle of the road. They might have stopped once they saw the accident, and I couldn't afford to drag anymore people in my abduction. "Let's get this over with!"

We both started running for the truck in the parking lot of the motel. I didn't know what was inside, but I was shaking from the anticipation. When he unhooked the hinges and lifted up the door, it was something I had feared. There was nothing inside except for a pair of chains on the back wall.

"Where are we going?" I asked him.

"To my home," he smiled. "You don't remember?"

I gulped a little bit. I remembered The Master of the House, but I didn't remember his children having the same eyes. Then again, I wasn't allowed to play with them. "What do you want with me?"

"Absolutely nothing." He mercilessly threw Adam inside the foot of the truck. "It's Lyla we want."

I clenched my fists. If he thought he was going to get away with treating Adam like that, he had another thing coming. "For what?"

He smirked. "To set the world free." I did remember a young boy with black hair playing in the backyard. He would have been about the right age. He must have been The Master's son.

"Our powers don't even work on whatever you are." I wanted to find a compassionate piece of him to make him let me go or even touch Adam, but I still couldn't find anything inside of him. I couldn't feel any emotions. I could only guess from his facial expressions. "We can't do anything for you, so what's the point?"

He smiled harder. "Get in the truck."

I looked at Adam as I climbed inside. He wasn't going to wake up anytime soon. There was a chance that he wouldn't wake up at all. I still couldn't feel anything from him either.

"Not yet." The man got inside and started nudging me toward the back. "The chains are for you, Roxanne."

I couldn't stand there and let Adam die. Something in me snapped, and I screamed and charged at him as fast and as hard as I could. I was determined to knock him on the ground, make him hit his head, and injure him long enough to heal Adam. I put all of my energy in my shoulder and meant to tackle him, but he was a brick wall. He grabbed me and carried me to the back. I couldn't kick or hit myself free while my eyes stayed on Adam, who was dwindling away. He slammed me against the wall. I couldn't even fight him off when he started putting me in those chains. After the shackle clasped around my right wrist, I went crazy. I started tugging on my chains, but he shackled my other hand effortlessly. He couldn't have possibly been human to be that strong and cruel!

When I was strapped in secure, he smiled and lightly slapped me in my face. I tried to rip the chains off so I could give him a piece of my mind, but that only made him laugh sinisterly. "You should try to enjoy your life. You don't have much of it left."

I stopped. I didn't know what he meant, but it scared me. There was no way that could have been true. I could always heal if I got hurt. I couldn't die, and even if I could, that would mean the death of Lyla. They wouldn't want that.

He must have been trying to trick me. It was the only explanation. He was nothing but a liar! "You told me that I could heal Adam."

"And you can…Right before sunset."

"He might not last that long!"

"If he's meant to live, he will live." He smiled and walked out of the truck laughing malevolently. It wasn't only because he was evil and enjoyed his cruelty. He enjoyed destroying me.

I looked at Adam. His chest was still rising up and down, but barely. He wasn't breathing deeply as he should have been if he were in a peaceful sleep. I honestly didn't know if he could hold on until sunset. "You have to hold on, Adam!"

My captor grabbed the top of the door and begun to slide it down, shutting off every bit of light until I was engulfed in darkness. How could I wake up with such hope of freedom, lose and regain my hope of love, and at the end be placed on the edge of insanity? Sunset was hours away, and if he waited too long, Lyla wouldn't be able to heal him. I didn't know if she'd want to even if she could.

I wondered what Lyla was thinking, watching me chained up in the dark as she had been so many times before. Did she think that I was getting what I deserved, or was there a part of her that wanted me unchained so I could heal Adam? I assumed it had to be the former. She could never have compassion, especially not when it would mean my happiness. Besides, how could a ruler not be such an example for her evil followers?

"Hold on, Adam." Once again, I had nothing left to do but cry for hours while I was driven down to my own personal hell. I had been humiliated, abused, and I had to face all of that while being indecent. I would not accept Adam's death on top of all that. Somehow, someway, he was going to make it and I would make us free again. "Hold on."

It was the first time in my life that I ever anticipated a sunset.

Chapter Eight

My eyes were beyond the point of tears. I wasn't sure if Adam was alive or dead. I couldn't see anything, and I didn't know what time it was. Every minute I wished for sunset, yet only a minute had passed and my goal was hours away. My mind was usually a shelter, but it was maddened with the thought of losing Adam. I didn't know how I could go on without him, but I knew that I would need to. I wouldn't have anything else to live for besides stopping Lyla and revenge didn't fuel me. Being stuck in an endless battle with her was rather depressing.

Then after I had nearly lost my mind, the truck began to slow down until it had stopped. I felt myself begin to slip. Sunset wasn't far away, and it was becoming harder to think. I fell into nothing when Lyla awakened, but I couldn't let her take me just yet. "Hurry!"

My eyes were fluttering and the light in the world started flickering—shifting from day to darkness. I couldn't feel anything. There was nothing to hold onto, so I was floating away...

No! There was something grounding me. I had to save Adam. I had to! My hands fell onto the ground from my hands finally being free, and I remembered how Adam needed me to save his life.

I didn't have time to fight my legs and make them work. I had to climb on my hands and knees until I felt his bloodied and mangled mess. "Adam!"

It was hard to search for that light inside of Adam. I knew it was there, but I wasn't enough of myself to find it. It was too hard!

But I knew there was a light inside of me. I had my love in my heart burning so brightly for him that I knew it had to work. I pushed it out as much as I could think to do. I watched his face. It was still expressionless for so long. I pushed harder until I began to feel cold and weak and then he began to move ever so slightly until his eyes opened and he sprung up, knocking me flat on my face.

"Roxy?" He held me in his arms, but I couldn't see him. I could barely feel him. His voice was more like the thought in the back of my head. "Don't let Lyla come back. Fight her!"

But there was no way to fight her. My body didn't have the will to do so. "Adam…"

I smiled. It wasn't often that I was held in the arms of a big, strong man. "Adam!" I hugged him back and pressed myself into him.

"Lyla…" He let me go and actually let me fall. What a perfect gentleman!

"I'll help you!" Alvin was such a polite boy. He rushed to my side and helped me on my feet at once.

"Thank you." As soon as he let go of me, I stumbled into his arms. Roxy didn't mean to, but she had seriously hindered us both. She had never healed anyone by releasing the energy from her own body. She usually unlocked the human's own potential. I felt like I needed a nap.

"Having trouble, Lyla?" Adam was as fit as a fiddle and got up with no problem. I suspected he was more than healed. He must have felt spectacular with Roxy's own energy released in his body.

"I'm fine." If Roxy had a little bit more time, I'm certain she would have healed herself of the fatigue, but it happened too close during the transition.

Adam was enjoying me in a weak state a little too much, especially with all the smiling. "You don't look too good."

"Would you like me to kill him?" Alvin asked.

"No. I've got grand plans for him." It was lovely that Alvin tortured Adam so, but I would have been very crossed if Adam would have ended up dead. "No one is to harm him except to protect me," I smirked wickedly, "or unless I get bored."

"Would you like us to continue our trip?" Alvin asked.

I observed my dear Adam. He couldn't exactly run away, and he wouldn't leave Roxy defenseless anyway. Besides, he already gave himself over to me willingly. That was truly the first step to making him mine. "We need a bathroom break and probably something to eat. You can go ahead and bring me a pair of pants. I assumed you grabbed our belongings."

"Yes, Ma'am." Alvin ran off to fetch the duffle bag and came back quickly with it. "Here you are, Lyla."

"Thank you, Alvin." I didn't care so much about having bare legs, but there was no point in causing a public scene. Alvin also brought me moist wipes and rags to wipe the blood stains from my body.

He bowed before me. "You're quite welcome, my goddess." I could get use to that.

Adam could have stood to be a bit more respectful. He was rolling his eyes like a fool. "She can barely stand up, and you think she's a god?"

Alvin moved fast and was about to strike him hard in the face, but I stopped him when he was just a few inches away from blowing Adam's eyeballs through the back of his skull. "There's no need to hurt him,

Alvin. Just because he can't see the web, doesn't mean he isn't entangled. He's very much mine. It is our destiny."

Alvin couldn't help but be upset. I assumed he was quite jealous of Adam. He was particularly fond of me when I was a child. He must have been crushed when Mommy and Daddy rescued me. It was quite amusing watching someone love me…If love were even possible.

"Stand down," I told him.

It was especially hard for him with Adam looking so lackadaisical. Adam didn't care about Alvin, regardless of the fact that he had nearly killed him. He was raging. It was clear by his shaking. If I were capable of letting down his barriers, he would have beaten Adam until his brain was mush on the floor. But he still had his obligations to fulfill my every desire. "Alright."

"Leave us," I told him.

Alvin left quickly, but with a hesitant heart. Adam wasn't in the best of moods, but I trusted that I knew him well enough to know that I was safe. "Did you miss me?"

"You know I didn't." He tried to be stoic, but I could read him like a book (not that I would need to). He told Roxy exactly how he felt about me.

"You said some particularly intriguing things to Roxy. Some were very sweet." I smiled, almost intoxicated from the memory of it. "Some were deliciously cruel. I'm proud of you."

"You're proud of me?" He was angry, confused, and frightened. I loved it.

"Yes." I placed my hand on his chest that I knew to be perfect when bare. He was indeed my favorite plaything. "You admitted to murdering Daddy. You also admitted that it was part of your nature."

He spoke up quickly and indigent. "You tricked me—"

161

"You told her that you would be willing to kill anyone to save her." I had silenced him. Sure, it was a noble and romantic sentiment. It was a manly thing to say. Roxy knew she would always be protected, but she didn't like the suggestion of death from his hands. I, on the other hand, was quite enticed by his offer. "Who else would you kill in the name of love?"

"You," he seethed.

I laughed. "No, I don't think you have spine for that."

He took a threatening step closer toward me. "I guess now is as good a time as any to prove it."

I acted quickly and forced him against the wall. I was not too weak to use my powers, and with some rest, I would be fine. "You think you can kill me because I'm a little fatigued?" It was insulting!

I unzipped the duffle bag with my thoughts and raised my knife out of it and brought it to my hands. It was such a simple and lovely blade, and it still reeked of death. I had such a fond memory of it. "This was the knife I slit my mommy's throat with. It's thirsty for more blood." Then I held the blade against his throat. "Shall it be yours?"

Adam was afraid, but not of the prospect of dying. He wasn't even intimidated by the knife. If I couldn't sense his fear, I wouldn't have seen it at all—not even in his eyes. "I'm not afraid of you."

"No." I smirked. "You're afraid of yourself."

"I'm afraid of what you can make me do."

"No. You're afraid of what I'll *let* you do. There's a difference." I took a step back and let him fall on his feet. There was no point in kidding with him. I had no intention of killing Adam or letting him die. "You're not too different than me. You have an entire different person hiding inside you. When will he come out and play with me?" I felt like a child waiting for a friend to come from across the street and knock on my door. There was no point in hiding his existence from me. The difference was night and day, just as Roxy and I were different.

"Never." Oh, Adam! He was so determined to keep his doppelganger at bay. He didn't realize that the more he tried to resist me, the more the rabid beast chewed at his chains from anticipation of being free.

"You're more valuable to me than you know and whether or not I uncage the monster inside of you doesn't matter. You'll be an enormous help to me regardless."

"And what do you mean by that?"

"That's a mystery I'll leave be for the time being." I could feel my words scratching at the tip of his mind. It made me happy. "Now, why don't we go get something to eat and freshen up?"

Adam always had to pretend like he wasn't pleased with me, no matter what I said. "Fine."

I washed the blood off of my skin and put on a pair of jeans. I wouldn't have minded being scandalous, but I wanted to hurry and get back on the road without any sort of hiccups. We were taken to a fast food place to get something to eat and to use the bathroom. Adam had to be watched by Alvin while he used the men's room. He was in there for a while, but he needed time to gather himself. I could feel him through the wall while I was inside the woman's bathroom. I leaned my body against the wall and indulged myself in all of his hopelessness. He knew there was nothing he could do, so he needed to talk himself up so he could endure the night. My poor sweetheart had no idea what was in store for him.

I came out of the bathroom first and reached out my hand so it would be right there when he came out. He glared at me threateningly and walked away from me toward the front counter. I wasn't offended. I laughed to myself, but Alvin was fuming. "You should let me kill him," he said.

I cut my eyes at him. "Don't you dare give me orders!"

Alvin could snap me in two, but he was terrified of me and he was right to be. "I apologize." He was such a strong man, yet he was shaking just a little bit. "I just don't see the reason why you keep him around. Is he your pet?"

I didn't need to explain myself to him, but I decided to be kind and not rip out his tongue with my mind. "I enjoy hurting Roxy, and this is the best way that I can."

"Wouldn't his death be more satisfying?" Regardless of the fact that I was unable to sense emotions from Alvin, I could obviously tell that he was extremely jealous of Adam. It was utterly ridiculous.

"No. The death of a man's decency is much more crushing than the loss of breath. Besides, I have other uses for him that will be revealed soon enough." I had to point my finger at him to stop him from speaking. He took his thoughts, sucked them right back up, and waited for me to finish. "You are not to question me. Ever. Is that understood?"

It was hardly noticeable, but he gulped. "Of course."

We ordered a couple of cheeseburgers, fries, and the largest drinks they had. Roxy hadn't properly been feeding us, so once again I had to pick up the slack. We took our meal back to the truck, and Adam didn't even make a fuss about having to get in the back of the truck. I did him a favor and turned the light on for him, since his hands were full.

"Should I chain him up?" Alvin asked, but he was wishing for an agreement and not an opinion.

"That won't be necessary." I smiled. "I'll be safe in the back with him."

Alvin was struggling while he tried not to explode all over the place. I wondered if he thought I'd be doing something wicked with Adam or if he was just genuinely disappointed that he couldn't sit next to me

164

while he drove to his home. "Can I do anything to make the trip more comfortable for you?"

"I'll live like a queen when I get to your home, but I'll be fine for now." I didn't care much for Alvin's disappointment. I found it much more delicious how frustrated and annoyed Adam was. "I'll see you in a few hours, Alvin."

Alvin's nostrils were flaring, and his mouth was twitching. "As you wish." Alvin reluctantly pulled down the door and left me alone with my dear Adam.

I sat my food down next to him and swung my body from side to side in a cutesy way that should have made him think of Roxy. I could be sweet if I wanted, but it was such a waste since he didn't bother to look at me! I cleared my throat, but he started paying more attention to his burger than me. I certainly wasn't going to let that slide! I plopped down next to him and started eating with him. A few seconds later, he started scooting away. I wasn't going to bother playing cat and mouse with him. That was stupid! I slid him next to me and he grumbled, but he knew better than to do it again. "I obviously want to spend time with you."

He laughed shortly and hysterical. "Why?"

"You know Roxy. I think you should get to know me too." I knew how to be Roxy. I knew about the way she would smile and giggle when he looked at her with his gorgeous blue eyes. I knew the way she swayed her hair to the side when she started feeling those butterflies and her head tilted a little bit. I even raised the pitch of my voice a little bit higher as she would.

"What else is there to know other than the fact that you're psychotic?"

I pouted. "Don't treat me so cruelly." I leaned my head against him. "Every minute I decide not to kill you is a minute your life is saved. You owe me everything."

165

"No, you owe me everything and yet there's nothing you could ever give me back." My poor baby was so angry! "I despise you. Don't expect me to ever worship you like that moron."

"I don't need you to worship me." Honestly, I kind of liked it. I would never admit that to Adam, but my struggle for his adoration kept life from being boring. "I just want us to be friends right now, and if that's out of the question, we can at least be friendly."

He rolled his eyes and began eating to ignore me. I followed his example and started eating myself. I got a couple of cheeseburgers. It always pissed me off that Roxy ate all of Mommy's crap. I ripped right through two and started on a third, even though I was stuffed. I didn't want Adam to accuse me of pecking again and then I noticed Adam staring at me.

"What?" I wiped my face, but I didn't have any condiments dripping from my mouth. "Why are you staring at me?"

I couldn't tell if Adam was shocked or appalled. "Roxy doesn't really eat a lot of meat."

"Yeah, and I hate her for it every day." I loved the gooey cheese, the grease soaked into the toasted bread, the texture of the meat tearing against my teeth, and the sweetness of the ketchup. It was probably the best thing I could remember tasting. "Eating is an experience, and I usually haven't gotten much experience—at least, not for a couple of years."

Roxy thought she had it so hard because she got strapped up for a few minutes and woke up with a full bladder and occasionally bloodied wrists. She got off easy. "You don't know how difficult it is watching the world trapped behind a glass wall without any power to do anything."

Adam glared at me, but he was amused. "Am I supposed to feel sorry for you?"

"You're supposed to understand me." I didn't need his pity, nor did I desire it. "You think Roxy is so perfect, and I'm somehow worse than the devil." I only wanted Adam to understand the truth about the righteous people who he admired. "Do you think I was born this way? Do you think children just become monsters?"

"You're going to blame your psychotic nature on your mom and dad?"

"Well, they did put me in a pair of chains every night. That doesn't exactly make a child feel loved."

"You can't blame your actions on two people that you've already killed."

I smiled. "I only killed one of them, remember?"

"Why do you want to be back here with me? I know you're weaker. What makes you think I won't take the opportunity to kill you?"

I don't know why, but I found his threats to be incredibly sexy. He mostly despised me, then he was scared, but under those complex feelings of wanting to get away from me, he genuinely wanted to screw me. "Let's not kid ourselves. We are both safe from one another." No, I didn't have any plans to rip Adam into little pieces. His fear of me would subside once he realized that I didn't plan on hurting or manipulating him. His hatred would dissipate once he learned who the true villains of the story were. Then after all that was gone, he'd happily let me seduce him.

Of course, he'd never willingly come to me while he was still emotionally attached to Roxy, but it wouldn't take much effort to convince him that was a fool's errand. "Why don't you tell me the secrets you've been keeping from Roxy? She's not listening." I leaned in closer to him and whispered. "It'll be our little secret."

"It's none of your business."

"But it is." I thought of the image of him with his shirt off and his glistening pectorals and my happy hand had a mind of its own and begun feeling on his chest. "I could help you in ways you can't even imagine."

Adam might have hated me, but he was still a man. I was making him feel uncomfortable, but it was more than being awkward. Of course he was afraid to reject me. He probably thought I would rip out his lungs if he moved away from me. I could feel his heart pounding through his shirt...As well as his beautifully pronounced man chest. But besides all that, there was a part of him wondering what life would be like if he just released all of his frustrations by indulging himself in me.

"I bet it has something to do with your twelfth birthday and how your mommy and step-daddy died." My hand was becoming naughtier and began trailing down his chest and abs to the bottom of his shirt. I then proceeded to lift it up slowly. "Am I right?"

Adam grabbed my hand so fast; he could have snapped my wrist without me being able to stop him—if he wanted to. "Just shut up." I loved when he stared at me with those burning, hateful eyes. They were so gorgeous and filled with such passion. Love could never produce such a thing. Hate was the blazing beauty that consumed the world in its flames. Love could never consume anything but the heart of a fool.

"Alright." I smirked seductively; because I wanted to remind him how attracted he was to me. "We'll bond with our silence." I rested my head on his shoulder and he sighed heavily, but he didn't move away. He was majorly pissed about having to be right next to me, which made me smile. Perhaps I should have been more cautious, but I was tired from Roxy's little stunt and I had a full stomach weighing me down. Adam was so comfortable; it wasn't long until I fell asleep.

"Roxy?"

My ears tingled from Adam's warm breath falling against my skin. I stopped myself from physically reacting in order to play along with whatever he was doing. Besides, I was in an exceptionally comfortable position. He was holding me in his strong arms with my head pressed up against his chest. Even though he must have known that I was still in charge, he felt such a strong connection to Roxy that he couldn't help but hold me.

"I don't know if you can hear me, but I'm at a loss of what to do." I could feel so much pressure on him, as if a string were holding all of his troubles back from making him snap. "I don't know what's gonna happen next. I just wanna keep you safe, but I need to stop her from unleashing hell on earth."

As if someone so small could ever stop me! He was much too weak. One pull on his stitches and his heart would unravel. "Tell me what to do, Roxy."

I wanted to bust out in laughter or at least snicker, but I was a decent enough actress to hold myself in and pretend to still be sleeping while pretending to be Roxy, offering the only sane option left. "Kill me."

He gasped, and his fingers gripped on tighter to me. I could feel his heartbeat quickening and his breaths deepening. He knew it was the right option, but it felt like his insides were shaking. Nothing about that sensible solution was cohesive with his mind. "I can't…"

"But you have to." I smiled and rose up giggling. He looked so funny! He couldn't strangle me because he was too emotionally raped. "It's the only way to stop me."

I watched his eyes. It was almost like they changed colors, because they burned so intensely. It was funny watching his nose twitch a little bit. I was prepping myself for that moment when he lunged at me and tried to start squeezing my neck. I waited patiently, but his fingers never even got close to pressing on my delicate neck.

He narrowed his eyes in on me. "You really think it's that easy to break me?"

169

I laughed to myself. "You're already broken, Adam. I'm trying to fix you."

I noticed that the truck wasn't moving. No wonder why Adam was desperate enough for that lame attempt of trying to reach Roxy while I slept. It was already too late for him. "It'll be over soon."

I felt much better and got on my feet with ease just in time for the door to open. This time, Alvin wasn't alone. There were ten other men with him, all bowing down to me. I slightly turned my head casually to Adam. He had an adorable pout on his face. "No need in stalling. We don't have long until daylight, and there's something I would like everyone to see."

He rolled his eyes and lazily got up and began following me out of the truck. I had four pairs of hands ease me out onto the ground, but the eleven subjects of mine were jealous of Adam and crossed their arms and steadily glared at him as he came out.

"This is Adam," I said to them. "The only one allowed to be wicked to him is me."

I didn't quite recognize any of them, but I was only six years old the last time I was at Alvin's lovely home, yet one of them dared to question me. "He is your ally?"

I took a deep breath in order to hold my peace. "Of course he is."

"No!" Adam said like a stubborn child. "I'm Roxy's."

All of the surrounding men were ready to pounce like feral beasts. They might as well have started pissing all over the place. "How dare you!"

"Silence!" I stopped them from saying another pointless word. "He is my ally."

I looked at my dear Adam. He was eyeing me down like I was actually his enemy. I smiled at his lack of intelligence. I was the only one in the world who knew the truth about who he was. I reached with my mind for my duffle bag and slid it close to me. Adam wouldn't take his burning eyes off of me, and I enjoyed the heat. It only made taking the knife out the bag that much easier.

"I could kill him for you," Alvin said. "There's no point in getting your hands dirty."

"Quiet, Alvin." He was becoming annoying, but I wasn't crossed enough to kill. I was too engaged by my sexual chemistry with Adam to needlessly slaughter my worshipers. "I know what I'm doing."

Adam eyes bucked ever so slightly when the knife fell into my hands. I smirked and tugged on his shirt and slashed it straight down the middle. He was probably thinking something naughty. I knew I was! However, my fingers wove inside his newly made vest until I made my way up toward his shoulders and nudged his shirt right off until it slid onto the ground.

"Are you done?"

"No." I gently nudged his shoulder until he turned around, unleashing a giant gasp from those around us.

I watched Adam carefully. He rightfully was afraid, but trying not to show it. However, I could feel it so much that I could taste it like sweet nectar. "What's going on?"

Roxy didn't know it when she saw it, but I did. I saw that odd marking burned into his skin, and I wanted to bust out from behind my wall and take control of my body. I had to wait patiently, but it was well worth it. "He's my ally, my Chosen."

From then on, I started taking bets within my own mind. I was curious to see who would react first and who would have the best reaction. I was hoping it would be Adam, but he was stuck somewhere between pure confusion and the smart choice of thinking that I was making it all up to screw with him. Common sense told me that it was undoubtedly going to be the boys though. Their reaction was almost instantaneous.

"A human?"

"Him?"

"How is this possible?"

Yes, the boys were pissed that out of all off those among me, my chosen guardian was an ordinary human boy. It was surprising to me as well, but I liked the fact that destiny had intertwined us together in such a remarkable way. Even his sacred marking was a miracle, created by a brute. It was enthralling, to say the least.

"No more questions," I told them. "Take us inside."

The property was beautiful. It was about eight acres of land. When I was young, I wanted to ride The Master's ponies across the trail and dip into the pool when it got too hot, but it was always too dark outside to enjoy his lands as I wanted. Most of the children were preparing for bed by the time I came in control. I did spend most of my time exploring the house and playing with my many dolls. Perhaps once I finally rid myself of Roxy, I could finally enjoy the extravagancies of a proper childhood, like swinging back and forth with your hair hanging down and the sun kissing your face on a swing. I could see Roxy living those moments, but I could never properly feel them for myself. All in proper time though. I didn't plan on abandoning The Master's side again.

Adam was by my side as we approached the front door. His thoughts were rattling wildly along in his mind. He had a solid front, but he couldn't hide his fear from me. That burn mark on his back changed everything and he didn't even know why, but in the pit of his stomach, he knew that he had a deeper connection to me.

"Let me get the door for you," Alvin stepped in front of us and opened the door with a big grin aimed directly at me.

"Thank you, Alvin." I eased past all of the boys and stepped inside. It was more glorious than I remembered. The mansion was pure decadence from top to bottom, from the giant white columns to the golden chandeliers hanging from the ceilings. I remembered running up the winding staircase to my room before the dawn came. I sprained my knee once and got blood on the white carpet. The Master punished the maid that was closest to me, saying it was her fault. They escorted her screaming into the basement, and I never saw her again.

"Isn't this lovely?" I asked Adam as he came up behind me.

"It's a little too classy for your type."

"You shouldn't speak to Lyla that way." The Master of the house was waiting for us at the top step with a manila folder in his hands. He began coming down to greet us properly with an uncontrollable swagger and arrogant air to him. He looked a lot like Alvin, only aged a little bit more. He actually looked thirty—not fifty as he should have been. "She's going to set this world free."

I smiled from remembering one of the few people who were ever kind to me. "It's good to see you again, Rider."

"The honor is mine." He bowed before me. "Hopefully, you'll have a much longer stay with us this time."

"Well, don't worry about the recuse mission. My parents are dead, and Adam won't be any trouble to you."

"Think like that and you might end up dead," Adam spoke under his breath.

Rider only glared at Adam, but I knew people who died for less in his house. "Does he have a problem with clothes?"

"No," I smirked, "but I had a problem with him being clothed." I watched for Adam's reaction, but he only rolled his eyes. "Besides, I wanted to show all of your minions the marking on Adam's back."

Rider seemed to know what I meant before taking a step behind Adam to observe it for himself. Once he did, his eyes bucked and he gasped. "He's The Chosen!"

Rider was just like his son and his minions. He was astonished and supremely jealous of that curse mark burned into Adam's skin. "How does a human get such an honor?"

Adam's eyebrows raised just a hair, but I could feel his emotions bouncing all over the place. He was freaking out so much; it surprised me that he could remain calm. "You all speak like you're not human."

I responded to him simply. "We're not."

It felt like Adam's mind was expanding at an incredibly explosive rate. He was probably going through every memory in his mind, combing through every detail to find the oddness in us and related it to not being human. It made perfect sense, yet it somehow completely blew his mind.

"You've told him nothing?" Rider asked surprised.

"I only found out his true purpose today."

"Well, I think it's important to know that he hasn't been honest with you." He placed the folder he had been carrying in my hands. "His name isn't even Adam."

Then, I felt a giant *pop*! He was terrified that all his dirty secrets were in my hands. That only made me so much more interested!

Adam stepped closer toward me to peek inside his file, but I stepped away and blocked his vision of it with my body as much as possible while I browsed through a couple of papers and pictures. "Your name is Blake?" There were specs about his height, blood type, and the names of is biological parents. I flipped through one page and saw a police report and grisly crime scene photos of a woman and a man bloodied and laid out across a kitchen floor. "Your biological daddy killed your step-daddy after he killed your mommy? Wow!"

Poor Adam. He tried to look crossed with me, but I could feel he was highly shamed of the whole situation. If he weren't such a strong man, he probably would have burst into tears.

I continued flipping through the files. There was a little bit of history about his mommy's alcohol abuse, his step-daddy's shady connections, and his father's string of petty robberies. They just seemed like a bunch of losers that got involved in an out of hand situation. "I see nothing in these files to explain how his step-daddy knew the sacred marking of The Chosen."

That's what I really wanted to know. If his step-daddy had never been exposed to the sacred text of my people, there was no way he could have burned it into Adam's back so neatly with a cigarette butt.

"It must truly be fate," Rider said.

"Indeed..." It was hard to believe, but I also liked it. It was actually amazing. The love of Roxy's life was always destined to be mine. How could I not appreciate that?

Alvin couldn't take being ignored and approached the front of the classroom. "What do you wish to do now?" He was so eager to do anything for me—they all were—except for the one who mattered the most.

There was much I wanted to do, and much I wanted to say to Adam, but I simply didn't have the time. "Dawn is soon approaching. Adam will come up to my room with me, and I'll transform. Then I suspect that he'll be honest with Roxy and then I'll know the truth as well."

I smirked at my dear boy. He glared the tiniest amount, which was tolerable when everyone else in the room bowed down to me once more. Then, Adam began to follow me up the stairs and down the hall to my bedroom without any sort of fuss.

Oh, the room was just as I remembered! My beautiful dolls were sitting up on a high mantle as if they had never been touched at all. Of course, someone had been taking care of them. They were in perfect condition. I floated one of them with rosy cheeks into my arms and cuddled it like a mother would do to a child.

"You think you've won, don't you?" Adam looked so self-righteous! He was going to do his best to escape and save the world from itself. Such a silly child, he was.

I thought he deserved a depriving laugh while I floated my beloved doll back to the mantle. "Adam, Roxy is incapable of defeating me, and I just figured out that you've truly been my ally all along." He was actually no different from one of those dolls. He was nothing more than something for me to manipulate for my amusement.

Adam had been biting his tongue for long enough, yet I felt him constantly pulling on me like an old wife nagging at me constantly. Thank God he finally bothered to ask his question aloud. "What is this marking on my back supposed to mean? How do I know if it's not a coincidence from my lunatic stepdad?"

I smiled at my dear boy. He wanted so badly for there to be some kind of catch, but just as sure as I could feel his soft skin when I gently stroked his face with my finger, I felt an internal connection that couldn't be explained by normal human connections. "It's not a coincidence, Adam. You're my Chosen. You're going to free me."

"From?"

"The prophecy isn't specific, but the only logical guess is—"

"From Roxy?" He looked like a frightened, little lamb.

His fear was quite delicious. "Yes. That's my assumption." Most everything about Adam was delicious, and I had a few interesting theories on how I was to get rid of Roxy with his aide. "You're going to help me get rid or Roxy and free this world."

Then I got to see those beautiful, burning, hateful eyes as he stared into my own and warned me in a tone that screamed domestic abuse. "Never!"

176

Of course, I had nothing to fear. "You don't have a choice." He was supposed to protect me, guide me, and make me greater than I was before. It had been so long since I heard the prophecy that I couldn't remember everything to it, but I remembered the marking quite well.

"We'll escape." He was so desperately confident that it was cute. "Roxy did it before, we'll—"

"Roxy didn't escape. When my parents fought their way in with some allies, I decided to leave with them."

There was something so satisfying about bursting his metaphorical bubble. He was so sure he had figured out every little thing about me. Roxy was the good guy; I was the bad guy with a bunch of evil minions. I loved when I felt his mind shatter from each new revelation. "Why?"

"Because, she was my mommy, and he was my daddy." It made me sick thinking about it. I was being treated like a god when one day, mommy and daddy came in shooting guns and killing whoever they had to with their friends in order to get me back. Rider was away, and his sons were only boys. There wasn't much that could have been done against their arsenal. The only one who could have stopped them was me.

Everyone probably suspected that I would. Daddy had started treating me coldly. Mommy didn't want him to chain me up to a wall, but she sure didn't stop him. I made them promise me that they would treat me better. They told me that I could sleep in my own bed and that they would love me forever. "I didn't think they would chain me back up and leave me to rot!"

I should have never believed them, but I didn't want to believe that they weren't my parents. After Daddy had gone back on his promise, I accepted that they were the monsters.

Adam seemed exasperated. "What are you? Where are you from? Why are you even here?"

It was time to explain everything to him, but I could see the light beginning to pierce through the darkness outside of my window. "I'll explain everything when I reawaken. I'll give you the decency you won't give to Roxy."

"Lyla?" Alvin knocked on the door frame since the door was already open, but he was anxious and stepped inside before I invited him. If Alvin wasn't bringing me my duffle bag, I might have thrown his snooping butt straight through the window.

"Thank you for our things." I levitated the bag onto the bed and started searching for my parents wedding album. It was on the very bottom. I picked it up and held it to my chest as if it were one of my dolls. All I had left of my horrid past was in that book.

"Feeling sentimental?" Adam asked mockingly.

"No, not at all." I placed the book in Alvin's hands. "Find everyone in that book and kill every single one of them."

"No!" I had never heard Adam protest with such hatred and disgust. He was boiling angry. I thought it hardly merited that level of volume. "I understand revenge on your parents, but why kill innocent people?"

I looked at Adam shocked. I had an obligation! "I have to keep my promise to Mommy."

"Lyla, I'm begging you." Within his immense and innumerable hatred of me laid dormant a speck of hope. Deep down, Adam hoped that I was a little bit like Roxy and would take pity on my relatives, go back on my word, and spare their miserable and insignificant lives. He dared to have faith in my mercy as if I were his god. "Don't do this."

Too bad I wasn't feeling very magnanimous. "Make sure they know why they died," I told Alvin with a purposely cruel smile. "And if their children are present, kill them too!"

My body collapsed and my face stung for a moment and then there was a rush of pain as I noticed the blood pouring down my face and dripping onto my hands and on the carpet. I thought I hear a *crunch*, but I was just so shocked that I couldn't remember. My nose hurt, but the thought of so much blood over flooded my senses.

Alvin roared like an animal, and Adam was smacked hard enough to be sent flying into the wall and bounce off of it and onto the floor. I trusted that Alvin wouldn't let Adam get away with such a heinous crime. He stepped over me while I was still staring at my red hands, and he pulled Adam off the ground by his neck alone.

"Wait!" I raised my hands and separated the two of them right before Alvin's fist impacted and exploded Adam's skull into pieces. Perhaps I should have let Alvin exact his revenge, but I could not let Adam take the easy way out.

I slammed Adam back up against the wall and held him steady and set Alvin down right outside of my room. "Leave us."

"What?" Alvin howled.

"I said leave us!" I pushed him back and slammed the door shut. I did not need someone so weak to rescue me from the likes of a human!

"That wasn't a good idea!" Adam talked big, but he couldn't break free of my hold, no matter how much he struggled. I very well should have slit him from his toes to his eyelids and stabbed his heart after crunching his nose into bits for busting my own. That's what he deserved for acting so brave when I knew how truly terrified he was of me.

"You know what I can do."

"Yes."

"You know what I can make you do."

"Yes."

"And you fear me?"

"Yes."

He baffled me beyond reason. "Then why would you dare strike me?"

"Because I am not a coward!" Adam yelled to the top of his lungs if only to prove a point. The sound of his testimony echoed throughout the room and it rendered me incapable of speaking one word at all. "And I believe I'm a good man. I cannot let you get away with destroying the world or hurting Roxy any more than what you have."

Then he swore to me with a covenant made by fire and singed into my heart. "I would rather die than do nothing."

Was Roxy truly that special to him? How could she be? She was weak. She was a naive fool! She didn't even deserve her worthless life. She didn't even know how to treat a man that desired her so strongly—a man who she could easily reciprocate attraction toward. She didn't deserve his undying loyalty. She didn't deserve his love!

Adam was my Chosen. He was supposed to be dedicated to me. He was supposed to be mine!

I was so furious I didn't know what to say. Life would have been so much simpler if I ripped his head off, but I couldn't. The day was beginning to break through the window, and I could feel myself losing control of my already limited body.

I reached out to touch his beautiful face that was still so angry with me, but bewildered when my bloodied fingers met his skin. He was so infuriating, so…Inexplicable! There was something so…

I'm not sure. He was something special—entirely different than any other human I had ever known. For some reason, I was fond of him and his tenacity. I wanted to push the boundaries of his devotion for Roxy and see if his borders would extend the courtesy toward me.

But soon, I felt as if I were watching him from behind my glass. He fell onto his feet, and I dropped to my knees and watched myself cry and cover my broken nose instead of admiring his mysteries.

Chapter Nine

"My nose!" I couldn't think. It really hurt, and when it stopped hurting and clicked into place, there was still blood all over my face and hands. "You punched Lyla?"

Adam was on the ground and tried to help me, but he was so guilty that he didn't know how to help. "Sorry if I hurt you, but she really deserved it."

The pain was gone, but sometimes I could still remember it. It lingered like a bad taste in my mouth. I could handle it though. I honestly liked the fact that he decked Lyla in the face. "You got her good, huh?"

Adam looked at me surprised and then started laughing all the sudden. "Yeah, I did." I could tell that he was trying to cover up his feelings. He felt terrible, almost shaky when he usually felt solid like a rock. I think I started to steady him a little bit, but something was bothering him.

And then suddenly, it started bothering me. "Oh no..." I realized where I was. I looked up, and Lyla's soulless dolls were staring at me with their beady, little eyes. Not one of them had a smile. They all looked at me as if they knew they were hers and it bothered me. "Open the window for me, would you?"

"Sure." Adam didn't think it over. He went to the window and lifted it up while I stood up on my tippy toes to reach Lyla's dolls. I hoped she was sick to her stomach as she watched me dirty their dainty and beautiful dresses with the blood she forced Adam to draw.

I hoped she screamed on the inside of me on the next part particularly. "This is for my stuffed animals!" I started chucking every single one of her creepy dolls out of the window. It wasn't much in the great scheme of things and maybe it was really petty, but I wanted them gone.

"We have to find a way to get out of here, Roxy." I wished Adam would have appreciated my doll throwing frustrations a little bit more, but he had probably been through a lot of hardships.

That's what was so hard about being back there. All I wanted to do was leave. I would have loved to jump out the window, break my legs, heal my legs, and run away. Unfortunately, that was impossible. "I'm afraid I can't leave."

"Why?"

I sighed and decided just to show him. I headed straight for the door and opened it harmlessly enough, but I couldn't step through it. Every time I tried, there was an invisible wall constantly blocking me. I must have looked silly pressing my body against an invisible wall like a professional mime.

Adam didn't find it funny though. "So you're like a vampire and have to be invited out?"

"No. The only way for me to leave this room is for me to be Lyla."

"Grab my hand." He reached out his hand and tried to walk me through the door, but he couldn't leave out as long as he was attached to me. "Are you kidding me?" He was frustrated, and he kept trying to break through, but he hit the same wall I did and he eventually stopped trying.

"There were enchantments on Lyla's chains at my house to keep her powers at bay and conceal her energy. These people must know some similar tricks. I'm stuck."

"First things first—"

"Why don't you have a shirt on?" I freaked out about so many other things that I didn't have time to freak out about that one. I needed to figure out a way to escape and figure out where I was, and Adam's body was...Distracting. Adam looked at me like I was stupid and I felt even worse. "I know it's silly to be so prude right now, but I wanna know what she did to you."

He pouted and took a deep breath. I started thinking the worst, because he felt really stressed. "I wanna tell you everything, Roxy. I will, but let's just get cleaned up. Okay?"

I didn't know how to question him, so I nodded. It would be an odd thing to fight about anyway. I didn't want to be covered in my blood all day long, and Adam was still looking scrappy from nearly dying.

I smiled for the simple fact that he was still alive. Things were beyond bad and a little past impossible, but it didn't seem like the end of the world when I knew that I still had Adam loving me. "I'm glad I was able to save you."

He returned a small, grateful smile. "However you did it, it managed to injure Lyla. Maybe we can use that in the future."

I injured Lyla? I was actually able to hinder her? I stood somewhat of an actual fighting chance? "Sure!" I was a little concerned with the fact that I felt so tired during my transformation, but it was worth my life if I could somehow stop her from carrying out her insidious plan.

I decided to go in the shower first, and I took a little bit more time than what I should have, but I started thinking about my life and what my next step was. If Lyla was too weak, she wouldn't be able to continuously overpower Adam. She wasn't his only obstacle when it came to escaping, but she was undeniably the biggest. I knew he wouldn't want to leave me, but if Lyla wanted to corrupt Adam, then him escaping the mansion was my number one priority.

But it would be better if he could somehow mount an escape during the day. If I could be myself, I could heal him when he got hurt during the escape. I wasn't sure if he could make it out alive if he were alone. Alvin would certainly be there to try and stop him.

I had to think of a way to get Alvin and his family out of the picture. I didn't know a lot about them. They wouldn't speak to me, and I was bound to one room. The only time I remembered seeing them was when Alvin was outside playing. His father came outside every day with his sons, and I would see them blaze the trail with their horses. They would be gone for about thirty minutes and then return.

That was my only window of opportunity, if they even still did it. It wasn't much, but we had no choice but to take it. It would be sometime around noon. Adam would try to make an escape, and if I could figure out how to get past the enchantments, I would be right there with him.

When I got done with my shower, I remembered that I didn't bring any clean clothes with me into the bathroom. I had to get some out of the duffle bag, or I had to have Adam riffle through my bra and panties and bring them to me. Both of them seemed really inappropriate, and I didn't know what to do.

I wrapped myself up in a towel and knocked on the bathroom door. Adam replied back confused. "Come out...?"

I gulped. My whole face was probably red by the time I actually opened the door. After all we had been through; I just wasn't ready to face Adam so indecent. "Um..." I couldn't even look at him. "Could you please hand me the duffle bag?" I gripped onto the towel with one hand for dear life and used the other to reach out my hand without looking.

Instead of the duffle bag, I felt a pile of cloth. I was intrigued and mustered up enough courage to look at them and then Adam. "What are these?" It was obviously a neat pile of folded clothes, but they weren't mine.

"One of the maids brought me clothes. She said you had a fully stocked closet." Adam was trying not to laugh at me for being so shy.

"They really like Lyla here…" If there were any deeper shade of red that I could have gotten, I was it. I felt my head getting hotter and hotter.

Adam finally couldn't hold it in any longer and started cracking up. "Roxy, go put your clothes on."

I practically ran back inside the bathroom and started to change. The clothes weren't as bad as I thought they would be. I thought if Lyla had her choice of clothes, it would be thongs, leather, and whips. It was just a pair of skinny blue jeans and a V-neck shirt that was a little too low-cut for my taste. I think the jeans were expensive though. I usually didn't like anything too formfitting, but it was a nice fit.

Adam got into the shower next, and he didn't take nearly as long as I did. He was probably only in the shower for about five minutes and came out fully dressed with his teeth brushed and everything less than another five.

It wasn't nearly enough time for me to gather all my thoughts. I was trying to figure out how to get Adam out of the mansion safely, but I was still stumped on how I could get out of the room.

Adam picked up on my disposition seconds after leaving the bathroom. "What's the matter?"

I didn't want to burden him with how I felt. I should have been more grateful for the fact that we were both safe for the time being. "I'm really glad that you're alive. I didn't know if I could save you and I didn't know if her minions would keep you alive."

Adam wouldn't return the smile, and he joined me on the bed with a heavy heart and a furrowed brow. "Roxy, they're keeping me alive because they think I'm of use to them."

That certainly was foolish of them. Lyla liked to play her games, but Alvin certainly wasn't the type. Why would they take the chance on Adam? "They must know you'd never help them."

"The burn mark on my back…It means something." It was an awful burn mark. It had healed remarkably enough into an odd symbol, but the thought of how much time his stepdad must have taken to make such an accurate design was terrifying. It was hard to believe that there was anyone that cruel in the world to do that to a little boy.

Adam was terribly troubled about it. He was when he showed it to me, but this was much worse. "Lyla says it means I'm supposed to set her free or something like that."

I instantly became angry. "What is that supposed to mean?" It couldn't have meant anything. Lyla was only trying to mess with Adam's head or turn him against me, and I was sick of it!

Apparently, it had some effect on Adam. He was too ashamed to even look at me. "She thinks I'm supposed to help her get rid of you."

That was ridiculous. "You would never and it's impossible. We're two souls stuck in one body. That's what we are." But for some reason, even I was shook up about it. I didn't think Adam would help Lyla, especially not voluntary. There was always a chance that she could influence him, but if Lyla freed people from stopping themselves from what they truly wanted, then why would he help her? But I did deep down think it was possible for one of us to be destroyed and for the other to live. My dad hinted that it was possible that I could be rid of Lyla. If it were possible for me to get rid of her, it wasn't impossible that she might have known a way to get rid of me.

"There's more. There's a lot more. She said she'd tell me more tonight, but I wanted to ask you…" Adam took my hand, and he looked at me with sad and endearing eyes. He wanted to protect me, but he knew he was about to hurt me. "…Were your parents your biological parents?"

"Of course!" I didn't even know why he would ask me that.

I had intimidated Adam with my response, but he timidly pressed through. "Then why do you have these abilities, Roxy?"

"I don't know." I had asked myself that question a million times, but I never suspected that I wasn't their child. "I was just chosen, I guess."

"Maybe so…" Adam was so kind and gentle when he looked into my eyes, but I could feel him so twisted up inside, and his words felt incredibly cruel. "But you're not human."

I lost my breath. Hearing it out loud didn't really shock me, but it just didn't sit well. It was as if I were punched again, but that terrible pain lingered in the pit of my stomach. "Then what am I?"

"Lyla's been called a god a lot lately, but I don't think she's literally that powerful." Adam mocked Lyla, but I could tell he was genuinely worried about her power and what other secrets were yet to be revealed. "Are you okay?"

I hadn't even noticed that my eyes had started welling up with tears. "I guess I should have known, but…Why wouldn't they tell me?" I was sick of always crying and not knowing anything about myself. I was at a complete disadvantage and Lyla used my ignorance to place us exactly where she wanted us.

"Why didn't they tell me any of this?" It's not like I would have loved them any less. It's not like I would have run away until I found the truth somewhere out in the world. It would have been difficult to hear, but I could have handled it. I was sick of everyone treating me like I was weak!

187

"Lyla was told everything when she escaped when she was six," Adam said. "Not even she wanted to believe it all. Your parents rescued you because Lyla decided to go home."

Now that I couldn't believe! "Why would she do that?" She was the reason why they were dead. Why would she agree to go home with people she hated and leave people who worshiped her?

"She thought your mom and dad were gonna treat her better." If I didn't know any better, I would say he sounded little sorry for her. "When did she get really bad?"

My mom and dad didn't talk a lot about Lyla, and they left out a lot of details. They didn't start to open up about her until I got older. "When she was a toddler, my parents were fascinated with what she could do, but they were becoming uneasy about it. Lyla had a couple of nightmares or something, and there were some incidents with her powers and someone eventually got hurt. My dad started to chain her up and in a week or two, she broke out. After that, things weren't ever the same.

"She was always a little creepy, but she didn't start getting evil until a couple of years ago. She's teaching me every day how awful she can be."

I watched Adam nodding over and over again, taking everything in. I was sure that he hated her. I didn't know how much. I wasn't so good at feeling the depths of something that negative. Maybe it was because I didn't want to, but I couldn't. What I could feel was that very tiny speck of pity he had for what my parents did to her, and it really upset me. "Why do you want to know about her? You're not taking her side, are you?"

"No! I'm trying to understand." He sounded honest enough, but there was something rubbing me the wrong way.

"Understand her side?"

"Understand how her mind works. She lives off of manipulation, but maybe I can manipulate her."

I shook my head over and over. "I don't like it." Lyla could hear what he just said. We couldn't sink to her level, because we could never go far down enough without drowning and killing our own characters.

"She's terribly psychotic, but even a psychopath has rules. She's completely ruthless, Roxy. If I don't figure her out, everyone is gonna end up dead."

I couldn't take any chances. Lyla wanted to take him away from me, and I couldn't let that happen. "You have to find a way to leave without me." I ran to the window and looked for any way for him to get out. Maybe there was some weak spot in their security, or maybe one of the guards was napping or something! I had to protect him from Lyla. "If they won't kill you, maybe you should take the risk and bolt it out of here. I don't want her to use her powers on you. She must figure it's the only way to make you cooperate with her."

He looked so pitiful, not even the least bit desperate. I'm not even sure if he was afraid anymore. "She thinks I'm bad, Roxy."

"How?" I kind of laughed a little. I thought about how he sweetly came to my front door and picked me up for school or how much he loved his grannie. "You've only ever been sweet to me, besides when we first met." He was a little cold at first, but not bad. Lyla knew that. "What aren't you telling me?"

"She knows about who I really am." He looked at me, and I felt such unbearable shame that was capable of breaking him into shambles. "My name isn't really Adam. It's Blake."

"Blake?" I didn't like the name. It sounded hard and bland, not the enchanting and romantic tone I heard when I said the name I knew him by. Adam was such a better name.

"I needed it changed when I went to go move with Grannie. I had to start my life over. My stepdad was just as much an alcoholic as my mother, and they fought like maniacs when they were drunk. I couldn't take it anymore, and I called my dad to come and save me from the two of them. My stepdad got angry and he started arguing with my mom even more.

"Next thing I knew, Mom had his gun in her hands. He calmed down and talked her out of it, but as soon as she dropped her guard, he took the gun and fired it into her chest." Adam was close to tears and his voice was breaking up. "I saw the whole thing."

There wasn't anything I could say to make it better. "I'm so sorry."

"There's more."

I wanted to make him feel happy and just pretend like everything was okay, but I had to let him finish. No, I didn't want to hear what he had to say next, because I knew it was going to be hard to stomach. I felt queasy inside from all of the negativity that he had, but I had to let him finish. I deserved to hear the truth and he deserved a strong woman to stand by his side, so that's what I did. I walked back over to the bed and sat beside him.

"He was an evil man, but I'm not sure if he meant to kill her. He dropped the gun and cried over her like he didn't mean to do it, like he was truly sorry." The way he talked about it made him remember all of the emotions that he felt then. "Then when he saw me, I ran for the gun and picked it up myself. He told me that it was an accident and how sorry he was for killing my mom, but I didn't know how to believe him! My mom believed his apology and she ended up dead. He tried to ease a step toward me, but I emptied the gun right in him."

For lack of a better analogy, I'll just describe Adam as a black hole. Every bit of good was being sucked into a void. That brilliant light that I knew he had was nowhere in my reach. I couldn't feel anything but cold. I was too caught up in the hopelessness to think clearly or try to make him feel better.

"You killed your stepdad?" It sounded even worse when I repeated it. I understood how it happened when he explained it all to me, but I couldn't help but think of my dad and how Adam had killed him. How could murder twice be an honest mistake?

"My real dad showed up about an hour later, and I told him what happened. He wiped off my finger prints and threw the gun away, but I think he planted his prints on the gun on purpose, because the police expected him."

I was hit again in the gut by an incredible pang of guilt.

"They never found us, because my dad had his friend change our identification. I started a new life with my grannie, and I haven't seen my dad since. I got a postcard from him once. That's why I wanted to try and find him."

It seemed like an awful lot of work. He was only a boy! "Why couldn't you just tell the police the truth?"

"I wasn't hiding from the police. I was hiding from the people my stepdad knew." His voice grew quieter. "Besides, it wasn't exactly self-defense."

"But you thought he was going to kill you if you put the gun down."

He made sure his eyes didn't meet mine, but I could feel it. He was unsure of whether or not it was truly an accident or self-defense. Did he honestly think his stepdad was going to kill him? Only he could be the judge of that, but he had been beating himself over and over again until he was a bloodied pulp.

"That's my secret, Roxy. I'm a killer. I've killed before. I could easily do it again." Each line there was a new level of disgust, until his nostrils started flaring and he yelled. "What can you say to that?"

It was a lot—much more than I ever expected—but just because there was a part of Adam I didn't know, didn't mean that part I loved existed any less. "Can I still just call you Adam?"

He was frozen in shock of my response, and it disturbed me. Did he want to be Blake? Was it that important that I accepted his past? But then, he smiled and laughed with a gorgeous smile and his eyes beautifully shimmered from his tears. "Yeah. You can call me Adam."

I took Adam's hands and clasped them tight. I knew he felt terrible, but I cleared my head and started to feel that goodness he had inside of him. At least I knew he had a love for me that would never go away. I focused on it and brightened him up until it was like a newly made star in the universe. "You're scared she might bring out a killer in you? I won't let that happen! I'm gonna get you free somehow."

I loved him more than anything in my life. He could never be Lyla's. She didn't see what I saw when I looked into his beautiful blue eyes. I saw a good man full of confidence and exceptional strength. He would do anything to protect me.

I was washed away in every emotion pouring from him and myself. My insides felt like they were constantly tossing and turning from all of the butterflies I felt and I suddenly started drowning in the passion I had for him. The only way to breathe was for Adam to give me breath. I came crashing into him, and we kissed. It felt like I hadn't been with him for an eternity and that moment should have lasted the rest of my life, until my seemingly immortal body withered away into nothing.

My parents treated me like a child, and Lyla and her people treated me like a joke. At long last, I was finally being treated like a woman.

Every part of me was tingling, even my toes. When our lips parted for a breath, my hands wouldn't dare let go of the back of his head.

"I can't leave without you." He spoke briefly and dived back in again. He had never kissed me before like that. Perhaps it was the rush of the possibility that we might die, but I didn't mind all that much about the future of our intimacy. I was wrapped up in the moment of what it was and how alive he made me feel. I honestly didn't want it to end.

There was a knock on my door, but our mouths were too busy to ask who it was. I shouldn't have been rude and ignored them, but I didn't want to let go of the incredible feeling that I had birthing out of me. I knew Adam felt it too.

The door slammed open, and Alvin entered in without an invite. Adam and I instantly pulled apart, and I felt a little embarrassed for being caught and even a little upset that our moment was ruined. The look on Alvin's face didn't help any. "Roxanne." I wasn't Lyla, but he was jealous. I couldn't feel his emotions, but I was no dummy. He was tense and glared at Adam with so much hate! Then he looked at me as if I were some kind of prize for him to obtain. "It's nice to see you again. It's probably for the last time."

"What do you want?" I stood up to him, because I wasn't afraid.

He took a step closer to me and looked down on me. It wasn't hard with him hovering, but he was trying to make me feel inferior. "My father wants to see Blake."

I crossed my arms and refused to be intimidated. "He doesn't want to be called that."

"He wants to play the lie, huh?" He laughed and looked at Adam. "*Adam*, you are to come meet my father in his study."

"He'll be down when he's ready!" He didn't need to ignore me like I was nothing.

"It's adorable when you pretend to be brave." I felt really uncomfortable with the way Alvin stared at me. It was like he didn't see me at all, because he didn't want to. He liked my body and desired it. "You always were the fool." His finger gently stroked my cheek quickly, but I swear it was like the hairy leg of a tarantula. It gave me the creeps!

"You'll be the fool when Lyla betrays you."

"She would never."

"She would never love you."

Something snapped within him. Sure, he found me revolting, but Mr. Impenetrable had very thin skin. His nose twitched a little bit, and before I could finish my blink, his hand was gripping around my neck.

"Stop it!" Adam got up and bravely tried to defend me, but Alvin acted quickly and knocked him across the room and into the wooden bed post, snapping it in two.

I tried to pull his hand off of me, but I couldn't even get his fingers to move. I knew I wouldn't die, but I sure didn't like having my throat crushed by his fingers digging into my flesh. I hit him in his chest and his arms, but I was nothing to him.

Adam got back on his feet and tried to tackle Alvin again, but he used his other hand to begin squeezing the life from Adam. We both must have looked pathetic, but we didn't give up.

Alvin would have usually laughed at our desperation, but he pulled me in closer for me to hear. "Soon, you won't even exist anymore and then Blake will be rendered useless, and I will kill him!" Then, he threw Adam down on the ground hard. "So for now, I'll play nice." He threw me on the floor as hard as he could on top of Adam.

My gut had made a violent impact with Adam's knees. Alvin probably wanted a decent scream, but I couldn't breathe. I held my left side and took a moment to try to get some air, but I think I damaged something when I collided with Adam. It hurt badly, but I refused to cry anymore for Alvin.

Adam rubbed my back and comforted me until I started healing myself and could properly breathe again. He was such a strong protector. He might not have been as powerful as Alvin, but he made me feel safe and as soon as I was okay, he glared at Alvin. "I'll come when I'm ready."

Alvin was angry again and stepped up to Adam like he was gonna hurt him, so I quickly acted and got in between. "You know Lyla's gonna kill you, right?"

Alvin certainly did look like he was going to hurt me. I knew he wanted to, but something held him back. Maybe deep down he knew he couldn't trust Lyla, but he'd never admit that to me. One of us would be proven right soon enough. By the way he started smiling, he must have convinced himself that he would live happily ever after with Lyla. "Enjoy these last moments, Roxanne. Cherish them well."

I felt sorry for him. "I always cherish my time with Adam. I'm sure Lyla does too." It was one of my first attempts at saying something stinging. It worked well. Alvin fumed up his face and left us alone.

I turned to smile at Adam, but he was holding his back and bending over while he tried to crack it. "Do you need me to heal you?"

"No. I'm okay." He flexed his muscles and threw his arms back until something cracked. "I've actually felt pretty good since you healed me yesterday."

I didn't know of any side effects that could have occurred from healing anybody. I hadn't done it enough and using my own energy was also new. I would eventually have to try it again, if it wasn't going to kill me.

"What do you think The Master of the house wants?" I asked.

He sighed and rubbed his head, probably missing his full set of hair. I know I did. "Nothing good."

195

"This could end up working out well for us."

"You've got a plan?" He sounded surprised. If I were anyone else, maybe I would have been offended, but I admittedly hadn't been contributing enough on our journey as far as good advice.

"Not really much of one, but maybe you should find out all that you can. The Master and his sons would go horseback riding every day. If they still do, maybe that's our only window of opportunity to get out of here."

"I'll do my best to find out about it, but we've got to find a way to get you out of this room."

I did want to get away, but there was still a part of me that wanted to know so much more about myself. They knew everything about me and my parents wouldn't tell me what they did know. I had to finally know the truth. "I also don't know what I am or where I came from. Maybe if you could find something out, we could figure out the next move. They'd be more inclined to talk to you, since they think you're on her side."

"They're all jealous of me!" Adam was almost whining. I could understand that he didn't want to be around them. I didn't either.

"Just do your best playing spy." The thought of it made me smile. He really made a cute spy, and I knew he could be dashing enough. "Then we'll try to get out of here."

Adam groaned a little bit, but he was a good sport. He pulled me into a hug and kissed my forehead. "You don't have to worry."

For some reason, that made me a little bit more worried. I guess it was because I knew how amazing of a person he was and it made me a little bit more desperate to hold onto him. "You're a good person, Adam. Don't let anyone else tell you different."

It felt really terrific to have him holding me. His arms were big, toned, and very muscular. I did start to blush a little bit. Maybe if we made it out of everything alive, he could be my husband, and I wouldn't feel so silly about being held by such a hunk.

"Hold tight. I'll be back when I can."

I nodded, and he let me go. I thought about telling him to stop before he walked out the door for half a second, but I bit my tongue and let him go. It was the only way to find out any information.

I sighed a big, heavy, and incredibly nervous sigh. I was trapped, but there had to be something I could do! When I was a kid, I didn't know why I couldn't leave the room. I just knew that I couldn't. It didn't occur to me until recently that the room was enchanted. There had to be something around the doors and windows that were keeping me from getting out.

I looked on the windowsill and the frames on the door. The floor was carpeted, so I couldn't actually look under a rug. It's not like there was some weird text painted on the walls. It was still the red paint...

I got closer to the wall. I guess I had barely looked at it, and I couldn't remember it from when I was small, but it wasn't red paint at all. There was paint on the walls, but the more I looked, I noticed there were imperfections. There were little creases and bubbles that occurred when wallpaper didn't all the way take to the paste. The enchantments had to be something I couldn't see and since I didn't think there was any invisible ink in the world, it had to be behind the wallpaper.

I decided not to start ripping paper down from the walls, because I didn't know when Alvin would come back to spy, and I didn't know what kind of trouble Adam would be in. Everything needed to be the same until it was time to make my move.

I sat down alone on the bed and waited for him to come back. It seemed like a really long time. Of course, I didn't have anything to do but worry, so that made time tick by slower. I was beginning to get seriously worried about him. What if The Master of the House had decided he was

197

better off killing Adam? I mean, he really couldn't be destined to help Lyla. They would have to eventually catch onto the fact that Lyla made a mistake. Maybe they wanted to punish him for punching Lyla! There were so many possibilities, and it made me sick thinking about it.

I tried to relax myself by lying down. The bed was probably the most comfortable thing I had ever laid on. I didn't even need to wrap myself up in a blanket to fall asleep, but it was just another reminder that the people I was with would be willing to do anything to benefit Lyla.

When fifteen minutes had gone by, I started counting every second that he wasn't with me. After I reached seven hundred, I became too nervous to keep count. I paced around the room for a while, but that only made me more anxious to see him again. I couldn't keep any straight thoughts. Every positive one quickly turned into a negative. I couldn't take being trapped alone in that room while the love of my life was probably being water boarded and all sorts of other terrible things! Two excruciatingly painful hours dragged their way tooth and nail out of my life until I was cuddled up into a ball, chewing on my nails.

The door finally flung open, and I spun around so that I could run into Adam's arms, but he wasn't standing. One of Alvin's brothers had an unconscious, sweaty, and shirtless Adam on his back. I gasped horrified as soon as I saw him. His back was red and bloodied with fresh black ink covering his scars and filling out the alien circular designs with much more finesse. Alvin's brother flung Adam onto the bed next to me without the slightest bit of concern.

I slowly touched his hot skin, getting some of his blood on my fingers. "What happened?"

This brother was taller than Alvin and skinnier, but still toned. He lacked the charm that their father had, as well as Alvin's wild passion. "He didn't respond well and started seizing until he passed out."

"What?" I started to lose my grip on reality and panicked so much that I couldn't think. I pushed Adam's deadweight body until I had rolled him over. His face still had a little foam residue at the side of his mouth, and I felt so guilty for letting him go out there alone and encouraging him to play spy.

I looked up just in time to jump in response of the loud slam from Alvin's brother leaving the room. I don't know why I felt so surprised that he would leave me alone with Adam to wallow in my troubles. It's not like anyone was on our side and the reiteration of that fact brought more unfortunate tears to my eyes.

But it didn't matter if I were alone. I placed my hands on his chest and concentrated. I could heal Adam the same way as always—by finding the light or energy inside of him and expanding it until he had healed himself—but there was something different about him. I couldn't quite explain it, but there was something inside of Adam waiting for me to poke at it. When I did, it exploded.

"Lyla!"

I think my heart literally stopped once Adam reached out and gripped onto my hand. It wasn't just that he slapped his hand on my arm and started squeezing with his incredibly strong hands. That only would have startled me for a quick second. Calling me "Lyla" freaked me out, but it could have been an honest mistake seeing that we shared a body. It was his silver eyes peering into mine that had me screaming and pushed my heart back into my chest until I had successfully pulled my arm away and pressed myself completely into the wall.

I couldn't breathe. What had they done to him? In that quick moment, I remembered how he said Lyla's name. It wasn't with the usual disgust. It was…It wasn't exactly like he admired or cared about her, but it wasn't terrible. It simply made me feel terrible.

What had they done to my sweet man? "Adam?"

His eyes began to flicker and he collapsed back on the bed unconscious. He had frightened me so bad; I couldn't properly heal him. I was too scared to get close to him and try to do it again. I could still feel him. He was oddly enough at peace—not a single bit of turmoil in him while he napped, and that disturbed me. He still must have been human, or else I wouldn't have felt him at all. But if he were human, how could he have silver eyes? Were his eyes even silver? How did I know that I didn't imagine it?

I started inching closer to the bed. I wanted to check. If I lifted his eye lid, I could make sure, but what would that even accomplish? If his eyes were silver and he was somehow no longer human, that didn't mean that he was on Lyla's side! Even if he were, what could I possibly do about it?

No! I wouldn't accept that he had changed. He was no different, and it was only my imagination getting the best of me. I was going to let him rest. He deserved it. I climbed back into the bed next to him, being very careful not to touch him or move the bed much at all. I watched him carefully, but he seemed to be sleeping normal. I certainly wasn't comfortable sharing a bed with Adam given those circumstances, but I decided to relax myself the best I could. Besides, there wasn't much of anything else I could do. Either he was mine, or he was hers'.

Chapter Ten

"Roxy?"

I opened my eyes immediately. I didn't mean to doze off, but I immediately woke up as soon as he said my name. "Adam!" I was staring right into his stunning eyes and thankfully, they were just as blue as they always were. "Are you okay?"

"I'm fine." He was smiling as if nothing had happened. I had started to heal him, but he should have still felt a little bit crappy. The memory of whatever kind of torture should have made him react in some kind of way. I couldn't believe that he was unaffected.

Of course, he might have been trying to ignore all that and was simply focusing on the fact that I was lying on his chest, and he was holding me in his arms. I immediately started blushing once I had really noticed and with his eyes looking into my eyes…I don't know! The world kind of did feel magical all the sudden and I realized how easily he could cast all of his cares off his shoulders and let them fly off into space like letting go of a balloon…A gorgeously, wonderfully, blue balloon. Then there was his smile that was making me all giddy all of a sudden. I don't know what sort of thoughts he had when he looked at me as if I was the only person on the planet, but I could feel that he loved me.

I wondered what I should do. Was it wrong of me to lie on his chest and listen to the way his heart began to beat faster the more he stared into my eyes? Was it wrong of me that I wanted him to hold me with his muscular arms while my arms spread across his ripped abdomen? Was it wrong of me to want him to stretch his neck toward me so I could comfortably kiss his luscious lips? My parents had a lot of rules for me, but they didn't know much about my powers. The one thing they were sure of was that I was supposed to be chaste. I always knew I could handle that, because I thought it would only be decent to be intimate with a man who had committed himself to me completely with an oath of loyalty that would last until we were no more than dust. I had never considered that I would die before being able to have a romantic and a full life with a wonderful husband. What if that moment were the last bit of intimacy that we would ever share? And then I truly began to consider if I were ready to go all the way with Adam.

But I was still naive. My parents might have kept many secrets from me, and it was very possible that they would fib about my necessity of purity so they could protect me from my hormones or my emotions, but I just couldn't doubt them. It seemed like it would dishonor their memory, so I never bothered to answer the question of whether I was ready. Even if the answer were, *yes*, it would still be, *no*.

I started to rise, and I could sense the reluctance from Adam before he let go of me and let me sit up. "What happened when The Master asked for you?"

"Nothing really." I couldn't just feel that Adam was disappointed, but I could visibly see on his face that he was. I think he was a little bit irritated too. He usually thought my need to be a constant prude was cute or even funny. Why did it become annoying all the sudden?

"The Master didn't hurt you?" I was hunting for information, trying not to prod him too deep. Maybe it was too traumatic for him talk about, but Adam eyed me suspiciously and confused.

"Not exactly…" He got out of the bed and started stretching. I guess he wasn't aware of his tattoo. The redness was gone. There was only a little dried blood from what didn't latch onto the bed and stain it. "Oddly enough, he's actually really nice…" Then he stopped stretching and noticed the blood on the sheets and looked even more confused the more he stared at it.

I didn't want to be the one to break it to him, but his brain wasn't gonna have a breakthrough any time soon. "They kind of gave you a tattoo."

His eyes bucked. "A tattoo?"

I nodded, and I just felt awful for him because he started to get so angry. "It's actually pretty cool except it's of that scar you got, so it's actually a really bad thing…" My voice trailed off until I was mumbling alone. Adam had run into the bathroom to look into the mirror, and I could see his horrified face in the reflection.

"What else did they do?"

"I'm not sure. You didn't say." I rushed inside the bathroom to help him. I soaked a rag and began to wipe the blood crud from off of his back. He was angrier than I had ever felt. I started concentrating some positive emotions and slowly started bringing them to the surface so he would start calming down. He was clenching his fists extremely tight, as he was getting ready to punch out a wall. I let that be my visual guide, and I knew I had done enough once his hand relaxed and rested at his sides.

"I guess it does look pretty cool." He smiled as he looked into the mirror almost admiring it. It wasn't quite what I wanted, but I would rather have him admit that his evil tattoo looked cool instead of him going on a rampage and destroying the bathroom. "Did you use your powers on me?"

"Why? Are you mad?" I felt like a little child being scolded.

Adam turned around and placed his hands on my shoulders. He was still visibly pleased with a big smile on his face. "Well, you know I can't be. You pumped me full of the happies."

Well, I knew that there was still a little bit of sarcasm in his voice, and I knew him well enough to know that he would have been quite upset if he were able to feel that way. "I'm only trying to help."

"I have a right to feel angry, Roxy." It was weird that he felt so strongly about it that he felt the need to argue with me. He should have still been happy, but he was a little melancholy. "I don't like what they did to me and sometimes, our passion fuels. It's not always love that drives us. Sometimes, the rage gets things done."

"I don't believe in that sort of thing."

He folded his arms and glared at me playfully. "Love never won any wars."

"That's because it's usually disguised as hate!"

Adam began to laugh. "Are you trying to say we should love Lyla to death?"

"No!" I was a little embarrassed, and I didn't know why. I guess I didn't like that Adam was mocking me, but I did feel strongly about it. "I've disliked Lyla my whole, entire life. I've got every reason to hate her, and so do you, but I don't believe that hating someone can bring peace. If I'm gonna stop her, it has to be my way."

"And how exactly is your way?" Adam asked with a chuckle in his voice.

I bit my lip as I thought about it. I didn't believe in total passivism or anything, and I would fight her, but I didn't exactly have any solutions yet. I just knew that no one was going to die. "I'll let you know as soon as I do!"

Adam smiled as if he were about to laugh at me, but he didn't. If I didn't make him feel positive, I think he would have been frustrated.

Instead, he seemed to be pretty amused with me, like an adult being amazed by how the mind of a child works.

At least he was calm. He walked over the bed and plopped down on his back. He was considerably mellow. I didn't want to anger him and tell him about supposedly seeing silver eyes or the seizures. Besides, it was more urgent that we escaped. We could figure out the rest later. "What about the horses?"

"He had a painting up in his study with some horses on it, and I asked him about it. I guess he figured I was buttering him up, but he fell right for it and told me that he goes riding every day with some of his sons."

I jumped up and clapped. I was so excited that I couldn't help it! "When do they go?"

He smiled. "In the afternoon, but he was considering going tonight so Lyla could ride with them."

"Oh no!" It was the only time we could escape.

Adam sat up and his smile became devilishly cute as he began to laugh. "But, I casually explained it was a lousy idea. Lyla hates animals."

"She does?"

He shrugged. "I don't know, but Rider now thinks she killed an entire farm, because she was bored and hated the nearby smell. He seemed a little confused and or troubled, but I think he bought it."

It certainly did sound like something Lyla would do. "I can't say I approve of the lies, but good spy work."

Adam tried to continue smiling, but I could feel him beginning to slip from the state I had put him in and the smile on his face began to fade. "I wish I had something more to tell you about yourself, but he wouldn't talk about you. He didn't want to reveal anything that Lyla didn't want me to know yet."

"Oh, I see…" I tried to remain positive, but after a big sigh, I plopped on the bed next to Adam and realized how disappointed I actually was. "So, you don't know anything new about me?"

"He had this book in his study with some kind of weird writing. It had a bunch of sticky notes, so I assume he works out of it a lot. He wouldn't let me go through it. It probably has some answers in there, if we could translate it."

"I wouldn't know how." I couldn't even read my own language from a planet I knew nothing about. It certainly bummed me out.

"There were plenty of pictures. One of them was of the symbol on my back." Then I felt the expansion of his worry and guilt like a sudden tumor on the inside of my chest. "There's no mistaking it, Roxy. I'm somehow apart of this." It upset him so much that I didn't know if I should ask him if he remembered what The Master had done to him. It was distressing enough that he questioned his morality. If he questioned his humanity, there might not have been a way back for Adam.

I got determined for his sake and stood to my feet. "We need to get that book! Even if we can't figure it out, maybe we can find someone who can help us."

"So, the plan is to watch Rider and Alvin like a hawk, find out when they go horseback riding, for me to sneak back into his study, for us to find out a way for you to escape out of this room, and…Jump out the window?" It sounded kind of stupid when he said it like that.

I ran to an imperfection on the wall and pointed to the bubble. "This is wallpaper. I think it's covering the enchantments. If we could peel it off the wall, all we'd have to do is scrape the marking and I can go!"

"It's that simple?" Even though Adam was asking a question, it certainly seemed like a shutdown. "What about the inhuman guards?"

"Only Alvin, his brothers, and his father are inhuman. I can sense everyone else's emotions, meaning that they're human."

I suddenly felt a beam of hope and Adam's eyes widened as he eased onto his feet. "Meaning that you could control them?"

I was instantly offended. "I can't control anyone and never have!"

"But you can manipulate people."

"Into feeling good." Honestly! What type of person did he think I was? Was it really so bad when I helped him feel better? I never meant to abuse my abilities, but Adam made me feel like some kind of criminal.

"Can you make them feel so good that they wouldn't want to hurt you if you escaped? Can you make them feel so good that they might want to help us?"

"Maybe. I've never done it before." I had honestly never thought about it, but I couldn't just go around poking in people's souls! That's not what I did, and he had no idea what he was suggesting.

"Besides," I said, "Alvin might not go riding with all of his brothers! I would imagine that some would stay behind."

"So…" Adam started giving me a look that kind of made me sink in my knees in a bad way. I kind of bit my lip and I couldn't say anything in my defense. "You have to make the human guards and workers like you so much that they fight to help you get out of here by whatever means necessary." Adam was definitely very manly, and he for sure had a moment when his word was law.

I just felt terrible about it. "I don't want anyone to die for me," I spoke quietly.

He grumbled and glared. "This isn't a small scuffle, Roxy. Either the world is saved, or it's destroyed. I've seen what Lyla can do. You have to suck up whatever reservations you have about using your powers to the max and just do it!"

He hadn't really fussed at me before. I didn't have much of a defense for it. I mean, I knew he was right in one sense. It was crucial that

I stopped Lyla or else everyone would suffer, but I didn't know if I had it in me to manipulate them like one of Lyla's dolls. "Okay."

I couldn't exactly look at Adam, because I was kind of mad at him. I knew he was only doing what he thought was best for me, but it didn't matter. I was still mad and maybe a little disappointed too.

Adam didn't like that either and I knew he felt remorseful, but he let out a heavy sigh and let it go. "There should be a maid coming to feed us breakfast soon. I informed Rider how much Lyla hates it when you miss a meal."

I crossed my arms and refused to look at him, like a stubborn child.

"You should test your powers out on her."

My little protest failed, and I looked at him with a hanging mouth. "You really want me to do this?"

"Yes, Roxy. I do." The more he talked about it, the more comfortable he became with it. I began to wonder how much he had changed as a result of whatever The Master did to him or if there were parts of him already that I just didn't want to see.

"Maybe you should get some more rest."

"I actually feel great considering everything." He did look impressive. Physically, nothing had changed. He was still the muscular hunk of a man he had always been. I had just seen a lot more of him recently, and I wasn't quite as scared to look at him anymore. He didn't feel that much different on the inside either, but I knew that there was something there that could dramatically change everything. It was kind of like the present under the Christmas tree that I had no idea what was inside the package. I hoped for something great, but it very well could have been something that I wished I could return. It didn't feel dark or sinister. It was just something unexpected.

"Roxy, is something wrong?"

I felt guilty. I couldn't take keeping Adam's new development a secret. I had to be honest about what I thought I saw. Even though I was quite shy and didn't have much nerve, I had to say something. "About what happened to you...I don't know what they did, but—"

There was a knock at the door just in time, and it caused me to stop. It was the moment I had been waiting for. "Come in!"

A plump, middle aged woman with black hair and dark eyes came into the room armed with a tray of cinnamon buns and chocolate milk. "I brought breakfast. Lyla always loved something sweet. I figured you'd enjoy this."

"Thank you." It did look delicious, and the scent of cinnamon and the glaze was powerful. I wanted to be helpful so I took the tray from her and sat it on the bed. "You're very kind to do this."

She sneered. "I do this for Lyla." She was a human being. I could sense that she was so disgusted with me. I wondered what sort of lies The Master said about Lyla because Lyla didn't care about humans, and she certainly wasn't going to be kind to anyone. She only cared about hurting people. I didn't think I could convince her otherwise, at least not by my word alone. She didn't strike me as a very nice person.

Adam looked at me, and I quickly realized that he was signaling me with his eyes to go forward with his plan. If someone had to die, I certainly didn't want it to be Adam, but I couldn't make someone do something that they didn't want to do. There might have been a terrible price to pay if I didn't win the battle against Lyla, but I didn't think it was right for anyone to throw their life away for mine, especially if they couldn't help themselves. Men signed up for the army. I didn't want to force someone to walk to their death.

I wanted to wait until the maid had left and tell Adam that I simply couldn't go through with making anyone my doll, but he kept giving me a look and little by little, his beautiful eyes were glaring at me! He didn't even know if I could do what he was asking me.

Then I figured, maybe it was better to try it and then fail. That way, he couldn't bother me about doing it and we'd simply have to figure something else out. I was certain I couldn't do it anyway. I was born to save the world—not control it.

"Still, it was very nice." I smiled at the maid pleasantly. I could sense that there was some good in her. There's good in everybody. It sounds terribly cliché, but it's true. No matter how deep you are in darkness, there was always a speck of light somewhere. I didn't have to dig that deep for the maid. She had a lot of love in her heart for people in her life that she felt obligated to. She probably had children she was working for. I shouldn't have pushed her and pulled her into my war. I was holding onto her future and everything that ever mattered in her life. In that moment, I realized that I was far beyond capable of meeting all of Adam's demands.

Adam walked behind me and placed his hands on my shoulders and kissed my neck. It tickled and I giggled. It was so unexpected. He had never done anything so sultry before and I'm not very proud to say that I kind of enjoyed it. I don't know why he did it. Perhaps he thought it would be enough incentive for me to go on and manipulate the maid, but it wouldn't have worked for that reason. It did work because I was so overcome with such an unexpected moment of pleasure that I sort of squeezed onto the maid's emotions until she started smiling uncontrollably.

"You're welcome." I honestly didn't mean to do it, but I had brought out so much more affection. The poor woman couldn't understand it. She looked so baffled, but joyful. "I...I ...Thank you so much!"

I still didn't have the full revelation of what I did though. "For what?"

"For being here. Thank you for…" She shrugged and just started laughing. "You're just so wonderful."

I always thought that what I could do was a complete gift. I had never forced my power on people before. It was just a little push in order to brighten up someone's day. Sometimes, I didn't even have to do anything, and it would seep out of me. That's really what happened with Adam. I didn't make him fall in love with me. It happened pretty naturally, but what I was doing was wrong!

But even knowing that, I closed my eyes and pushed a little bit harder. I needed to know how far I could go and what I was capable of. I made her feel uncontrollable, uncompromising love, and it was so gorgeous that she burst into a fit of tears and giggles. "I've never felt this way before!"

I was more than her supposed children and any man she'd ever love. I was more than the flesh on her body and blood in her veins. I was her everything and I knew how wrong it was and it disgusted me and yet, it rejuvenated me. It made me feel stronger. I'm sad to say that it also made me happy. I couldn't radiate someone's feelings without magnifying them within me.

Adam lightly pulled me back from the maid and stood in between us. "You know the feeling will go away if Rider gets his way. He wants to kill Roxy."

Her eyes grew enormous and she gasped terrified and dramatic. "He can't! He can't! He just…" She fought off more tears—the sort that was made out of true desolation from losing someone that you care deeply about. She looked at me with her glistening eyes, and it was clear that she'd do anything in order to keep me safe. She reached out to grab me, and she shook me. "You're too wonderful!"

Adam was still in between us and began to pull the maid away from me to keep her focused. "You'd do anything to protect her?"

"Yes! I swear!" I had never pushed someone so far before. Some say love is fleeting, but I asked myself if it would ever go away. The maid wanted to protect me more than breathe. I'm not sure if that kind of love ever goes away. She was trapped.

"There's a book with writing from Roxy's world in it," Adam told her. "We need it in order to leave. Bring it to us as soon as Rider goes horseback riding. If any of his sons stay behind, you have to cause some kind of distraction. Roxy and I have to escape."

She nodded a couple of times with pure determination on her face. She only asked me one question. "Is this what you want?"

I certainly didn't want any human slaves. I certainly didn't want to use love as a weapon. "Yes, please." I just didn't have the heart to stop her because I loved Adam and I needed to get him out before he was corrupted. "If you don't mind, I'd like for you to help us."

"Of course!" She bowed quickly a few times before heading for the door. "I would do anything for you! Count on me!"

"You can go." I sat on a bed and wore an ugly pout on my face. I was nothing but a bully!

"Leave us." Adam was stern with the woman and confident. Why didn't he care that I was playing puppet master? He should have been more disgusted with what I had done, but he showed her to the door and forgot about her as soon as she left.

"I can't do this—"

"This worked out great."

We both grew silent after hearing each other's thoughts. He probably thought I was weak, because I could feel a massive amount of frustration that I had never quite felt from him before. If I didn't have such a soft spot for Adam, maybe I would have reflected that feeling. Instead, I was extremely disappointed.

No. I was more than that. I was disgusted. Heck! I was even angry. I couldn't believe what he made me do. "This is wrong. People aren't puppets. This isn't what I do!"

"I know, Roxy. I understand that." I wasn't sure if he did, and that's what hurt the most. He thought I was corrupted, and he encouraged my behavior.

I couldn't stay mad at him though, because Adam got real sad. He kind of looked adorable when he got all mopey. "I just want us to get out of here. I don't know what comes next after we escape, but I know we have to leave. I don't feel the same. I feel physically strong, but there's something wrong with me."

I realized how wrong it was not to tell him. I hated that I knew nothing about myself. I couldn't be a hypocrite. "You were sick when you got back. I don't know what they did, but you had a seizure. Then I think I saw silver eyes, and I freaked out. When I woke up, you were fine."

"But I'm not fine!" I should have noticed it. He was masking it so well, but he was scared of whatever he was becoming. I never imagined that Lyla could physically change him into anything. She was playing more than mind games, and I wasn't sure how to compete with that and I didn't know how long he could resist it. "We have to leave!"

He was masked with so much desperation. I couldn't take it, and I rushed into his arms. It was all I could offer him in the meantime. I didn't feel like using my abilities. Maybe he had the right to feel frustrated, angry, and terrified about what was happening to him. Besides, he wouldn't need to feel that way anymore once I had somehow defeated Lyla, but the first step was to escape.

We ate our breakfast, and it was delicious. Things were still a little uneasy between us, but I think it's because we felt like we had both let each other down. That was progress.

213

After a while, Adam kept looking out of the window. From his gaze alone, I could see that he was far off in his thoughts. Perhaps he was dreaming of freedom somewhere beyond the cold walls of a castle and out among the woods. Maybe he was dreaming of his grannie and of the life the two of us could have had together. Maybe he was considering all what his life could have been if he had never encountered me.

"Hey, Roxy."

"Yeah?"

He turned from the window and looked at me, and I knew it was something heavy. "Do you believe in God?"

I hesitated, but only because I was a little bit surprised by his question. "Yes."

Adam's mouth dropped. "How?" He had never asked me a question like that before. I suppose he was bitter about how some of his life was playing out, and it was easier to blame God than be angry at me. "You're not even human and you're a part of Lyla. You know what evil is. You know how unjust the world is. Look at what happened to your parents!"

"I know, and I think that's why I believe." It was hard when he slammed that in my face, especially knowing that he killed my dad. With all that terrible chaos in the world and people like Lyla who thrived off of it, maybe it was easy for most people to question God. However, I wasn't most people. "I don't think we could have invented something as beautiful as love."

Adam was intrigued, but also stupefied. "That's the reason? Really?"

"Look at the way I just abused that privilege!" I laughed about it, even though there was nothing to really laugh about. Adam thought I was so perfect, and I thought I would always be morally upright myself. I never meant to become the bad guy, but I messed up.

214

"I think love is something more than an emotion or something that sets off chemical reactions to make you respond a certain way. When a mother has a child growing inside her womb and she feels that unique bond of always wanting to protect it regardless of never seeing its face, that's divine purpose. The way a brother feels when his sister is getting picked on and how he has to defend her honor—even though she annoys him to no end—that's divine purpose." I had already begun to smile thinking about all the wonderful emotions of love I had felt through other human beings, but none was quite as remarkable as when I thought about what I had felt myself. "The way I feel when you look at me is divine purpose. I don't think a species could have created this feeling that I have for you, not even in millions of years. I think it's too good and too pure, and sometimes, I don't feel worthy of such a gift and yet, it's mine."

The way Adam looked at me confirmed everything I had just said. His eyes were full of such conviction and pride, and it made me feel like the most beautiful girl in the world. Before I knew it, he rushed over and kissed me with everything that he had, while still being so gentle. I tremendously enjoyed kissing Adam. It was like every butterfly in the world had come inside of me and was trying to burst out of my stomach so they could escape. I wondered what it felt like when normal people kissed. Not only could I feel my own magnificent feelings, but I could feel Adam's emotions like the taste of a sweet peach in my mouth. The more I felt him, the stronger it grew, and the stronger I felt.

He held my face and rested his forehead on mine while he gazed into my eyes. "You don't have to use your powers to escape. We can manage some other way."

I smiled at first, but he reminded me why I needed to leave that terrible place so badly. "I think I could do it for you though. This wonderful gift of love can be so terrible. It's a dangerous weapon to wield, and if you're not careful, you can cut yourself." I laughed to hide how

215

nervous I actually was about it. "I know I'm taking a risk, but I have to protect you. If your life meant mine, I'd gladly lay it down."

He placed his finger on my lips before I could make another bold promise of death. "I promise I'll be fine! Your integrity is more important than my life, but no one is going to die."

I was glad he was so sure. Well, I guess he wasn't all the way sure, but he was so manly and convincing. That handsome smile certainly helped. I just felt extremely good about our chances of making it out of that terrible place.

There was another knock at the door, and I could sense the beaming amount of admiration and commitment through the walls. There was no mistaking who it was. "Come in."

The maid quickly came in and shut the door behind her. "Hello, Roxy." She was so giddy about seeing me again that she even waved her hand and smiled like a school girl meeting a pop star.

"Hi." I felt terrible for what I had done to her. She was ready to jump in front of a moving train for me, and I didn't even know her name. "Breakfast was delicious, Miss…"

"Susan! You can call me Susan." Then she started to laugh so loud and with such abandonment that it became an odd cackle. "Roxanne Harris knows my name!"

I looked at Adam and we both tried smiling at one another, but we were only kidding ourselves. We were both really freaked out at how Susan was worshiping me. I barely knew how to accept compliments about looking nice in a new dress! That was beyond awkward.

"What about the riding schedule?" Adam asked. "Do you know anything about it?"

"Uh…" Her voice started quivering, and her hands were actually shaking. "Master Rider is going riding with four of his sons at noon, but four are leaving for a lunch outing."

"Is one of them Alvin?" I asked.

"Yes."

I clapped to myself and hopped up a little bit because I was so excited. Alvin was sure to try to kill Adam any chance he had. "We can actually pull this off!"

"They should be far away enough at a quarter after. That's when you should make your escape."

I was quite freaked out by Susan, but I couldn't help myself and I wrapped my arms around her as tight as I could. "Thank you so much."

I heard Susan gasp and then she was still and very quiet until I heard her sobbing to herself. My eyes bucked and I let her go to see what was wrong, but she was smiling. "You actually touched me!" I couldn't believe that my touch could mean that much to anybody. Ever. The scariest thing to me was how fulfilled Susan felt. "I'll make sure you'll have that book before you escape."

"I don't want you to risk your life for that book!" Adam must have sensed it or seen it too. Susan was heading straight toward a cliff, and her eyes were wide open. She just refused to look down. We couldn't predict the future, but we had the eerie feeling that Susan would die if we didn't somehow do the impossible and convince her to abandon her only dream of helping me be free.

"But I want to!" She reached out to grab me, and I jumped right before she started shaking me out of desperation. "You have to escape. I can't let them kill you. I couldn't live in a world knowing that you were gone."

The true horror of what I had done was revealed. If anything happened to me, she would die. If she wouldn't have killed herself, she certainly would have died from a broken spirit. She wouldn't be beneficial to anyone in that state, dead or alive. I didn't have any other options. "I understand."

She loosened her extremely tight grip and clasped her hands together as if she were praying to me. "I'm so pleased to do this for you!"

"Thank you." I could barely watch Susan as she left the room. I had done such a terrible thing to her. Would she ever be able to love her children the same way because I had completely seized control of her heart? Was she capable of having any more hopes and dreams or was my will her only goal in life? Would she even be able to function if she couldn't see me anymore? I always wanted to be more powerful so I could defeat Lyla, and even though I had found a way, the price of victory was simply too high.

"Do you know if you can change her back?" Adam asked, full of guilt.

I shook my head. "I can't make people feel negative emotions. If she's lucky, maybe it will fade away."

"I don't know if it can." He smiled and bumped into me playfully. "I know I could never stop loving you and you didn't even do any of your hocus pocus on me."

I knew he was trying to cheer me up, but I felt way too ashamed. "We've got about a half hour to go."

Adam took in a deep breath and sighed. "Then we escape."

It was impossible for me not to be nervous. A woman's life hung in the balance and I stood a reasonable chance of losing Adam. If I were caught, I wouldn't be living so cushy. Even after we made it out safely, Lyla was still going to return at sunset, and she very well could have been upset enough to use her powers on Adam. Whatever the case of the future, I had to put that aside and think of what was happening in the present. It was the only way I would survive. "We escape."

Chapter Eleven

Watching the little wall clock was nerve-wracking. It just wasn't the fact that we had so much riding on our escape attempt, but it was also the clock itself. It was one of those clocks shaped like a cat with big eyes and a whopping smile. They had a funny idea about what was appropriate for children in that house. I didn't really remember it, because Lyla's dolls were such a prominent memory, but the clock was incredibly creepy. As it ticked, its eyes shifted from left to right while it smiled like a little demon. It was meant to drive me crazy and make me anxious. It worked so well when I was a kid. I felt each minute of my life slip me by when I was trapped in that room.

No more.

"It's time."

Lyla kept that atrocious knife in our duffle bag. Alvin shouldn't have left us with such a thing, but he was probably afraid to return Lyla's bag to her without everything inside. I hated to touch the knife. It's not as if the knife had any feelings, but I knew she hurt people with it. It had a bad vibe to it, and it had nothing to do with my powers. There was just death on it.

"I can do it, if you want."

I handed the knife to Adam, and he began using it to cut and scrape the wallpaper right around the window. It was a long way down, but it certainly wouldn't kill me. Adam was sure he could climb down using the bricks and the vines crawling up the walls. I wasn't comfortable with that plan, so we were going to see if the coast was clear enough to use the door when Susan came back with the book.

"Do you think we can pull this off?" I asked Adam.

He sort of laughed to himself. "I've been running my whole life, Roxy. I think I can make one more great escape."

I thought it was really sad, and it reminded me of how he was safe in his secret identity with his grannie. I owed him a life! "I don't want you to have to run anymore."

He tried to shrug it off like it wasn't a big deal, but everyone wanted a home. "Maybe once you save the world, there will be a tremendous parade or something. You'll become the president and give me full pardon."

"I don't think I'm a naturalized citizen."

"You don't know that. Maybe your mom was vacationing here when she had you. Besides, no one can deny you. You're too adorable."

I started blushing. "That's how I feel about you sometimes."

"I'm not adorable." He turned and smirked at me. "I'm handsome and sexy."

"Yeah." I didn't mean to say it so dreamily. After I heard what I sounded like, I got all flustered and started becoming red. Adam noticed, and he cocked his eyebrow and looked real cute too. I covered my face to hide from him until I could calm myself down. "I mean, yes."

I left it at that because I could sense Susan coming. "Please, get the door."

He looked a little confused, but walked over to the door to open it. "Susan."

220

She had a massive pile of white towels in her hands and put them on the bed. It was heavier than what it should have been. "They're gone. The rest of the boys are playing pool in the billiard room."

"Do you have the book?" Adam asked.

"Of course!" She lifted up half of the towels and the thick, brown leather-bound book was revealed. "I would never fail you."

I picked up the book and didn't bother to open it. I held it into my chest. I was just so excited to finally have some answers about who and what I was. I cradled it in my arms like one of my stuffed animals. Soon, I'd know everything. "Thank you so much!"

"You're welcome. I hope you get out safely."

"Stay safe yourself. I hope you don't get in trouble for this." Maybe it was terribly naive to think that there was a possibility that she would get away with it, but I was trying to be positive.

"Oh, I'll be fine. Believe me." Susan was fidgety and all smiles until she overloaded and couldn't help but reach out and hug me. "Thank you for letting me do this."

Letting? I was *making* her do something. There was a significant difference. "Please leave us."

"Okay." She giddily waved her hand a lot and started walking backwards out of the room. Her eyes never left me until she closed the door.

"If she gets caught, she's dead," Adam said.

I pouted. "I know, Adam. I know."

At least Adam was managing to peel the wallpaper off. Unfortunately, the wall behind it was black and even though he scraped around the door, we couldn't see anything. It would have to have been some kind of full circle around the window to keep me from leaving. I didn't know what the symbols would look like, but they had to be there.

Adam touched the wall and started feeling on it. "There has to be something that we're missing."

I looked, but I didn't notice anything out of the ordinary. "I can't be wrong. It has to be on this wall around this window.

"They must have painted it in black. It's devilishly clever of them."

"So, what will we do?"

"Let's just slash it." Adam started on the sill of the window and worked his way across the wall, carving it out as easily as a good piece of meat, but it certainly wasn't quiet. Someone was bound to come and check it out. Just to be safe, he did it over and over again on different sides. "Tell me when you feel something different."

"I don't know!" I thought I would feel liberated, but I didn't really. I mean, the enchantment didn't make me feel any different than what I normally did. I was getting so anxious that it was kind of hard to feel anything, and I still had the door trapping me.

After making about ten slashes all around the window, Adam stopped and opened it up for me. "Try it."

I don't know why I was so nervous, but I closed my eyes and stuck my hand out. I felt a brisk breeze on my hand, firing off every nerve into a pleasurable sensation. I opened my eyes, and I realized I was free. "Oh my gosh!"

"Congratulations, Roxy."

I stuck my head out of the window and took in the fresh, clean air scented in roses from the bushes below. "We should move quickly."

I heard Adam sniffing in something like a dog trying to analyze a scent. I turned around, but I didn't speak at first. I didn't want to break his concentration, and he looked very concerned. "I smell gas."

I tried to smell myself, but I didn't know what I was searching for. "I don't smell anything."

I screamed and grabbed onto Adam not even five seconds later from the house shaking and from the sound of an explosion. Dozens of smoke detectors sounded off and so did screams and shouting from all over the house. I still couldn't smell the gas, but I started to smell the smoke. "What happened?"

Adam's eyes zoned out. "I told Susan to cause a distraction."

My eyes bucked and my mouth dropped. I certainly didn't think she would try something as insane as blowing up the house. I thought the most she would do was show the sons baby pictures or something time consuming, not completely life-threatening.

I could hear shouting and feet pounding everywhere. It wasn't gonna be very long until someone came into my room to check on me. "What should we do?"

"Jump out the window!"

I looked and it was way far down. I was three stories up, and I knew I was gonna hurt myself, especially while holding such a heavy book. "Here I go!" I closed my eyes and shut my mouth tight so I wouldn't scream, but as soon as I stepped out of that window and felt myself falling so fast, I did. Even though it was muffled by my tightly closed mouth, it still seemed pretty loud. Then I definitely let out a scream once I hit the ground, and my tiny body and the massive book turned into a ton and destroyed my arms.

"Roxy!"

I wished I couldn't feel pain, but I could, and I knew that I had broken probably both of my arms. I wished for a smoother landing, but of course, I would land in a way that would make me hurt all over with my face in the grass. "I can't move!"

I heard yelling and screaming from everywhere around me, and I could smell the smoke from the mansion burning. The thought that so many people could have gotten hurt over me started to block my

223

concentration, and though I didn't always need concentration to heal from injures, it sure did help with the speed. "Adam!"

I moved my head up from the grass so I could breathe in better. There was no sense in dying of grass suffocation and then *bam*! I saw two feet in front of my eyes, and I recognized the new pair of running shoes that was given to Adam by the maid. "What?"

"We need to go!" He grabbed me and I immediately began screaming. I couldn't hold onto the book, and I couldn't hold onto him. He had to toss me over his shoulders and held the book himself. The pain was a lot, but it couldn't distract me from wracking my brain about how Adam managed to not only jump out of the window and land on his feet, but to do it without hurting himself at all.

"How did you do that?"

"I don't know." He started running, and I realized how sore I was from my head to my toes. My back and rib cage felt especially terrible as he started sprinting across the lawn faster than what seemed humanly possible.

"Adam!"

"I know!"

Alarms started ringing and then Rottweilers started coming from everywhere! There were at least twenty dogs simultaneously chasing us. I focused on healing just so I could be ready for when they caught us and started ripping our flesh off. "Adam!"

"I know. I can hear them, Roxy!"

I heard a crack for just about every part of my body, and it hurt until I wasn't sore anymore. That was a small consolation prize to my imagination running wild and seeing all of my flesh being ripped off by all those dogs. "Adam!" I closed my eyes and continued to scream. They were gaining on us. I quickly looked behind me and saw that, in front of us, a giant stone gate had us blocked in. It must have been twenty feet high! We weren't gonna make it. "Adam!"

He grabbed the back of my shirt, and the next thing I knew, I was flying through the air. I was too afraid to open my eyes, but it was all happening so fast and I felt so high that I knew I wasn't going to be okay once I landed, especially once those dogs got me. I thought it was reasonable to keep screaming, particularly when I landed on my arm and broke it again. "Adam!"

I opened my eyes and sat up. I was extremely sore and my body was still in shock, so I couldn't sit up on the stone cement rather than the soft grass. I was bleeding and scrapped up pretty bad, but at least the dogs were on the other side of the massive stone wall. I still didn't understand how I had gotten to safety though. "Adam!"

I looked up just as he soared over the top of the wall like a heavenly angel with the sun right over him and his arms outstretched. He was athletic, but nothing explained what I had seen from him. Then he landed on his feet again like some kind of man cat. Had Alvin made Adam a man cat? I didn't know if I'd like a man cat. "What is happening to you?"

"I don't know, but we don't have time to chitchat about it."

I felt the presence of a shadow looming overhead, and it chilled me like a frost on a winter's morning. My whole body froze completely. I couldn't even warn Adam when the shadow morphed into human form before my very eyes, and I realized that the dark blur was one of my inhuman captors, who were simply too fast to stop from punching Adam in the face and knocking him straight into the thick wall.

Whatever had happened to Adam, he still bleed like a normal person, and he appeared unconscious from being hit so hard that his indentation was left in the wall when he fell face first into the sidewalk.

"Leave him alone!" I forced myself to stand, but my body wobbled and my unintentional charge became a stumble into a palm slap from him.

"Roxanne." It freaked me out how emotionless he was. At least Alvin cared for Lyla, and that's what pushed him over the edge. He showed no compassion or contempt when he brought an unconscious Adam to me. He didn't even care about breaking my nose and making me bleed all over the ground. "I can't let you escape. You know Lyla has to remake this boring world."

"Boring?" It infuriated me! "You mean to tell me that you wanna help Lyla because you're bored?"

"Well, I have been waiting for her to remake this world for close to eighteen years. I would think it's a little reasonable."

He made me so angry, but he slapped me so hard that I knew how weak I was against him. I couldn't fight him off. Even if he let me go, I wouldn't be able to lug Adam's bulky body away to safety. I simply wasn't strong enough.

I was about to accept the worst until I heard Adam grunting. My attacker even managed to let himself look surprised as the two of us watched Adam slowly getting up. His body was trembling a little bit, but I started smiling from relief that he was still alive.

"That's interesting." He even started to laugh. I certainly couldn't appreciate his twisted sense of humor. I was horrified watching Adam struggling onto his feet. "You started seizing when we dosed you with our power. I didn't think it would take. You at least seem human enough."

I could see and sense that Adam was rattled. He had every right to be, because I was far beyond rattled! Ironically, The Master's gift was the only chance I had left of escaping, but it still scared me like no other to think about what the gift would mean.

"Don't worry," Adam told me while wiping the blood from his mouth, "we'll get out of here."

"Just try it."

Adam yelled and charged him as fast as he could. Adam managed to ram him into the wall, but he wasn't stopped. He started pounding in Adam's back over and over again, and Adam grunted in pain every time. I was flinching and gritting my teeth at the brutality of it. Their fists pounding into each other's flesh so hard that it was cracking their bones just made me wanna vomit. I wanted to shield my eyes, but I couldn't help but look at it.

Adam rose up and socked him in the face so hard that the blood splattered on my shirt. I should have been happy that Adam stood a fighting chance, but it was too vicious for me to enjoy and I hated how visceral Adam felt. I knew he was fighting for my freedom, but if his mind always went on a rampage when he started fighting, it suddenly made sense how my dad ended up dead.

Adam couldn't keep him down, and he plunged forward and rammed Adam's back straight into a tree, splitting the bark apart. From then on, it was blow for blow. I couldn't stand watching them beat each other into bloodied, mangled messes. I tried closing my eyes, but then I opened them to check if Adam was still standing. Adam always got back up and pushed hard. I don't even know if he was fighting for me anymore. All I felt was hot rage.

The Master's son lost his footing and tripped on a tree root and landed flat on his back. Adam wouldn't allow him the chance to get back up, and he took the advantage of the higher ground by continuously punching his opponent in the face over and over again until there was no fight back.

I had tears in the back of my eyes as I watched Adam drive all of his rage into a body that he had already defeated. I was shaking and

227

wishing that he would take it upon himself to stop. I wanted him to be able to look at his blood covered hands and realize that he had won, but he couldn't. He was still stuck in rage. "Adam!" I ran toward him and grabbed his right arm. I was so weak compared to him. Even with my whole body working against his arm, he still managed to get in a few more punches before I could get through to him. "Stop it!"

And then he did. He froze with his fist in the air, shaking it from the rage and his silver eyes shimmering from sheer disbelief of himself. "This has never happened before..."

"It's okay." I don't know if I should have believed that his rage was a problem born from whatever was put inside him, but I was a sucker and I bought it completely. "But we have to get out of here, Adam."

He couldn't take his eyes off of his fallen foe. Even though his brothers would come very soon to make Adam pay for what he had done, he didn't budge. "Is he dead?"

"No." I could see that he was breathing...Barely, but I certainly couldn't heal him. I wouldn't be able to use his energy to heal his body, because he wasn't human and he wasn't worth risking my life to force feed him my energy. We had no choice but to let God sort it out. "But we have to go!"

I pulled on Adam's arm until he got up. I picked up the book myself, since I was far less bloody than Adam. I was scared that I didn't have time to heal him, so we both started running. I realized that I wasn't bleeding or feeling any pain. The only thing I felt was a little numb.

There was nowhere to run to. I wasn't exactly a track star and Adam was wounded. After a couple of minutes, the adrenaline wasn't enough, and I came to a stop to catch my breath.

Adam wasn't out of breath though. "Are you okay?"

Alvin and his father should have been hot on our heels. They would drag me back to their burning mansion, make me watch Susan's execution, and torture Adam until sunset so Lyla could decide his fate. No, I wasn't okay. "I should heal you now. I don't wanna sound lazy, but I think you can probably carry me faster on your back than running by my side."

"At least now, anyway."

"Hey!" I knew what he meant by that. I could feel it on him like a heavy, irritatingly big, uncomfortable coat. "It doesn't matter what they did. You're still you." I meant that, even if I was looking into his silver eyes instead of blue. I believed that he was good, and he could get better. Everyone could be better.

Adam could barely look me in the eye! "I kind of don't want you to heal me."

"Why?" He wouldn't answer me. He was being stubborn and wouldn't look at me, so I had to keep tugging on his arm until he answered me. "Why would you say that?"

"Because you're gonna make me feel good, and I'll be totally contempt with what I am and what I'm becoming!" He eventually lowered his voice, but he was still just as angry. "I've never lost control like that, Roxy. I know I was only protecting you and if I had to kill him to do it, I would have. I just…I don't want anyone to turn me into anything."

He had said a lot of hurtful things in his burst of anger. He was still willing to kill anyone in my way, yet he resented me. It was reasonable that he would resent me for being on the run and Lyla trying to ruin his life, but not for all of the good I had done! "I thought you were thankful. I thought you liked that I helped you become a better person!"

"I am grateful, believe me. It's just different now."

"But it's okay for me to do it to other people?"

He was stumped at first. Maybe he realized how much of a hypocrite he was being, but sooner or later, he didn't care. "Yes. It is."

I had never been so disappointed in him. "We should keep moving."

He turned around, and I rolled my eyes. I kind of wanted to be away from him for a little bit, but I had to ride on his back like a helpless, little girl. He was hurting, punishing himself even. I mean I didn't weigh much, but running by himself must have been taxing to his body. I certainly couldn't have been helping. I should have just healed him without his permission, but I didn't wanna force myself on him.

Adam was still moving pretty fast though. He was as agile as a deer running through the woods like he belonged there, leaping and treading so lightly that his grace was quite stunning. It wasn't very long before we began to hear the distant sound of cars, meaning that there was a road somewhere leading to civilization. I didn't know where we were, but we could certainly find our way if we found a road.

There was a small creek before the road. Adam stopped at it and set me down. "Let's try to get as much blood as possible off."

"Yeah." That was easier said than done. It was a simple matter of washing off blood for me, but Adam was still bleeding. Alvin probably could have tracked us from the blood Adam left all over the place. Adam had gashes all over his body, and his shirt was soaked. Then he was bruised, and his face had started to swell. People were gonna ask questions no matter where we went. "It'll be safer for us if I heal you."

Adam wasn't so angry anymore, just concerned. But he did know I was right. "When you healed me in the truck, I felt different. It felt extremely amazing, but it was weird."

And I felt like I was gonna die! I guess I healed up a little bit, but Lyla must have been real angry that I left her so weak. "I'm not gonna give you any of my energy and put it inside you. I'll use your own energy to do it, like how I healed your grannie. I promise you'll be fine."

He nodded, but he still looked worried. "Okay."

I tried not to make it weird or long. I tried not to make it feel too good, but I didn't know any other way to make him feel. It was just my method, and I didn't know of one that worked any better. I held onto the positive energy inside of a person and used it to help them help themselves. Joy was just a side effect.

"Thanks." Adam was beaming from ear to ear, and I knew he didn't want me to make him joyful, but I couldn't help it. Besides—this might be selfish—but I loved to see him smile. "You're welcome."

Before, I couldn't imagine what The Master and his boys did to Adam, but it suddenly dawned on me. If I could somehow use my own life force, they could too. "That's what they probably did to you. The Master and his sons probably gave you some of themselves."

"Why would they do that?" I didn't quite get that myself. If I were Alvin, I wouldn't risk my life to empower someone I hated. He was much too petty of a person. He must have thought that Adam would die or something.

"Maybe it's because you're Lyla's chosen vessel, or so they say. I guess that's why you seized. It was too much for you."

"Well, I survived. So, does that mean something?" It was only a question. He was incapable of being normal Adam and having a negative outlook, but I knew him well enough to know how he'd really feel about it if he could help himself.

"Oh, it means something alright." I stood up and placed my hands on my hips, very determined and in an attempt to be inspiring. "It means they're gonna be sorry that they messed with us!"

Adam blinked a couple of times before busting out into laughter. I guess I didn't look much like a leader, but I knew we could somehow overcome our enemies! We still had good on our side. "Let's keep moving."

We kept running, following the sound of the distant cars until it was right in front of us. We exited out from the tress and saw black, beautiful pavement. I was surprised about Alvin not catching up with us yet. Surely he must have been faster than Adam and even if he didn't have enough sense to follow the trail of blood that Adam left behind, he would certainly think to let the dogs smell our clothes and viciously track us down. Instead, we seemed to be making a clean getaway.

When we got to a road, we lucked out and spotted a bus stop about fifty yards away. We saw it coming from down the road and started sprinting for it. I started waving my arms and screaming so the driver wouldn't dare pass us. Adam surpassed me and got there before the bus, which made it come to a stop. Then he waited for me patiently so the driver wouldn't leave me.

The driver was a thickset man who looked and felt incredibly sad and impatient. "Sir, please! We don't have any fare, but—"

"No fare, no entree."

"Please!" I had to stick my hand inside to keep him from closing the door on us. "It's a life or death situation!"

He took a moment to look at us both. Adam did have a lot of blood on his clothes, and I had some on mine. We had obviously been injured or on a killing spree, and he wasn't concerned about either. "You need to go to a hospital?"

"No, but—"

He rolled his eyes and started to close the door again. "Off my bus."

Adam grabbed the door and held it open long enough for me to step inside. It was clear what I had to do, and I didn't like it. "It would be very nice of you if you let us ride the bus. I'll pay you back when I can." I smiled sweetly, but that wasn't enough for him. I had to push, prod, and poke inside of his soul to bring out enough compassion and joy to make him want to do anyone a favor. It wasn't that difficult. He wasn't pure evil. He was just grumpy.

In a matter of seconds, he had a full-sized smile on his face. "Oh, that won't be necessary! You can ride."

"Thank you." I curtsied for him a little bit. I didn't know why, but I did. When I was walking to a seat near the front, I noticed that I was getting a lot of glares from upset people who were mad that I didn't have to pay. You'd think they'd be more concerned about the blood. Some of them looked at us strange, and a couple of them were concerned, but there was this guy in the middle eyeballing us as if we had punched a baby! I rushed to my seat and wouldn't look at anyone else out of guilt.

There was a man in the back who was just so irritated. He jumped out of his seat and pointed toward us. "Why don't they have to pay, Louie?"

"I'll spot 'em," the bus driver said. "They're in a rough spot."

"They can't even be sanitary!" He was one to talk. Of course, Adam must have looked gross with all that blood, but the man in the back needed a bath. He was grungy and coated in dirt. "Louie!"

"They need some help," Louie said. "I'm gonna help them. I'll bleach the bus myself if I have to."

"Thank you, Louie!" I was extremely grateful. All I had to do was make him feel good. I didn't even need to control him like Susan.

Adam slyly took a seat next to me and leaned over to speak quietly in my ear. "I thought you weren't gonna do that anymore."

"I thought you still wanted me to. You aren't being very clear."

He sighed. The guilt had to have been weighing on him too, but he was much more relaxed than me. "Getting out of here alive should be our number one priority. Screw everything else, even my feelings. Even yours."

I guess I really didn't have much of a choice, but I still wasn't very comfortable with having to do it. "I understand."

"Excuse me," said a woman sitting across us, "are you two alright?" She was probably in her thirties, very motherly. She was terribly afraid for us.

"Yeah," Adam said laughingly. "We were out hiking, and I fell into a berry bush." He was so skilled at covering his tracks. He didn't miss a beat, and he actually looked embarrassed about it.

"Oh!" She placed her hand on her chest, took a deep breath, and exhaled. "I'm so relieved. I thought that was blood."

"No." He laughed again, even more convincingly. "Sorry to have scared you."

There was a little awkward moment when she started looking at his shirt again. He didn't smell fruity, so it wasn't hard to poke holes through his story, but Adam was so charming and sly that you wanted to believe him. Besides, he was either too hurt to be conscious or a serial killer, and who would have believed either? "My mistake."

At least some other people who must have been eavesdropping heard our story. I felt a lot of tension beginning to ease up.

With that out of the way, Adam sat the heavy book down in my lap. "So, let's look at this book."

It was funny that I wanted to look inside it so badly, because suddenly, I was nervous about seeing what was actually inside of it. I had to open it though. Adam would have made me do it anyway, and he would have fussed at me for taking so long.

It was just as he said. There was a lot of writing that I couldn't understand. The markings looked familiar, like the markings on Lyla's chains that kept her powers at bay. Still, there would be no way for me to decipher any of it. "Is any of this jogging your memory?"

"I can't say that it is. I can't really jog if I've never seen it before. I've had human parents my whole life, remember?"

"Maybe something will catch your eye." He smiled, and it made me want to look on the bright side.

There were a couple of pictures. Most of it was of stuff I didn't understand. I figured maybe most of it was metaphorical, because there were lots of pictures with animals and such. The first picture that I got to that I recognized was a drawing of the tattooed and scarred symbol on Adam's back. I watched Adam to see what he would do. His face didn't change. He only slumped his shoulders a bit. "It's weird, but not the end of the world."

"No, it's not." I kept turning the pages until I found a picture that was very intriguing. It was of a girl (who I guess was me) standing on some kind of stone platform, trying to pull some sort of scepter out of it. I didn't know what to make of it, but I had a gut feeling that told me how significant the picture was. I found myself wishing that it was a picture of me and not Lyla. I mean, the girl looked pretty heroic with her hair blowing from the energy or wind—whatever the swirls were meant to illustrate. I wanted to stop her so badly.

I turned the page to see if there was another illustration similar, but there wasn't. The next couple had nothing but text. But then, I finally found a page with a yellow sticky note with English and numbers written on it. "Jackpot!"

"What is it?"

Adam tried to reach out and take it from me, but I fended him off with my arms so I could look at it myself. I picked up the sticky note and read the address. "This is an address for Priest Porter...Who can open a portal."

"What kind of priest do you think he is?"

I flipped a couple of pages back to a picture with a swirling black hole with little stars inside of it. I thought it was literally a black hole or at least an evil force, but maybe it was an actual portal. A page after that, there was a picture of the staff the girl was holding onto. It just looked like a complicated, expensive stick with jewels on it. But then the next two pages were the picture of the heroic girl. "Whatever I'm supposed to do to stop Lyla, I think he's our ticket."

"What makes you assume that he'd help you?"

There was no way I could be sure, but I needed to try and remain positive. "I'm just gonna have to have a little bit of faith here."

He rolled his eyes. "You always assume the best in people, and that's not always a good thing. He could try to kill us."

"He's our only lead away from Alvin and his terrible family. I think this is a chance we're gonna have to take. Besides, I have to be lucky tomorrow. It's my birthday."

Adam probably had millions of things to say, but he refused to speak his first initial reaction. "Tell the bus driver to take us there."

I slumped my shoulders. I was glad he agreed, but I didn't want to push the driver again. I didn't have a choice, so I didn't bother to protest. I kind of eased out of my seat and walked over to the driver with my head hung low. "Um…" Then I spoke so quietly, it was a surprise that he could hear me at all. "I need you to take us to this address."

I tried to hand him the sticky note, but he wouldn't even look at it. "Oh, I'm sorry Miss. I'd really love to, but I have a set route and all these people need to go somewhere."

"I know…" I bit my lip and looked at all the people behind me on the bus. They all looked pretty miserable, but maybe that's because they were in a hurry. I felt guilty, but they'd never care enough about anything to ride the bus again if Lyla had her way. "…But you want to do this favor for me. Everyone else will understand."

"Like hell we will!" The man from the back shouted. I predicted that he would be the biggest problem out of everyone.

"Yeah, Lady!" said another man that was angry about the suggestion. "I've got somewhere to be."

"It's fine." I wasn't sure if my powers could work on multiple people at the same time. It was a day for firsts, for sure. I didn't want to try some kind of massive wave, because I didn't want to change Adam into someone without an opinion. I would have been in a bad spot without him.

I just cleared my mind and felt them all out. I could sense everyone's common frustration with me, and that's how I singled out Adam and managed to leave him out. Once I had them all, I started picking inside them. They all had a common goal of wanting to get off the bus for various reasons. There must have been close to thirty people, but I picked them off easier than flies. The process seemed much more difficult than it actually was. In reality, it only took a couple of seconds.

I smiled. "You can all get off at the next stop and wait for the next bus. It's a beautiful day. It'll be a lovely wait."

The same man who sounded as if he wanted to punch me in the face was beaming like a little child. "Yeah, it sure will."

The motherly woman clasped her hands together and smiled. "That sounds like a wonderful idea."

The bus driver nodded. "Then it's settled." He took the sticky note from me. His eyes got a little big, but he kept smiling. "It'll probably take a few hours though."

It was best to be far, far away from Alvin. "That's fine. Thank you."

I sat next to Adam again, and he was questioning me so fast with the delicate raise of one brow. "That's not draining you too much, is it?"

"No." I felt really good. "It's scarily pretty easy." I never would have thought to do it if Adam hadn't made me, and I certainly would have never thought I'd not only pick it up quickly, but be able to do it faster and faster. I didn't even have to stop in the middle of a sentence or anything. It's not like I made them like Susan. I didn't need to, but it was still a manipulation and I was truly skilled at it.

"I think I need a nap," Adam said.

"You're tired?"

"Not really, but I need one mentally." I thought it was a good idea. His eyes hadn't changed back to normal yet. I could love him with silver or no eyes if need be, but I'd feel better if he went to sleep and woke up normal as he had done earlier. We had been through so many changes already. I missed my blonde hair; I missed Adam having hair. I just wanted something to be normal.

"Well, the seat behind us is empty. You stretch out and try to relax."

"I should help decipher the book."

"I'll ask when I need you, but you're not an expert."

"Fine. You win." He leaned over and kissed me on the cheek. It was comforting to know that no matter what did change, he would still always love me. "Just wake me up if there's any trouble."

I nodded, and he got up to walk to the seat behind me. I think he wanted to try and fall asleep so he could reset the day himself and just be normal Adam. I hoped he could do that, and I hoped that he would live to accept whatever happened to him, just like I knew I would.

I started looking through the book again where I had left off. There were a bunch of different symbols, and there were fewer pictures as the pages went on. I started to get impatient and began flipping through it, bypassing a couple of pages with more pictures until I got to the back, which was just one blank page after another. I sighed, because it was a bit disconcerting. It didn't seem like a whole lot of history. I wondered who even wrote it.

I flipped backward and landed on a page with a beautiful woman dressed in a wonderful flowing gown and bedazzled in spectacular gems. Her face was very delicate—soft and round—yet she had a look in her eye that showed such inspiring strength. Her hair was very long and wavy. I could tell she was tall, but she was slender like me and her posture was perfection, unlike my klutzy self. I wondered who she was. I thought she kind of looked like me, only older, powerful, mature, and obviously much more graceful.

Wouldn't it be something if she were my mother? What if I could meet her and she was actually a decent person? What if she loved me and taught me how to be as strong and confident as I knew she was from her picture alone? I wanted to be that poised and beautiful. Heck, I'd even settle for being a little taller.

When I was done daydreaming about something so silly, I turned the page and everything changed. I was staring at a picture of me. I knew it was me. I had seen my baby pictures. I wasn't that tiny in any of my pictures at home, but I could recognize myself.

But there were two babies.

I didn't know what it meant. Lyla and I were two different people? Was that even possible? How could we have ended up being stuck in one body? But more importantly, if we were two separate people, what happened to the other body? Was the body I was in actually mine, or did it belong to Lyla?

Chapter Twelve

Hours had gone by, and Adam had been asleep for a while, so it was only Louie and me. I asked him politely to stop talking to me once I realized he was so boring. It's not because I was in a mean mood. I was just busy being a nervous wreck about the picture. I kept gripping on the book wishing for it to be different. Lyla and I were twins, not some mystic, schizophrenic person born with two souls. The *how* didn't bother me so much. I was more concerned about my body. I hoped it was mine. She was intruding in my life, but I guess she would say the same about me. Was that why Lyla always seemed more powerful? Was that why she could remember what I did, but I couldn't remember her life? What if our two bodies were somehow joined together? Did that mean we were both the owners? Could we be separated? Was that what my dad meant when he said there was a way for things to change, or did he mean that one of us had to die?

I should have told Adam about what I felt. He would have made me feel better, but I couldn't bring myself to do it. What if I weren't even a real person? Was I worth sticking around for if I were merely an infection in Lyla's body? I didn't know.

The driver wasn't kidding when he said it would take a couple of hours. We drove about six. Adam managed to sleep through it all, or he at least pretended he slept through it all. I couldn't have slept if I wanted to.

240

I kept looking outside and stared up at the beautiful blue sky and praying to God that He would make the sun stand still so I could win my battle.

But just like every day, the sky was beginning to darken just as we were pulling into a little neighborhood. The houses were tiny but very quaint with a charm that I liked. It was peaceful, and I didn't like that I was about to ruin it all.

Louie pulled the bus right up to a house with a white picket fence and pink daisies. I certainly couldn't be intimidated by a place like that. But I wasn't gonna judge the priest by the house or the neighborhood alone. It felt like a nice place, and I didn't sense any danger. Of course that could have all changed when I knocked on the door.

"Adam."

He opened his eyes immediately. "I'm awake." That's why I thought that he was pretending to be asleep. He didn't sound groggy. His eyes certainly weren't heavy. I think he just didn't feel like talking, and by the way he shied his eyes from me, I don't think he wanted me to see him either.

"Are you worried about your eyes?"

I'm surprised that he did, but he nodded.

"Don't be." I smiled. "They're blue again." I tried not to be too relieved. I didn't want to make it seem like the end of the world if they weren't back to normal.

"They're normal until I snap again."

"You won't snap!" Of course there was a chance that he would, but I wasn't gonna give up on him. He didn't give up on me, and I was part Lyla. "I'll be here to help you."

Adam gave me a tiny smile, and we both got up. Louie still hadn't said a peep since I asked him to stop talking to me. I felt crummy for making him go so far out of his way. He must have been fired for sure. "Thank you for everything, Louie."

241

"No problem. I'm glad I could help you."

"Do you have a family?"

"I've got a wife and two girls." I could tell how much he cared about them. They were probably worried about where he was. I wondered what he would do to support them after he lost his job for disappearing for so many hours. I owed him something, but I didn't have anything to give.

The only thing I could do to make up for everything was to beat Lyla. Nothing would matter if she somehow succeeded in freeing the world. I tried to be as optimistic as possible, but there was a fifty percent chance that I was gonna fail. "You should go home to them and hug them and kiss them and let them know how much you love them. You never know when everything is gonna end. Be grateful."

"That's good advice." He smiled. "Take care of yourself."

"I'm gonna try very hard." I started walking off of the bus, and Adam shook Louie's hand before he followed me off the bus and onto the sidewalk.

I didn't bother hesitating when it came to approaching the front door. I wanted my battle with Lyla to finally come to an end, and I believed the priest would help me. I reached over the fence, unlatched the gate so I could get through, ran up the porch, and then started pounding on the door.

Adam was dragging his feet though. "You sure this is a good idea?"

I laughed. "Adam, the house is yellow. Evil people don't live in yellow houses!" It was a silly distinction, but I just didn't think I had a real reason to be intimidated.

Adam lifted up the back of his shirt, and I noticed that Lyla's knife was in his back pocket, just in case. I thought maybe he had left it at the mansion. I was sad to see it again. It was as if the stupid thing were haunting me!

I reached out my arm to knock on the door again, but I froze when I heard it unlock. My eyes bucked, and I had to catch myself in order to stay calm. The door opened quickly, like a man welcoming a friend instead of a stranger, but I didn't know him. He was an older man, probably about sixty with frosted white hair. He didn't look like a strong warrior like Alvin and his brothers, but I knew he couldn't have been human because of his silver eyes. "Hello." He still sounded friendly though.

"Hi." My voice shook a little bit, so I cleared my throat so I wouldn't seem like such a child. "My name is Roxanne, and this is Adam. I don't know if you know why I'm here, but—"

"Of course I do! Come in." He signaled us both inside and took a step back. "My name is Porter, but I'm sure you already know that." He was smiling so much that it actually started to make me sort of suspicious—like I expected a large cage to fall on us as soon as I stepped through the door.

Adam gave me a little nudge in the back, and I stumbled inside. He followed right after me. "So you know about what Roxy is and what she can do?"

"Yes." He closed the door and then I got even more nervous. He just seemed way too friendly. I couldn't even think of anything good to ask to confirm that we could one hundred percent trust him.

"And you're not playing on Lyla's team?" I thought Adam had lost his suspicion since he came inside, but I guess he didn't have much to be afraid of anymore.

"Oh, I'm not on anyone's team. I'm very neutral in the matter." He certainly didn't look like a priest. He was dressed in a button-down, long-sleeved shirt with a plaid sweater vest and khakis. He looked like a spry grandpa who was waiting on his grandchildren to arrive. He was very humanistic, or what I thought a human grandpa should have been.

"You're not human?" It was a stupid question, but I asked it anyway.

"No. I'm a mediator between those who would follow Lyla and Roxy." He started tapping his chin and looked up toward the ceiling. "No. Perhaps mediator is the wrong term. I'm more like a referee."

"Meaning what?" My voice shrieked on an accident, but I was appalled! "You're keeping score?" It wasn't a game what Lyla was doing. Good people died because of her!

"No. I just want the game to end, be interesting, and fair."

I looked at Adam to see what he thought, but he just shrugged his shoulders. I guess it was my call. I opened up the book and started flipping through the pages until I got to the one with the heroic girl clinging onto the staff. Then I held up the book toward him and pointed at it. "So, you'll open the portal to this for me?"

He bent down to get a closer look, but then smiled and nodded. "Yes, but it'll take some time."

"I don't have time! Lyla is coming very soon." I gasped. "Does that mean when she wakes, you'll have to open it for her?"

"If she asked me to, but I won't be done until at least tomorrow afternoon."

"Seriously?" I shrieked again and jumped. I couldn't help myself.

"Opening a portal is serious business, Roxy. It's not an easy task, especially by myself."

I started to calm down. I felt dizzy all of a sudden, and then I remembered how close I was to the night. It was like the world was sinking and I was drowning into nothing, but I was rocking back and forth, about to fall off my feet.

I saw Adam and the man talking, but I couldn't understand them anymore. I was falling too deep. The man pointed at me, and Adam noticed what was happening. He tried to shake me out of it, but then I had to let go completely.

"Lyla?"

I raised my head up, finally having control of my own body. I was hoping to be totally myself and stare into his silver eyes, but I settled with his sexy baby blues and smirked. "Hello, Adam."

I flung him toward the closest wall and held down his arms and legs once he tried to escape, but he wasn't going anywhere. No, he was finally mine, and I had no intention of letting him skip out on his destiny.

I looked at the old man. He was not afraid and neither was Adam. I thought maybe I should hurt the old man in case they thought I was getting soft or something, but I did want him alive and up to full strength. "Start opening the portal."

"As you wish." He walked out of the room and opened a door leading down into a basement. I was a little surprised that he left Adam all alone for me to do whatever I desired, but I couldn't blame him. Adam was technically still a human, and they meant nothing.

I walked toward him slowly. He was struggling in vain to move his limbs, but he could never break free from my grasp, even with the extra strength. I planned on doing naughty things to him. He must have anticipated it, but he hid behind a brave smirk. "You're not mad at me, are you?"

I laughed. I hated to admit it, but I was quite fond of Adam. He was funny, he was idiotically brave, and he was so yummy on the outside. I wondered if his insides would look so appealing once I laid them all across the floor. "You want to know if I'm crossed about you breaking my nose. Or do you want to know whether or not I'm pissed about you escaping with Roxy?" I thought I would be angry. When I first threw him against the wall, I planned on gutting him like one of Roxy's vomiting worthy stuffed animals. He should have feared me and respected me. I couldn't have a lowly human punching me in the face and making me look weak in front of my admirers. He had to die for his treachery!

But for some reason, when I got up close and personal with Adam, I wasn't as angry as I should have been. I wanted to give him a chance to fulfill his true purpose. "Well, you heard the priest. I'm supposed to be here."

"And the portal won't be ready until Roxy wakes up." He tried not to smirk for a millisecond, but he had to rub it in my face that he thought he'd won.

I shrugged. "It doesn't matter. Roxy won't be here tomorrow morning anyway."

And then he looked so hurt and concerned for the poor baby! "What do you mean?" Why did he even like her so much? She was so annoying! I knew she was. I had to watch her all day long. Every time Roxy looked at Adam shirtless, she was practically going to faint. She wasn't even a woman! How could he even be attracted to someone like that?

"Promise you'll behave, and I'll let you down."

He hesitated, but then he nodded.

I took a couple of steps back in case he wouldn't keep his promise, but I knew his word was good. Then, I let him go. "You're gonna help me kill her."

He crossed his arms. "And why would I do that?"

"Because, it's your destiny."

"Destiny is mine to control. It doesn't own me and neither do you."

"Wait!" He was sexy when he struggled, but I was excited to finally let it all out for him. "Don't give me silly speeches on rebellion when you're just gonna do what I want anyway. Ask me questions. I know you've been dying to find out the truth about me."

"And you're just gonna tell me after all this time?" He had every right to be suspicious, but I genuinely wasn't playing any games.

"Yep."

"Okay..." He kept eyeing me and waiting for me to shut him down, but I was seriously ready to be totally honest with him. "What—"

"Roxy is hiding something big from you!" I had a systematic order that I wanted to tell everything in, but I couldn't help myself from busting Roxy's bubble. She was finally the bad guy.

Adam sighed and rolled his eyes. "And what would that be?"

Roxy had dropped my book on the floor when I started emerging. I grabbed the book and turned to the exact page of our baby pictures and pointed to it for Adam. "She found this, and she didn't wanna tell you about it."

Adam couldn't keep his calm composure. His eyes bucked a little bit and he snatched the book right out of my hands. Rude much! "What does it mean?"

"It's obvious." How many theories could they have actually come up with? He and Roxy simply didn't want to accept it. "We're twins, and Roxy's soul got put into my body and she's been the bane of my existence ever since."

He looked at me and then back at the picture and then that process repeated a couple of times. He felt so conflicted, but I felt the revelation like brightness. He knew the truth, yet he still asked dumb questions. "Why do you think this is your body?"

"It makes sense, doesn't it? That's why I'm the strongest and why I remember everything." I watched him furrow his cute brows as he dug deep and hard into his brain. He was trying to find some kind of rebuttal. He wanted to figure out something so he could have accused me of lying, but I knew even Roxy figured out that our body was really mine. It made too much sense.

"So, what does your moral compass say about that?" They treated me as if I was some kind of cancer, but it was Roxy who was ruining my life. It wasn't fair to me. "Don't you think we should eradicate the virus now?"

I loved the hurt in his eyes. It was delicious! He didn't have a single thing to say about Roxy, the body snatcher. What could he say? What could Roxy say? It didn't matter if I were a terrible person who would kill a human at the drop of a hat. I still had a right to my own body.

Adam threw the book down on the closest piece of furniture. "Are you an alien?"

"Foreign?"

"From outer space, you smart aleck." Testy, testy!

I smirked. "No. I was born on earth, but my people are from another dimension."

He pretended not to be impressed, but he totally was. "And how did you crossover?"

"Duh! We opened a portal."

"And why are you here?"

"Well, my home isn't like this dimension. You guys have worlds spanning across the infinite and ever expanding universe—more of it than you could ever explore. We only have our world. Our people aren't weak like earthlings, we don't have wars, and we don't murder each other. It's a very peaceful and civilized place, but that also means that we have an exceptionally low mortality rate. Our scientists predicted that, in a short ten thousand years, we'll be terribly overpopulated."

"That's why you came to earth?" Adam asked.

"We observed it at first. We wanted to know what kind of place it was before we started expanding. We were horrified at what we discovered." I remembered the first time Roxy learned about war in school. She literally started crying. She was such a baby, but even I thought it was terrible. "There was so much hatred in the world and over such trivial matters. We couldn't live peacefully among you humans. You're afraid of everything that's not like you and you live to destroy it. Your governments would only ally themselves so they could kill us and then they'd get right back to killing each other as soon as we were all hunted down, examined, and slaughtered."

"Why don't you crossover on earth and then go to another planet?"

"For the same reason your people haven't. We don't have the means."

"So you sought to conquer us instead?"

"Not quite. That's not exactly our style, but the more we watched, the more we started to debate that you all didn't deserve your planet and your magnificent possibilities." I mean humans really were disgusting creatures. They couldn't even keep their streets or their water clean. "We could have easily destroyed all of you, but some of us felt that wasn't right. Humans deserved a chance to prove themselves."

I smiled and threw my hands up in the air. "That's where I came in."

"You?" I was glad I could amuse him so.

"Yep. My mother—the queen—decided that she would give birth to a child who could bring out the true nature in human beings." I was quite proud of my real heritage. Screw Mommy and Daddy. Roxy could have their filthy memories if she wanted, but I was glad they were dead. My real mother would have never treated me in such a way. I was far too important to her. "By her design, humans could either live in harmony, or

249

they would destroy themselves. I would be the one to determine whether or not they would be worthy to continue on."

"And what about Roxy?"

"Oh, she was a happy accident. You see, our mother lived among the humans. She grew to care for them, so she thought humanity deserved a handicap. Roxy and I were created at the same time, to test and redeem humanity."

The entire time I was explaining, I could feel Adam slowly simmering on the inside. Finally, he boiled over. "How can you be such a hypocrite? You kill and hurt just as easily as any human would, even more so."

I figured my mother wouldn't be pleased with some of my impulsive behavior, but that couldn't be blamed on me. "That's one of the tricky bits of being half human. My mother mated with an incredibly kind human male. He's the sole reason why Roxy was born." I couldn't help that I was a little trigger happy. It was a side effect that couldn't be helped. Even Rider and his sons were corrupted after living among them for so long.

"So how can you despise humanity if you're a part of them?"

"Besides the fact that the humans who called me 'daughter' locked me up every night and left me to sleep in my own excretions? Gee, let me think!" I hoped he enjoyed drowning in my pool of sarcasm. My people would never treat their own so cruelly, especially not their children. "My biological father was murdered by a human. He was gunned down because he wanted my father's watch, which was a treasured gift from my mother."

Adam felt sorry for me, but he wasn't going to tell me that. That was fine. I didn't know the man anyway. His pity would have done nothing for me.

"My mother was struck with such grief that she could hardly give birth to us. I was the first born and I came out perfectly healthy. Roxy wasn't so lucky. Our powers didn't work as babies, so her healing factor couldn't help her. Her tiny, weak body was failing her. Maybe it was because my mother finally decided to give up on humanity. Maybe it was because Roxy was always doomed to fail. I don't know for sure, but my mother died the moment Roxy was born. The indestructible and all-powerful queen died from a broken heart." I laughed. "Isn't that ridiculous?"

Adam didn't comment, but his opinion didn't matter on the subject anyway. The queen of an extraordinarily powerful people died because she got attached to a human. Roxy was going to lose to me because she was attached to Adam. I wouldn't make such an unbelievably stupid mistake. After Adam outlived his usefulness, I planned on carving my name on his throat.

"A trusted friend of my mother believed in her vision of an equal chance for humanity. He took Roxy's soul and put it in my healthy body." Sometimes I just wanted to leave the little twit a message saying that she wasn't real, but she would have never believed me. Sure, she would have freaked out at first, but Mommy and Daddy would have made up a fancy lie to bribe her from the truth. She was a disease, yet she thought that of me. I hoped that when Adam told her the truth, she would be looking in a mirror so I could see her face.

"Mother's friend also made a series of different incantations to bind our powers and smuggled us away to some good people looking for redemption. He didn't tell them everything. He has that oath to remain neutral and all." Rider told me everything about Mommy and Daddy, but I didn't want to believe they were bad people who used to be drug addicts. You'd think people like them would learn to forgive mistakes.

"I had one bad dream when I was asleep in a car with my parents and caused an accident. But that's what it was: an accident!" A minivan got flipped over and a little kid ended up dying. I never meant to hurt that little boy, and I had enough grief over it anyway. Mommy tried to tell me that it wasn't my fault, but it was hard with Daddy whispering twisted words in her ear. "That wasn't enough, and they never treated me the same. I escaped, and Rider found me. He told me everything, but I was six. I wanted to believe that the people who tucked me in were my real parents! That's why I went home with them. They promised they would treat me better, but that was a lie!"

I still remembered how Mommy took my hand. She said we were gonna go outside and sit on the porch and watch the stars, but we had to get a pair of binoculars from the basement. Daddy was waiting for me with the shackles. I should have fought him off, but I didn't wanna hurt them. That was way back when I actually still cared about them and lived with a false hope that they still cared about me.

I cried and cried until my eyes hurt too much to continue. I couldn't sleep because I was too uncomfortable and I eventually got sick of begging for Mommy to come and save me. After a few more nights, I just started screaming to the top of my lungs until my throat was raw and my voice was raspy. Then I started to hear the television from the ceiling. It dawned on me that they would ignore my pain forever. After that, I let go.

I smirked and struck a sexy pose for Adam. "From then on, I started to accept it. When you're cast as the villain, you might as well play the part as brilliantly as you can."

Adam did hate me. I could clearly feel that, but there was some pity mixed in there and it did make me feel a little sick. I would have much rather had him feel contempt for ripping Daddy's heart in pieces with metal bullets. He always took his time while trying to understand everything. He was picking apart every line of what I said, so he could make a fair assessment. Most people wouldn't do that. Most people judge and never change their minds once a decision is made. "Lyla, what does all this have to do with me?"

252

I walked over to my dear Adam with my hips swaying back and forth and placed my hands on his strong, broad shoulders. "You're the chosen one who will set me free."

He cocked his brow. "How do you think that will happen?"

"You're going to choose me over her right now."

"Never." He responded so quickly, it was as if he knew what I was going to say before I even spoke it. "I love Roxy. I despise you. That won't change. Ever."

I sighed and shook my head. "That's just a technical error." He had absolutely no idea about anything, especially when it came to women.

I let go of Adam and started looking around the room. I picked up little knickknacks and such. There were little random statues of sweet looking people with rosy cheeks and clothes stylized like they were all named Hansel or Gretel. Porter had no attractive pictures of himself, no photos of friends, and the most artistic thing he had in his home was a painting of a bowl of fruit. Porter was so bland it was hard not to want to kill someone just to keep myself from snoozing.

I looked back at Adam, who was being tortured by my dramatic pause. That was planned, of course. "I hate having Roxy inside of me. There are few upsides. She always heals me." I smirked. "She brought you to me, but I'm sure we would have crossed paths anyway. Destiny and all that stuff. But the biggest upside is that it's temporary."

I loved watching his eyebrows raise the tiniest bit, his mouth widening just a smidgen, yet the inside of him was preparing to panic if my information called for it.

"Roxy and I were born for one purpose. Roxy failed because she was weak, but someone took mercy on her. However, as soon as she fulfills her obligation, she will fade into nothing."

Then it was time for one of my favorite moments. He became so shocked and terrified that when he asked the question, I knew that deep down, his guess was probably correct. "What do you mean?"

"It means that there's this ritual that one of us is gonna do as soon as that portal is open. We'll grab the Staff of Power, and it'll amplify our abilities enough to let us reach the entire world. Roxy could cause peace on earth or I could unleash humanity on itself. Once she fails in stopping me, or if she actually succeeds, she goes bye-bye!" I waved goodbye for him with a smile on my face from the pure thought of being alone in my own body. "Her duty is fulfilled, and I'm free. It's actually a win-win situation for me."

Oh, Adam! I loved how distraught he was. He was usually so calm and reserved when it came to his emotions, but he was so scared and concerned over his dear Roxy. He covered his mouth with his hands and began breathing into them. He should have covered his eyes so I wouldn't have been able to see how rattled he actually was. It was fascinating watching him squirm like the filthy insect I knew he truly was. Roxy was going to die, and there was nothing he could do in order to stop it. He felt worthless, insecure, and he was a man without a way out. That was quite the tasty appetizer indeed.

Then suddenly, I had a terrible taste in my mouth. It was sweet, innocent, and oh so desperate. He had the smallest, tiniest, most insignificant bit of hope, and it steadily grew into an audible thought. "What if you two don't perform the ritual?"

"Come again?" I needed him to repeat it, because it was too crazy to be a real question in the first place.

"Just don't do it." He smiled, even laughed as if it were a clear and plausible solution. "Nothing changes."

"No!" Out of all the most brain-dead things I had heard in my life that was probably the one that topped them all. "We both hate being a part of each other. It's hell." I knew he was ignorant in the art of complete and total hell, but it was still painfully idiotic for him to even suggest it. He might as well have tried to catch a flight by jumping in front of a train, hoping that the impact would send him into the plane's trajectory, because that was dumb! "Not even she would agree to this."

"But she doesn't know that she'll disappear. I'm sure she'd rather come to some kind of agreement than die." The dumbest thing about it was that somewhere in his calculations, he made the assumption that I cared about Roxy enough to spare her life when she was stealing mine!

But that wasn't the most puzzling thing. I wasn't even really that angry at him when I had the thought. "So, you would deal with me for half of the rest of our life just to have her for the other half?"

Then he started to look so pitiful. He probably wasn't going to cry, but he certainly was on the way to doing something of the sort. His lip quivered, and he sounded so pathetic that I didn't know what to do with him anymore. "I can't lose her."

I didn't understand him. Any other human being in his shoes would have taken their freedom and ran with it. If Roxy failed, there was a very high chance that humanity would be destroyed, but at least he'd be rid of me. He said he hated me. He should have wanted me gone. If Roxy was gone, there was no obligation to me. He could finally be free!

But I could understand him loving her and wanting her to survive, but he always made it seem as if I was so unbearable to be around. He led me to believe that he was tolerating me until he somehow found a way to stop me. He honestly thought Roxy was worth putting himself through so much misery. I wasn't going to treat Adam kindly. He must have known how lousy his decision was, yet he cared about Roxy so much to endure someone that he despised.

"No." He might have been crazy enough to give up his entire future for some chick, but he had another thing coming if he thought I was that brain-dead. He was being borderline offensive. "I was born to do this. I have to."

"No." He walked over to me, grabbed my arms, and shook me. "You're Lyla! You only do what you want." It was nice of him to try reverse psychology on me, but it was easy to see through such a thing.

I forcibly removed his hands off of me. "I want to do what I was born to do, and I want to get rid of Roxy by any means necessary." I laughed. "Besides, what kind of life would you have with her? She has to be pure to perform the ritual. If she can't perform it, she's gone. You two have sex and *poof!*"

"So, wait…" I was laughing at the confused look on his face. What didn't a man want more than sex? I bet his whole brain started recalibrating. He was probably deciding to help me just so he wouldn't have to deal with Roxy's whining after he dumped her for not being able to put out. "…You think I'm about to have sex with you to make her disappear?"

"Absolutely!"

He surprisingly looked offended. "Why would I do that?"

I smirked and wrapped my arms around his neck. "Because, I'm about to seduce you."

Adam grabbed my hands and threw my arms away from him. "I don't want to do this!"

I wasn't really surprised…Only a little bit, but I got it. Adam was playing hard to get. He was a marvelous boyfriend, so it was necessary. But it was only a formality. "Don't tell me that you're not attracted to me. I know you'd be lying." I always felt passion between the two of us. When he wasn't terrified of dying or having my powers used on him, he thought of me in naughty ways. I couldn't read his thoughts, but I could feel his lust rising like a burning sensation inside of me. That moment was no exception. He couldn't fight physical attraction. The need to mate was written within his DNA, and he couldn't fight his genetics.

"You expect me to sleep with you and kill my girlfriend?"

I ignored his yammering and proceeded to rip of his shirt with my mind. I certainly did enjoy doing it, even though the horrified look on Adam's face wasn't exactly attractive. It was the geekiest he had ever looked. I wasn't turned off, seeing that I was more interested in his flawless body. "You need someone that can actually please you. She's just a silly child, and that won't ever change."

I reached out to touch his chiseled abs of stone, but he grabbed my hand and squeezed it tight. "No! That is not gonna happen." He was actually serious. Even though I could feel his attraction to me just as real as I could feel his increased pulse as our hands touched, I felt his will building up like a solid, unbreakable wall growing higher and higher with no way to infiltrate it.

It angered me and I threw his back into the wall, forcing his arms and legs still. Who was he to deny me of anything that I wanted? He was only a pitiful human, and I was a princess of a world far greater than earth. "I can make you!"

He was a man. He couldn't have possibly enjoyed having all of his pride ripped from his body. He was pouting his tensed mouth and beaming his beautiful, hateful eyes at me. He wasn't seriously struggling to break free. He must have come to realize that I always got what I wanted. "Then you'll have to make me!" Adam said.

I gave away my poker face, because I know my eyes bucked. He obviously didn't want me to take advantage of him. It would have been better for his self-esteem to just take me like a man. How could I have been such a forbidden fruit that he didn't want me? Shouldn't that have made me sexier?

I couldn't even pretend. "No! That'll be weird." I let him go. I couldn't do anything to him. It was far too awkward. He didn't even bother to run from me, because he knew I wouldn't go through with making him do it. I just couldn't.

"Just…" It was more than an issue of wanting to get rid of Roxy, wanting to fulfill my destiny, and genuinely wanting to fulfill my naughty desires that I had for Adam. My own pride was being tarnished. "Why won't you have sex with me?" He wanted to live a life with Roxy, even though she blushed and covered her eyes in health class during sex education and asked to leave the room while they were going through the male anatomy diagram, yet he couldn't screw me? I knew we looked the same, but I was the hotter one. I was the one with the sexy personality. Roxy didn't even know how to talk seductively. She couldn't speak without raising our voice an octave higher. It didn't make any sense. "You're a guy and—"

"Listen to me very carefully." He grabbed me and looked me straight in the eye. "I love Roxy, and that means something. You can feel emotions, Lyla. You should know how much I care about her."

I sort of had an idea. I mean, I was there the first time he held our—or rather *my*—hand. It was in the eighth grade and Roxy was going to slip on some ice. He grabbed it, and my heart started racing. Then, he smiled at me for the first time. Of course I was there for the first "I love you", and the first kiss, and every kiss since then. That was truly yummy. I experienced those things right along with Roxy, so I had just about enough assurance as any other human girl. I could feel emotions, but I never tried to feel love. I didn't like how it made me feel. It was nauseating. Besides, I didn't believe in such a thing. Love meant redemption, and there was no redemption for humanity. In a world where a mother could hurt her own child, there was no justice and no reason why humanity should be saved. If a father could cause his own child harm, there was no peace. They all deserved to die. Love was something writers made up to sell fairytales to little children who grew up into silly women with stupid romantic notions, and expected their boyfriends to buy them flowers and chocolates on Valentine's Day, because some advertising company said that they should.

Adam didn't know what he was saying. I thought he was smarter than that, but apparently he wasn't. Love? Ha! It was nothing. It wasn't real. It was impossible.

But he seemed so convinced. I could sense his conviction and his sincerity, and there had to be some sort of explanation for his unbreakable will. I was curious about what he claimed that he felt. The darker emotions of a human were much more interesting, and it empowered me. It was like taking a drug that I had mastered, yet couldn't live without. I never really thought of dealing with any good ones. I never realized how useful they could be until I watched Roxy manipulate human beings like puppets. Not even I could do something like that.

Was there truly something to the goodness in humanity—if there was truly such a thing? Adam had already proven to be such an intriguing fellow. If I was going to try to feel anyone's love, it was only fitting that it would be his.

I reached inside and concentrated. It was there. It had always been, like a stone castle so gorgeous that I wanted to go inside, yet so intimidating that I never did. I was apprehensive to break through those walls, but I did remember what Roxy had done. There could be great gain in mastering all of human emotions, so I opened the door and the army came through.

I felt his passion, his kindness, and his recklessness. There was such abandonment, that I understood how he could sacrifice all that he had and who he was just to please her. There was such strength that it felt like someone had hurled a javelin through my chest and I nearly gasped. It was so immense that I didn't know how he managed to take a feeling so big and squeeze it into his flesh. I could sense him directing all of those emotions at me, yet his eyes were looking through me to someone who wasn't even watching. But just because Roxy wasn't watching, didn't mean that I didn't see. I understood him far greater than I did before. Love was real to him and he believed in it so strongly that he actually formed it into reality.

"I could never do anything to hurt her intentionally, especially not with you." Then Adam made me a promise. "You'll literally have to kill me."

I laughed out of disbelief. "Sex or death and you choose death?"

"Without hesitation." It was hard not to be offended by that, even after feeling his so-called "love". He was dead set on never touching me.

I felt like I was going to throw up. I knew it would make me sick to my stomach. Even my chest hurt. "But you're my Chosen. That's supposed to mean something! You're supposed to set me free from her."

"No!" He became a bit frustrated. "If I have to be a eunuch for the rest of my life just so we can be together, I'll do it."

"That's impossible!" I yelled.

"As long as I love her, it's possible."

I wanted to find some sort of rebuttal, but I knew he was serious. He really could elude me forever for her. That's how powerful his love for Roxy was. I didn't think she deserved it, but whatever. "Fine! I'll go find someone else. I don't need you. There are tons of guys who would love to be my first and you can't stop me."

He was stunned and then incredibly sad. "No, I can't." That was more like it! I enjoyed watching him squeal in his thoughts, but it wasn't quite as satisfying as usual. "But if the sun rises and if Roxy doesn't rise along with it, I'm gone."

I tried my best not to have a reaction, but I definitely had one internally. I didn't want Adam to leave. It's not like he was all the way human anymore and I found him to be interesting. He was disposable before, but I had a right to change my mind. I wanted him to stay with me.

But I couldn't let him know that. "Is that supposed to scare me?"

Then he narrowed his eyes in on me just in the slightest way that made me think he had some kind of trick up his sleeve. "Have a pleasant evening, Lyla."

He didn't have to say that. He didn't mean it. He didn't want me to find anyone and be happy at all. I couldn't stand him! "Fine."

I waited for him to say something else, but he turned away from me and started heading for the kitchen. He didn't say one single thing to me. He should have begged me not to go out and kill the supposed love of his life. That's what he should have done! Better yet, he should have had the decency to do it himself instead of letting some stranger handle his love's body. He wasn't a man. He was only a mouse. No. He was worse than a mouse. He was an ameba. He was an insignificant ameba who was about to lose the only person he had in his life because he was an idiot too prideful to stop me from going out the front door.

Chapter Thirteen

Porter had a set of keys attached to a magnet on the bottom of his car. I suppose he felt safe enough in his sickeningly quiet neighborhood to trust that no one would steal—but alas—there was me. Unfortunately, I still didn't know how to drive, and I didn't want to take any chances of wrecking the car, since I wouldn't have Roxy to heal me up in the morning.

Luckily for me, Porter had a bicycle in the backyard, and I did thankfully know how to ride a bike. I didn't know where I was going, and I didn't know how long I would be riding, but I just wanted to find some guy who was worthy of me. Now I didn't have a lot of time to find this special man, so I knew that I would have to settle somewhat. I wouldn't play twenty questions. I just wanted him to be mildly attractive.

Unfortunately, I was in a neighborhood with a cluster of little, cute homes. I had to ride around three miles before I could start to sense what I needed. I needed passion, lust, and rebellion. I needed a wild and free young man. I didn't want to defile myself with an older man. They'd have to be a bit of a pervert, because I very much did look like a high school girl. I didn't want a young loser. I deserved so much better than that. It really pissed me off that Adam wouldn't suck up his stupid honor for a couple of minutes. It's not as if Roxy would mean a whole lot in the great scheme of things anyway. She was a skid mark on the pages of history, and I was the entire tale.

I sensed a bunch of ravenous feelings and began to follow the trail they left. The closer I got, the more mixed it was with feelings of desperation, depression, and destitution. It was a collection of different people who felt very hollow. I enjoyed feeling humans so distraught, but it wasn't exactly what I wanted to feel before losing my virginity. I wanted to feel that confidence and inner strength that made Adam so freaking attractive. I didn't want someone who was slumming through life, wandering soullessly through an irrelevant existence. I wanted to be with someone that mattered.

I realized why I was sensing those certain emotions with the ravenous one once I got to my destination. I parked my dinky bike next to a beautiful motorcycle and walked straight into a bar. I got a couple of looks. It was a little bar filled with older men who looked like they escaped from their nagging wives and wanted to piss their lives away, because they simply didn't have any reason to live. There were also the middle aged wenches who should have realized they were too old to live without a shred of dignity. To all of them, I probably looked like a fourteen-year-old. But there were some younger guys who could gage ages in years instead of increments of twenty.

The youngest one I saw was the ravenous one that I sensed. He was flirting with a girl at the bar, and she slapped him hard in the face not even ten seconds after I first laid my eyes on him. He was a pervert. There wasn't much in him besides lust. I suppose he had a great sadness within him, but it was so far buried under the need to be a whore that I don't think he realized it was there.

Oh well. At least he was sexy. He was a little taller than six feet, had dark hair and dark eyes. He wasn't as physically fit as Adam, but he wasn't fat or anything. I just didn't think there would be abs of steel when I ripped off his shirt, and that let me down a little bit.

He was acceptable enough, and the obvious best choice I had since Adam rejected me. I walked over to the man, who was enjoying watching the woman he had offended walking away by staring intently at her rear. He was quite the devil.

I prepared myself for seduction and leaned on the bar. "Don't worry about her."

He turned around and smirked at first, but then there was a slight pause. "Hi there."

"Aren't you gonna offer to buy me a drink?"

He smirked and leaned on the bar lazily while staring me down creepily. "And what would I get in return?"

"Well, nothing since I'm not actually old enough to drink." I only mentioned it to see how much he would panic on his face. I wasn't surprised that he wasn't that appalled. "Don't worry. I'm legally old enough to consent to having sex with you."

He laughed, probably because he was already enjoying my company so much. "Is that so?"

"Yes. Are you ready?"

He cocked his sexy, full brow. "To?"

"To consent." I placed my hand on his chest. I was right about him not being as built as Adam, but there was hardness there. At least he worked out a little bit.

"You don't need to know my name or anything?" He wasn't asking to slow our process; he merely wanted to know if I were going to back out or not.

"No, but I know you're not the type to need mine, but I'll give you some information anyway. I don't have any diseases because I'm a virgin."

That made him laugh. "And you want to lose your virginity to a stranger?" I could sense the lust within him intensifying. He wanted to rip my clothes off right then and there. He very well could have been a pedophile by the way he wanted me. It wasn't because I was young. He was excited to strip me away from my innocence. It was a thrill for him— a game for a pure hunter. Then there was the fact that he was illuminating so much attraction from himself toward me. He didn't give the shapely older woman as much attention as he had given to me, and though I knew I could be sexy, I still looked like a little girl.

It didn't matter to me what he did in his private life, especially since he was about to become the savior and the destroyer of mankind. "This world is a nightmare—not a fairytale. There's no point in saving myself for a prince that doesn't exist."

"So into the dungeon with the scoundrel you go?" He brushed some hair out of my face and caressed my cheek. He had uncommonly soft hands for a man, yet there wasn't anything gentle in that moment. He was sleazy and disgusting and maybe I would have liked that before, but I had changed. My heart should have been racing and my blood pumping with incredible lust, but my heart slowed down and I felt cold as my heart fell into my stomach.

"I'm used to the dungeon."

He left a hundred dollar bill on the bar and signaled me to follow him. That was a good sign. Hopefully he was taking me somewhere up to my true standards, so I could destroy humanity in class. He had a silver new Cadillac, and I was becoming pleasantly more pleased with him by the second. He even opened up the passenger door for me like a gentleman.

I was comfortable sitting in those leather seats. That's how I should have been traveling since I began my journey with Adam. He had a fantastic car, but he got rid of it in order to protect himself and Roxy. He was such an imbecile for always protecting her and sacrificing everything.

I understood that he loved her, but you had to be smart about it. He couldn't have a life with her. It was never possible.

My stranger entered on the driver's side, and I realized that I was nervous. I never thought I would be, but it actually was a bigger deal than I calculated. "So, what is your name?"

He wouldn't answer. He bombarded me as soon as he closed the door, and his slimly tongue was shoved in my mouth, and I didn't know what to do. I had actually never kissed someone before and the only man who had kissed my body was Adam. I figured I could do an excellent job, but I was caught totally off guard.

"Is something wrong?"

I wiped the slobber off of my mouth. "I wanted to know your name."

"This isn't gonna turn into a thing, is it?" He started whining like a little brat. "I just want to have sex and leave it at that. You're not gonna stalk me, are you?"

"No!" I was offended by his arrogance to presume such a thing. "I have no interest in you."

"Good. You already told me that you didn't need to know my name. I'll hold you to that."

He started lunging for me again, so I pressed myself into the seat as much as I could. I needed a moment to think and to breathe. "You wanna do it in here?"

"You don't need to come to my house." I knew he was hiding something from me, but it shouldn't have mattered.

I was being ridiculous. I was about to complete my goals and rid myself of Roxy forever. She was about to be wiped out of existence, and I'd have my body all to myself. That was enough incentive to have sex with the guy. Besides, I didn't need to be a virgin, especially if sex was so amazing. "You're right. We can do it right here, right now."

He smirked disgustingly. "Good."

Then he started kissing me, and I kissed him back. I knew I could keep up with him, but something was weird. His hands explored my body, and I followed. He kissed me on my neck and all over my face, but it didn't tickle and there was no burning sensation. There was no wild passion as I imagined my first time would be. He was only supposed to be my piece of meat, but I didn't appreciate being tasted and savored like I was one myself. I tried to get into it. I tried feeling his inferior body and tasting his less luscious lips, but there was no spark. I wasn't the least bit interested.

"Wait!" I pushed him away from me, and he was still for a couple of seconds, but I could still feel him pulling at me, and that disgusted me all the more. "I can't do this."

"What?" His anger outweighed his lust. He was furious. "You can't just—"

"I did, and I am." I opened the door and started walking away as fast as I could, but he did the same and began to follow me. "Just let it go," I warned.

"No!" He caught up with me and grabbed my arm and squeezed it enough to make it hurt. "You can't just tease a guy and get out of it."

I agreed that I thought it was unfair. I wasn't a tease, but it just didn't feel right. Besides, he lost all of his chances when he thought he could control me. "Let me go." That time, it was a genuine threat.

He squeezed my hand tighter and started to pull me back toward his car. That was the last straw. I looked at his index finger tightly gripped around my arm with the rest of them. A guy like him probably used his hands to feel up on women and only God knows what every day, so I bent it back until I heard his bone snap. He let go of me and dropped to his knees and started screaming.

I looked at my discolored skin and knew that I had a bruise coming. I was lucky he didn't break my arm. For that, I broke another finger and another until his screams brought a pleased smile on my face, which happened around eight fingers. He started rolling on the ground, crying like a baby. He could have at least taken it like a man!

"Don't take this too personal," I told him. "Everyone who defies me has to pay a price. I don't particularly care if you're a disgusting whore, but I deserve respect!"

Then in that moment while I was watching the little man beg and plead for his life with words I didn't care to listen to, I realized how right I was. Adam needed to stop fooling around because I deserved him. He belonged to me. He chose to stay by my side, not just Roxy's. He needed to get over himself and realize that he wanted to be with me.

With that revelation, I was at peace again. The only thing left was the crying and broken man lying on the ground in the parking lot. I really wasn't in the mood to enjoy his screams anymore. I had things to do, so I snapped his neck and put him out of his misery. It was a show of good faith and the least I could do after teasing him so.

I got on my bike and rode back over to Porter's house with a song in my heart and whistling lips. I just knew that when I got back home, I would be able to convince Adam that I was the one he wanted to be with.

Sure enough, he had left the light on for me. I could see him from the window in the kitchen. He was bustling about over something, probably anxious about seeing me again. He was so tense and worried that I figured he must have been thinking about me with another man ever since I left. There was no reason for Adam to be jealous. I was about to make all of his desires come to life.

I threw the bike on the lawn and ran back inside and to the kitchen. There were a couple of vegetables and condiments laid out on the counter and pans in the sink. Adam was in the midst of biting into a very delicious looking chicken submarine sandwich when I stepped in. He looked surprised to see me, yet still a little unfazed.

I didn't say anything. I wanted him to say something. I wasn't sure if I was accidently allowing myself to feel love again, but maybe I was. I kind of had a churning feeling in my stomach, and it was kind of hard to think and even breathe. Only love usually made me that sick.

He finished chewing his first bite and sat his sandwich down on the plate. He wiped his mouth with a napkin and took some time to think or whatever. "I didn't think you'd be back so soon."

"I didn't have sex with anyone!" I didn't mean to blurt it out the way that I did. I was just really fidgety for some reason.

He smiled and laughed relieved. "That's great." The poor dear was worried that he wouldn't be my first. He must have realized while I was gone how much he missed me. He would have felt like the world's biggest fool if he missed out on the opportunity to be with me. It's not every day that a girl like me would condescend themselves to be with a human. He was very lucky indeed.

I waited for him to pour out his heart and apologize to me for making it seem like he loved Roxy more than he worshiped me. I understood he was confused. That's why I wasn't going to kill him. He deserved the chance to set things right.

I waited, and I waited, but there was an extremely nervous and awkward energy between the two of us. He folded his arms and stared at me as he was waiting for me to say something, and then his muscles bulged even more. "You didn't find a shirt?"

"I figured you'd just rip it off again."

"You're right about that…" I smiled and laughed like…Like I was Roxy or something! It was nerdy and completely not me. I didn't understand what was happening to me. Feeling his emotions toward me must have been making me go crazy.

269

Even he was concerned and confused with how antsy I was. He should have just come out and said what was on his mind, but I couldn't blame him. He was probably nervous. It was the biggest honor ever.

"I want to have sex with you." There! I had said it. I just blurted it out and waited for him to run into my arms.

He stared at me. He was probably shocked from the glory and the honor of it all. "That is not gonna happen."

My mouth dropped. "Why?"

"I told you why." He rejected me. Again! He was ignoring me too. He started eating his sandwich like I wasn't a big deal. "If you really wanted to do this, then you would have found someone else."

I was angry and I threw the plate against the wall, shattering it to pieces and spilling his precious sandwich all over the floor. Adam was about to start yelling, but he stopped himself and held it in. I was glad I made him angry. He deserved the worst kind of pain for rejecting me.

"But no one else is good enough!" That's the only reason why I didn't kill Adam. I had spent the past couple days with him, but really, I had spent years with him. I had seen how confident he was. He wouldn't back down from a challenge, even if it were impossible odds. I liked trying to corrupt him, but I liked how much he fought against me. It was like a game of cat and mouse, and I enjoyed it. No one else had ever stood up to me. Everyone else was boring. He was the only true exciting thing in my life. "You're the only one worthy of me."

"What?" Adam yelled in disbelief. "Out of all the guys in the world, I'm the best one?"

"The best one for me, yes."

"Wait..." He was being such an idiot. I don't know why that confused Adam so much. It was a very clear concept to grasp since I explained it so plainly. There was no one else besides Adam. There would never be anyone else besides Adam. It wasn't rocket science. I wanted him, and he should have appreciated that fact, and I knew that he secretly was wildly in love with me.

But for some reason, he took a step back and raised his finger up in the air for me to stop talking, while he wandered through his muddled brain. "Are you..." He laughed, in an oddly attractive snort kind of way. "...Are you in love with me?"

I gasped. "No!" How dare he say such a thing to me? "Of course not." Why, would I ever love someone like him? I would never love anyone!

Adam was afraid to approach me, but he gulped and gathered his courage enough to do so. He stepped forward until we were only a couple of inches apart and he beamed his blue eyes into mine and tried to search out my emotions, as if he had the special ability. "Oh no..."

"What?" He couldn't read my emotions. It was impossible, and I didn't have any emotions to read anyway. I was lusting after Adam, and that was all. I needed him, because he was the means to an annoying end. There was nothing to read!

Adam stepped away horrified. "You are!" But he was wrong.

"No. I'm not in love with you." He was a filthy, dirty, disgusting human. Mommy and Daddy tried to trick me. They tried to make me think that they cared about me, but they didn't. I wouldn't be tricked again, and I wouldn't be a hypocrite and pretend that it was possible to actually love someone myself. Humans were incapable of such a thing, and I was sadly half human. I wasn't stupid enough to lie to myself. "Don't insult me."

"How could this happen?" He wasn't even asking me. He had snapped and started talking to himself, a clear sign to show that he didn't know what the heck he was talking about. "Well, I guess you were there with Roxy while we were falling in love, but this..."

271

"I'm not in love with you!" I yelled. He was making me so infuriated.

He laughed hysterically and pointed his finger in my face. "Oh, yes you are!"

"No!" I had tears welling up in my eyes, and I hated it. I didn't want him to think he was right, but I couldn't help myself. I was getting too upset.

Then he spoke to me condescendingly, as if I were a child. "You are in love with me, Lyla. That's why you don't want to have sex with anyone else and that's why you won't kill me." Then he smirked. "And that's why you won't use your powers on me, and that's why you're not gonna win."

He turned away from me and started laughing as a tremendous weight had been released from his shoulders, but it felt like a giant slap in the face to me. He was wrong about me. I was not in love with him, and I only kept him alive to amuse myself. There was no other reason than that. And if he thought I was going to lose to Roxy and Team Good so I could live in a world where everyone talked about bubbles, unicorns, and rainbows all day long, he had another thing coming. His supposed love for Roxy made me want to vomit. I would not suffer with that taste for the rest of my life!

And while he was rejoicing in his supposedly sealed victory, I remembered that my butterfly knife was securely resting in the back pocket of his tight butt. I didn't need it to put him out of his misery, but it only seemed appropriate after all we had been through. If I did love anything in life, it was one thing. I absolutely loved to set people free, and Adam didn't deserve to be caught up in my war with Roxy. It was messy business. It was time to release him.

The knife came into my hands, and it felt like an extension of my body. My dear friend and I had been on an incredible journey together, and there was just one more fool to kill before everything came to a close.

I flicked my wrist to open it and stabbed Adam in the back while he was still laughing to himself. He grunted in pain, and I knew that one stab wouldn't be enough to kill him. I had to make it good and make it hurt. I stabbed him again and again and again before he hollered and turned around to stop me, but I wouldn't let him touch me. I restrained his body and continued stabbing him in his gut until my hands were coated in his blood. Adam tried not to yell out in pain, and he did an exceptional job until I twisted the knife inside of him. I loved that look on his face. He was so confused. He thought his thinking was flawless. He actually believed that I would ever love such a creature. What a fool!

I did have to stare into those beautifully blue eyes. I waited for them to burn with that tasty hatred that I craved so much, but I didn't see it. He furrowed his brows and looked pitiful, sad, and still so conflicted. "Why?"

"Because, I don't love you." I pulled my knife from his mangled body and threw it over me and through the wall, missing the doorway on purpose. I wanted him to enjoy his death and the only way to do it was to feel every single second of it.

I looked at my pretty knife. Once again, it had done me proud.

I began strutting over to my latest victim. I took a moment to look at the exploded wall, still crumbling apart from having Adam's big body tossed through it. It made me giggle thinking about how much pain he must have been in. It's what he deserved for defiling my name with accusations of love toward him. Who did he think he was anyway?

He should have been unconscious or dead already, but he did still have some inhuman powers within him. Still, it wasn't enough to keep him from dying. He struggled to get up, but he barely had the strength to raise his hands a couple of inches off the ground. His legs could only twitch a little bit, and when he tried to speak, blood began to ooze from his mouth. His body had crashed uncomfortably on the coffee table. He probably had glass and a bunch of Porters cute knickknacks stuck in his back. What a terrible way to die...

It was so precious!

His blood was beginning to soak into the carpet, and I took off my shoes in respect for the dying. I also wanted to feel the carpet squish in between my toes. It wouldn't be long before he was gone, so I leaned down beside him and stroked his face. If he still had his hair, I would have run my fingers through it, but I sort of liked his shaven head with only a little fuzz on top. It made him look so much harder and so much more attractive.

"Oh, Adam. You had to die a fool, didn't you?"

I could see that his eyes were beginning to dim with life passing from them each second. He couldn't hold on with blood pouring out through all those holes in him and sunrise was still hours away. Roxy couldn't save him, and he very well wasn't immortal. He was going to die.

He was going to die. "No..." I had made a mistake. I started feeling all of these terrible things I hadn't felt in such a long time. The last time I felt that way was when I found out about that little boy in the car accident. My chest ached, and I couldn't breathe. Was I really feeling guilty about what I had done to Adam? How was that possible? Didn't he deserve to die?

Then why was I crying uncontrollably? Why was I shaking? "Please, don't die!" Why did I bother to ask him that? He couldn't do anything about it. "I didn't mean it. Just don't die. Please!"

I had to think of something. I couldn't let him leave me. The thought was suddenly unbearable. Who would take care of me when I turned into Roxy? Who would stare into my eyes with such unrestrained heroism that literally sent chills down my spine? Who would amuse me? Who would hold me and kiss me? Who could I feel those weird feelings for?

"No..." Crap! I think I might have possibly—at least a little bit—been in love with him. I didn't know what to do about it. I had never been in love before. I didn't want to be in love! It felt so terrible. I wanted to throw up all over the place. Maybe it would have been better just to let Adam die, but I couldn't stand the thought of what the next few minutes of my life would be like without him. Then Roxy would cry a lot, and I'd have to watch that, and we'd both be a mess. I just didn't wanna deal with that.

Adam's eyes started to roll into the back of his head, and I freaked out. "No!" I tried slapping his face, but his eyelids only fluttered, but he still lost consciousness.

"Porter!" No. He couldn't do anything. He was too busy making that stupid portal that would have been ready for Roxy to use if I didn't somehow find a way to make Adam wake up, forgive me, and help me destroy her by having sex with me.

I couldn't save him! I didn't know how. I didn't have the power. Only one person did. "Roxy!" I didn't know what I was doing or what I was expecting to happen, but I needed her. I needed her to save Adam or...I don't know. I just couldn't bear the thought of living a life that he wasn't a part of. "Roxy, please! Save Adam!"

Chapter Fourteen

Everything had changed. I usually felt myself come back, almost as if I were waiting at a train station that I couldn't quite remember being at. I didn't understand why, but it was almost like a hand had reached for me and pulled me back to where I belonged. The world felt different and something was wrong. My face was stained with tears with fresh ones still pouring from my eyes. My arm hurt, but that quickly faded away. Then my hands felt wet, yet they were warm. I couldn't yet process anything in front of my eyes, but in my heart, I knew everything was falling apart.

My eyes began tearing up as if I already knew and I began to scream. "Adam!" My hands were covered in his blood. My clothes had his blood splattered all over them. It was on my feet and all over the floor and he had lost so much! I still had Lyla's evil knife clutched into my hands. Its blade was coated in the same blood. I let it slip out of my hands, and I started to tremble.

"Please don't leave me." I wasn't feeling anything from him, and his color was already leaving his face. He was pale, but when I touched his blood stained face, it was still warm. There was time, only seconds.

"Forgive me…" I knew he didn't want me to put my own energy in his body, but I didn't have a choice. There was nothing from within him to hold onto. There was nothing I could find to bring out of him to heal him in time, and I didn't know if I had enough courage and focus to find it.

I was beyond the point of desperation. My life was worth giving up to save him.

I closed my eyes and more tears rolled down my cheeks and onto my neck. My shaking fingers came to a halt on his bare chest that was shredded by so many stab wounds that I didn't have time to count. The blood was pouring from him even still, but I couldn't let it rattle me.

I took all that I had for Adam and focused my will. I had loved him for so long. I was more than the nice, naive, little girl who needed to be protected and watched over like a lamb. I had a lot of power in me, and I could wield it however I liked. I refused to live a life that he wasn't apart of!

I gathered it all together and pushed. I felt incredible warmth inside of my stomach. It rose up and I concentrated it through my hands, then I shot it out into his chest. He didn't budge. He didn't seem to change at all, but I collapsed on top of him.

I didn't know if I was going to live. I knew it was terrible to lay on top of Adam in his condition, but I couldn't even raise my head up. I had never felt so drained before. It was hard to breathe and every thought was a challenge. If I had truly lost Adam, I didn't have the strength to cry anymore. "Adam…" I mumbled his name and felt even more exhausted from only speaking it.

He gasped and shot right up, rolling my body over onto the floor. He got up and backed straight into the wall, heavily panting while he caught his new breath. I had fallen on some broken glass and my right arm was beginning to bleed, but I couldn't move to make myself comfortable, and I certainly didn't have enough strength to heal myself.

I watched Adam and waited for him to help me, but he must have thought I was Lyla by the way he looked at me. He was incredibly defensive, angry, and perhaps even a bit afraid. How come he didn't realize I was myself? Hadn't the sun come up?

He banged on his chest and tilted his head back to stare at the ceiling. After a couple more deep breaths, he regained his calm composure and glared at me in a way I had never quite seen before. I had seen him lose himself in a fit of rage during a fight, but not with a hatred that seemed so much a part of him. It frightened me. "Lyla..." He seethed, even though he wanted to yell her name in fury until our ears started to bleed.

"I'm not her..." I didn't even know if he could hear me.

"I won't fall for that again. It's still night!"

I didn't have the strength to cry all on my own with my head held high, or my head hanging low, but they managed to slip out fine without any force or much emotion at all. I wasn't sad. I was in pain from being stabbed continuously by the shattered glass, but the pain wasn't worse than being so weak, so that's not why I started to cry. I began to cry from all the possibilities that were suddenly presented to me. What did it mean that Lyla was gone? Was I finally free from her?

"I promise it's me."

"You stabbed me near the point of death!" He was furious. I would have been furious myself if I had the strength. I couldn't believe that she hurt him. I would never forgive her for trying to take Adam away from me and neither would he. I'm not sure what he was thinking to do while he stared at me, but maybe he thought to do what he really should of.

"I can't be Lyla," I said. "I just healed you."

He was still enraged for a couple of more seconds, but then it all evaporated into nothing but calm. But after the calm was over, he went into a full on panic. "Roxy!" He rushed toward me and picked me up in his arms. It was then that I realized how badly my arm was cut up and even worse, the fact that I wasn't healing. "What did you do?"

"Giving you some of my energy was the only way to save you."

"I didn't want you to risk your life like this!" If he weren't so worried, he probably would have been mad at me. He had just received a dose of something inhuman, and it showed through his silver eyes again.

"It's the least I could do after Lyla tried to kill you." I slowly lifted my weak head and saw how conflicted he looked. I couldn't pinpoint what those furrowed brows meant though. My powers of perception weren't working. "What's the matter?"

He sat me down on a couch and began observing my bleeding arm that still hadn't begun to heal. "I knew I wasn't safe with her. She's obviously an evil individual, but most villains have their rules. Now I see she's just crazy."

"I can stop her!" I didn't know what kind of experience he had with Lyla, but I got the sense that he trusted that she wouldn't hurt him. With that trust gone, I couldn't allow the two of them to be together again. "After the portal opens up, I know I can find a way to stop her. That staff—whatever it is—it's the key. I can feel it."

"About all that…" Whatever Adam was about to tell me, he held his tongue until my fingers managed to somehow raise and touch his kneecap, triggering his eyes to fall into mine. He then saw how badly I needed him to tell me the truth and he couldn't keep it from me. "Lyla told me everything, even what the ritual was and what will happen if you win or lose."

"And you trust her?"

His lip quivered. "I don't think she had any reason to lie about it."

Adam always appeared so strong, but I knew he was beginning to break. I don't know if my powers were beginning to come back or if I were able to read his face like a book, but he had the sort of grief you have when you're about to lose someone you love. Perhaps I recognized it from when he went to go visit his grannie. "Just tell me how bad it is."

"The staff will amplify either one of your power. You could change the entire world or she could." I could certainly understand the magnitude of the situation, but seeing that I was aware during the middle of the night, he should have been ecstatic.

"Well, the portal should be ready in the day and Lyla has apparently fled from the scene. I'm in charge." I breathed out a sigh of relief and began to smile nervously. For the first time since I geared myself up to defeat Lyla, I truly knew that I could beat her. "I'm gonna pull this off, Adam."

He glared at me in the slightest bit, and I already began to feel guilty. "The picture you didn't wanna tell me about is serious."

"Oh…" Lyla must have told him about it. She would jump at the chance to make me look bad. I wasn't trying to be devious. I was just scared. "How serious?"

"Lyla says that you're in her body. When you were a baby, your mom got sick from grief over the murder of your human father. You were dying, so a friend of your mother—the queen—placed your soul in Lyla's body."

That was a lot to swallow. The woman in that book was probably my mother, but she was gone. I was actually of some kind of royal blood, but I was still part human. My human father was gone too and apparently, he was someone who deserved to be missed. On top of all that, I had nearly died myself. I owed my life to Lyla?

It was too much! "And you actually believe her?"

Adam was surprised that I chose to remain ignorant of the fact, but he wouldn't have any of it. "You know that it makes sense."

I didn't mean to, but I became so overwhelmed by my emotions that I started to tear up. "I know that it does." It made sense why Lyla was more powerful than I was. It made sense why she would remember my life, but I wasn't entitled to remember hers. All of that time when I thought of her as an infection in my life, I was really the parasite shoved into hers. "I'm so sorry."

I couldn't help myself. I tried to fight off my tears, but I was too weak to really even wipe them from my eyes. I gave up on trying to be so strong and waited for Adam to pull me into his arms, but he stayed on his side of the couch, thinking of how cruel he had to be in order for me to know the whole truth. "That's not the end of it," he said.

I sniffed and muttered out my heavy and erotic breaths as silently as I could, so I could hear him speak things I knew I didn't want to hear. "You're both born to test humanity. Lyla pits humanity against themselves, but it's almost like a rigged race. Of course we'd lose if we all only cared to do what we wanted to do. You were the only way to make it truly safe. You were saved to keep the game fair."

"The game?" How could something as serious as the future of mankind be referred to such a thing?

"And when you finish—win or lose—you..." Adam paused in fear of losing himself to his premature grief. "You'll disappear, Roxy." A stubborn tear tried to escape from his eye, but he wiped it away quickly and began sniffing and trying to reassemble himself. "You were only saved to complete your calling. It looks like Lyla wins this time."

I was numb. I couldn't say or do anything, because there wasn't really anything to say. No matter what I did in life, I was always set up to fail. No matter how hard I fought, I was going to die and leave Adam alone to deal with Lyla. So what if I won and managed to save the world from Lyla? She would still be free. Adam would still be in danger from her and so would anyone else in her path.

Very quickly, I thought that I should ask Adam to kill me. If there were no way for me to win, it was best to make sure that Lyla couldn't either. But then I realized that I was being fearful of her and of failure. I suppose I was always afraid of those things, but I covered it up with naivety or artificial bravery. I was terrified. If I had the strength to shake from it, I would have. I probably would have run across the world until my legs fell off.

I couldn't live what little time I had left in fear of failure. My dad told me that I was going to save the world, and I believed him. Whether I would die and go to heaven or if I would slip away into an abyss of nothing, I still had a job to do. I couldn't let my parents' deaths be for nothing, and I certainly couldn't let their entire lives be lived in vain. "I'll do what I have to." My final tears slipped from my eyes, and I decided, no more. I was going to be the Amazon—not the Princess.

"I don't want you to do the ritual!" Adam yelled. "We'll run away together and live our lives in peace." He grabbed a hold of me and his eyes told me thousands of tales of how happy our lives could be. He did proclaim that I would marry him. He had so many ideas thought over countless of hours spent in his bed and dreaming of me. I knew, because I dreamt of our life together too. To have a nice, simple home and a beautiful baby resting peacefully in its room while we made love in our bedroom was more than impossible, but that was the beauty of a dream.

But it was only just a dream. Lyla would always be there.

"I might have to deal with Lyla, but at least I'll have you." He was so amazing. I thought it would be too much to ask for, yet he offered himself. "Maybe we can restrain her as your parents did. We can find a way. She might not even come back."

It was so tempting—not just the life, but him. Still, I couldn't do it. "I could literally make the world a utopia. I could make everybody so happy and giving that everyone would prosper. There wouldn't be wars. There wouldn't even be jealousy or spite. I don't know if it's right to just let that go."

"That's not your responsibility! It's not fair for you to die just to make a bunch of strangers' lives better. We have to be who we are. You're not obligated to be our savior."

"I wasn't obligated to save your grannie, but I did. Aren't you happy she survived?"

"I am but—"

"But nothing!" It was one of the hardest decisions I had ever made, but it had to be done. "I have to do what I can."

Adam became frustrated, desperate, and he yelled at me, "You're not God, Roxy!"

Though he appeared angry at me, I smiled. I knew he was only holding on so tight in fear of reality when he had to let me go. "I thought you didn't believe in God."

For some reason, he smiled also. "Well, you're quite the miracle, Roxanne Harris. You make me believe in the extraordinary."

I was finally able to find enough strength to wrap my arms around him. "Then believe me when I say that everything will work out for the best."

The pain in my arm had subsided and the bleeding had stopped. My strength was incredibly low, but at least I was beginning to recover. I imagined I would need a lot of strength to save the entire world from itself.

"Could you help me get cleaned up?" It was quite the scandalous request, but I was still too weak to do it, and I didn't like the fact that I was covered in Adam's blood literally from head to toe.

"Sure." He took me into his arms and began to carry me up the stairs. There were only a few rooms upstairs. We found two smaller rooms and then a bathroom with a tub. Then we found the master bedroom with a bathroom attached. The big walk-in shower made it a winner.

I couldn't even manage to stand on my own two feet yet, so Adam carried me inside the shower and turned it on with the two of us still fully clothed in his arms. I wasn't thinking anything sensual about it…At least, not at first. We were washing our blood off of our bodies, so it would have been grotesque to be involved in any naughty thoughts. I could only think about washing away all of the awful things in my life and finishing my journey.

I wasn't sure what was happening in Adam's mind while he was with me in that shower, but to me, he felt like my protector. I knew according to destiny, he was supposed to help Lyla, but he was still mine. He might not have been the perfect prince I remembered, but I needed him to be a warrior fit to handle the amazon I had no choice but to be.

All of the blood washed from our bodies, but it was still stained in our clothes. Adam turned off the water, and my steaming body was quickly turning cold. His body had kept me warm, but he very carefully sat me down on the tiled step in the shower and I was suddenly freezing. "Can you take your clothes off by yourself?"

"Excuse me?" My voice quivered and I started blushing.

"You shouldn't keep these on. I'm gonna find you something to wear."

He seemed pretty calm, but I certainly wasn't. It was bad enough he walked around with his shirt off all the time. I didn't need to be naked with him! "I'll manage."

He left out of the shower and got me a towel to wear. I took it and held it to my chest. I should have asked him for help, but I was too shy and afraid to be indecent. Adam was acting strange too. He seemed like he barely wanted to look at me and he sounded nervous himself. "I'll be back soon."

I tried to take off my pants as soon as he left, but I had trouble pulling them off with my little body feeling like it weighed as much as a freight train! I leaned up against the wall for support and used all of my might to push myself up on my feet. I took a second to catch my breath and mentally prepared myself to pull my pants off. I counted to three and tried, but my I lost my balance and fell onto the tile. Hard. I don't think I broke anything, but it didn't make any sense how tired I was. If I didn't recover soon, I wouldn't be strong enough to perform the ritual.

Adam came running back into the bathroom and picked me up and carried my aching body onto the bed. He was concerned with my well-being, but he was mad too. He still wouldn't really look at me. "Don't be so full of pride, Roxy. I can help you."

I knew that I needed his help. If it weren't for him, I'd still be sitting on a pile of glass. But I was afraid to let him get close to me in mature situations. I had to keep myself pure, but he was a boy, and boys had thoughts, and they tried to make you think thoughts with their good looks and their perfect bodies. I had to come to terms that I wasn't as shy or prude as I used to be when we were sitting next to each other in the classroom. I was still pretty chicken, but I knew what I wanted. "It's not really pride that I think I'm full of."

I expected him to get it, but he looked confused. "What do you mean?"

I started blushing so hard! My face was hot and I felt so nervous. I could barely speak. "I'm ashamed of how I feel about you right now."

His eyes grew bigger. "Oh." He chuckled. "I'm really not even thinking about that right now. I just wanna take care of you."

"Oh." I should have been relieved. "Okay." But for some reason, I was a little disappointed.

I decided to let him help me. He very carefully took off my pants while I caught my panties and made sure they didn't follow down. I didn't know what he felt, and he wouldn't really look at me while he was helping me. I sure did feel funny and certainly not in any way that would make me wanna laugh out loud. Then when he pulled my shirt over my head, his face was there right in front of me and I wanted to kiss him. It felt right. It felt perfectly right, so I leaned in closer to touch his lips. His eyes bucked when it happened, but it was only a second, and then it was over. He still wouldn't look at me, and he grabbed a towel and pressed it against my chest. "Here."

I held it as tight as I could in an attempt to comfort myself. I was totally rejected, and things felt really awkward. I knew that it was a bad time, but I couldn't help myself. Then to make things worse, he got even closer to me and came behind me to unhook my bra. I knew he wasn't going to do anything, but that didn't make it any less awkward and I felt even more embarrassed and ashamed of my feelings.

He left out of the room, and I tried to stop blushing and feeling like such a fool. It was wrong of me to want him...Or maybe it wasn't. Wasn't it natural? But even if it was, it surely didn't matter. We would never have a life together, and I didn't have the strength to be intimate.

Adam came back with a white, floor-length nightgown in his hand crafted out silk and lace with a matching robe. Adam was very careful while he helped me put it on. I held the towel around my bosoms with one hand while I raised my hand up and put it into the sleeve and then reversed it so he would never see my bare chest. Once the dress had draped down to my waist, I took the towel and my bra out from underneath the gown. Then he helped me stand to my feet, and the gown fell to the floor. It was meant for someone much more womanly than me with more shape and height. I had never worn anything so sexy before, yet I had never felt so ugly in my life.

Adam set me back down gently on the bed, and he crouched down in front of me for a while, but he wouldn't say anything.

I was so embarrassed to ask, but I needed to know. "Do you not find me attractive?"

Then he finally looked at me. He was certainly surprised. Then, he started to laugh and I wanted to run away and hide from my own skin, but I couldn't do any of that. He grabbed my face and held me still. "You're adorable and so, so very sexy. You are."

I found that hard to believe. I did hate it when everyone treated me like a child, but the truth is that I generally felt like one most of the time. It was hard to believe that my eighteenth birthday was only a couple of hours away. I was going to be a legal adult, but I still didn't feel I could match up to his manly physique. He was certainly acting like he wasn't interested.

"I know about how you need to be pure, and I'm not gonna endanger that."

I suppose I did believe him. Even if I wasn't his or anyone's ideal woman, the way he stared into my eyes made me feel like the most beautiful woman in the world. That's what made tomorrow so incredibly painful for me. "After the ritual, I'm gonna disappear. We'll never get our chance to…"

"Make love?" He smirked so adorably, it was hard to keep my train of thought.

"Get married, make love, and start a family." Even if I didn't have the ritual, we couldn't exactly have those things anyway. We were on the road, running from the law. If they found Adam, he was going to go to jail. Lyla might have broken him out, but it would only make things worse. My dad could never walk me down the aisle, because Adam had killed him. We really didn't have a future together.

"When this is over, please stay away from Lyla." Adam managed to start a life over before. Maybe he could find his dad and make it happen again. I took his hands and continued to look into his eyes, because I wanted his word that he would do what I asked. "I want you to find a nice girl who will love you perfectly, and I want you to live the happiest life you can possibly live. I—"

He placed his finger on my lips to force me to stop talking. Even that made me want to use my lips on his, but it wasn't the proper time. He was staring at me so intently that it felt like I wasn't wearing anything. I was vulnerable, completely helpless, and drawn to the passion and conviction that dwelled within his silver eyes. "Roxy, I don't wanna live my life with anyone else. There is no one else. There is only you."

It was hard to argue with a proclamation as powerful as that. It was selfish of me to ask him to never love anyone again, but it would have been foolish to deny him of me. I didn't care what he said and what he was trying to protect me from. I used what strength I did have, and I pulled him into me for a kiss. He didn't fight me. That would have also been selfish and foolish of him. It was something that the both of us simply needed in order to get through the last day of my life. We couldn't make love. Frankly, I didn't have enough strength do so, but sharing that kiss with him was worth more than a thousand different lifetimes I could have had with any other man. There was only him.

"Can you take me outside?" My head fell onto his chest and my hands on his shoulders. I was drained, but it was well worth it. "I want to see what a night sky really looks like."

He kissed my forehead and sent shivers throughout my entire body, and they were certainly the good kind. "Sure."

Adam left out of the room to find a pair of black sweat pants and a white cotton T-shirt that was too small, so the shirt really hugged his body. After being exposed to his chest for so long, I didn't mind his muscles rippling through. I wondered what sort of people wore the clothes we were wearing. I didn't think they belonged to Porter. I didn't think he could fit Adams's borrowed outfit either. I wondered if they belonged to a man and woman who loved each other very much and I wondered if they were just as happy as I knew Adam could make me.

288

I held on tight to him while he carried me down the stairs. I didn't have a fear of him dropping me, but I didn't want to let him go. I didn't want to forget the way he looked, the way he walked with such a swagger and air of importance and character, or the way his strong arms lifted me up like a feather. I took in the scent of him. Sometimes he smelled like motor oil, and I could tell that he had been working on his car for countless hours. Sometimes he carried the scent of the wind and the trees from when he would go out jogging to prepare for a big race. Right before the end of the school day, he would smell like cinnamon, spice, and carnations in the manliest way possible. He didn't have any of those scents embedded in his skin. His clothes smelled like stale air, but his skin was something else entirely. It was familiar, but I couldn't describe it, yet I knew I had smelled the scent a lot recently. I don't think he smelled human at all, but I did like the smell of him.

Adam opened the door and took a moment before crossing over the threshold. I always told myself that I wanted to see the night, but part of me imagined that there was something dark and twisted about it. The night belonged to Lyla, and anything that belonged to her must have been evil, yet my imagination would often get the best of me. I wondered what it would be like to be immersed in all of that darkness.

He didn't ask me if I were ready. In reality, he didn't really hesitate for more time than it took to finish his step. When we stepped outside, I was blanketed with the darkness, yet I was hit with a spotlight of the full moon overhead, shining down like the world was my own private stage for me to dance upon. I was amazed once I threw my head back and gazed up at the shining lights spread across the sky in an array that couldn't compare to anything I had ever seen. I had seen pictures of a night sky, but their essence couldn't be captured on film any more than a human soul could. They glimmered and danced like the way the light would hit a diamond. I never imagined a star to be so beautiful. Once I blinked to check my eyes to see if everything I was experiencing was real, the heavens blessed me with a star shooting across the sky looking like a streamer of light at hyper speed. There was something spectacular about all of the beauty living infinitely throughout the universe—always growing, dying, being reborn, and ever expanding to create even greater extravagancies.

I was in awe. "I've never seen a star before."

"You've seen the sun," Adam reminded.

I felt silly and chuckled at myself. "I suppose you're right." The sun was a star, but it was different. It stood alone when I saw it during the day. It was nice to know that it truly wasn't alone, nor was it gone. It was still fulfilling its purpose, even though I couldn't see it.

Adam was watching my reaction very carefully. "I can't imagine all of the things you've gone through, Roxy."

It was a lot. I don't mean to sound like I'm bragging, but most people wouldn't have been able to go through what I did. I was also very sheltered and deprived. What kind of child could never look up into the sky and make a wish on a shooting star? Well, I was still a child for a couple of more hours. It was time to close my eyes and make my wish.

I didn't speak of it out loud. I didn't want Adam to know what I was doing, because he would ask and I think I would have blabbed and ruined the wish. He would have also been able to guess it, because it was so obvious. I wished that somehow, someway, the two of us could live our lives together. It didn't have to be perfect. We didn't have to grow old and grey with a bunch of grandchildren to play with by the fire on cold winter days. I just wanted to be a little bit more selfish and to have him be mine for just a little while longer. I would make the time count.

"Do you think we could sleep out here tonight?"

"You really wanna do that?"

It was a warm night. I didn't think the temperature would drop so drastically and even if it did, I would have Adam's body to keep me comfortable and warm. I always wondered what it would be like to sleep under the stars during some sort of camping trip. It was my only chance to really experience it. "I'm sure."

"Then your wish is my command." Adam was such a gentleman. He sat me down so carefully, and he let me lean against him, wrapping his arms around me. His grandmother would have been proud of how well he took care of me. I hoped when everything was all over, he would be able to somehow show everyone how hard he fought to save the world from evil and how desperately he desired to be a good man himself.

"Adam…"

"Yeah, Roxy?"

I started blushing. I felt so silly for asking, but I wanted to hear him say it. "Promise me that you won't forget about me and how I made you feel."

"I could never." He held me tighter and kissed my forehead.

It felt so good to have him hold me and admire me. I wrapped my arms around him as well. I figured he needed to be held and showed how much he was admired and adored sometimes. "Promise me that you'll always be a good man."

"I'll try." His voice was beginning to break up, but I knew he wouldn't start crying for me. He was too tough for that. If I could manage not to cry, he most certainly wouldn't.

Besides, there wasn't anything to cry about. "You are a good man, Adam. I know you've made some mistakes. I've made them too, and we've both been awful, but that doesn't mean we can't do right in the end."

His chin was resting on top of my forehead, and I felt a wetness slide from his chin onto my forehead, and it started to slide down my face until I wiped it away on my cheek. I knew the feeling all too well. Those were tears, and they weren't coming from me.

I looked up and saw Adam struggling not to cry. He wasn't bawling like a baby, but lightly crying like a man with a broken heart. He hated the fact that he was. I could see the stubbornness in his tight jaw as he cursed himself in his mind for letting it happen. He didn't have to be so ashamed of it though. I thought it was beautiful that he opened himself up to me so much that he was vulnerable enough to be hurt.

I was reassured how much I meant to him. "I believe in you, Adam. I know how wonderful you are." I smiled. "And after tomorrow, you get to brag about how you helped me save the world."

He laughed and though it was a genuine laugh, it became harder for him to maintain his composure, yet he did. "Tomorrow, you're gonna save the world."

When my dad first told me that I was meant to save the world, I felt heaviness. It wasn't even the appropriate amount, but it was still very intense. It wasn't like that. I really wasn't afraid anymore. "I'm gonna save the world."

Chapter Fifteen

I felt something tickling my neck so gently. I started giggling until I realized that my neck was wet. My eyes bucked and I rose up yelling. "Adam, stop!" A little white dog started harping and running away, the same time Adam sat up startled. Once I realized what had happened, I took a big sigh of relief.

"What happened?" Adam asked surprised.

"Nothing." I was too embarrassed to talk about it. "It was an honest mistake." I wiped the salvia left on my neck away. Then I saw that the puppy was accompanied by a morning jogger who was staring at us like we had committed a crime. "Maybe we should just go inside."

"Yeah. I didn't mean to fall asleep." He stretched and yawned before helping me up to my feet. "I was just so peaceful with you in my arms."

I started to blush once I realized that my body was cold from missing the touch of him. He held me through the entire night. I smiled, because I couldn't think of a better way to spend my first and last night of life.

I was grateful that I was still myself when I woke up in the morning, though I wished I would have stayed awake to experience a sunrise. It seemed like Lyla was truly gone for good. I couldn't feel her or anything. I usually couldn't, but I was choosing to look on the bright side. Maybe when I died, she would die. Adam could be free.

The two of us came inside the house, and I was reminded just how much damage Lyla had caused. There was still glass, rubble, and blood splattered around the living room. Adam wouldn't let me stand still to observe it. He pulled me into the kitchen, but that didn't get us away from the destruction. There was a hole in the wall, and Adam's blood was still on the floor. Adam tried to ignore it, but it was soaked into the wood. I began feeling nauseous and stumbled back.

Adam rushed behind me quickly to catch me. "Are you still weak?"

"I am, but it's the blood that's getting to me." That was his blood on the floor. There were pints of it soaked into the carpet. I did my best not to step in the wet parts that were still squishy. "It doesn't bother you?"

"Well, I apparently regenerated some more. I don't exactly miss it." It really didn't seem like it bugged him at all. Adam washed his hands and started riffling through the cabinets, pulling out all sorts of pans and setting them on the stove. I didn't see how he could cook with that reminder of death on the floor to taunt him.

"But she could have killed you!"

"And you saved me. I'm here right now because of you and you'll be gone soon." His hands were full of eggs and oil, but he stopped and looked at me. I realized that my powers were working greater than before. I could sense his distress and annoyance with the severity of the situation and even how his mind was fighting it off by being anxious and needing to keep busy. "That's the only thing that bothers me. For that reason, I'm gonna make you some breakfast and you're gonna enjoy it. It is your birthday after all."

"Yeah. I guess it is." I tried to smile about it, but I couldn't. I could feel how much I was tearing him apart with my decision. I thought he had accepted it, but he was only putting on a brave face. It made me feel incredibly guilty, but I wasn't ready to start doubting my intentions.

I decided I would let Adam do what he felt he needed, but I had to clean up the kitchen in return. There was a mop in a closet and a bucket and soap under the sink. I was still pretty tired, and I didn't do a lot of physical labor, but I wasn't lazy and I liked things to be kept pretty tidy.

"What are you doing?" Adam rushed over and tried to take the mop from me. "It's your birthday."

"And I can't eat with your blood all over the kitchen floor. It's too much, and it's downright unsanitary."

"Then I'll do it."

"No. Let me do this." I fought back and took the mop from him. "You are making breakfast, so I'll clean."

He looked concerned, and that worried me a bit. "You can cook right?" I felt silly that I couldn't really do it, or do it well. "Mom always had food for me when I became myself. I never did it before."

"I had to learn how to cook when Grannie became ill. I became pretty good at it." He started working. He seemed to know what he was doing, and there were plenty of ingredients in the fridge. There just wasn't a lot for portions for two. That's why Adam decided he would make a bunch of different food.

I was able to clean up most of the blood, but some of it was stained. It looked like someone had slaughtered a pig right on the kitchen floor. After the soap and water failed, I tried scrubbing it all away with a sponge, but all that did was hurt my fingers. I found some bleach and just before I doused the floor in it, Adam took it from me. "You're in my way now."

"Sorry." I got some paper towel and started drying the floor so he wouldn't slip while he was working in the kitchen. He was getting irritated from having to walk around me, but I finished up as fast as I could. "I'm finished. I swear."

"I'll be done pretty soon myself." He was working four pans at once. There were hash browns, pancakes, bacon, and eggs. It certainly did look very delicious and smelled yummy.

I sat down at the kitchen table and waited for him to finish. Maybe I should have tried to help him finish cooking, but I figured I would only be in his way again.

Besides, there were some things on my mind that I hadn't really gotten the chance to talk to Adam about. "So, I'm an alien?"

He was silent at first. I watched him while he tried to bury himself in the art of flipping over pancakes without them losing their perfect form. Mom always messed them up. Adam was quite remarkable in every way, but I wasn't going to stop burning holes into the back of his head until he answered me. "You're from a different dimension. You guys have an unusually low mortality rate, so you need some more territory."

"And earth was the perfect place?" I wanted to be disgusted, but after seeing a night sky, I couldn't lie and pretend that I didn't understand. "It is a beautiful place."

I guess he was done, because he began powering down everything and started plating the last meal I would ever eat. He even dressed it up so my pancakes were smiling out of bacon and strawberries, which was a drastic contrast to the expression on his face. "Should I tell you more?"

I knew he didn't wanna talk about it. He had all his answers, but I was left in the dark. But having the answers didn't make him any happier. I could feel and see how much they were ruining his life. Talking about it would jeopardize any chance of last minute happiness that we would have. The truth would have been an excellent birthday present, but my naivety would serve the both of us best. "No. For the first time in my life, I don't care. I just wanna spend my last day with you."

296

I reached out across the table and smiled as he looked at me. I could sense that offered him a small piece of condolence. It was all I knew to do for him.

We enjoyed the simple moment that we had together. His food was delicious, and I savored every bite from the sweetness of the strawberries to the saltiness of the crispy bacon. I licked my lips when some of the syrup dripped on my mouth, and Adam shook his head and chuckled at me. I suppose in a lot of ways, I was still a child, but I hoped that he'd remember how much of a woman I was.

He was trying to be normal, like we were together at lunch and joking around. He would like to eat alone with me sometimes. He was really private that way. But just because it felt familiar, didn't mean I couldn't tell that there was something bothering him. "Tell me what's going through that head of yours."

He smiled. "I guess you know me pretty well, Roxanne. I've been thinking about your powers."

"And?" I was hoping that he had figured out a way for me to keep living in my body after the ritual.

"I find it fascinating what the similarities and differences between you and Lyla are. You can both sense emotions, but you choose to focus on the good, Lyla focuses on the bad, and you both try to ignore that there's an opposing side at the end of the spectrum."

"Yeah, so what?"

"Lyla can pinpoint certain ones and make it so dominant that it's your only point of focus until you're satisfied or dead. She enjoys the chaos, but she could never truly manipulate anyone. She can to a point, but technically, Lyla couldn't make anyone do anything they didn't genuinely want to do."

"I don't think that's right. You didn't see what she did to my mom." When I went into her room, I could feel such a dark presence in there. She wasn't herself, and my dad didn't even want my mom to ever see Lyla again. She was more powerful than what he knew.

"Lyla just knows how to work people. Maybe she could entice them a little bit with her ability to free. Maybe she can free just parts of you, but she can't control anybody."

"She manipulates all the time!" I found it hard to believe that she could ruin my mother the way she did without using her powers.

"Yeah, but let's say that she cared about me and wanted me to love her."

"What?" I yelled, and I was pretty angry about it too. "Lyla said that?"

"I'm speaking hypothetically," he said quickly.

I breathed a sigh of relief. That would have been just freaky! I knew Lyla wanted to corrupt Adam and no doubt that she was highly attracted to him, but he wasn't her type of guy. No guy was her type. She was too selfish to ever love anyone.

"If she used her powers on me, I could very well snap and break her neck." I could hear and feel the animosity in his voice. I was sure that he would do it if he had the chance and I wasn't in the way. "She couldn't make me do anything I really didn't want to do, but you can!"

Hearing that made me a bit uneasy. I certainly didn't like to be compared to Lyla, and I didn't like that I could control people. I mean I did use that ability, but I shouldn't have. It was wrong of me. Taking away freedom of will was probably the greatest injustice that could be inflicted on a human being. I was grateful that Lyla was incapable of doing it, but out of the two of us, how could I be the one capable of such a thing?

Adam didn't share my concern. The revelation even pleased him. "You thought Lyla was the most powerful because she can float a book across the room. Well, the truth is that you're the most powerful!"

It's what I always wanted to hear, but it was a little too late. "What does it matter if you think I'm the strongest? I'm not going to survive."

Adam hesitated. He was worried, but he pressed through. "What if you're not supposed to save the world in the way that you think?"

"Meaning?" I couldn't help but be at least a little bit interested. I wasn't one hundred percent positive on how I was supposed to save the world anyway.

"You can make me feel great. You could make me want to hug an alligator, but sooner or later, it would be possible for me to get upset and fall back into old patterns, unless you pushed me like you did Susan."

"But my powers would be amplified." I didn't know what that meant, but I assumed the obvious. "Maybe I would wipe out negative emotions entirely."

"I don't believe that's true. Our perception is what decides what is and what isn't negative. It's not evil to hate evil. Greed isn't wrong as long as it motivates and doesn't control you. And jealousy..." He laughed. "God is jealous! He sends you straight to hell for not making him number one and were we not made in his image? It won't damn me if I'm jealous over the right things. You're very black and white, Roxy. You can't remove negativity, because you don't understand shades of grey."

"I went to kindergarten," I mumbled. "I know my colors."

"I'm serious." He reached across the table and bumped me on the arm.

I smiled. It was too bad that we'd never be able to have moments when we could joke around with each other. I didn't know if I'd be able to remember or really miss Adam. I knew he'd miss me though. "Then what were you thinking?"

"Maybe..." I could sense a hint of fear. Then he spoke quietly. "Maybe you're supposed to do what you did to Susan..."

I couldn't believe my ears. "To everyone? In the world?" I kept waiting for Adam to say something to correct himself, but he wouldn't say anything. The more I waited, the more I swear he looked like he was becoming more confident in his decision. "That's insane! I would be crossing so many lines."

"Listen. You were at a disadvantage from day one. Lyla is using human nature to destroy itself. That's why it's so hard to fight against her." How dare he try to reason such a terrible thing?

"No." I didn't want to be that angry with Adam with so little time left of my life, but I couldn't help it. "Humanity can decipher what is and what isn't right."

"Really? I'm sure there were lots of Germans who stood against Hitler and risked a lot just to stand up for what was right. Then there were some who ignored the reality and pretended to be naive so they could sleep through the night. Then there were those who were brainwashed into believing that they were so great that they deserved to wipe out an entire race. Right and wrong are opinions."

"Well, my opinion is that human beings deserve free will!"

"Roxy, they would be worshiping you with their own free will!"

"After I corrupted them!" I was horrified with each thing that he said. He was a human being. He didn't like being controlled, held captive, or even influenced. How dare he even consider me destroying free will? "You're being a hypocrite. You wouldn't want me to do it to you."

He started to laugh to himself and that made me even more upset. "You're right. It was just a thought, Roxy. Besides, with you being gone, it would be useless. I guess I'm just thinking out loud."

"If you say so…" I leaned back into my seat and pouted. I accepted that he was joking around or just asking difficult questions because he was curious, but I still felt uneasy about the conversation.

Then Adam kept staring at me with this dreamy, mysterious smile and a wandering look. It began to worry me. "What is it?"

"Nothing." He was smiling, but I could sense how sad he was. "I just wonder what the world will be like without you."

"It's not like I've been around forever. This world was fine without me."

"Well, mine wasn't."

I was flattered, and that led to some serious blushing. "Hush up and eat." We finished eating mostly in silence. There was so much nervousness in the air. I wasn't exactly calm about dying and I knew he was terrified of the prospect of losing me. It was just something the two of us would have to deal with.

Then suddenly, I nearly jumped out of my skin at the sound of the crack of lightening. I even screamed a little bit until I covered my mouth. I thought Adam would laugh at me, but he looked just as surprised as me. I began to realize that everything in the house was shaking. I had never been in an earthquake before.

Adam got out of his seat and grabbed my arm. "Come on!" It was hard to walk with the whole house shaking. I thought we were gonna find a doorframe to stand in, but he led me to the basement door and reached out to open it, just as the shaking came to a complete stop and Porter opened up the door himself.

"Roxanne?" Porter was surprised, deathly pale, and covered in sweat.

"What's going on?" Adam asked.

"Do you think it's simple to open up a portal?"

I felt terrified all of a sudden. "Is it ready?" My heart started pounding incredibly fast. I guess I wasn't quite as ready as I once thought.

"Not quite. It needs to stabilize. It'll be ready in an hour or two." He finished walking up the stairs and was horrified to see what had become of his home. I felt terrible for what Lyla had done to mess it up so, but so many of his peculiar trinkets had fallen during the earthquake and had shattered into pieces.

"I'm sorry about the damage," I said.

"No. It's alright." He walked over to my book—which was sitting on a couch in the living room—and began to hold it for a while like he hadn't seen it in ages. It was almost like when I was a child and held onto one of my stuffed animals after becoming myself in the morning. I wouldn't be able to cling onto anything like that again. I had to fully let go of everything for the sake of everything.

"Did you author that book?" Adam asked.

Porter began flipping through the pages as he was rediscovering an old friend. Each page made him smile in a new, richer way. Then when he got to a certain page, he wouldn't dare turn it, and he smiled the way Adam did when he looked at me. "I did."

I was curious to know which page could have made him so happy, so I hovered over him to look at the page of the beautiful woman. There was no mistaking his expression. When Porter looked at her, he gave away his feelings all too plainly, without the slightest bit of encryption. "You loved her, didn't you?"

"Very much." When he touched the pages, his fingers traced each strand of hair as if he could remember what it felt like to actually touch her once when she was alive. "Your mother was wonderful in every sense of the word."

I shouldn't have been surprised, but I was. That incredibly pose, beautiful, and strong woman was my mother. "Is this her gown?"

He didn't have to look at me. He had noticed it when he first opened up the door. "Yes. I kept some of her things."

"Did she and my father live here?"

"For some time. Yes."

I looked around. I didn't think a great queen of a world of such powerful people would be in such a cozy home. All of the smashed up statues of cute characters didn't seem like something a queen would have, but Porter could have redecorated the place once he moved in. "And what were you to her?"

"Only a friend," he said with unmistakable sadness masked with a smile. "I watched over her, helped protect her in some ways. There aren't many of us who can open portals. I had to come to this world with her in order to fulfill her plans." He closed the book shut. "I always wished that she would have chosen me, but she loved the human instead."

I felt awful for Porter, but I very well couldn't apologize for my mother choosing my father if I valued my life at all. "What were their names?"

He faced me. Though he was saddened by old memories, he did have a sense of admiration for the both of them that truly pleased me. "She was Queen Avariana of Avarian. He was a carpenter named Samuel. He was murdered by another human, and she lost her will to live after a difficult pregnancy. It was difficult to will such powerful children into the world, and she had only originally planned for one. Samuel was more than the human used to create you. Without him, you wouldn't have even been a thought."

Hearing what he said made me feel better about my side that wasn't human. Not all Avarians were like Alvin and his family. My mother must have been incredibly kind and had such an unshakable strong will to stand up for humanity and to even conceive a child by a human. She was beautiful and a queen. She probably could have had any Avarian that she wanted, including Porter. "And did you put me in Lyla's body?"

"You would have died otherwise, and it was your mother's will for the two of you to contend for humanity in different ways."

"But how could Lyla contend for humanity?" Adam asked. "She's constructed to make us destroy ourselves."

"Not if humans were like Samuel." It was odd. There wasn't one speck of jealousy that I could sense from Porter. He genuinely believed that a human being could be the better man. "He was born with goals to help others. He worked, and he worked honestly, but he would give everything away if it were only to help someone in need. His generosity sparked a curiosity within your mother and she eventually fell madly in love with the kind human. She believed that if humanity could be like Samuel, then we Avarians could learn a great deal from them. Things changed when her kind and gentle Samuel was murdered for his watch. But even as he was being robbed, he tried to talk to the robber and help him make the better decision. He was trying to help people right up until the end."

Adam placed his hand on my shoulder. "I guess you were a lot like your dad, Roxy."

I smiled. "I suppose so." I couldn't blame my mother for being upset about his death. I felt grief for him, and I had never known the man. Some might have found that silly, but his life was something to be proud of and he deserved to be missed, even by those who knew him from reputation alone.

"With someone as pure hearted as Roxy performing the ritual, earth will become like a paradise." Porter stroked his chin as he thought. "Well, in theory anyway."

I couldn't forfeit humanity's chance at paradise. That seemed wrong beyond any doubt. I had to go through with it and execute it as perfect as possible. "What exactly is the ritual? What do I have to do?"

"Once you enter through the portal, you'll enter through the Great Hall of Truth. The Staff of Power will be sitting in a stone altar. All you have to do is pull it out, and the rest will be made plain to you."

"And that's all?" I remembered the picture in the book clearly, but that hardly seemed like enough. "It seems pretty easy for something that's gonna destroy me."

"You will be tempted by your other half."

"Lyla isn't gone?" Adam asked terribly disappointed.

"No." Porter narrowed his eyes in on me and just stared for what seemed to be the longest time. It made me uncomfortable. It was as if he were peeking in on me while I was in the shower. I hoped it didn't feel like that when I poked through people's emotions. "I sense Lyla's will over her body isn't as strong as it once was. She must have given up the right to her body."

My eyes bucked. "But why would she do that?" I turned to Adam, but he wouldn't say anything. Oddly enough, he had something to say, but he didn't want to share.

Porter forgot about it easily enough and patted me on the shoulder with a great smile on his face. "Whatever the reason, this body is now yours. She probably won't be able to come back until you relinquish the right over it."

"Well, I'd never do that!"

"Whether you would or not, her body will belong to her once you fulfill your calling and fade away."

My shoulders slumped. "And why did you do that exactly? Why do I have to disappear?"

"This isn't your body. By all accounts, you shouldn't be alive. You shouldn't complain, Roxy. You've gotten more than you ever would have."

Was he right? Was I really being selfish for wanting to have more to my life? I was lucky to be that young and to have found someone that I truly loved. I hadn't experienced a lot, but the moments I had with Adam were more than most people would experience in a lifetime. Being in

305

Adam's arms while we danced in the gymnasium or when he jumped out of the car to kiss me goodbye on my doorstep was perfection. Was it selfish to want more time to have more perfect moments with Adam?

"You're not being fair!" Adam exploded, yelling at Porter with such fury that I thought he was going to lunge at him. "She's about to give up everything for the world, including me. That isn't easy for her, and it's certainly not easy for me either."

He was being so calm, but that was all just a clever lie. He buried his fury in so deep that I didn't sense quite how angry he was about losing me. I held my chest and silently moaned to myself. I had to fight with everything I had to stay strong with my decision, or else Adam's demand to have me would have weighed too heavily on my soul.

Porter seemed so kind and gentle, but then he became the cruelest of beings. "She doesn't have a choice otherwise."

"She could decide not to do anything."

Porter's eyes widened. "She wouldn't dare!" He was shocked that we would do something so undignified. Our duty was brought upon us by the queen's orders, and we weren't meant to disobey them. "The ritual must be performed, or there will be consequences. This prophecy will come to pass. The princess shall enter the Hall of Truth, and she will unleash great joy or suffering upon humanity that will either save or condemn them."

"That's not true!" Adam yelled. "That doesn't have to happen. Look at me. I was supposed to serve Lyla, but that hasn't happened."

"You're supposed to set her free, and that will happen as well." When Porter spoke, it felt like a creepy omen. A chill surfaced all over my body and tickled my back like a knife grazing my skin. It was like the breath was taken out of the room and we lost our ability to refute him. "Our fates have been set in stone. There is nothing else in this world but our destinies. Everything else is irrelevant. I learned that the hard way when I tried to stand in the way of Queen Avariana and Samuel."

Then I knew that Porter wasn't trying to be cruel. His warning was his idea of compassion, so I wouldn't get my hopes up and waste my time on wishes that would never come true. But even still, I couldn't accept that Adam would betray me. I knew him too well. I loved him too much. Our bond was too strong. I curled my fingers into fists and shook at the thought of it. "Adam can't possibly free Lyla. I know him. As soon as I'm gone, he's going to kill Lyla, regardless of whether I tell him to or not."

"And are you okay with that?"

Lyla wasn't the only person who had earned the right of my hatred, but she was the only one who had received it. I don't think I hated her before, but I couldn't forgive her for almost killing Adam. There was no hope for her. She would never change. "I don't want him to hurt anyone, but if Lyla needs to be stopped, I would much prefer if Adam survived."

Porter seemed surprised. "Lyla might be your bane of existence, but she still is your sister. You were once the same life form entirely. You could sever a bond so easily?"

I never thought of us as being sisters. I wasn't sure that we were related in any sort of way until I found that picture of the two babies. She could have been a demon who crawled up from the depths of hell who was assigned to ruin my life. It was better to imagine her that way. No one knew how difficult it was for me to know that I was the ghost living in her body. I certainly didn't want anyone to throw the fact that she was my twin sister in my face. "She's not interested in being my friend and I'm only interested in protecting the man that I love. Besides, it won't matter how I feel once I'm gone. I'll be gone."

"Very well. You'll be able to save the world very soon." I don't know why my answer disappointed him so. He saw the damage that Lyla had done to his home. She was nothing but a monster!

"Guys." Something had happened. Adam's eyes had grown large and his body was still, except for his shaking fingers.

"What is it?"

He snapped out of his fear and channeled it into a fire to fuel his anger. He clenched his fists and grunted. "Alvin and his family are on their way here."

"What?"

"They'll be here soon. I can feel them coming. They're extremely close."

Memories from how badly Alvin had beaten the both of us came to my mind in a continuous flash. I couldn't forget about the blood and how he wouldn't let me heal Adam. Adam would be a dead man if they got their hands on him. "We have to run!"

"The portal will not wait for you," Porter said. "After it stabilizes, it won't stay open by itself more than an hour or two, and it takes far too much time and energy to continuously keep opening them. I could probably only do it once more. You don't want to chance that it will be for Lyla."

It was clear that Porter wasn't on my side, despite saving my life when I was only a baby. The only person I could depend on was Adam, but Alvin and his family were going to rip through him like tissue paper. I didn't even think it was possible to really outrun them. If Adam could sense them, they could probably sense us. "What do we do?"

"I have to fight them. I can hold them off while you—"

"No!" I clung onto Adam in an instant, hysterical panic. "They'll kill you, Adam."

He had to laugh at me somewhat to keep himself from being infected by my rational fear of him being dismembered by psychopaths from another world. "I'll be okay. I'm just as strong as them now."

"You're outnumbered. Don't kid yourself."

Little by little, my rationality was seeping into him. He was quiet, but I could feel that fear growing inside of him. I could see it in his eyes. If he even bothered to try to fight Alvin and his family, he would be killed. Even with that truth fully developed in his brain, he smiled and wrapped his arms around me. "I have to do this. If they get their hands on you, Lyla wins."

I knew he was being so strong, but it was too hard for me to be brave and let him accept the inevitable like a hero and a gentleman. "I want to build a better world, but I need you to be in it." I wrapped my arms around him as tight as I could and promised myself to never let him go for as long as I had breath in my body.

"Roxy, you have to let me save you."

"Just so we can both die?" I couldn't let him be a casualty in my war! "Please don't tell me to do this."

"Roxy, you have to let me go."

There was a crack of thunder and a bolt of pain shot right through me, severing my spine. I lost the feeling in my legs and collapsed into his arms, determined still not to let him go, no matter what the world threw at me. The thunder wouldn't stop, and it came like a percussion filled orchestra. I had closed my eyes on instinct when I first heard the noise, but I peeked and saw dust and smoke flying all around me. A splash of red flew out from the corner of my eye like a falling ribbon, and I looked up at Adam, who was coughing up blood. It had splattered on my face, but he couldn't have splattered as much as I felt on my face coming from my own mouth.

He lost his strength and fell to his knees. My fingers were losing their grip, but I didn't want to let him go. "Adam…"

He sat me down as gently as he could in the pain he was in. The bullets were still flying in over our heads, so he stayed down as close to the ground as he possibly could. "Stay down." He was once again covered in blood from all of the holes in his body, but it was different this time. My eyes had fallen on a wound in his shoulder. The bullet had just grazed him, but it had taken out a chunk of his flesh. I could see his white meat being eclipsed by the flow of blood pouring through, but that wasn't worse than the wound in his chest. He would die without my help, but I could barely sit up.

"Be still!" He took my hands and pressed down on my stomach that was covered in blood, but there was a puddle under me that continuously grew and I felt like I was soon going to drown and lose consciousness in my ocean of pain. "I think it went right through you."

The bullets continued flying through the house, destroying the walls as if it were built out of crackers. Feathers and cotton from fabric were tossed in the air along with blood and screams from Porter. I couldn't even look behind me to see if he were somehow holding on after his giant thud. Then everything went silent.

It was silly for me to think about how I was ruining my mother's nightgown, but it bothered me that I had on something so glamorous and I ruined it with my rotten luck. Would the queen of Avarian ever be caught lying on her back, shielded by her lover, while her attackers tried to take everything away from her? I bet she wouldn't. I bet she would stand up and fight, but I couldn't even feel my legs.

I looked at my dear Adam. He looked well considering that he had several bullet holes in him. I looked at his shoulder as his flesh came back together before my very eyes. "You're healing."

He didn't care. "And you're not."

310

I knew I wasn't back up to one hundred percent, but I didn't think my healing power was still stalled. I tried to concentrate and heal myself, but it was so unbelievable that Adam had completely stopped bleeding. "How is this possible?"

"I must have some of your ability." He looked at his hands mystified for a couple of seconds before placing them on my stomach. "Maybe I can—"

"Don't! You don't know how, and if you accidently give me your own energy, you could die." I was hurt, but I wasn't going to die. I wouldn't let myself. I just needed some time to concentrate. I would be okay. I had to be!

"What about Porter?"

Adam looked up and back at me like he didn't want to say. He didn't have to.

I didn't have any choice but to somehow get to the portal and perform the ritual. But even if Adam somehow stalled for me, I wouldn't be able to make a run for it until I got my legs miraculously working again.

"Roxy!" It was Mr. Rider. He was understandably furious. "I'm assuming everyone in the house is dead besides you. Come out now without any resistance and we won't kill you."

They wanted to kill Adam, and they didn't care about Porter anymore. I didn't know how to save Adam or stop them from kidnaping me until I somehow became Lyla again. "What do I do?"

He wasn't sure himself, and it wasn't fair to put that much pressure on him. He was frustrated and angry, but he let those emotions go in one grunt under his breath before yelling to confirm that he was alive. "Roxy is hurt. Something is wrong with her powers!"

"No—" Adam placed his hand on my mouth and warned me with his eyes to keep quiet. He should have pretended to be dead or run away. What was he thinking?

311

"You expect me to believe that?" Mr. Rider yelled.

"It's true!"

There was a pause. Uncomfortable silences filled the crumbling room as we waited to see whether they believed Adam, or if they would charge in like bulldozers and tear everything else down. "Is Porter alive?"

"No."

There was more silence and it was literally maddening! I closed my eyes and concentrated as much as possible on my wounds. I envisioned myself getting better. I could feel it working. It would just take time. I needed more time!

"Then come outside, Adam. We expect no resistance from you. We might even let you live."

He started to get up, but I opened my eyes and pulled on his arm. "Please, don't!" As soon as I opened my eyes, tears poured out of them and rolled down my cheeks. I really didn't mean to. Promising not to cry was my only fruitless promise. I decided I wouldn't make promises like that anymore. Whether I was being weak or not, didn't matter. I didn't want to see Adam brutally ripped apart by men who hated him for being mine. "Don't go, Adam. Stay with me."

He bent down and kissed my forehead affectionately but still ignoring all of my desperate pleas. "Stay and concentrate on getting better."

"No…" I tried to hold onto him, but he was too strong and he slipped right through my fingers.

He stood up straight and faced the outside window that had been demolished. The sun was bursting through so much that he was swallowed up by darkness and was only a silhouette. However, he still looked heroic with his muscular frame tensing up and preparing for a fight, swearing to me by stance alone that he would die in order to protect me. One step at a time, he headed for the front door and disappeared into enemy lines.

There was no more time to waste. I couldn't think about how he was gonna be torn to bits if I didn't somehow stop Alvin and his ruthless family. I couldn't think about Porter's dead body laying a couple of feet from me, and how he had to die for knowing me and fulfilling his duty, even though he was never on my side. I couldn't think about whether or not Lyla was coming back or not, or how she would deal with everything if she were in my shoes. I had to close my wounds and restore my busted organs. I had to regenerate everything from tissue to blood. The only way to do it was to be positive that I was able. I had to in order to save Adam's life!

I felt my stomach for my different wounds, but I couldn't find any holes—only the blood splatters from where they once were. I was still incredibly sore, but at least I was able to sit up. I looked at my toes and willed them to wiggle or twitch, but they wouldn't do anything. I grunted and lay back down and tried to concentrate on my spine.

Then I heard Adam scream. It was agonizing, and I'm sure the whole neighborhood heard it. It was one more thing the neighbors could report when they called the police for the millionth time. He might have been able to last a little bit longer than usual with the newfound ability to regenerate, but he very well couldn't heal himself if he was dead.

"Come on!" I pounded my fists into the carpet hard enough to hurt my hands, but I did it over and over again. I needed to get better so I could save him. I wasn't cutting it. "You have to get better now!"

I sat back up and stared at my toes with sheer determination, grinding my teeth and glaring like I was about to tackle an invisible enemy. I needed to win. I was going to win! "Now!"

And just like magic, all ten of my toes began to wiggle. I was okay. I could move my legs, but I wasn't over the soreness. If it didn't actually exist, the mental lingering was enough to make it real. I didn't care though. I forced myself to get up on my own two feet. My legs

313

wobbled until I thought I would collapse, but I slapped them as hard as I could. "Don't you dare!"

I straightened myself out and took a clumsy step forward, but I caught myself before diving head first into a pile of glass. I took a deep breath and took another step forward, and each step was better than the last. By the time I got to the door, I was no clumsier than usual. I bravely placed my hand on the doorknob and flung it open.

It was a bright, beautiful day in a little neighborhood that looked like paradise—except for my bloodied and bruised boyfriend being head locked by a jealous man prepping to rip his head clear off his shoulders. Alvin was surrounded by all of his brothers and father. Though they honestly didn't need guns, they were armed with big ones strong enough to make Porter's house look like Swiss cheese. The only reason why Adam still had a head was because they all stopped to look at me and they were all waiting for my reaction.

I could have begged for Adam's life, but Alvin would have killed him just to see me cry. That wouldn't be the only reason, but it would be a powerful motivation for him. I could have tried to reason with Mr. Rider, but they wouldn't care about how Adam was supposed to free Lyla. No one knew what that meant, and it just didn't matter anymore.

There was only one thing I knew to do. "I see my boys have been naughty while I was away." I smirked as wickedly as I could. "You're all picking on your new brother, my Chosen. How very naughty indeed!"

They all began to look at each other baffled, but Adam was the most confused of all. "Lyla?"

Chapter Sixteen

Adam was so heartbroken that it was hard for me not to break my composure and admit everything to him. I was never a talented actress, but I had to put on the best performance of my life if I expected the both of us to make it out of there alive.

"It's the morning," Mr. Rider said. "How is it possible that you're Lyla?"

"Fun fact: the two of us can give up our time in this body. Roxy was hoping that if she allowed me to take over, I would stop all of you from killing Adam. Unfortunately, she was right." I walked over to Adam who looked at me in ways difficult to describe. He really hated Lyla. If he weren't in such a tight grip, I think he would have bitten my fingers off when I stroked his cheek. "I need my Chosen alive."

"To do what?" Alvin exploded. "He's just a human."

"You and your family have made that statement a lie. He's both Avarian and human now, like me. It's fitting that he'd be my Chosen."

I thought Alvin would be much calmer around Lyla, but he was only becoming angrier. "You don't even know what the prophecy means. You don't know if he can set you free!"

It took a lot of me not to cower at the might of his crazed rage. I still remembered what it was like to be hit by Alvin, but Lyla wouldn't be afraid. She wasn't afraid of anything, so I couldn't be either. "Of course I do. He's going to live, and he's going to set me free."

Adam started grunting or growling or…I don't know. He was just so angry until he exploded. "I'll never have sex with you, Lyla! You might as well kill me!"

I lost it. My composure was gone, and there was nothing I could do about it. I was far too surprised. I hoped that everyone was surprised like Alvin clearly was and didn't notice how afraid, disgusted, saddened, and angry I was. I recovered as quickly as I could with a smirk, but it felt extremely uncomfortable.

"She's not Lyla." Mr. Rider pointed his finger right at me. "That's Roxy."

One of the boys started laughing hysterically. "I take it that you didn't know that Lyla was trying to seduce your boyfriend, huh?"

It made me so mad! That's how she thought she could get rid of me? And why didn't Adam tell me that? Did he secretly want her? I couldn't even think about it, or I was gonna lose my mind completely.

The brother, that Adam had beaten so savagely, came from behind and wrapped his arms around me so tight that I couldn't move. "Game over."

"This isn't a game!" As futile as it was, I tried to move and somehow get free. "This is the future of humanity and you creeps don't deserve this planet."

Mr. Rider smiled. "Humanity will decide that for us, Roxy. We were never meant to decide their fates. Since you have such hope in them, you should let Lyla do what she was born to do instead of trying to be their crutch." Mr. Rider, who was always so elegantly cruel from a distance, walked toward me with his superiority complex swaggering across the grass. He thought he was above everything, and maybe living in a huge home with a bunch of servants answering every thought will do that to most men over time, but he didn't deserve to have that much pride. He was no better than those worms living under the grass, tending the soil as they squirmed about. He didn't realize his place. He was nothing to Lyla, but he thought he was a god. I wanted to puke all over him once his arrogant finger began grazing my skin. It didn't matter how smooth and gentle he felt. He was still a squirmy, little worm.

"Sometimes, we all need crutches. If it weren't for Adam, I wouldn't have made it this far, and he wouldn't be the man who he is without me. Even Lyla needed him. Whether our impact is good or bad, we all leave some sort of imprint on someone's life. We can teach what to do or what not to do. It's not wrong to need someone."

"Maybe, but it is incredibly stupid." He smiled. "Kill him."

"No!"

Alvin was going to do it. He had been waiting for the order, itching to pull Adam's head from his neck—the only sure way to kill him with my powers. Adam needed me, and I was powerless to save him. There was only one person who could, and I didn't have time to doubt myself or question what would happen to the world five minutes after their bodies had been ripped to pieces. I barely thought it, but she came so easily.

"Ahhh!" I didn't know Alvin could scream like such a little girl, but I suppose that's what happens when someone gets both of their arms ripped off of their body. Even when he looked to his right and to his left where his arms used to be, the poor dear was still so terribly confused, and the only way he could solve his confusion was to scream.

Adam fell to the ground. I had never seen him so terrified of anything before, but considering the circumstances, I could forgive him for looking so pathetic, and he didn't lose any of his immense sexuality.

Alvin, on the other hand, wasn't being sexy at all. I mean, he was making a mess with all of that blood squirting from his arteries. It was gross, and the screaming was so not dignifying.

I wanted to greet him to his death properly, but Alvin's pesky brother had uncharacteristically decided to freak out. He was gripped with such fear that he was stuck and wouldn't let me go. He was squeezing me tighter than I would have liked. I had to take control of his arms and release myself. But when I saw how truly terrified he was, I had to explore the depths of how far it would go. How wide could his eyes and mouth open? How much would he quiver? Would he scream? I couldn't sense how much his brother's misfortune was affecting him. I needed him to paint the expression clearly on his face, and I believed the silent ones were always the true artists.

I took his left hand and uncurled his tightly wound fingers until they were spread and cupped like he was about to pick a ripe fruit. He was trying to figure out what I was going to have him do, but I don't know how any sane person could have guessed. I raised his hand so he could get a good look at it. I wanted him to know what he was about to do with his own hand. Then, I shoved it right into his chest. He wailed and started screaming until it filled my heart with such glee. I wondered what it felt like for him to reach inside of himself and continuously go further, despite the innumerable pain surging throughout him. I was especially curious how he felt when his fingers touched his heart and slowly began to grip around it one finger at a time. It must have been excruciatingly painful. I noticed he started to grit his teeth by then. But I wasn't as wickedly cruel as some would believe. I soon put him out of his misery. He clung tightly to his heart and ripped it out of his chest. That was when my scientific nature went to a deeper level. I figured he would have fallen right over, but he still had time to look at his heart with his shaking hands, screaming quietly one last time as the blood poured from his mouth. And then he died.

With that out of the way, I freely walked over to Alvin and kicked him in his chest until he fell flat on his back, still moaning and whining like a freaking baby! "I don't know why you're freaking out. Roxy told you that I would kill you."

Then his eyes started welling up with tears and his lips were quivering. Couldn't he face his death like a man? Did he really have to be that sniveling on his way to hell? "Why?"

"Because you overestimated your worth to me. You're less than nothing." And then with a thought manifesting into physical motion in the slightest way, his neck went: "Oh, snap!"

I guess Adam didn't like my sense of humor. He quickly got up after that, grabbed the gun that Alvin had on the ground, and took off running back inside the house. Why he didn't run away from all of us, I didn't know. It didn't matter though. I'd get to him soon enough.

I had to deal with the rest of my pesky followers that were trying to murder the love of my life (who was secretly in love with me). They had to pay dearly.

I was surprised that Rider and his family were so broken up about their missing members. I mean, Rider didn't charge me when I started ripping his sons apart. That showed me a lack of loyalty. If that were the case, why was he so upset with me? He wouldn't dare reveal the answer. He rightly feared me too much.

"Now, what am I to do with the rest of you wicked boys?" I eyed the rest of the survivors carefully, trying to find out who my next victim would be. I couldn't be too long. The sirens were getting louder. The cops would arrive in a few seconds. That was too bad for me. I wanted to

319

ruin what was left of their little lives. "No, not boys. You're all like little mice scurrying about as soon as the master leaves the house. Did I not say that Adam was only to be harmed by myself?"

"He aided in Roxy's escape!" It certainly did sound like Rider was begging. How dare he! He knew he deserved to die.

"To the exact place I needed to be on the exact day!" Of course Roxy was an idiot who fell right into my hands. She was better than my actual henchmen. "You're such a fool."

"But the portal is open now. I can sense it. It's at the wrong time." And he was panicking. Good. That made me feel a little bit better.

"You didn't believe I would find a way to be here during this time? Well, you underestimated me." They had insulted my intelligence for the last time. They brought those pretty guns with them. I had grown fond of my knife, but it would be gratifying to have something that powerful aiding me. But I didn't need any of that. It was all just for show, and I too was an artist.

I aimed, I shot them a couple of times in the head, and it was over. It was less gruesome than my first two examples, but I didn't need to always be so flashy. Sometimes, less is more. "I hope all of you incompetent losers enjoy death!"

Even though everyone was dead, there were still screams. Those nosey neighbors who called the cops must have been watching through their windows. I should have killed them too, but I was on a short leash as far as time.

The cops arrived just as expected with their sirens blazing. There were four cars total, which made things extremely easy. I didn't have any desire to fight them one on one. Before they could put their cars in park and order me to put my hands in the air, I put two of their cars into their air. It did put pressure on my head. Roxy wasn't at one hundred percent when I took my body back. I didn't need to keep them in the air for long. I only needed to place them on top of the other two.

Those poor fools had no idea what they had walked into. Insistent do-gooders like Roxy would always pay for being nosey. I didn't even bother to enjoy their screams. I slammed the cars together until they were mushed together like two clumps of clay. I did always like clay.

The neighbors seriously started screaming after that, so I decided to hurry up and free the world before the freaking army came to get me.

I busted the door down in case he had tried to barricade it. It fell easily enough. I stepped inside and didn't see him. "Adam?" Why was he hiding from me? "Adam?"

I didn't think he would be hiding in the basement. He wouldn't want to be near the portal knowing that I would follow him. He must have been waiting for me upstairs.

I smiled and rushed up the stairs and opened the master bedroom. "Adam!"

I was constantly hit with a barrage of bullets and manly yells that he probably got from watching too many action films. If I weren't as skilled as I am, I probably wouldn't have been able to stop all of them. He probably shot at me twenty times before he was shocked enough for me to take the time to pull the gun from out of his hands and toss it out the window. "What are you doing?

"Stay away from me."

Why was he so afraid of me? It made me feel bad. "Adam…"

"Stay away!" He had backed himself up into a wall. I had never seen him like that. Yeah, he hated me still, but he was also scared.

"I wouldn't hurt you."

"You've proven otherwise."

"But that's in the past."

"You tried to kill me!"

321

"But I gave up my body to bring you back." I honestly didn't know what would happen to me when I let Roxy take over my body. I could have died, but I couldn't think about that. I couldn't let Adam die, no matter what the cost. "Doesn't that mean anything?"

"No!" He yelled.

"But it should mean everything." I didn't understand. Service and sacrifice usually meant so much for humanity. Didn't Christianity spread because God in human form sacrificed himself for a bunch of ungrateful human beings? Why was Adam being an ungrateful human being? "I just risked everything for you!"

He shrugged his shoulders as if my feelings were some kind of game to him. "Why?" He laughed exasperated.

I felt so shy all of a sudden. I had never felt the way that I felt before. I felt like a hypocrite for even giving into it, but I couldn't help it. He made me feel like a child and children only care about what they want. "I love you, Silly."

I started blushing. I touched my face and my cheeks felt like they were on fire. That had never happened to me before. My heart was pounding, that nauseating fluttering had come back, and I finally realized that I experienced what the humans referred to as "butterflies". I even giggled like an idiot. "Now it's your turn."

He cocked his brow and he looked so adorable. "My turn for what? To be doped up on crazy pills?"

"Don't be so silly!" I laughed. He was so funny. "Be honest with me. Tell me that you love me."

He raised both of his brows. Maybe he hadn't realized it before, but I could sense that he had become assured in something. I had yet to feel the overpowering love toward me seep out of him like a sickening (yet somehow pleasing) array, but I figured it was coming. "Lyla."

"Yes?" I couldn't stop smiling.

"I am absolutely one hundred percent certain that I am not in love with you."

I guess I could stop smiling. "What?"

"As a matter of fact, I despise you." I didn't get it. I still felt that reassurance. He wasn't torn about anything. There was no inner turmoil or conflicted emotions, but that wasn't possible. "There is no one else worthy in this world of this much hatred than you. I like Hitler and Genghis Khan more than you. I might like Satan more than you."

I tried to laugh it off. "Well, you question the reality of hell, so that's not too bad."

"Oh, I believe in hell. I've been there since I met you!" He was so angry with me. How could he feel that way about me when I told him that I loved him? "You've got to be insane to think that I would ever love you."

I couldn't believe myself. I felt tears in my eyes. I didn't cry unless I wanted to. I hadn't cried since I was a little girl chained up in the basement. I couldn't let some boy make me cry! But I was so confused, and it hurt. The inside of my chest was aching. My heart couldn't literally be breaking, could it? "But I feel a connection between us."

"I'd rather screw a cactus."

I was so hurt, I could barely speak. "You're lying to me."

"No. I'm not." He was no longer afraid. It was like my torment gave him some kind of unknown power, and he actually approached me and placed his hands on my shoulders. "I promise to God that I'm not. I hate you. You should do us both a favor and kill yourself."

"You would lose Roxy just to not be with me?" I knew how much he loved her, despite being so inferior to the both of us. Hearing him say that it would be better if we were both dead was the breaking point, and I actually started to cry over that stupid boy!

323

"I'm gonna lose her anyway. You might as well give me some sense of relief and die right here."

Then it became an annoying cry that just exploded out of me. I didn't recognize the person I had become. I was like any regular weak human. If that's what love was, then I hated it!

"Oh, and now you're gonna cry?" Adam mocked. "You can't be that evil and then cry when someone calls you out on it. You're being pathetic!"

"And you're a liar." I knew that I was, and I tried to do my best to suck it up, but I didn't know how. I was acting no better than a child finding out that Santa wasn't real or that their parents were getting divorced or something like that. I just couldn't help that I was upset.

"No. I'm not."

"Yes, you are!" I finally couldn't take it anymore, and I flung him up against the wall and pinned him down tight. "And I don't like lies, Adam."

"What are you doing?" He suddenly wasn't in the mood to mock me anymore.

"You're only lying to me because you're afraid." He suddenly became all too clear for me. I could feel who he was right at his core. He was a boy afraid of the truth. He weighed himself down with lies to keep himself from rising to the surface. "You're afraid of what it'll do to Roxy and what it would mean for you. I understand!"

"No. Lyla—"

"Shhh!" I placed my finger on his lovely lips and closed them tight with my mind so he could plainly hear me while I whispered his salvation so softly in his ear. "I'm gonna set you free."

"No!" He knew how futile it was to fight against me, yet he bothered to try it anyway. "Please, Lyla, don't do this!" He was so desperate for me to save him. It amazed me how confused he was. Humans didn't know themselves at all.

"I have to do this. It's the only way you'll realize who you belong with."

Then he became so desperate, the most I had ever seen him. I had seen him look at Roxy at the brink of death and never give such a look as in that moment when he tried to stop me from making his life better. "If you really do love me—even a little bit—you will not do this to me."

How could Adam believe he was a good man and be afraid of the darkness that lay dormant within him? I truly wanted to know, because I didn't understand how his mind worked. Was it better for him to live his life in a lie if he could live in peace from himself? I didn't believe that's how anyone should live. If anything, I could alleviate his burden of fear from not knowing.

"I'm sorry, but this is the only way to save you." I didn't give him the time to refuse me again. I placed my hand on his face and looked deep into his eyes, connecting him with me. I wanted to feel what he was so afraid of. It was literally nothing! He was afraid of nothing. He was scared of feeling nothing. He deserved to know that. When I pulled myself out of his soul, I cut the string and let the true mastermind of his life rise as I let him fall to his feet.

He kept his head down for a while. He was trying to process, but there was nothing left to figure out. He must have known how much he cared about me. "Adam—"

He grabbed my neck and pinned my back into the wall. He was squeezing my neck so tightly that I couldn't breathe. He was still super strong and he was a tiny bit shy of totally snapping my neck into pieces. Those hateful eyes that I found so wonderfully attractive suddenly became my undoing. I was going to die in his beauty.

I didn't know that he would actually kill me. He was going to do it if I didn't kill him first, but I couldn't. I was really in love with him.

Then something changed. There was something else in his eyes and something else I could feel. It felt like a ravenous hunger. I could feel it in myself, so I recognized what it was. Then, a little smirk appeared on his face right before he leaned right into me and kissed my lips.

I chose to forget the pervert encounter and dubbed that my first real kiss from a boy and I could seriously start to enjoy it once he stopped choking me. He still tasted sweet from breakfast, but he had never been so passionate with Roxy. He was unbound and fearless, and I knew how much he wanted me.

He swooped me off my feet, and I realized why Roxy was so blown away by his strength. I even enjoyed touching his broad shoulders. He was my Chosen and I deserved him. I made people honest. I didn't force anyone like that twit, Roxy.

He threw me onto the bed and I knew he was preparing to give me exactly what I asked for, but I couldn't let him do it. "Wait!" I had to physically stop him with my powers, because he was so riled up.

He started laughing from unbelief. "I know you want me."

"Of course I do, but now isn't a good time." It was what I wanted. I was in the perfect position to exile Roxy forever in the most perfect way, but I just couldn't do it. "If I let this happen, I won't want it to stop, and we're short on time. I've got to get into that portal, and I've got to free the world." I felt like such a tease and I hated being a tease. "I hope you understand."

"I do." I let him go, but he was only acting so he could sit on the bed with me and move in to kiss me. I was flattered that he couldn't keep his hands off of me, but I had to push him away.

"Adam, I'm being serious."

He smirked and traced his finger on my arm starting from my bare shoulder, tipping my strap over on his way down to my hand. He tickled and electrified every inch of my skin and to top it all off, he looked back at me out of the corner of his eye and his smirk grew. "Do you know what I really feel about you right now?"

He was too charming not to play with. "What?"

"I'm grateful." His hand snaked behind my back and pulled me into his lap. "I don't feel it anymore."

"And pray tell what is 'it' that you don't feel?"

He continued to stroke my skin, tempting me in the simplest of ways. "I've been so concerned with being a monster after I murdered my stepfather that I made myself feel such guilt over what I had done. I made it this colossal mistake that I let hinder my whole life and it made me feel less than human. But now, I can admit the truth." He ceased teasing me and smiled like a child instead of my sexy lover. "I don't miss him. I don't care that I shot him. I'm glad that I did it. He deserved to die."

He certainly sounded exceedingly happy and content with being so cold. It didn't matter to me that when he opened his heart, the draft rushed in and frosted everything. As long as he was happy as a result of something I had done, I was pleased. "I'm glad you feel so renewed."

"I do." He laughed to himself while he found it too difficult to keep from touching me and kissing my lips and my neck. "I thought you were gonna make everybody devolve into a bunch of howler monkeys until we ruined the planet. This is amazing."

The way he was with me was more than I imagined. He was sexy, sultry, and almost romantic. "So what now, my Chosen?"

"I want to help you."

"Really?"

"Everyone should feel this way."

I was grateful, but I couldn't entirely believe him. It was too perfect. He couldn't keep his hands off of me, and he wanted to fulfill his calling to aid me. Adam was incapable of lying to me after having a free mind, but he must have been playing some kind of game on me. "What about Roxy?"

"Roxy?" He stopped and looked at me pitifully, and his emotions exploded all over the place. I felt his love for her burst inside of me. "I love Roxy."

"I know you do." Even with him being freed, he didn't express any of those emotions toward me. Maybe he really wasn't in love with me and even if he were, it didn't compare to what he felt for Roxy. "Helping me would destroy her."

"She's determined to be destroyed anyway." Just because Adam knew that to be true, it didn't stop him from grieving over her. He became even more pitiful, and his grief overcame me like a tidal wave. "I'm gonna miss her."

I was starting to feel...Bad for him. I actually found myself wishing I could do something to keep Roxy alive...As long as she was living outside of my body in Siberia somewhere. There just wasn't anything I could do. I didn't decide that she had to die for my cause. "And that's it? You're still gonna help me?"

"Well," he sexily smirked and leaned into me until he pushed my back into the bed. "I do wanna sleep with you."

I was so over the guilt thing. It wasn't my style. "And why is that?" I touched his face and felt his wonderfully structured cheek bones. He could have been a model, and not one of those slender ones with delicate features that made them look ambiguous. He was the epitome of male perfection from his strong jaw line to his appropriately protruding chin. His nose wasn't too wide or too long. He had such pretty yellow skin, and whether his hair was short and wavy or peach fuzz, he was still incredibly sexy, and I rather enjoyed his new pair of silver eyes. He was literally so good looking that he could have had any girl in the school. Roxy didn't flaunt or exploit our strengths enough to catch a man like him.

"I know I'm pretty and powerful, but I'm like a bundle of adorable. This body doesn't exactly scream sex symbol."

"You're incredibly sexy, Lyla. You could be taller, but I'm wildly attracted to you. It must be from all of those times I imagined this body naked." He smirked unbelievably naughty! Adam had never once implied to Roxy that he was checking her out in a sexual way. He was always such a gentleman, consciously never wanting to make her feel uncomfortable since she was such a prude.

I giggled. It might have been from his sweet kisses or from the fact that he was finally letting his true self show. "All of those sweet nothings you whispered to Roxy about not wanting anyone else was all for nothing."

"No, I meant every word." He shrugged it off. "Things are just different now. I'm different." How fickle of him.

As much as I was enjoying Adam, I pushed him off of me before he started taking off our clothes. "Should I continue to call you Adam or can you acknowledge the real you, Blake?"

"I don't honestly care." He was persistent and tried to kiss me again, but I held him back once more. There would be plenty of time for that once I freed the world.

"I'm not gonna free the world in a bloodied nightgown. I'm gonna find something more appropriate for a queen. Prepare yourself. All those guns outside should come in handy."

"What's beyond the portal?"

"I know *what* is there, but there's no telling *who* is there. Roxy's brigade of allies was far too pathetic. There might be last minute resistance."

"Well, I don't know if you've noticed this, but I've got super strength and the ability to heal." Adam—or Blake rather—had such a cocky attitude. He always had a sexy confidence to him. I liked it.

"The strength is yours to have now, but the healing is probably temporary and I don't know when it will fail you."

"Why don't you give me some of your ability?"

I laughed at his blind arrogance. "Because if you don't seize to death, you'd have a brain aneurism if you tried to levitate a spoon."

"You think I'm that weak compared to you?" He laughed, but he was offended. All of that time he was terrified of becoming something other than human, he was only forcing himself to feel that way because it was the proper thing to do.

"Humans get a little bit of power and then it always goes to their head. Trust me, Blake, you can't handle it." I wasn't trying to underestimate him or make myself more superior—though I already was. He'd be in true danger if he took on my powers. The only reason why he wasn't dead from having Roxy's abilities was because it replenished his body constantly, but he wouldn't retain it forever. Roxy and I were just different from all other Avarians, far more powerful and of royal blood.

"Blake, do yourself a favor and get armed." I started heading for the bathroom, so I could take a quick shower and wash all of the blood off of my body.

Just as I had turned around, I felt his hard chest against my back and his hands easing their away across my tiny waist. "I'd rather join you in the shower."

It was hard to resist him when he started kissing my neck again. If that portal weren't already open, we wouldn't be having that conversation at all. I had to be strong, and I broke free from him. "We're on a tight schedule. No time for games!"

He laughed. I think he enjoyed playing with me. "Tonight then."

330

"Tonight." I closed the door and locked it so he wouldn't join me. Of course he could have always busted the door down, but that would be a bit extreme.

I was so excited about everything. Soon, I would fulfill my destiny and be rid of Roxy forever. I had often dreamed of such a day. While I was strapped up in those chains dealing with those fools and pretending to be ignorant, I knew that it would pay off one day. Everything had gone according to plan.

I slipped off the straps to my mother's gown and let it slip off my shoulders and onto the ground. It was soaked in my blood, and I didn't feel it was appropriate to start the new world off in my blood. I wanted to be sitting pretty in my new world. I didn't exactly know what was going to happen, but after the humans destroyed themselves, I knew I would become queen of the Avarians. I'd have to manage my life without Roxy's convenient ability, but it's not like anyone could really hurt me.

I didn't stay long in the shower. As soon as I washed off all the blood, I got out and dried myself off. I tried to slick my hair back, but my natural curls were quite insistent and informed me that they would not be restrained unless I had a blow dryer and a flatiron.

I unlocked and opened the bathroom door and saw a black party dress. It was velvet and strapless with a gold trim around the outline of the breast, studded with diamonds. It appeared that Mother could be quite the diva when she desired.

"I thought you'd look lovely in it." Blake was watching me from the doorway, leaning against the frame like a skank, armed with a couple of machine guns strapped to him, while he gazed upon my naked body. "I guess wishes do come true."

I laughed to myself and put the dress on. It didn't fit quite right, and I didn't fill it out as nicely as my mother probably did, but it was a pretty dress for it being so out of date. "I love it."

331

Blake began taking off his guns and setting them on the floor. Then he took off his shirt and dropped it on the ground. He was also covered in blood, but I was still turned on by his rock hard abs. "You never want me to get to this ritual of mine, do you? It's like you're trying to stall me."

"No. I meant what I said." He smiled, and I sort of became putty in his hand. It would have been clever of him to stall me in that way, but I don't think he was capable of lying to me. Besides, what I felt between us was sensual and genuine. It wasn't constructed, and I could certainly feel his desire for me. Those weren't lies, but there could have been some manipulation hidden within his truth.

"You really want to help me? You don't wanna live in paradise?"

"People like my stepdad don't deserve paradise. That's why God made hell." Once again, he was quite cold. I really liked it.

"Wash your face a bit and then we'll go."

"Yes, Ma'am." It was too good to be true. I knew I was worthy for him to leave Roxy for me, but I knew how much he cared for her. He must have truly believed in my cause and what I was doing. I was glad that setting him free gave him such peace. Roxy couldn't do that. Sure, she could make him feel happy for a while, but only as long as those weights were slowly sinking him into the ground. Only when you were free of attachments could you truly be yourself.

Roxy was buried deep within me, and if she did come back, it probably wouldn't be until the next dawn. It would be too late by then. She had failed. "I win."

Chapter Seventeen

"It's pretty wild, isn't it?"

"That's putting it lightly." There was literally a hole in the universe floating in the middle of a basement in a tiny suburb. It had a diameter of about six feet. There was a blue sparking energy surrounding it, but the inside was like a shimmering silver liquid screen over the air, but I could see through it. Inside the portal, there was the inside of a temple made out of white stone. I couldn't see the altar or the staff of power, but it must have been farther down from the long walkway that I saw. I walked behind the portal and saw the same image of the temple. It was definitely trippy.

"Are you ready?" Blake asked rather impatiently.

"Of course I am. I've been waiting for this day for at least twelve years of my life." I stepped through the portal, and I can't thoroughly describe much what it felt like. It was most certainly weird, but it was over as soon as I stepped inside of it. I looked around, and I was inside of the temple. I turned around, and there was Blake, still standing inside of the basement looking amazed that I had just disappeared to the other side. I still had a sensation left on my skin. It was sort of like being moist from when you've gotten out the shower and haven't quite dried all the way, but I wasn't wet.

I noticed all of the hairs on my arm were standing straight up. There was a chill on my skin, but I didn't feel cool. It was like a shock from rubbing your feet against the carpet.

I watched the portal to see what it looked like when someone came through. I saw Blake reach his hand through from the other side and then he disappeared in shimmering golden light. I stepped back and gasped. I was concerned that my lover had been digitized and wouldn't reassemble himself by my side, but then there was a speck of light that came through the portal. It grew as it reached out toward me until it formed his hand and spread out and became his body. The light then faded away into his normal form.

"Did it look amazing? It didn't feel as I expected."

I think my mouth was still hanging low, so I closed it and gathered myself mentally. "It was interesting, for sure."

Blake's body suddenly became still, except for his fingers that became clinched in a tight fist. "We're not alone."

I didn't see anyone around us, so I set my sights up above our heads. "Oh joy…"

I was right about Roxy's last ditch effort resistance. The Great Hall was enormous with a walkway that was about the length of a football field, floating on seemingly endless water. The runway led to an estimated fifty steps that led to top of the altar with the golden, jewel encrusted Staff of Power. There were pillars all around the temple and large ledges overhead that spread across the entire temple. On those ledges were men dressed in white cloaks, armed with swords.

"Are these friends of yours?" Blake asked.

"I'm afraid not."

Blake and I circled the room quickly to count as many as we could, but there had to be at least a hundred men. We didn't have enough time for the exact number and we ended up being back to back, preparing ourselves for our toughest battle yet.

"Do you think they would forget about trying to kill me if I told them that I was Roxy's boyfriend?"

"Considering that you're with me, I don't think that's gonna help." It didn't matter. Blake had nothing to worry about. I could handle an army of Avarians, especially with him by my side. "Do me a favor and don't die."

"Yes, Ma'am."

They charged us all at once like a storm cloud. Blake drew his guns and began to shoot while I stopped them all in midair. It wasn't the easiest thing to do. I was still feeling weak from before, and they were somehow different from Rider and his boys. I didn't know if they were physically strong, but they were certainly more powerful.

I tried to hold them still long enough for Blake to kill them one at a time, but my head started pounding. I looked behind me at those Blake had slaughtered and let them fall one by one. Some of them fell into the white marble floors while other poisoned the clear waters with their insignificant lives. They were strong and persistent annoyances. Blake had to shoot them several times before they would stop moving.

I felt a sting in my arm, and it shocked me enough to let go of some of my grip. I shielded my newly made cut and eyed the weapon stained with my blood as my attacker fell perfectly on his feet. Roxy wasn't very athletic and she made my body less than ideal for combat. I was fit, but hardly built like a warrior. I had no chance in a physical confrontation and the black pumps on my feet wouldn't help me either. I did the dishonorable thing and sent the sword flying straight into the wannabe ninja's head. He was killed instantly, but my brief victory cost me some more of my focus and more of them began to fall.

"Lyla!" Blake complained when they started charging after him. He shot a couple more, but they continued moving quickly until they were fast enough to forcibly remove the guns out of his hands. Blake was still quick—perhaps quicker than them. He dodged a couple of sword swings from two of them and maneuvered his way until they clumsily stabbed each other in the chest.

"You can take care of yourself, Blake." I had enough on my mind while they were coming after me. I wasn't any faster or stronger than the average human female. I had to rely on my wits and my incredible power to survive. Blake's guns weren't being used by him, and I doubted he had any time to worry about them. I floated them to myself as fast as possible and fired the guns down into the ground, constantly circling me as my own personal force field, so no one would try close contact fighting while I worked. Restraining me was about all they could do anyway. They wouldn't want to kill me and consequentially kill Roxy.

The bullet frenzy came to quite a surprise to them, which I used to my advantage. I yanked the swords out of five of their hands, stabbed them in the gut, and twisted the swords until it was enough to make them fall to the ground dead.

The more I used my powers offensively, the more of them fell free. I continued killing them with their own weapons, but it was becoming more difficult in the heat of battle.

I was also concerned with Blake. He should have been able to prove himself to me, but I was worried that his lack of combat skills would get him killed. He wasn't fighting the army of men unscathed. He was continuously getting slashed with each new opponent.

As soon as I ran out of bullets, I tossed the guns straight into a couple of heads. I didn't hit them hard enough to kill, but it knocked them to the ground pretty hard. They were smart and didn't get back up.

I heard Blake scream, and I turned around to make sure he was still alive. He had gotten slashed terrible across his back, splitting his seal of loyalty toward me in half. I really liked that tattoo. They had to pay. "Stay away from him!"

I was angry and wouldn't risk Blake's life anymore. I concentrated and picked up everyone who was still standing. They thought they could throw me off by tossing their swords at me, but I stopped those as well and turned them back on them. I didn't want to play any more games, so I rammed their swords straight through their hearts. They were remarkable creatures. Some of them were even still squirming. They reminded me of insects who still twitched a little bit after their bodies has been severed, but they died just the same.

I dropped their bodies in the in water with the other stragglers. I didn't want to trip over anyone while I strutted on the runway to my destiny. It was an admirable try for Team Good, but they were always doomed.

I heard Blake grunting in pain and I hurried over to him. "Are you alright?"

I watched his wounds, but none of them were closing. He had cuts on his face, on his arms, several on his torso, legs, the big one on his back, and a stab wound in his shoulder. He was bleeding a lot, but it was nothing he couldn't heal from with some medical attention. It was sad that Roxy's healing abilities had already faded, but a human like him could have never truly retained the power of immortality.

"I told you, Blake, you're only a human!"

"Why are you mad at me?"

I didn't know why. Maybe it was because he tagged along and risked himself in the first place. "Just take better care of yourself, or I'll have to kill you."

"That sounds a bit conflicting."

"I'm serious!" I would never have Roxy again. If anything happened to Blake, he'd be gone, and there was nothing I could do about it. "I want you to be by my side always." I took his hands and smiled.

For some reason, Blake didn't appear to be wildly enthused that I was offering myself up to him forever.

"Do you…" I don't know why I was hesitating. I wasn't afraid of anything. "Do you still hate me?"

He tilted his head as he thought. "Not nearly as immensely as before, but definitely enough to be alarmed about."

I didn't understand. I thought things were different. He said he was grateful toward me. I made his life better. I rebirthed him into my world. He was exactly as I pleased and of his own free will. How could he hate me? "Then why are you here with me now?"

I felt a pang in my chest created from a bolt of anger that struck our hearts simultaneously. "Because no matter how much I understand and respect Roxy's decision to make the earth a paradise, I don't buy it. I don't think it's possible. It'll never last, because we humans aren't good. We're just not. I'm not sure if I completely believe in God, but I believe he'd give everyone exactly what they deserve, meaning we'd somehow screw up paradise and her sacrifice would be in vain. What she's doing is idiotic!

"She might be doing it with pure intentions, but I resent it." Blake was incredibly hurt. "I resent her for making this choice and for leaving me and…And…" He paused, trying to form his difficult feelings that came to his mind easily enough, but translated poorly. "You're a good rebound."

He began to stroke some of my lose strands of hair that had gotten in my face during the battle and brushed it back, almost like he was affectionate and felt something for me. "It's because you look just like her. You remind me of that girl who I always wanted, and in some way, being with you would be like having a piece of her."

338

I tilted my head away, so he wouldn't touch me anymore. I enjoyed the way he was with me all the sudden, but it wasn't because he loved me or even liked me. It wasn't because he thought I was pretty or because he thought what I was doing was right. When Roxy was gone, he wanted to look at me like a soulless vessel and remember the girl who used to dwell within. That was probably the most hurtful thing that had ever been said to me. I never had anyone who made me feel that low since I was first chained up to my basement walls. I thought something was wrong with me, but I didn't think I did anything wrong. I said I was sorry for hurting that little boy. I didn't mean to hurt anybody. They said they forgave me. So why didn't Mommy and Daddy love me anymore?

I was struggling not to cry and to push those worthless emotions out of my mind and soul. They shouldn't have meant anything to me. All they did was make me weak! I shouldn't have cared about what any human thought about me. As long as they feared me, that was all the respect I needed.

But then why was I so heartbroken by Blake's constant rejection? "So, you don't think you could ever grow to love me?"

"No," he said quickly with self-assurance and a no-nonsense tone that made me aware that there was no room for growth. "Too much has happened between us."

Then he smiled and lightly patted me on the arm. "But I think you and I can have some fun."

"Fun?" I laughed, but it was the saddest and most pitiful laugh in the existence of time. That's all I really was to him. I was just the body that his adolescent body craved to bang; because he could never make love to the woman who he believed earned it rightfully. I wanted him as well, but I wasn't sure if it was enough, and I didn't have enough time to figure it out.

"Now go and fulfill your destiny or whatever. Everyone is waiting."

I forced myself to smile. It was the brave thing to do, and I didn't want him to think I was scared. I wasn't. There wasn't a thing in the world that frightened me, not even the thought of living the rest of my life never being loved by the man I would literally crush the world until it leaked out blood for. No! I wasn't afraid—not even in the slightest.

It's not like Blake was the same man I fell in love with anyway. I admired Adam for his endless devotion toward Roxy, for his abrasive attitude toward me when we'd banter sexily with each other over silly matters like right and wrong, and for always standing up confidently against me in an act of heroism, despite being totally terrified of my power. I fell for how relentless he was in his effort to stop me. It wasn't because I needed someone to fight against. I just appreciated the fact that while I was surrounded by sniveling cowards, he actually had a spine. A queen needed a man like that.

Blake wasn't like that. Sure, he'd probably argue with me and would have even snapped my neck if I made him angry enough. He was still physically a hunk of flesh that made my mind wander into X-rated places. He was wild, honest, and brave enough to execute whatever he felt he needed to get done, but his bountiful unrelenting sense of loyalty was gone. He didn't really have loyalty toward me. He thought I was fun for the meantime, and he had completely betrayed Roxy. The only thing I could trust about him was that he was going to betray me. Blake was a sluty, uncaring, unsympathetic, selfish, psychotic, murdering, douchebag.

He was no different from the rest of the humans. Did he even deserve to be loved anymore, or was I holding on to who Adam used to be a couple of hours ago?

It didn't matter. I held in my tears and began taking the long walk toward my destiny. My destiny was all that mattered and all that was ever truly mine. Taking a hold of the Staff of Power and setting the world free was what I was born to do—what I was expected to do. It's why my parents treated me like a monster and why my followers worshiped me like a god. The staff was calling out to me. I could feel it yanking onto my heart and expanding my chest as its power circulated through me. I had to fulfill my purpose.

"You really shouldn't do that." It was my own voice spoken inside of my head, but I wouldn't be thinking that.

"What?"

"You know you don't wanna go through with this. Look what you did to my Adam." It wasn't how I would talk. It was the wrong pitch.

"Roxy?" I stopped about midway down and looked around me. She wasn't behind me. It didn't even sound like she was anywhere except for inside me, but I was the one who was supposed to be in control.

"What's going on?" Blake asked.

"Nothing." I tried to keep walking, but I heard her voice again.

"You can't ignore me, Lyla!" No, I couldn't ignore her. She was much too loud in my head. *"I'm right over here."*

I turned my head toward the water. The blood from her slaughtered followers was contaminating the water, but it wasn't all of the way run over with red. I could clearly see my reflection, but it wasn't exactly me. It didn't move as I did. "How are you doing this?"

"Porter told me that I would be tested by my other self when I entered the temple. I assume the same goes for you."

"If this were a test, you'd have to be somewhat of a challenge, and I've already made it very clear that you've lost." I flipped my hair back and continued strutting.

"Please don't do this, Lyla." She was so annoying! How could she cry inside of my head?

"It's no use, Roxy. I'm not letting you turn humanity into a bunch of bobble heads. That's not what's supposed to happen."

"Don't act like you're pleased with what you did to Adam."

I shouldn't have let that stop me, but it did. Blake was fine. He wasn't Adam, but he'd be good enough. I'd make it work. "You don't know what you're talking about."

"I've been aware ever since you entered this room. I know you have regrets, and I'm in your head whether you say your thoughts out loud or not."

Jeez, that sucked! She invaded my body, and I couldn't even have any thoughts to myself.

"If you aren't good for him, what makes you think you're good for the entire planet?"

I wasn't aware that little Roxy could debase herself long enough to come up with a low blow. It was well played, but I preferred to aim for the jugular. "Well, then you must know how much Blake hates you for deciding to disappear! Don't try and stop me so you can break his heart."

I watched her in the reflection as she began to frown up her face. She was going to start crying a freaking river. She was always going to be a pathetic baby! *"Maybe he's right, you know. Maybe humanity doesn't deserve paradise."*

I rolled my eyes. "I could have told you that."

"But you know taking away humanity's ability to judge is wrong."

"I make them more of themself!"

"You take away their ability to love, and be loyal, and to make the right decisions. You can't make the entire world selfish. Look how far it's gotten you, Lyla. You're completely alone, and the man you love will never love you back."

"That's because you're always in the way!" I snapped.

"No. It's because you're not worthy of it."

Why that sniveling, vile, ingrate! I had never been so insulted in my life! How could I be unworthy when he sunk to such filthy levels to care for her? And she was so confident and smug about it. If Roxy had her own body, I would have ripped her eyes out!

"You're so full of yourself that you can't truly let anyone else in, and you're so stingy that you could never really give yourself over to anyone else. That's why it'll never work out between you and Adam, or anyone else."

She didn't know what she was talking about. Blake had plans with me. We were going to be an item. She just refused to see the truth because she was jealous! "I don't need a tongue lashing from a dead girl. Excuse me, but I've got a destiny to fulfill."

I started walking again. I could still feel the Staff of Power pulling on me. I wanted to touch the gold and let its power resonate all throughout my body as I poured my desire out into the world. I wanted to touch each soul and usher in a new age of humanity until they ran themselves into the ground. I wanted to stand in that mysterious light that surrounded it yet had nowhere to come from other than its own energy. It must have been incredible. Nothing could stop me from taking my victory.

"Sister, stop!"

"Sister?" I mumbled it. The word was foreign to me. I had never uttered it myself, nor had I heard it directed toward me. It held such value for other human beings, but I didn't recognize its value. My experience with the world was far too minimal, yet the only person who I knew was my "sister" seemed to hold it with such merit, as if it was supposed to stop me and correct all the wrongs in the world.

"Sister?" No, I didn't recognize what the word was supposed to mean. It was supposed to mean comradery. It was supposed to mean that even though you might fight, you could make up because you were blood and still loved each other. It was supposed to be a bond that no one else could understand—not even the closest of friends. It was supposed to mean trust, and honor, and that someone would always have your back.

"You dare call me sister?" I went into a full rage and got on my knees, so I'd be close enough to lash out at my reflection in the water. I hit Roxy's form and splashed her image until she rippled and waved away, but she shimmered back into the calm puddle again and looked at me with confused, doe eyes. "You have some nerve! Where were you when Mommy and Daddy locked me up every night like a monster?"

"I was right there with you!"

"No, you weren't. You were too busy dreaming about how to get rid of me. And when you were yourself, you never once asked them to stop treating me so cruelly. You thought I scratched and bruised myself up? No! They did that when they were angry or afraid, but you didn't care. You bought into their bravado and believed I was the Boogeyman that hid in your closet, waiting to eat you alive. You're just as responsible as they are for making me the way that I am!"

My voice was beginning to rasp up. I hated that my face was stained with tears. I certainly didn't like crying, and I certainly didn't want to do it in front of Roxy. I couldn't help myself. I was so angry for what she had done to me. I was angry for what they had all done to me.

"I'm sorry for not standing up for you." She must have accepted what I had said. She shed her tears in the mystical reflection and wiped them away just as I did. It was her fault that my life was hell!

"But…" Roxy began to look angry and yell. *"Don't you think it's time to take some responsibility for your own actions? How old do you have to be before you can be held accountable for what you've done, huh? Eighteen? Thirty? Fifty? It's not always gonna be someone else's fault. You're the one who killed all those people and you're the one who ruined Adam!"*

"Shut up!" I didn't want to hear any more of what she had to say. I pounded my fists into her reflection. I just wanted her to go away. And just as I did, the blood flowed down and covered her up.

"What are you doing?" Blake grabbed me by my arms and helped me on my feet. "Have you finally snapped all the way off?"

I was a little amazed. "You can't hear her, can you?"

"I only heard you yelling at your reflection like the crazy person I know you are. This is a little bit farther off the deep end than usual." I was surprised he was concerned for my wellbeing. Earlier that morning, he wanted the ritual to be disbarred completely, yet I found him anxiously waiting for me to complete it.

I smirked and grabbed his face while I kissed him—full tongue and all. I knew Roxy was watching. If she were aware like me, she could see everything and almost feel everything, but not enough. It was a personal hell. She wouldn't be able to kiss the man she loved goodbye and had to instead stand by and watch while he embraced me.

"What was that for?" He asked with a smirk.

Roxy was speechless, so I had to do it again. "Just shut up and kiss me."

I didn't care that Blake was bleeding or covered in blood. I didn't care that I would need another good shower, or that all sorts of military officers were probably closing in on Porter's house and would soon arrive in that basement to find us. I was too busy hurting my dear sister to care.

"You're so cruel, Lyla." I had done what I set out to do, but it wasn't nearly enough.

"Roxy is about to die." I hugged Blake and pressed my head up against his firm chest. Roxy could see me touching him; she could almost feel it, but not quite. She was like an echo living inside of me—never the real voice. "Are you okay with that?"

345

"You know that I'm not." I felt that overbearing, puke worthy love rushing out of him again. The only consolation was that it was mixed in with such resentment and anger that it sullied his positive feelings to probably leave Roxy paralyzed with guilt. "I would have forsaken the entire world a hundred times for her, but she apparently didn't feel the same way about me. I don't have much of a choice in the matter, so screw it. You can both do what you want."

I held him tighter. Roxy wasn't saying anything, and that's how I knew that I had won. "I'll do this, and then we'll have our fun." I made sure to say it seductively, so even Miss Naive could understand the sexual implications behind it.

I let go of Blake and started making my last twenty yards with a satisfied grin on my face.

Then there was a tremendous splash of water, a wild force of energy, and I heard Blake scream. I turned just in time to see him fly across the right side of the water, at least a hundred feet back. "Blake!"

One of Roxy's followers had survived, and he had hit Blake with some sort of power that I didn't understand. I sensed that he was different, but I didn't know how. "How dare you!" I lashed out at him and snapped his neck so hard that his face became part of his backside. He died easily enough, but I didn't know what he had done to my dear Blake.

"I'm coming!" In a wild panic, I stepped out into the water but fell completely in. I thought it was shallow, but it turned out to be as immense and as big as an ocean. I couldn't anticipate how far down the bottom was, and there was no way for me to know how wide it was either.

"Don't be an idiot, Lyla."

I realized how much of a child I was being. I didn't need to rush in after him. I lifted myself out of the water and did the same for his body. I could hear him gagging, and it became difficult to concentrate. I was overrun by the thought of losing him, and my emotions began to get the best of me. I was trembling. "Hold on, Baby!"

I sat us both down on the marble walkway, and I fell to his side. He was having another seizure, and I didn't know how to make it stop. "Blake!" The only way I knew to save him was to have Roxy do it, but I was not going to be tricked into turning into her. He was going to snap out of it someway. "Blake?"

Then it stopped. He was perfectly still, and then he breathed a sigh of relief that extinguished all of the strength from him.

"He's alright!"

He wearily opened his eyes. "Roxy?"

I was hit with a sudden pang of worry. "No. It's me, Lyla."

"I'm right here, Adam!" That twit just wouldn't shut up. *"I won't leave you!"*

"Roxy!" He sprung up and held on tight to me.

"No. I'm…" It was impossible. "You can hear her now?"

He didn't even hear me. He couldn't stop looking through me, like I was just the vessel and she was the soul. He grabbed my face, and his eyes were so loving, but I didn't feel that any of it was for me. "How is this possible?"

"I don't know, but I'm glad I get to tell you this." I looked at my reflection, and I could see her holding and speaking to him, as if I didn't exist at all. *"I'm sorry if I made you feel like I was bailing out on you and our relationship. That's not how I ever wanted to make you feel. I love you more than anything, Adam. I love you more than glory or duty. Maybe it's incredibly selfish of me, but I think I'm willing to forsake the world for you too."*

He clasped my hands with such desperate hope. "Are you saying you won't do the ritual?"

347

"I won't." I couldn't believe it. That selfish nitwit was breaking all of the rules.

"I'm glad." Blake couldn't help himself. He forgot that I was in control, and that Roxy was only a voice in my head that he could somehow hear, and he kissed me. When he did, it was different from all the other times. It wasn't sexy, and it wasn't sultry, and it didn't make me want to take me clothes off. It made me want to weep at the beauty of how he made me feel and that he didn't even mean it for me.

I pushed him off of me. "Hello!" I had enough of their little freak show. "It doesn't matter what the two of you want, because I'm in charge of this body. I'm the one who's gonna perform the ritual. I'm going to be the champion of the Avarian people. I'm going to set the world free!"

I got up and started to charge for the altar, but his strong hands grabbed a hold of my wrist. "No!"

I warned him with a glare. "Unhand me."

"Please, don't do this, Lyla!" Was he honestly begging me for mercy? What had happened to the careless and sexy Blake?

I tried to remind him who he was and what he desired with a sexy smirk. "I'm going to do this, and then we can have our fun."

I tried to move away, but he pulled tighter on my arm until I was eye level with him. "I don't want fun, Lyla. I want to live my life with the woman I love. Screw you. Screw the world. That's what I want."

"That's what you want?" I felt rejected in every sense of the word. He wouldn't accept me, he wouldn't give me affection, he saw right through me and made me feel useless, and he wouldn't let me become one with him. I couldn't stand it, and he'd pay for how inferior I felt. "Well, I want to watch the world burn!"

I forced him to let me go and I sent him flying back about fifty yards. I hoped he remembered how useless he was once Roxy was ripped from my body.

348

"You have to stop her, Adam!"

"Oh, give it up, Roxy!"

"Lyla!" Blake got back up on his feet and started running toward me. "You don't have to do this."

"Yes, I do." The Staff of Power was still calling out to me. It was the only thing that truly belonged to me in the world—it, and its power that it would grant. I longed to touch it and feel all of the human souls around the world. I wondered what it would feel like to have that many lives in my grasp.

I stepped on the altar, and I could feel its power growing stronger within me. Its mystical light fell upon my skin and bathed me in only a foretaste, and my mind became clearer. Things I had never wanted to feel before, I could understand. I could understand all of it. I could feel all of it.

Blake ran to the steps, but something prevented him from coming up. There was a force field of light that shimmered and repelled him back a few feet when he tried. "Why do you have to do this? Who said? Do you really even want this?"

"What else am I supposed to do?" I asked while still walking toward my golden prize. Its gems were dazzling. There were so many different colored stones sparkling for me and me alone. When it was in my grasp, I reached for it.

"Run away with me!"

I slowly drew my hand back and pulled it into my chest. It was a perfectly fine request. It was a perfectly, beautiful request. After all, I enjoyed his company during our journey. It just became excruciatingly complicated once I fell in love with him. "You mean run away with you and live in the shadows until the morning when you get to play house with your little doll? Watch you love her while you never love me? I don't think so! That's not a life."

349

"And how would you know? You've never had a real life. You've been given all these titles, restraints, and responsibilities. You don't know what it's like to live for yourself. I bet you don't even know what you want. Do you?"

I looked behind me and down at the sniveling human below me. He was beneath me, and he didn't deserve to have the power to make me feel so helpless. He didn't deserve to have such stunning eyes—whether they were blue or silver—filled with such conviction that it was capable of making me stop in my tracks and reconsider everything about who I was. He didn't deserve to be so wonderful.

I cried my last few tears and let them slip from my eyes so he could see, because I think he did deserve to know that he shattered my heart into so many pieces, that I questioned whether it truly belonged to me. "I wanted you."

I grabbed the staff, and I felt its power surge inside of me. My heart started pounding as an incredible energy circulated all around me. I could see Blake—Adam—whoever he was. I knew everything about him and exactly how he felt. I could see the humans back through the portal in that subdivision and how panicked and distraught they were from the damage. I could see the determined and curious SWAT team on the way as their fearless leader inspired his rowdy men, who were bored and excited to have something to do. I saw people angry because they were hungry, abandoned by their mothers, and doomed to live their life as products of the streets. I could feel the girl who felt violated, because she put her trust in someone that she thought she loved. I could feel the mind of a man who was on the brink of exploding all sense of his sanity, because he was so worried about how he was going to provide for his family. I could feel the innocence of a little girl who pecked a boy on the cheek for the first time, because he gave her a pudding cup. It was too much, yet I knew I could control it. I was connected to them all, and all they needed was a big tug to remove all of those cares. They didn't need any fear. They could all be free.

"Stop it, Lyla!"

I laughed and opened my eyes. "You're too l..."

Blake had snapped. He had grabbed one of the swords from Roxy's followers, and he had the tip pressed to his gut with his hands gripped onto the handle.

I tried not to care, but it was hard not to care when you were connected to over six billion people! "What are you doing?"

"Either Roxy and I get to live together, or we both die right here!" He looked crazed, definitely desperate. He said dozens of times that Roxy changed his life for the better, but I didn't think he was suicidal. That's not who he was.

I didn't exactly have the best poker face, but I was game. "You're bluffing."

He wasn't. He pulled the blade back and I screamed and cried like a baby as I saw him twist the sword inside of his body until he gritted his teeth from the pain, but that didn't stop the blood from seeping through his teeth and dripping out of his mouth.

"Blake!"

He fell over, and he wasn't moving. I knew his regenerative powers were gone. He was going to be dead in a few seconds if I didn't let Roxy come back, but I was already in the process of freeing the world. I didn't know if I would get a second chance or if Roxy would be selfishly selfless and let him die to fulfill her own call.

"Adam..." I remembered the first day I met him through Roxy. He wouldn't speak to her or anyone else. He sat in the back of every class with his head down. Even when the teachers called on him, he wouldn't answer. He looked so pathetic I didn't even know if he wanted to live. But when it was time to go home, Roxy hugged him. Adam hated it, and he pushed her away and yelled at her, causing an uncomfortable scene. She said he looked like he needed it and she offered to be his friend. He rejected her, calling her an idiot and a bunch of nasty insults. Roxy somehow managed to keep herself from crying or even getting upset. She eventually smiled and told him that she would give him all the time that he needed, and then she walked away. He was a jerk, but Roxy felt something that day. It was only a speck, but it was a strong speck. She felt his goodness, and she knew that one day, she would fall in love with that boy.

When I first laid my eyes on him—my true eyes—he was only trying to save me. He was only wanted to protect me, and I manipulated him into murdering Daddy. He stuck with me the whole journey just to keep Roxy safe, despite not wanting to deal with me.

He wanted to deal with me again, just to be with Roxy. There was still an amazing loyalty and goodness within him. He was still…"Adam!"

I couldn't let him die.

Chapter Eighteen

It was too much. I had won, but it was too much! There were so many people in so much pain and suffering. I didn't imagine that it would be so overwhelming. I was attached to everyone, but I didn't know if I could reach in everyone and find all of the goodness in the world. There were men who wanted to kill for no good reason. There were girls full of insecurities that took their clothes off for dirty old men full of lust; it made me want to vomit. There was so much negativity, and the power on me was too strong. I needed time, but I didn't have enough time!

Adam had made the ultimate sacrifice for me. He was dying on my road to destiny—a future casualty of my war. I was confused with Lyla. I was surprised that she cared about Adam enough to give up everything for him. I was conflicted and maybe a little bit jealous, but that was beside the point.

I had a decision to make. I could either end the suffering of the world or I could save Adam's life.

It was extremely selfish of me, but the choice wasn't hard at all.

"Adam!" I released the staff and started running toward him, praying to God that he would be alive when I got there. "Don't die!" As soon as I let go of the staff, its power was swept away from me. I couldn't feel the world. I wasn't connected to anyone except Adam, who was quickly fading.

I fell by his side and threw my body on top of him, crying hysterically while I searched for the dying light within him. It was fading, but it wasn't gone. It was just a speck, but it was a strong enough to save the man that I knew I would love forever.

"Roxy?" He opened his eyes slowly once his wounds were closed. I wasn't done healing him, but he wouldn't be still. "Are you, you?"

"I'm me." I pushed him back down so I could finish repairing all of the damage. That was way too close of a call. "That was too big of a gamble."

He sat up with a charming smirk on his face. "It's not a gamble when it's fixed."

I didn't believe that Lyla giving up her body was one hundred percent guaranteed. She was too selfish!

But maybe I was being too judgmental. After all, she gave up everything she had for a man she knew didn't love her back. "Let's go home."

The ground began to shake and Adam had to catch me, or else I would have fallen down as I tried to stand up. "You're still clumsy."

"An earthquake doesn't constitute as an excuse?"

"That's no earthquake."

We both looked back at the altar where the Staff of Power once was. "Where did it go?" I asked.

"This isn't good." He grabbed my hand and pulled on it until I started running behind him. "We've gotta get out of here!"

We started dashing for the portal that was shrinking before our very eyes. Adam kept pulling harder on my hand, trying to make me run faster, but it was really hard to run in those shoes, let alone run a lap on a football field sized runway! Then, I (of course) fell and sprained my ankle in our desperate time of need. "I'm sorry."

"No time for that!" Adam swooped me up in his arms, and I held on tight. I didn't mind him being the hero and running us straight through the portal. After all, I had just saved his life. "It's gonna be close!"

I closed my eyes and hugged him tight. Then I felt him leap through the air and then a rough landing on something that wasn't smooth enough to be marble. It felt like concrete and luckily for Adam, I broke his fall. "Ow!"

"Sorry." He rolled off of me as soon as he could.

I opened my eyes and observed the new scrapes on my arms from the rough landing. It was better than being trapped in a portal for all eternity, and judging by the fact that I didn't see the portal at all, I assumed that we barely made it out ourselves. The little cuts faded away before I even had time to bleed, and my ankle felt better by the time I kicked those stupid shoes off of my feet.

For some reason, Adam started laughing. It wasn't a chuckle or a normal laugh when something funny happened. It was hysterical and so out of the blue, that it was almost a crazy kind of laugh that alarmed me.

"What's the matter with you?"

He could barely speak out, "Nothing." He laughed so hard that he held onto his stomach and rolled over on the floor.

"Adam, come on!"

He wiped his eyes, which were welling with tears. I had never seen him laugh that hard. It took a while for him to calm down. "I just wanted to laugh, so I did."

It was such a simple thing to laugh about. I blinked a couple of times for lack of a comment, until we both burst out into a fit of hysterical laughter. We had been through so much; that's all we could do. I could cry tears of joy, but I think I had enough crying for one lifetime.

"Some kind of police or military force will be here soon."

"I know." I still couldn't stop smiling though. "I felt their presence when I touched the Staff of Power. Do you think we should run?"

"Maybe not. I think they'd catch us. Then we'd be in an even bigger mess."

There was only one thing I could think to do in a situation like that. "Then let's go wait for them." I got up, dusted myself off, and reached out my hand to help Adam up. He was so heavy that he nearly made me fall, which only made us laugh some more.

We hid my book on a bookshelf in the basement amongst a bunch of other books. Hopefully, plain sight would we be enough. It was the best we could do in the short amount of time that we had.

Sure enough, a SWAT team pulled up to the house. There were four trucks and a couple of regular police cars with them. Men had guns pointed at us at all times, and they screamed at us over and over again, even though Adam and I showed no resistance. Strangely enough, they didn't ask us any questions. They didn't read us any rights. They loaded us into the back of a prisoner truck and chained us down.

I don't know where they decided to take us, but the ride was longer than I would have expected. I imagined a military lab somewhere with creepy doctors and long needles. Why wouldn't they want to experiment on the girl who could heal or move objects with her mind? Even worse, they would want to study Adam to see why a normal human was no longer pure human.

Wherever they were taking us, they needed to be careful. Lyla would probably be coming soon.

"Adam, do you think this is what Porter was talking about when he said there would be consequences for not performing the ritual?"

"I hope this is all he meant."

I couldn't help but feel a shiver go down my back. "What do you mean?"

"Maybe you and Lyla didn't spark a war where your people physically fought each other, but it is a war. Now instead of you two being patriots, you're traitors. I assume there might be people who would want to make you pay for that, and we don't know what happened to the Staff of Power."

"It was destroyed after Lyla and I both refused to use it."

"All we know is that it disappeared. This might not be over yet." It felt like he was prophesying a dark future on me and it did scare me.

"I don't know what is gonna happen."

He shrugged. "I'm not worried about it."

"You're not?" Excuse me if I found that hard to believe, but he was chained up in a SWAT car, riding to only God knows where, his criminal record was bound to be discovered, and then they would pin him to the murder of my parents. Worst of all, he was about to be shackled next to a crazy girl who's life he ruined.

"No." He smiled the same way he always did when he looked at me. "As long as you're by my side, screw everything else. We'll get through this—all three of us."

It wasn't the most romantic speech in the world, but I was sold. I leaned into Adam and kissed him, because I didn't know what tomorrow would be like. I just knew that no matter what, I wanted him by my side and to know that I loved him more than anything. I could feel myself beginning to slip away, but I held on as long as I could into that kiss.

And that kiss was certainly yummy! I pulled his face in closer, and I think he realized which one I was. He should have pulled away

357

immediately, but what did he care? Two lovely lady lips were two lovely lady lips.

He pulled away from me and wiped his mouth, but he was sort of smiling. "Lyla."

Then I remembered what he did, and I punched him in the arm. "Why did you try to kill yourself?"

He had a confident and relaxed smirk on his face. "I knew you would save me."

My mouth dropped. "You couldn't have!"

"You and Roxy are both pretty easy to con. It must be the sister thing."

I didn't like being tricked or manipulated. I couldn't stand him. "You ruined everything!" I punched him in the arm again.

"No, I freed you."

"You freed me?" I raised my hands so he could see the silver chains around my wrists. "Please, elaborate."

"With your destiny gone, you have no more obligations. You don't have to be someone's monster or someone's god, Lyla. You get to reinvent yourself and be the person who you want to be. You get to be you—whoever that may be."

He sounded ridiculous. "And that's freedom to you?"

"It's freedom to everyone." He wasn't trying to con me again. I think he genuinely meant what he said, and maybe it wasn't so ridiculous. I hated Roxy, but she was right. It was time to take responsibility for the things I had done, and I planned on starting immediately. There was no one left in the world that treated me cruelly or worshiped me. I could start over completely fresh. I was renewed.

"I want to be the woman who you love." I blushed and shied my eyes away from him, but I couldn't help but be drawn back to his silver eyes.

"That won't be easy." He sighed. "It's probably impossible." But impossible didn't mean that he would never. Impossible didn't even mean that he wildly hated me anymore.

"Well, I've got time to kill." I didn't care what I had to do. I didn't care how long it took. I was going to make the boy of my dreams fall madly in love with me.

I didn't like those heavy chains weighing me down, so I busted the metal open until they fell right off of me. Then I stood up, looking at the closed door that I was about bust wide open, so I could escape and remake myself in my own image. "But in the meantime, how about you and I blow this Popsicle stand?"

He had been waiting for me to show up, because he ripped the chains off of his hands easily enough. He and Roxy could have escaped, but I think he just wanted to have some fun with me as the two of us became outlaws by human and Avarian standards.

He smirked wickedly. "Yes, Ma'am."